THE SPANISH DAUGHTER

Jillian Taberner

 **New Generation Publishing**

My thanks to my husband John for help and advice; my daughter Anna for proof reading, editing and translations into Spanish; my sister Janet for reading, commenting and for her encouragement. Also to friends Sheila May Bird, Laura Cooper and Lisa Beecheno for information and suggestions, thank you.

"Something of vengeance I had tasted for the first time; as aromatic wine it seemed, on swallowing, warm and racy: its after-flavour, metallic and corroding, gave me a sensation as if I had been poisoned."

Charlotte Brontë
(Jane Eyre)

PROLOGUE

Autumn 2007

Conchita leaned back resting her head on the soft pillows of her bed. She was warm and comfortable with the late afternoon sun falling onto the terrace outside her room. From time to time she raised her eyes and looking beyond the wide open doors she could see the vines that marched in straight lines across the dry land, now dressed in their autumnal colours. She took in the brilliant yellow of the leaves turning to orange, some deepening to red, and finally to rust before they fell. She lifted her head a little to bring her gaze up to the distant hills poking up out of the valley with the backdrop of the familiar Cantabria Mountains behind them. She sighed deeply. Though comfortable she felt listless and the pen, held loosely in her hand, would not move across the page. She could hear the words in her head but today she could not make them visible. She began to feel a strange ache in her chest and she closed her eyes, shutting out the colour, as the pain intensified. She lifted the diary and held it against her heart. With eyes closed, and as if from far away, she heard someone calling her.

'Nana? Nana?' Mercedes came across the west-facing terrace, through the billowing white curtains and into the room.

'Oh there you are, enjoying the view. You've dropped your storybook Nana.' Her granddaughter picked up the diary as though to replace it but saw that her eyes were closed.

'Asleep Nana, that's good.' Mercedes leaned over and gently laid her hand on her grandmother's arm and looked at her fondly. She gazed at her for a moment as she lay tranquil, and then Mercedes began to feel uneasy. There was something different about her grandmother's mien; the lines of strain had left her face and her head had rolled to one side.

'Nana, are you all right?' Suddenly Mercedes was frightened. She stood up straight and ran into the house calling for her mother.

Rosita caught the urgency in her daughter's voice.

'What is it Mercedes? What's wrong?'

'It's Nana, Oh, *Mama* I think....' Before she could finish Rosita pushed past her daughter into the room. Even before reaching her she knew it was too late. Her mother had gone. She knelt beside her and lifting both her hands kissed them softly as tears began to slide down her cheeks.

Mercedes was still holding the diary. She enfolded it in her arms and pressed it hard against her chest, trying not to let out the huge sob that she could feel rising in her throat. She stood beside her mother, watching the tears drop onto her grandmother's hands. But Rosita was smiling. She turned to her daughter.

'This is how she wanted it; to fall asleep, in the warmth of the sun, looking out across the vines to the distant hills. How we shall miss her.'

How could her mother be smiling when her darling Nana had gone, gone forever? She turned and ran into the house clutching the diary. It was too much, the sob rose and burst out in a great howl.

1

January 1938, Yorkshire, England

AMELIA

Amelia Hampton was shocked to learn that her son Philip had married, she felt thwarted at not having been involved with any part of her son's courtship to Flora, nor was she, or Philip's father Charles, present at the wedding ceremony. How could he go off and get married without her having seen, let alone approve, his intended wife?

Amelia's strength lay in her determination to manage things in life. It was not through selfishness, or a desire for power, but to get things right. She wanted her fine-looking, intelligent son to do well in life. Her own childhood and youth had been difficult. As the youngest of seven children she had come last in every sense; the last child born to a worn out mother, the last in line for an affectionate hug, the last to wear handed down well-worn clothes, even from brother to sister, the last to leave home, having taken care of her mother before her early death. Her motto, taken up from her father, a staunch, hard-working Yorkshireman, had been during those years, 'Never give in, never give up'. She was unwavering in her efforts to get things right and give Philip something better. She loved him with a fierce intensity.

Amelia pulled at her steel grey hair, permed twice a year with a 'Toni' home perm, she kept the tight curls in place with vigorous brushing. No need to waste money at the hairdresser she told herself. She dressed more often than not in a grey or navy blue pleated skirt, with a white blouse and a hand knitted cardigan. She was not a big woman but the cardigan was inclined to emphasise her ample bosom; the whole was in her opinion in good taste and underlined her no nonsense approach to life. In warmer weather she wore a short sleeved dress of white polka dot on a background of navy blue or black which was her smart outfit accompanied by a plain jacket.

Amelia's thoughts clamouring in her head made her scowl. Had she not guided her son from birth, helping him make the right decisions, protecting him from life's knocks? And here he was at twenty-nine having married without a by-your-leave! His university life had distanced him from her emotionally, as well as geographically; she knew it was responsible for the loss of her influence over him, and she had known in her heart that it was inevitable. He had learned to act without her opinion and advice and it had frightened her. Now this; his marriage to someone she'd never heard of, let alone met, and a southerner to boot!

'Don't get so upset Amelia,' Charles said. 'Aren't you happy he's found a nice girl?'

'Of course I want him to be happy in marriage,' she responded. 'But how do we know she's a 'nice girl' as you put it? How do we know if she's the right kind of wife for him? How does he know how to choose a wife?'

'My dear, we none of us know how to *choose*,' Charles said with a wry smile. 'We fall in love. Love is what makes us human you know, forbearing and charitable. And makes us happy,' he added, looking straight at Amelia nodding knowingly.

'He's not a child anymore Amelia,' Charles continued. For a moment he was silent. Then he said,

'In any case, no parent has the right to choose a partner for their child. If he's fallen in love that's good enough for me.' This, following his earlier remark, was quite an assertion coming from Charles who normally let his wife have her say. Amelia knew that Charles did not like to argue with her. She always managed to have an answer, especially if it was anything to do with Philip – most of their differences of opinion during their married life had been, and still were, about their son. All else in their married life was in accord. For the moment her resentment was appeased.

'We'll see,' she said.

'Aye, we'll see. But Amelia...' Charles hesitated. He'd already said more than he usually did in their discussions, as he preferred to call them. She looked up and her eyes challenged him.

'Go on, say it!'

'Well, go easy on them love. Give the girl a chance.'

'Don't worry, for Philip's sake I'll hold my tongue. As I said, we'll see.'

***

Amelia did see. She saw all too soon how the land lay when Philip and Flora came to visit them in mid-April, to tell them their good news.

'A baby? So soon?' she exclaimed.

'Well we didn't want to wait, did we Flora?' Philip said. 'I'm nearly thirty. I don't want to be an old man when my children are teenagers.'

'You haven't announced it yet I hope. I mean to anyone else? They'll think there's been some hanky panky before...'

'Amelia ! 'They', whoever you think they are, will think no such thing!'

At this outburst Charles started coughing and wheezing. Amelia was immediately contrite and quickly tried to make amends.

'It was a joke, Charles,' she murmured as she went to his side.

Flora had turned crimson at the remark and sat with her eyes lowered.

'I'm absolutely thrilled, my dear,' Charles said recovering from the coughing. He got up out of his arm chair, took her hands saying, 'Ee, I'm going to be a grandfather. Isn't that wonderful?' His Yorkshire accent intensified at moments of deep emotion or excitement, as he added,

'By gum, it's marvellous.'

He turned to Philip and taking his hand he shook it vigorously. With tears in his eyes and in a cracked voice he said, 'Congratulations, my son.'

'Amelia, you're pleased for them, aren't you?'

'Yes, of course,' came a rather subdued remark from Amelia. 'Well, I'll try to be a granny alongside you Charles as a grandpa,' and she smiled at him.

It was Charles who took the initiative again.

'Well how are you my dear? Are you well? Now you are looking after her aren't you Philip?'

'I'm fine thank you.' It was the first words Flora had uttered throughout the whole conversation. 'And don't worry, Philip is being very attentive.'

'Good. Good boy. Keep it up. Don't forget Flora's the one who has to do all the hard work. You've done yours!' He guffawed at his rather earthy comment.

'Charles, really!' Amelia said, though she was smiling.

Philip thought this a good moment to impart the rest of his news, whilst his mother was smiling.

'Now we have something else to tell you,' Philip began.

9

His mother looked round at him sharply with alarm in her eyes.

'I hope this will please you also,' he said.

'Well come on then, spit it out,' Amelia butted in. 'We've had enough of a shock for one day.' The tone was not lost on Flora, though she could not tell whether it was an intended rebuke or not.

'Amelia, let him speak.'

'I will be starting a new job in July and we shall be looking for a house, probably here in Bradford.'

Charles almost swooned at his words. His cup overflowed with emotion and he couldn't speak. It was Amelia who responded first.

'That's grand news Philip. I knew you'd come back home one day.'

Philip paid no heed to his mother's somewhat smug remark but rose and kissed her gently. He turned and took his father's hand.

'How's that then Dad? I hope you're as happy about it as we are.' Charles still couldn't speak. He just squeezed his son's hand and grinned.

And so Amelia saw how things were.

2

CHARLES

Philip's father, a gentle, easy going man, had opted for the quiet life, letting his wife make the decisions about their son. It wasn't that he didn't care, but he lacked the energy to stand up to her on a day to day basis.

He'd suffered physically in the First World War and on returning home experienced psychosomatic problems. His memories plagued him still, and there were nights when he couldn't sleep, even twenty years on. He dreamed of his pals lying wounded in the mud of the trenches. He heard their moans and cries in his sleep; he saw them dying and could do nothing to help them; and then they were dead. Sometimes he called out in the darkness of the night and Amelia would lay her hand on his brow and gently stroke until he settled again.

He knew that he was lucky to be alive at all after having taken that bullet in the left lung, and then being invalided out from the Somme. It had been removed in the field hospital but the conditions were notoriously poor, there were just too many of them needing medical attention, and he had developed an infection. Despite the fact that it had left him with only one good functioning lung he felt guilty that he lived when so many died, it humbled him. For the rest of his life he had a tendency to breathlessness along with a wheezy laugh which sometimes sent him into a bout of coughing when he told one of his many Music Hall jokes. He had been forced to sit back and take life a little easier.

His disability meant that he could not take up a full time job after the war. He wrote a weekly column for the local paper, the Telegraph and Argus, and articles for some of the national newspapers. The writing didn't bring in a great deal of money but working part-time in the local library and his war pension just about kept them solvent.

Charles was tall, a good six feet, but even when he stood erect, as he still did, he had to lift his gaze to look into his son's blue eyes.

Although he had put on a little weight over the years he still appeared fit and healthy. His rosy cheeks belied his underlying imperfect health.

He wore loose fitting corduroy trousers, check shirts and knitted cardigans; 'comfortable clothes' he called them. Even though they were casual in appearance he always looked smart and his neatly clipped moustache added to the slight air of authority he bore. It was a left over from the War. His ability to command was still there although buried for the most part, but he could and did occasionally over-ride Amelia's strong views.

He admitted that on the whole Amelia's course of action for Philip had been good. He admired his wife for her principles and for sticking to them, he remembered how she had coped during the war whilst he was away. He saw that Philip, with his own personal resolve, had repaid his mother's efforts with high achievement both at school and with a First Class Honours Degree from Cambridge, working hard throughout his years of education and beyond. Philip had proved himself as a gifted mathematician but not content with that he had read German alongside his other studies and left university as a fluent speaker in the language.

Charles was secretly very pleased that Philip had found a girl without Amelia's assistance. He felt it was right. He knew falling in love was something one did without anyone's help. He was looking forward to meeting Flora and was determined that he was going to make her feel welcome.

**

It was a bright, sunny day in mid April when Charles took up their morning post from the doormat. He took it into the kitchen to Amelia.

'One from Philip, if I'm not mistaken. I should know that writing by now.'

'You open it,' she said smiling.

He opened the letter, his cheeks already crinkling with a smile that became a grin as he read the opening lines. Charles had an endearing mannerism when pleased; he would push out his strong chin and tilt back his head, as though nodding upwards. The more he made the movement the more he was pleased. Amelia saw it.

'What?' she said.

'Eh, they want to come and see us,' he said excitedly. 'Philip's bought a car and they're going to drive up. They want to know if next weekend is all right.'

'That'll be nice. Send them a note straight away Charles, I know you like to do the writing.' Amelia paused. 'I wonder what she'll think of our place?'

'Our place' was a modest bungalow in Duckworth Lane, at the top end as Amelia called it, near the Bradford Royal Infirmary. Charles had often joked that it was very convenient; 'I could almost walk to the hospital – if need be!' The house was just off the main road only a matter of yards round the corner to the trolley bus terminal right outside the main hospital gates. The trolley bus took them right into town, to the bottom of Sunbridge Road every Saturday morning. Here they dismounted and made a beeline for Brown, Muffs Department Store, where they treated themselves; Amelia a coffee and Charles a cup of tea, before doing their shopping.

'I'll have to start thinking about what to make for dinner,' Amelia continued with a note of anxiety in her voice.

'Now Amelia, don't start getting het up, it's only your son, not the King of England!' and he laughed at his own joke.

'Aye, and his wife, I don't know what she likes, or doesn't like more to the point. It's a bit difficult when you've never met anyone before.'

'Don't start going on about that anymore. Just do what you normally do, roast beef and Yorkshire pudding. Nobody can find fault with that. And a lovely apple pie after.'

Amelia couldn't help smiling at Charles' childish enthusiasm at the thought of seeing their son, and his wife.

'Yes, I'm good at that; I make a lovely Yorkshire pudding, even though I say so myself.'

'You do that. Now I'll get on with the letter straight away so it can catch tonight's post.'

***

Charles' dream had come true; Philip and Flora were going to have a child. He couldn't believe it. He could see Amelia was a bit taken aback at the news. It was a bit of a surprise, especially as the news came on their first meeting with Flora. It was sooner than he had dared to hope, he had to admit, not that he knew much about these things as he often told his wife, with a shy grin. What was important to him was that Philip loved Flora, Charles could see that. Later he said to Amelia,

'She's a good looking lass, isn't she? I can see why he fell for her.'

'Yes, I just hope she's going to be as capable as she is nice-looking. She's going to have a tough time having that baby, she's very small boned. I hope it's not a big one, she's already showing, I could see that despite that loose shirt she was wearing.'

'Right away you start worrying, don't you? But you mustn't Amelia.'

'No, especially as they'll be living in Bradford by the time it arrives. I'll be able to help.' Amelia's expression brightened at the thought of the young couple living nearby, and of being a grandmother.

'I'd like her to call me 'gramps', not grandpa, not granddad – there's nothing 'grand' about me - or even worse grandfather!'

'Who? What're you talking about? Oh, you mean this baby! Anyway, what makes you so sure it's a girl?'

'Just a feeling in me water, you know,' Charles said with a grin.

'Charles, I wish you wouldn't use that expression, it's common. You know I don't like it.'

Charles turned his head away so that Amelia wouldn't see his mischievous grin; sometimes he said things like that just to get a rise out of her and see that frosty expression flit across her face. It made her amber eyes glow, which, even now, he found exciting. After over thirty years of marriage she still hadn't tumbled to his little game.

'You'll see,' he said, remembering Amelia's words of only a few weeks ago.

3

PHILIP

Philip had surprised himself at the swiftness with which he married Flora. Normally a cautions man, deliberating on serious issues particularly if they involved his emotions, he could hardly believe that he had acted with such alacrity, but then he had fallen in love. That had never happened to him before.

Philip knew that he wanted to marry Flora the very day he met her but convention ruled that he must give her time, to accept him that is. Accept him she did, after only eight days' acquaintanceship, with the words, 'Yes please,' when he popped the question. He couldn't believe his good fortune.

On their return from honeymoon Philip and Flora settled in Philip's rented flat in Barnes on the outskirts of London. It had been barely a long weekend. A honeymoon seemed something of an extravagance, having so recently spent eight days skiing in Öbergurgl, in Austria. But going on a honeymoon was what one did after getting married.

That skiing holiday had been a long awaited experience for Philip. When the opportunity came up for him to join some of his former Cambridge contemporaries, he jumped at the chance. He wanted to relax mentally, if not physically, to have a break before he started what he thought of as his career.

The holiday had been all that he had hoped for; physical exercise, fresh air, good food, meeting old friends and congenial people of his own age, and not a small amount of gluwein, that ubiquitous spiced red wine which warmed the insides, dispelling the cold after several hours on the slopes.

Flora's presence had been a surprise and he had fallen for her immediately.

She was not the first girl in whom he had had a romantic interest, but Flora was different. He knew the moment she walked into the breakfast room, and saw her short, curly brown hair, springing up round the green bandeau she wore on her head; he wanted to pull that band off and sink his fingers into her hair. She was petite and he wanted to hold and protect her. This was something he had never experienced before and his heart beat harder with the desire of it. The feeling startled him.

As a couple they attracted attention. Philip, tall with an erect bearing, looked rather lanky next to Flora's small, neat figure. His height emphasised her petite frame. She looked almost like a child standing next to him.

He watched her in the company of other members of their party and saw she was bright and smiling, and within minutes of speaking to her himself he was conscious of the fact that she was an intelligent young woman. It pleased him. He soon learned that she spoke French and Spanish and she apologised to him that she did not speak German. Philip immediately took advantage of that fact, helping her translate the menu and asking for drinks. It wasn't necessary, most of the people in the resort seemed to understand English but Philip pretended that was not the case, just so that he could stand next to her, and help and guide her. To his amazement and overwhelming joy, Flora responded to his attentiveness.

Introducing Flora to his parents was not going to be easy; he knew his parents would be disappointed not to have been at the wedding and regretted that he might have hurt them but Philip had selfishly wanted to keep her to himself for as long as possible before presenting her to his mother and father. He loved his parents, recognising in them the sacrifices they had made for his sake. For the first time in his life he had been overwhelmed by emotion. It surprised him and scared him a little but he married Flora anyway. He was a man now.

His mother would be ready with her questions; 'Why didn't you get married here in Yorkshire, love? Surely, that would have been so much easier. What was the hurry? You didn't give your future wife time to arrange a proper wedding.'

A 'proper' wedding was, in her eyes; the bride in a white dress, the service in a church, a suitably stylish, but not showy wedding breakfast in the Wedding Suite at Brown, Muffs of Bradford.

'And then we could have been with you,' would be her final remark. He knew his mother well, but he loved her.

He also knew that both his mother and father would be wondering what he was going to do with his life now that he had finished his peregrinations, as Amelia called them; travelling in Germany and throughout Europe. The fact that he was fluent in German meant little to her. How useful it had been in Austria!

He was glad he had got out of Germany some months ago, the political situation was frightening and the atmosphere forbidding. Travelling across Europe had been more difficult than he had expected; strict border controls, police on every corner of the streets demanding one's papers, and the transport system shot to pieces. Talk of war was in the air with unrest, demonstrations and arrests already taking place in some areas.

They were no sooner unpacking after their honeymoon when Philip explained to Flora that they would be moving; soon to be going to Bradford in West Yorkshire, and taking up a new post in banking. Philip realised that they would have to find a house, not a flat, as now they would need more space.

His post in the Westminster Bank was going to be a surprise to his parents. Applications and interviews had already taken place before Philip left for his skiing holiday but he had said nothing to his mother and father. Always mindful of his mother's aspirations for him he felt it better to present her with a success rather than a 'maybe'. Of his father's reaction he had no doubts. The Westminster was an old and respected establishment, it could trace its history back to the seventeenth century and Philip knew that his father would be impressed that he had secured a position with them. His father would, as always, be delighted at his son's achievement, showing his love and faith in him in whatever he chose to do.

When he left on holiday he already knew that he had gained a position of some standing for a young man of his age, and had, therefore, no qualms about the financial side of being married. Thus, he was able to explain to Flora that he had a 'good job'. He was proud of the fact that she would not need to go out to work, it seemed that more and more young wives were doing so these days.

What Philip had not reckoned with was the fact that he was going to be a father sooner than he had expected. Actually Philip had not expected anything on that topic, never having even thought about it. Even so he was delighted that he had immediately demonstrated his masculine vigour, and was excited at the prospect of being a father. This was the main news that they had to impart to his parents.

'But it's what we wanted, isn't it Flora?' he said turning to her as he proudly announced the fact to his parents when they visited and told them. It didn't occur to Philip that it could be difficult for Flora meeting his parents for the first time to be already sharing such momentous news. His mother's reaction had nonplussed him slightly but in his ingenuous way he put it down to her concern for Flora's wellbeing.

The news that followed, that he had secured what his mother would see as a 'good job' and that they were to move back to Yorkshire, had brought about the smiles that he so hoped would be forthcoming from both his parents, and the near tears from his father had surprised and moved him.

Now, as far as he was concerned, all that remained was to get on with the house-hunting in Yorkshire.

4

FLORA

Flora was nervous. Philip had painted quite an alarming picture of his mother; strict and determined, but 'loving' too he had added, even if not very demonstrative. As for his father Philip's description of him had left her in no doubt that he would be uncomplicated and ready to accept anything that his son made up his made to do.

The skiing holiday receded like a dream, still there in the memory but the details becoming blurred. What was not at all hazy in her mind was the fact that Philip had obviously been smitten with her on meeting. She was flattered, what young woman would not have been?

She thought back to Rhonda's hesitant phone call only ten days before Christmas. It was uncanny the way she and Rhonda had met up again after they had left school. Separated by six school years, they had never been friends; it was not the thing for Upper Sixth-formers to fraternise with the First Years. And then to the amazement of both they found themselves entering London University at the same time.

They had come together in their third year at university to work on a joint French language project. Flora would not have chosen Rhonda as her working partner but Rhonda had approached Flora, no - rather bounded up to her with resolve - and claimed her. Flora knew exactly what Rhonda was doing, having noticed her watching her own attitude to her studies. Rhonda left most of the work to Flora but they still never became more than colleagues. Rhonda finished her degree at twenty-one like most of the students, whereas Flora, a mature student by their standards, was nearly twenty-six. The gap in their ages, still as significant in their twenties as it had been at school, was one of the reasons they had parted on not exactly affable terms. An awkwardness had arisen between them, it seemed to Flora that there was a smattering of resentment on Rhonda's part at Flora's First Class Degree. But there was another deeper reason.

It was towards the end of their third and final year that Flora met Ramon López Garcia. He was tall and suave and at twenty-nine appeared mature and experienced. It happened in the Common Room one evening when she heard him speaking Spanish amongst a group of language students and she moved closer to listen. It was when she laughed out loud at some amusing comment he made that he turned and noticed her.

'You speak Spanish?' he asked her.

'I'm sorry, that must have seemed very rude. I wasn't really eavesdropping but I thought ....'

'Don't worry. It's refreshing to meet an English girl who speaks my language well enough to understand my jokes. I'm Ramon López Garcia by the way.'

'Flora Swinburne,' she replied and they formally shook hands. As she did so she caught sight of Rhonda's hand hanging on Ramon's elbow. She was leaning against him and smiling up at him, her eyes fixed on his. As he spoke she turned to look at Flora and said,

'Oh, it's you.'

'Yes,' said Flora trying to maintain her smile despite Rhonda's cool gaze.

Rhonda was still clutching Ramon's arm which he had stretched out to shake hands and in so doing had loosened Rhonda's grip. She looked peeved as she said to Flora,

'What are you doing here? You don't often come into the Students' Bar?' Before Flora could respond to Rhonda's unfriendly remark Ramon stepped in.

'You should come more often, I visit frequently and we have quite a laugh, don't we?' He turned to Rhonda as he said this and she simpered, smiling at Flora with her lips but her eyes were hostile.

Flora sensed that Rhonda was wary of her as a contender for Ramon's attention.

Thrown together whilst studying, it was clear that Rhonda's level of Spanish language competence was adequate but no match for Flora's fluency, nor, to make matters worse, did her aptitude in French reach Flora's excellent standard. Rhonda's attitude there in the Students' Bar spoke of jealousy, that emotion just a little more unkind than envy. It was not surprising that she had glowered at Flora's response to Ramon's joke, which she, along with some others, had clearly not understood.

It was his Continental brand of courtesy and air of good breeding, giving him an allure and an air of mystery that made Ramon stand out amongst the younger, seemingly immature English young men. All the girls fell in love with Ramon, which was not surprising, but it was Ramon and Flora who became lovers.

It was ironical that later it should be Rhonda who would save Flora from despair when Ramon abandoned her. His desertion, which is how she viewed it, remained unexplained and Flora took up a job she had secured just before he had left to return to Spain. Flora felt ill for weeks after his departure, sick of a broken heart, she told herself. She took to drinking red wine in the evenings in order to 'blur the edges' as she thought of it. Rhonda's telephone call came as a surprise but Flora was grateful for some kind of diversion.

'Not sure what your situation is...I mean, whether Ramon is around. Perhaps you'll be spending Christmas with him?' Flora knew full well that Rhonda had heard gossip that Ramon was not 'around'.

'Well, I'll come straight to the point. I organised a skiing party with Erna Low Travel Group, and one of the crowd has dropped out at the last minute. It's damned annoying. I suppose it seems just awful ringing you up like this at the last minute, but I thought you might be interested depending on.. .well... Ramon.' It was as though Rhonda were deliberately repeating his name, jabbing at a tender spot, knowing it would give Flora pain. There was a pause as though Rhonda were expecting Flora to confirm one way or the other her position with Ramon. She didn't respond and Rhonda rattled off again.

'You'll actually be doing me favour,' she continued. 'You see, as the organiser I get a free place providing it's a party of sixteen. So if you come I'll not have to pay. And as things are, well they're a bit tight at the moment, I've overrun my allowance rather badly. My parents have finally refused me another 'loan', mean devils. I don't know why they're filthy rich.' Rhonda paused for breath once again.

'Well, if you're booked or something, I expect I'll find someone else.'

The pause had given Flora just the few seconds she needed to come to a decision.

'No. I mean yes, I'd love to come. What do I have to do to join you?'

Rhonda described the other members of the party; her elder brother and girl-friend; some chums of his girl-friend from university; a cousin and his wife, and her present flat mate.

'All really nice people,' she added.

Philip was one of the really nice people.

With the fresh air, exercise, camaraderie and good food, Flora began to feel better. She stopped drinking the red wine, the feeling of hopelessness began to dissolve and her lethargy diminished.

And then, Philip's proposal swept her off her feet. Why not? she thought. He's attractive with his bright blue eyes and thatch of boyish floppy fair hair. His nose was just a little too big and straight to make him handsome but his looks were striking. Standing next to her they looked a little incongruous, she so short and he, with interminably long legs, towered above her, which obliged her to look up to meet his eyes, a gesture Philip took for respect and admiration, even love. His smile was slow to come but generous and once she had said 'yes' he never stopped smiling.

The date was set.

'There is no reason why we should wait, is there?' And no, she said there was no reason.

It was fixed for the 20th January in the Registry Office near Regent's Park. After asking Flora if there was anyone special she would like as a witness, to which she had replied no, Philip asked two of his colleagues in the office in which he was currently working to stand witness.

Flora bought a new dress, apple green silk with a matching jacket, the colour setting off her new light tan acquired on the slopes. She made a headdress with an orchid and a piece of net attached to a hair band, the circlet framed her small face, the contrast of the pale flower upon her bright curls was eye-catching. She had put the thing together herself to keep down the cost, mindful of her low funds.

The honeymoon in the Cotswolds was short, in a country hotel with a wood fire burning in a huge fireplace in the comfortable sitting room. It was quiet after the New Year flurry of clients, the atmosphere welcoming, its menus good if not too adventurous, and a cosy feather bed in a snug old-fashioned bedroom.

Cocooned in the calm ambience and warm comfort of the country hotel with Philip's devotion to her well-being, Flora was happy, happy enough to push aside that niggle whispering at the back of her mind – *rebound* – and to feel that perhaps she probably had got over her love affair with Ramon.

All that remained to mar her complete contentment was the thought of the journey to Yorkshire and the meeting with Philip's parents.

***

22

Flora was not normally nervous at meeting new people, she had a pleasant confidence and could make small talk, discuss the latest political situation, or the news headlines, with ability. This was not her worry.

The real apprehension, at this first meeting with Philip's parents, was with regard to how they would feel about the 'surprise' news they had for them.

As Flora had guessed Philip's father was kind and thrilled at the prospect of being a grandparent.

Ameila's response of shock and something nearing bewilderment was unnerving. Her concern about 'what the neighbours would say' had shaken Flora. It was only Charles' evident joy that had rescued her from bursting into tears. Amelia's later smiles began to reassure Flora that perhaps as they got to know one another they would get on.

What really saved the day was Charles' and Amelia's evident joy that their son was going to return to Yorkshire and that he and their daughter-in-law were to live close by.

5

RHONDA

Rhonda Shaw was pleasant looking rather than pretty, with a winning smile which she could use to advantage. She could switch it on like a light and as such it lit up her face for as long as she wanted it to shine. There remained though, an unattractive element to it; the smile rarely reached her eyes. She had a habit of narrowing them, peering through the slits as though she were short sighted but the trait gave more the impression that she was making a judgement on whom she was bestowing her gaze rather than having difficulty focusing. She was an intelligent girl and did not find it difficult to get into university but once there she abandoned her academic diligence in favour of sport and leisure pursuits, becoming a member of almost every club on the campus. Because of this, and the fact that she seemed to have plenty of money, she became well known as a good-time girl. She embraced ballroom dancing with a vigour she did not know she possessed, she joined a choir – only to find that her voice was not quite up to standard when it was politely suggested that she might 'enjoy' some other hobby. She played hockey, her athletic prowess standing her in good stead giving her a place in the first team. After organizing the trip to Austria she discovered skiing for the first time in her life and that she was a natural. She was candid and outgoing, displaying an acerbic wit which made her fellow students laugh, usually at someone else's expense but the fun and laughter in her company also made her popular. She was spontaneous which somehow sat at odds with that strange way of looking at people. Above all she was happy, free from the restraining bonds of her parents.

Her acquaintanceship with Flora at university was passing until the need for a partner to work on a project sent her in search of someone also reading French. It was an unlikely partnership right from the start given that Rhonda cared little for her studies. Rhonda knew Flora by reputation; rather bookish and taking her work seriously.

The project progressed with, not surprisingly, Flora doing most of the work. Rhonda soon realised that Flora seemed to enjoy the research and writing.

'Don't you mind doing all this work?' Rhonda had asked.

'Not at all, I'm quite enjoying myself, after all I am doing something I want to do.'

'You're strange, you know that? Anybody else would be resentful, but I reckon you knew what you were letting yourself in for, didn't you?'

Flora just smiled.

'Each to his own; you like sport and well...I like this,' Flora had replied.

'Yes, I reckon you're a bit of a swot, aren't you Flora?' Rhonda accused her well into the work.

'Still, I suppose it's a good thing one of us is prepared to do the work,' she laughed, as she went off to a hockey practice, leaving Flora to translate the latest piece of research.

Rhonda appeared not to have any scruples about her input, or lack of it. At the same time she did say to Flora one day;

'Are you going to include who worked-on-what in this boring tract? I mean, are you going to squeal so that you get all the kudos?'

Flora was baffled by Rhonda's question. The notion had never occurred to her. She didn't know how to reply without sounding condescending.

'Don't be silly, it's teamwork, there's no need to say who did what.'

'Ah but *they* know your translation is far better than mine. *They* will know all right. Anyway, it's too late now. It's just about finished. Isn't it?'

'Well yes, but I'd like you to run through it and see what you think, I mean, if you can see any inconsistencies.'

'You're joking of course!' But she could see from the look on Flora's face that it was no joke. 'O.K. I'll read it, but don't expect me to make any changes.'

It was two weeks before Rhonda got round to 'looking through' the work. It was dangerously close to deadline date for presentation when she returned the manuscript, Rhonda knew Flora was angry but it reached the head of department in time. After its submission Flora and Rhonda had no call to spend time together. Both were relieved.

The final year came to an end with parties and celebrations. It was at one of these celebrations in the Student Bar that the resentment between Rhonda and Flora was widened.

The Bar was not one of the places Flora regularly sought out for a let-up in her self-imposed, disciplined time-table. Besides she was on a strict budget and she had found on one of her initial visits that the money had trickled through her fingers as easily as the lager and lime had slipped down her throat. It was only on specific occasions that she paid a visit and now that the term was coming to an end she felt this was such an occasion when she could relax, and enjoy the camaraderie of her colleagues.

Flora was the last person Rhonda expected to see in the bar, their eyes met as she approached. Rhonda was determined that she would make no effort to be sociable with 'this unfathomable young woman', as Rhonda had been heard to describe Flora. Standing beside the bar, Rhonda was hanging on to a tall young man with her hand on his arm. As Flora approached she pushed her hand into the crook of his elbow; he was hers, even if he didn't know it yet and she was signalling the claim. What she hadn't bargained for was Flora's quick wit and fluency in Spanish. It was Rhonda's undoing.

The bantering within the group had suddenly broken into French and this attractive fellow had then started to tell a joke in Spanish. He was extremely popular; with his olive skin and dark hair he was the epitome of a Latin *amour,* all the girls fell for him. His wit and affable manner, without any touch of arrogance despite his more mature personality, made him well-liked among the students. His presence at the Students' Bar gave rise to some speculation; he was older than the norm; he was Spanish; he appeared well-to-do. All of this lent him an air of mystery - so what was he doing here?

Rhonda never had the opportunity to find out.

6

ANNIE

Annie came from a working class background and a large family; she was used to the arrival of babies. Other than looking after them, one after the other, Annie loved cooking. She had learned from her mother; basic foods, nothing wasted, touched with a magic that could not be learned from a cookery book. At sixteen she had gone to work in a factory works' canteen. From there she progressed to the kitchens of the local primary school. She had married at nineteen but no babies came along during the eleven years of her marriage. After some happy years in the school Annie decided that despite the weeks of out-of-term holidays, she wanted something more home-based, family orientated, more personal. If she was destined not to have children of her own then she was prepared to look after other folks' bairns she told her husband.

When Annie saw the advertisement in the local paper she thought she would give it a try. She brushed her pale straight hair, put on her plain navy blue coat, a dark beret, her flat navy shoes, and walked less than a mile from her home to Amelia and Charles' bungalow. Philip had placed the advertisement using his parents' address as a contact whilst he and Flora were staying with them. It was a stepping stone for a short time prior to taking up residence in their new house nearby. As soon as she rang the doorbell she realised she should have written a note to make an appointment. Annie was not yet confident with the new-fangled public telephone in its brilliant red box; she had pressed Button A too soon and lost her money the one and only time she had tried to use it. She was very impressed that there was a telephone at all in this household. Perhaps they were wealthy people. It was a Saturday – one shouldn't bother people at the weekend, she thought. It was too late now, she was on the door step.

It was Philip who answered the door.

27

'The advertisement...' she began, pulling off her beret. She couldn't think of anything else to say.

'Yes, of course. Come in. How nice of you to come round. Flora's resting at the moment but you can come into the kitchen and we can talk.'

Amelia appeared in the hallway on hearing the doorbell but left Philip to deal with it as soon as she heard the gist of the conversation.

Philip liked the look of this young woman. She was plainly dressed but neat. She held her head up and smiled though it was obvious from the twisting of her beret between her hands that she was nervous. They talked about Annie's family and she told him about her husband Frank, who worked as a print setter on the Telegraph and Argus newspaper. Philip was very relaxed, chatting in an amiable manner which gradually put Annie at her ease. He admitted that they had never thought of having any help but it now seemed that they needed someone, for he was extremely busy settling into a new job, there was much to do to get the house straight and of course there would be a baby in a few weeks' time.

'I'm sorry I can't show you round the house, we don't take possession of it until next week. Would you rather wait and see it before you make a decision?' he asked her.

'You mean you want me to start like? To do the 'ousework and cook? Perhaps I could give a hand with the bairn as well?'

'Yes, that's exactly it. Do you think you can do that?' Philip asked her.

'Oh aye, I can do that a'right,' she said with enthusiasm. 'I love cooking and I've had plenty of practice looking after bairns.'

There was talk of hours and pay. Then Philip said,

'Well what do you say?'

Annie said yes with a big grin which lit up her plain featured face.

She came to help the day Philip and Flora moved into the house in Heaton, a suburb of Bradford, up the hill behind the Royal Infirmary. It was to be a day she would remember forever.

Having left London some weeks before, Philip and Flora's furniture had been taken by the removal company to Bradford where it was now stored.

Philip had explained to Annie, they were staying with Amelia and Charles during the weeks of waiting before the keys of their house were released. His mother, Amelia, had said it was an ideal opportunity for Flora to put her feet up. She had noticed that as time went by Flora was increasingly tired and Flora had been grateful for Amelia's thoughtful suggestion.

The move was planned early enough for them to get established before the baby was born. The intention was that Annie would take some of the burden from Flora; unpacking, finding places to store their as yet modest belongings, do some shopping to stock the larder and generally help to settle in. And, of course, to cook. One of her duties was to help prepare a room for the baby, clean it and install the cot ready with its blankets and sheets.

Philip asked Annie to be at the house by eight o'clock on the morning of the move to meet him and open the house. The removal van was timed to arrive at nine. Amelia and Charles' plan was to drive Flora to the house at ten so that they could help to set up the kitchen and serve cups of tea and prepare lunch.

But it didn't work out like that.

***

Amelia knew nothing of Flora's pains as she got up on the morning of the move; pains that were rapidly becoming more regular and increasing in frequency. Flora was terrified but could not bring herself to tell Amelia, knowing that the arrival of the baby at this stage would cause some disruption to their plans. But Amelia was not easily fooled by Flora's struggle to conceal her discomfort, it was obvious to her by mid-morning that all their planning was about to fall apart. She made her way to the kitchen where Annie was washing up cups and saucers which she had just unwrapped. She closed the kitchen door and said to Annie,

'I think we are going to have to manage by ourselves Annie.'

'What is it? Is Mrs H bad?'

'I think the baby is on its way. I'm not surprised, looking at the size of the girl.'

'But it's not time Mrs Hampton is it? Ee, I hope everything's a'right.'

'So do I! What a good thing Philip was able to get a telephone installed so soon. One of the perks of his position I suppose. We'd better get him to call an ambulance straight away.'

As the removal vans pulled out of the drive of their new home, their work done, Flora watched them leave and seconds later saw with relief the ambulance hurtle into the crescent shape of the gravel entrance. She was ushered into the vehicle gently but with some haste. It was obvious there was no time to lose.

As the ambulance doors closed it was Annie who called out,

'Now don't you worry, we'll get everything straight ready for your return.' She waved as Flora was driven away shouting 'Good luck! See the two of you soon.'

Philip was in a state of near panic.

Charles hurried forward and pushed the car keys into Philip's hand.

'Follow them. Wait at the hospital until there's some news. We'll just get on with things. It'll be fine. Give her our love,' and he waved him away.

Philip followed the ambulance, its bell clanging. He was relieved it was only a matter of minutes to the Maternity Department of the Royal Infirmary. How right his father had been about the convenience of a hospital so near, not that he had envisaged a scene such as this when his father had made the joke.

***

Annie was excited at Flora's return within the week with a daughter; healthy, rosy cheeked and already with huge dark brown eyes. She had weighed over eight pounds at birth and had caused a little concern at the Maternity Unit after the midwife in the delivery room had examined Flora.

'This is a big baby for someone as small as you Mrs Hampton. I gather it's arrived earlier than predicted? Well, it's a good job, goodness knows how big she would have been if she'd been full term. It wasn't easy for you, we know but it could have been worse. Nevertheless you did very well. It must have been quite a burden carrying around that weight during these last weeks. You'll need to rest quite a bit every day for some time until you get your strength back. I hope you've got some help.'

Annie could see after only one week of going in every day that Flora was not going to manage, she was not the domestic type, never mind having just given birth. It didn't take long for Annie to be involved in looking after that 'cuddly bairn', as she called Connie. Annie was kind and sympathetic with Flora's continued post-natal fatigue but at the same time she was efficient and firm in her routine, especially where the bairn was concerned.

'Connie, well what a name!' Annie had murmured to herself. She wasn't sure whether she liked it but then it was none of her business. Goodness knows what she might have called her own, if she'd had any that is. What she did know was that she loved that child from the moment she came into the house.

7

Yorkshire 1939

After nearly six months of arriving every day as regular as clockwork Annie saw no effort on Flora's part to cope with the running of the household, Annie knew this was to be the pattern. She had waited patiently for what she had thought were 'baby-blues' to lift but it was soon evident that Flora had no intention of taking over. Annie could not fathom whether it be by design or because she truly was not the managing type domestically.

She also saw Flora's reluctance to bond with her daughter which did not diminish as the days went by; it puzzled her. Annie found herself more and more responsible for the care of the bairn.

Annie spent Christmas Day at home with Frank having shopped, cooked and worked right up until Christmas Eve in order to leave the new family home neat and tidy and with but a few preparations for their Christmas meal.

'You know Frank,' she confided to him as they ate their meal, 'she's a reet clever lady; Mr 'ampton told me she speaks French *and* Spanish. But she don't seem able to organise the 'ousehold.'

'Ye mean the Mrs? Aye well, p'rhaps she doesn't want to.'

'I've wondered. But what worries me is she's not looking after that bairn the way she should, after all she's 'er mother. She doesn't cuddle 'er, or talk to 'er, and it's me what feeds 'er. It's just as though she doesn't luv 'er.'

'Now then, stop your worrying. You look after 'er don't you?'

'That's what I mean. It shouldn't be me, it should be 'er, 'er own mother what looks after 'er. I do the cooking and cleaning and a bit of help with the bairn, that's fine, that's what they took me on for, or so I thought.'

'If you don't like it Annie, leave. You don't have to do it. We can manage luv.'

'Leave? Eh, I couldn't do that. I luv that bairn!'

32

'Well then, eat up, and stop worrying.'

***

In late February Philip went away for two weeks. He was invited to join a course in cryptography at Broadway Buildings, London. Philip knew the venue, somewhere between the Admiralty and the Foreign Office, and had no difficulty in making his way there directly. He was intrigued to find that the course was attended by other young men mostly mathematicians, some linguists. They all enjoyed being taken out to a good lunch at the Travellers' Club and it struck Philip that this little venture was as much for their hosts to scrutinise them in congenial surroundings, as it was to instruct them later in cryptography; for they were to discover that is why they were there.

This was Philip's first absence since Connie's birth, returning home after two weeks he knew that he would be going to London again quite soon, but this time it would be for an indefinite period. He kept the information to himself so that they were able to enjoy their first Christmas as a family together, without the cloud of a longer-lasting departure hanging over them.

When the time came for his second departure Philip felt uncomfortable; he was not at liberty to speak of his work. All he could say was that he had been asked to join others on a special project which was confidential.

'We all have to be located in the same centre so that we can work together,' he had told them. 'That means that I shall be away from home for a while.' At first Flora naively assumed it was to do with his work at the bank. She was aware of the rumblings of war but she did not sense any kind of foreboding and took Philip's departure as a temporary arrangement. Charles Hampton knew otherwise. He was alert to the signs and general news broadcast on the wireless and to articles that filled the newspapers every day. He was uneasy, he had seen it all before. What he did not know was that by September Britain would be at war.

***

In the spring of 1939, before the general population of the country knew that they would be at war before long, Philip was one of several young men pulled out of every-day life to join the unusual assortment of classical scholars, mathematicians, linguists and puzzle addicts, who were sent to Bletchley Park, in Buckinghamshire. Many of them had never heard of Station X, the alternative name given to Britain's code-breaking establishment, housed in what was formerly a mansion, its extensive grounds an ideal location for top secret war work. Code breaking, the intercepting and reading of messages of other powers, had been going on – in every capital – for two decades. Everyone seemed to be reading everyone else's codes. But it was Poland, learning code breaking after the First World War to a height of achievement that was not matched by any of the other great powers, who gave information to this newly formed team at Bletchley Park, as a basis for working on decrypting German Enigma signals.

The first group of members of the Government Code and Cypher School were moved to this country setting from Room 40, the curious and unofficial name for the code breaking cypher bureau of the Naval Intelligence Division in Broadway Buildings in London, where Philip first joined the swelling number of recruits. As many staff as five hundred by mid-1939, were now working on British cryptography. More space was urgently needed. These early 'guests' to Bletchley Park were obliged to disguise their visit, and were known as Captain Ridley's shooting party, in order to conceal their clandestine activities.

In February Philip arrived to find he knew some of the other members from his days in Cambridge. It was a surprise and pleasure to meet again a fellow mathematician and worthy chess opponent who was much admired by Philip for being British boys' chess champion. He could almost have believed he was a young man of twenty back at university with his fellow students.

Eric, with whom Philip found himself sharing the tasks of translating, had worked and studied in Germany for four years at the same time as Philip and they had had the good fortune to meet several times. Philip had returned from Germany in 1937, but Eric had only recently returned when suddenly he was summoned to a briefing in Broadway Buildings, and subsequently joined the party at Bletchley Park. Neither Philip nor Eric ever found out how they came to be invited to join the Government Code and Cypher School but they were both ideal recruits.

Philip was relieved to find that he would never handle a gun, never be faced with having to kill the 'enemy'; instead he would be amongst colleagues of like mind and ability, doing what he knew he did best – using his intelligence and language skills.

In May after three months away, Philip was given a forty-eight hour leave, his first visit home since becoming established at Bletchley Park. It was a happy visit despite the fact that Philip revealed he had to return to his duties indefinitely for the foreseeable future. At least he was able to tell Flora, without disclosing any details, that he was doing valuable war work.

One of the pleasures he looked forward to, going to visit Amelia and Charles, with Flora and Connie in her pram, was marred by an overheard remark as they walked along. 'Why ain't *'e* in uniform? There's nowt wrong wi' 'im that I can see.' The words were spoken loudly and Philip knew they were meant to shame him. Flora gasped. 'Don't take any notice,' he said, 'Just keep walking.'

Later he spoke to her of the incident.

'You know I'm doing something worthwhile, don't you? I'm sorry that I can't tell you about it. But that's how it is. I'm even more sorry that you had to hear that remark. They're only showing themselves up in fact; conscription is in age groups and there are many men who haven't yet had their call-up papers.' Flora nodded and said, 'It's all right. I can take it,' and she smiled at him.

***

Some weeks later Frank received news that he had been expecting for some time. His call-up papers arrived. As a long-term member of the Territorial Army, young and healthy, he was not surprised to hear the Army Despatch rider roar up their short garden path and rap hard on the front door. Annie opened it and blanched at the sight of the brown envelope.

'Frank Bates?' he directed at Frank standing close behind her. 'Orders. Bet it's to report to Catterick Camp,' he said grinning. 'And I bet it's *toot sweet.*' He laughed at his own attempt to lighten the moment with what he thought was a fair imitation of the French expression. He climbed back on his motor bicycle and sped off down the path leaving the gate open, shouting 'Ta ta for now!' Trying to disguise his trembling hand Frank tore open the envelope.

'Is it?' Annie asked. Frank took her in his arms and whispered in her ear,

'Aye, next week.' He felt Annie shudder. 'Don't worry luv, it's for training you know, just in case. I'll be back soon.'

''Ow did he know it were Catterick? Clever devil! Does he read 'em all?'

Frank laughed at Annie's indignation at the cocky Despatch Rider.

'Actually, he were wrong; I'm going to Pontefract. So he doesn't know everything does he?'

Frank wrote home that first night in the camp,

'...it looks as though I'm going to be here for twelve weeks, I'm told I've been recruited into the West Yorkshire Regiment, how about that! I'll let you know more later but I'll have to be careful what I say, they're already checking what we write to our loved ones. I'll get some leave I expect, so I'll see you afore long...take care. Love you!'

Within a month of the declaration of war on the 3rd of September, Frank's fighting role began. Given a forty-eight leave from his training at Pontefract, Frank went home excited at the prospect of rejoining his Regiment and beginning what he saw as an adventure. Even so he was uneasy about telling Annie that they had such a short time together, not knowing when they might see each other again.

Annie greeted him on his arrival,

'Eh, ya look reet 'ansome in uniform.' And she hugged him.

'What do ya mean – 'in uniform'? I've allus been 'ansome, haven't I?'

'Get on with ya, stop swanking.'

'I'll have to make the most of this smart outfit, I don't suppose it'll stay looking like this for long.'

Annie's smile dropped. 'What...

'Well, ya know, I 'spect it'll get a bit grubby 'ere and there.'

Frank's war was just beginning but Philip had already settled into his new role. Frank was seen as a soldier in uniform, going to fight for King and country and Annie had news of his posting but Philip did not wear a uniform and his whereabouts and duties were unknown to the family.

Philip hardly dare admit to himself that he was enjoying his work, perhaps even more than his job in the bank. He felt twinges of guilt when he read his father's letters; news of men in Bradford, like Frank, receiving their call up papers. They left their wives and families behind, as Philip had done, but they were seen as heroes. It was hard not being able to tell his father what he was doing, or where he was, and he knew it was hard for his father too. Philip realised that had he known anything of his son's work he would never have divulged it to others

36

but Philip, sworn to secrecy himself, didn't put him in that difficult position of having to conceal the facts. He would have been even more troubled if he had known that it would be at least three decades before he would be able to tell him anything of his life and work at Bletchley Park.

October 1939

Philip and Flora had never thought of having permanent 'help' let alone a housekeeper but the offer that Annie Bates boldly put forward came when both the family and she needed to make a change.

'If it would be more convenient I could... like... well, ya know, live in so to speak...while Frank's away,' Annie uncharacteristically stammered. She watched Flora's expression and hurriedly added, 'You being on your own like, ye'll be needing more 'elp and company... but I wouldn't expect any more money you know. We none of us know what's going to 'appen and you said, just the other day, that Mr 'ampton would probably be going away for a while, so you thought, but of course we all 'ope it's not for long.'

Annie was out of breath after the outburst and then felt uncomfortable as she waited for Flora's reply. Perhaps for once she shouldn't have been her usual outspoken self. Perhaps it was a bit of a cheek, but Annie knew there was adequate accommodation – that small bedroom just off the first landing would do her just fine. She had thought out the practicalities of it all. Nothing ventured, nothing gained she had thought.

'Well, what do you think Mrs 'ampton?'

'Won't your husband... won't Frank mind if you let your house go?'

'Oh no, it's only a rented place and I'm sure we'll find another when the time comes. To tell you the truth...we had a chat about it, Frank and me, and he thinks I'll be a bit lonely.' What Annie didn't tell Flora was Frank's unexpected remark that it would save them a bit of money; not having to pay rent. They would both have a roof over their heads and both would be fed. Annie knew that Frank had aspirations to buy a house one day and she saw the sense in it, a way of saving towards it.

'Frank says he doesn't really know when 'e'll be back and as you know I've got no bairns. It's all so sudden and uncertain isn't it? All this 'itler business. It might sound a bit selfish but I reckon Frank's right I could rightly do with some company too, I'm already feeling a bit.. you know.. on me own like.' There was another long pause before Flora said,

'But what about when Frank has leave? Wouldn't that be a bit difficult; he'll have no home to go to?'

In truth this had not occurred to either Annie or Frank. They had mulled over so many aspects of such a move, their saving money and Annie not being lonely being uppermost in Frank's mind, but neither of them had thought about leave. It was almost as though they had accepted that they wouldn't see each other for some time. It was Annie's turn to be silent until Flora broke in on her thoughts.

'You have a cousin in Shipley, don't you Annie? Perhaps she could put you up for a day or two if... I mean, when Frank comes home.'

'Aye I do, you mean Beatrice. Of course, I never thought of that Mrs H. She'd like that, we don't see much of one another and neither of us 'as any other relative. The only thing is, well...it would mean me being away from 'ere for a couple of days or so, depending on Frank's leave. Who would look after... I mean, would you be able to manage everything, not having been well a while ago?'

'I think we would manage well enough Annie. My mother-in-law is very helpful, always asking if they can have Connie. I don't suppose it would happen very often.'

'No probably not.'

'Sorry Annie, I didn't mean that to sound quite so selfish, of course I hope you *do* see Frank often.' Flora paused and then, 'I think I like your idea Annie.'

So it was settled there and then. Flora was comfortable with someone with a forthright manner like Annie's and she recognised straight away that she would never want to have to manage without her help; her moving in made it likely that she never would.

Annie became known in the area as the Hampton's housekeeper, a position she relished and a title she enjoyed. She was right about the help and the need of company for both of them.

8

Annie's settling in was well-timed, coinciding with the next surprise. Flora, knowing Connie was well looked after, saw the opportunity to find herself some work, something interesting, something useful. She saw all too clearly that domesticity was becoming tiresome and that it would be seen as patriotic to 'do her bit'. So many of the able bodied men were leaving and Flora realised that she would have no difficulty finding a responsible job. She was a little rusty perhaps but she knew she could soon work up her practical skills and play a valuable role.

She felt some sense of duty and though it might not be *expected* of her with a small child to care for, she didn't have a valid excuse for staying at home. She knew of many young mothers who left their little ones with grandparents whilst they worked in the factories and offices, after all she could rely on Annie to care for Connie. Since Philip's short leave in May Flora had found the routine of daily life monotonous. Taking Connie out in her pram was quite a pleasant pastime, people stopped and looked at the baby, cooed and smiled, declaring Connie a beautiful child commenting on her huge brown eyes. Sometimes Flora walked to Amelia and Charles' bungalow which pleased them, they couldn't see enough of their grandchild. Nevertheless, Flora found there was a limit to her pleasure in these walks.

However, her plan to find work came to nothing. It came as no surprise to Annie when Flora told her the news. She had seen Flora's paler than usual complexion and her hasty dashing to the bathroom first thing in the morning. Nevertheless she exclaimed with delight at the prospect of a new baby in the house. It was difficult to tell whether Flora was pleased or not.

Flora kept the news to herself for as long as possible. Her letter to Philip prompted him to telephone home straight away.

'Darling, I'm absolutely delighted. What a surprise!' How naïve Philip could be at times, Flora thought.

'How are you? Do you need me to come home? I don't know whether I can get time off, we're frantically busy here.'

'It would be lovely to see you but don't worry I'm fine, we're managing very well. Will you be home for Christmas?'

'That I can't say. It depends…on many things. But of course if it's at all possible I'll be there. I wouldn't want to miss seeing Connie open her Christmas presents.' There was a pause and then he said,

'And be with you of course. I do feel bad not being there … at a time like this. And Flora – I don't want you to get a job.'

'I'm not ill Philip, only pregnant. I'm fine. But Philip, do try to come, Connie hardly knows who you are.'

Sadly Philip did not see Connie open her Christmas presents but his request for compassionate leave in January for the birth of his second daughter was granted.

He arrived home to discover that public air raid shelters had been built, gas masks issued and barrage balloons loomed overhead. The family's Ration Books had been locked in a drawer in the kitchen dresser. Flora had handed them over to Annie's keeping instructing her to use them shrewdly. Annie's typical response had been that there wasn't much chance of her doing otherwise! Shops in the centre of Bradford were boarded up – one with the cheerful and optimistic sign *'Called up Chums! Back as soon as we beat Hitler'* to which Philip responded with a rueful smile. Shut away in the Berkshire countryside he was unaware of some of the inconveniences, even struggles, taking place elsewhere.

He was concerned to find that his father had joined the Air Raid Precautions organisation. As an air raid warden he was the proud owner of a brass bell with red handle.

'Dad, I'm not at all happy about this ARP business you know. It's not good for you to be out and about patrolling the streets in the cold night air.'

'Now then Philip, you're doing your bit and I want to do mine. I'm sixty-one not ninety-one, there's life in the old dog yet,' he laughed which caused a deep wheeze, belying the assurance of his words.

'You don't know how much I enjoy knocking on a door shouting "Put that light out!". You'd be amazed how many people leave doors open and forget to draw their blackout curtains. The tiniest crack is as good as a searchlight beaming into the street.'

He knew that if it came to it he wouldn't be able to help police or householders when the bombs came, his shortage of breath would limit his aid. His earlier Army experience during the First World War gave him the ability and confidence to keep an emergency situation under control, co-ordinate services and give directions, he knew he could do that, but as yet, no bombs had fallen on Bradford, for which he was grateful.

Philip returned, secretly very happy to be going back to the challenging work. The train rumbled out of Forster Square Station in Bradford, packed to the hilt with young men in khaki. He received more than one questioning glance at his conspicuous lack of uniform. He made himself as comfortable as he could squashed into the full carriage and raised his newspaper to block questions though it wasn't the first time he had heard the words 'What's he up to then? Coward or what?'

He closed his ears, safe in the knowledge that he was making a contribution. Once more he felt a twinge of guilt when he thought about Flora. He was thrilled that they were to have another child, he could hardly believe it. He would be relying heavily on letters from Amelia and Charles as well as Flora, to set his mind at rest. His knowledge that capable Annie watched over them raised his spirits. How thankful he was that Annie's coming to them had happened when it did.

1940

Annie was in her element caring for both Connie and Garnet, cooking and generally keeping the house in good order. Flora found housework tedious but could see that perhaps she was expecting too much of Annie. It was time she spoke to Annie about her plan.

'Annie, I'm feeling much better these days and things are running smoothly here at home, thanks to you, so I've decided to look for a job.' Flora paused as Annie slowly nodded her head.

'Aye, well I know you were thinking about it before Garnet came along.'

'I've made some enquiries at the Royal Infirmary and I'm told they are desperate for someone to run the Admissions Department. The young man who was in charge has been called up and apparently things have become a bit disorganised. I know I'm a bit rusty but I think I could soon get things in hand.'

'I think that's a good idea Mrs H. I think you'd enjoy that. I can manage everything 'ere at home.'

'Now I don't expect you to look after everything Annie. My job will only be part-time but I shall be earning enough to pay for some extra help.'

'Eh, Mrs H. you don't need to do that.'

'Well, lots of women are looking for work these days, with husbands away incomes are a bit stretched, so we'll be doing someone a favour won't we? I will be able to pay someone to do the cleaning and you can concentrate on the cooking and looking after the girls. How do you feel about that?'

'Well, it's not up to me Mrs H but I 'ave to say I'll be more than happy with that.'

'Good. Then we all benefit.'

What Flora did not admit to Annie, or anyone else for that matter, was that working would not only free her of the boredom of the domestic routine, but would also help to keep her thoughts occupied. She had been dwelling too much recently on Ramon.

She knew that he and his family had been through hell. The civil war in Spain had torn the country apart, set brother against brother, friend against friend, neighbour against neighbour. Poverty, famine, destruction of their homes and land, and even murder, had brought the proud people of Spain to their knees.

She had never understood how Ramon had come to be in England in 1937 and had stayed despite the fact that he must have known what was happening at home.

She had tried more than once to ask him about his home and family but he had brushed her questions aside. His smiling lips had hardened into a thin line and he had snapped at her when she broached the subject again. It was the only time she had seen him display any kind of bad humour. She had learned so little of Ramon's background and his life when she had loved him, now, when she could no longer afford even to think of him, she tried to parcel up the memories and pack them away in her mind. This vulnerable parcel of thoughts and emotions must be pushed deep into her subconscious. She had a new life and knew that she must live it as a wife and mother. She had broken away once before as a young woman and by her own diligence had given herself the chance of something better. This life of domesticity was not what she had envisaged as her future but this time she was trapped. Having a responsibility outside the home would free her to some extent.

She couldn't escape from the hardships of this war, and the awful 'goings on' as Annie called them, but she knew that the Hampton family was more fortunate than many. She listened to the wireless regularly, never missing the six o'clock news, and the voice of Alvar Liddell reading the reports of the blitz on London depressed her. And yet she knew their own needs were small in comparison to those people who had lost their homes and loved ones.

Annie's words came to mind once more; 'We just have to get on with it' and that is what she knew she would have to do until this war was over and Phillip came home again.

9

April, 1951

Diary:

'*A new family, a new school, a new language! How am I supposed to cope with that? I'm being sent away, they clearly don't love me and now they don't want me around anymore. I'm obviously an embarrassment to them. How convenient; just get rid of me, dump me on somebody else! Well good riddance to them all, see if I care!*

No, I don't mean that. I do care. Oh Nettie, what will I do without you. Who shall we each share our secrets with in bed, before we go to sleep. And my darling puppy, Bella, how will I manage without you? And Granny, and Gramps - I'll miss them dreadfully. But Daddy, Daddy how can you do this to me? I thought you of all people loved me. Why are you letting this happen?'

***

Connie was twelve years old when her mother called her into the study to tell her the dreadful news. Nearly thirteen, a number considered by some to be an ill-fated number but this was not how Connie saw it, she was eagerly awaiting her birthday; she would be a teenager. For Connie the ill-luck associated with the number had indeed arrived, but early, it was the end of her normal life as she would know it.

Flora was dressed in a smart suit, the jacket was shaped in to her waist which emphasised her neat figure. Even in her high heeled shoes she was still only five feet four inches tall. She was facing the bay window, gazing at her own reflection it seemed, her back to Connie as she entered the room. She did not turn or acknowledge her daughter's arrival. Connie waited knowing that to speak before her mother spoke to her was inviting a reprimand.

Flora had no idea how to begin. How could anyone know when was the right moment to tell a daughter of a shattering deception that had lasted over thirteen years? There never was a right moment of course, but Flora had no choice, it had to be now. The years had rolled by and Flora had persuaded herself that her secret would never be revealed. It had never occurred to her that one day when Connie grew up she might look at her birth date and that of her parents' marriage and then wonder. Flora had not worried at the time about what anyone else might think or say concerning Connie's 'early' arrival. She had held her head up and met their gaze. All that mattered at the time was what Philip thought. And Philip had been in raptures at the sight of his child, overjoyed to be a family man.

From the moment Connie was born Flora did not have a loving relationship with her elder daughter; she kept her distance not allowing tenderness and affection to creep in. She knew that it was her own dishonour, the lie she had been living, that prevented her from giving her love to Connie. Of course she loved her but Flora was terrified, and wrong, about the fact that if she had shown her love it would have unravelled her. She knew that then she would have told Philip everything; and *that* she could not do, their marriage would have been at stake; she stood to lose him and she realized that now she loved him.

At this very moment as she began to speak to her daughter she was sick at heart; this revelation was going to tear her family apart.

There was no going back, she had told Philip that she, and she alone, must do it and he had left her to the task.

Connie waited patiently.

'I have something to tell you,' her mother said after a few moments.

'This isn't going to be easy, either for you or me, but I have to do it. I don't know any other way of doing it Connie but this.'

There was another pause and then she said, 'The man you think of as daddy, isn't actually your father.' Flora turned round slowly.

It didn't make sense to Connie. She gaped at her mother. Was it some kind of a joke? Connie was not used to her mother joking, their relationship had never been easy; reprimands and criticisms yes, she was used to those, but not jokes.

'Well, say something Connie,' her mother's voice was so quiet Connie could hardly hear her.

'I…I don't understand…' she offered.

'No, I didn't expect you would.' Her mother turned back towards the window and gazed out again. 'It's all too complicated Connie. I can't go into details but there are some things you should know.' She stopped speaking, affecting an interest in the garden.

Connie waited in the silence.

'What things Ma?'

'*Don't* call me 'ma', you know how I loathe it.'

'Sorry.' She waited, then 'What things?' she asked again.

'Well, it's your name, it isn't Connie, not even Constance. It's Conchita.'

'What sort of a name is that?' she asked incredulously in a tone she wouldn't normally have dared to use to her mother.

'It's Spanish. Your father is Spanish,' Flora whispered.

'Spanish?' Connie almost spat the word. 'How?'

'Because he was born in Spain of course. Don't be tiresome Connie. It's obvious.'

Flora was lost, she could not keep the irritation out of her voice mostly because she did not know what to say next.

Nothing was obvious to Connie at this point. There was another long pause and Connie approached her mother at the window. She was already inches taller than her mother and took care not to stand too close. Flora had told her many times not to 'tower' above her.

'You said "a few things" Ma – Mother. What else?'

'You're going to live in Spain. It's all arranged. You're leaving next week. I can't help it Connie I have no choice, it's the only thing to do, believe me. Annie will help you pack, of course, I can't cope with all this upset and I'm going to be rather busy anyway.'

"Busy" Connie thought, doing what? She went white and started to sway on her long slim legs. She sat down quickly on the window seat trying to take in the third shocking revelation that her mother had just thrown at her.

Her father wasn't her father. Her name wasn't Connie and she was being sent away to a foreign land.

'But what about Daddy? What does Daddy say?' Connie said as she felt the hot tears stinging the backs of her eyes. 'He won't let me go, I know he won't.' It was almost a whisper.

'Daddy, as you call him, has no say in the matter. As I have just told you he is not your father anyway, and it's not up to him. So you needn't think you can go twisting him round your little finger like you usually do.'

It was a cruel remark and an unfair accusation. She and her father had a natural, loving relationship, with respect for one another. Connie thought him handsome; he was tall, with sparkling blue eyes, fair hair that fell over his forehead like a small boy; a gentle and quietly spoken man. To her he was the most wonderful man, far nicer than the fathers of any of her friends. Despite her age and long legs she still sat with him, half on his knee, half lolling back in the big old leather chair in the study, the very room where her mother had just told her the devastating news.

Every evening, after her tea when he came in after work, she told him about her school day. It was a ritual, before she settled down to do her homework. She was looking at the chair now and imagining him draping his long loose limbs over the worn seat of the chair, feeling the comfort and warmth of him, as she nestled in his arms. She loved him deeply. She had always thought she was a bit like him; with her long legs and quiet disposition. She wanted to be like him – kind and gentle. She admired him so. Suddenly she thought about her hair – thick like his but not fair, hers was brown, so very dark brown. Almost black. And her large eyes, deep brown eyes, were quite unlike her father's sparkling blue. It was Garnet who had fair hair, and the blue eyes. Pattie her American school friend had once said to her,

'I guess you're not really English with all that dark hair.' At the time Connie had laughed at the very idea, with the words 'Of course I am!'

Remembering Pattie's words brought her quickly back to reality.

'I- will- not- cry,' she whispered to herself. 'I will not.'

Connie's ability not to cry, in any given situation that might normally warrant it, had grown from sheer practice. She called on it often when she was determined that her mother should not see the frequent hurt she caused her. Besides, it helped her to push away the pain for a while, though inevitably it returned at bedtime when the tears then ran and soaked into her pillow, unheard and unseen, even by her sister Garnet in the twin bed beside her, who fortunately often fell asleep before Connie.

How many times had she brought home a poem, a drawing, a piece of written work from school to show her parents, only to be met with barely a glance from her mother and the remark 'very nice dear'. Connie knew no-one else who used that word 'nice' with the same cold intonation as her mother did.

Connie would say, 'But you haven't looked Ma.'

'Don't be tiresome Connie. Of course I've looked. It's just another piece of school work after all.'

Daddy, the man she had thought of as her father until this moment, would call her over.

'Let *me* look darling,' and he would take the drawing and commend it, picking up its good points and praising her.

'Well done, my love,' he would say. Her mother, sighing audibly from the other side of the room, would bid her daughter to run along and play. It was always the same and Connie grew to expect the format and yet she still brought her work home in the hope that one day her mother would look at it and say -

'Very nice darling,' and mean it. She did not understand her mother's coldness and attitude towards her which, of late, Connie had begun to question. She was grateful to her father for his well-meant words and for his obvious love but she still craved her mother's recognition of her efforts. It wasn't the praise she wanted but the love she needed, a love that she had grown to recognise her mother would not, perhaps could not, give her. She didn't understand why.

Connie lifted her head and took a deep breath.

'I can't go to Spain Mother, this is only my second year at the Grammar School, and I like it there. I thought you and Daddy were pleased that I got a scholarship to go there.'

'I'm afraid it's the other way round; *not* you can't go to Spain because you are at a good school in Harrogate, but that you can't continue at Donnington's because you are going to Spain.'

'But what about my place? I worked hard for that, you know I did M...Mother' she said in a voice the nearest Connie had ever got to being impertinent.

'There are schools in Spain you know. Your father will find a suitable one for you.'

Connie could barely control the tears but frustration was also rising in her chest. She didn't seem to be getting anywhere with her mother. Every question was blocked. Except one – her passport!

'If you say my name is... different, how can I possibly go abroad, next week, unless I have a passport? It's against the law.'

'You have a passport. I sent your birth certificate to the passport office sometime ago. You are registered as Conchita López, father Ramon López, and that's what it says on your passport.'

'Does Daddy know about that?'

'He does now.'

'Why? Why did you register me as Lo..lo..whatever. Why not our name, Hampton. Daddy's name?'

'That's enough Connie,' she said quietly, and Connie thought she heard a sadness in her mother's voice, a tone she had never heard before.

'No more questions, I can't cope with them now.'

Connie could have guessed her mother's ensuing words;

'Run along now. I've got things to do.'

Connie turned, grateful to escape for the tears were coming and there was nothing she could do about it.

*****

Philip Hampton arrived late at the bank that morning. He did not want to leave the house at all but Flora insisted that he leave her to do what she must - alone. His late arrival, noticed by his Personal Assistant was remarked upon with the question,

'Everything all right Mr Hampton?'

'I've got a bad headache Maggie, I'd better have some tablets.'

Maggie departed to fetch water and his preferred medication.

Maggie watched her boss go through the motions of the business day, shuffling papers, and delegating to deputies to take calls. It was obvious he was unable to concentrate. Her frequent questioning glances gave away her concern but Philip insisted that it was 'just a thumping head'. She knew him well enough to realise that there was something very wrong, she had never seen him so distracted.

*****

Philip was still in a state of disbelief and shock. For over three years Flora had kept the blackmail to herself, and the deception of Connie's true parentage for thirteen years. It had been a nightmare of a day and he could take no more. He left early with a message to Maggie to deal with the rest of the mail.

As he entered their smart, double fronted house in a leafy suburb of Harrogate he hesitated. He wasn't ready to face Flora and he was dreading seeing Connie's expression for he knew what it would be; incredulity, confusion, hurt and fear. All the things he himself had experienced as Flora told him of her debts. Sheer extravagance and overspending was something he could have coped with but how this debt had come about was like something out of a bad dream, a nightmare in fact.

He had been duped for over twelve years and the hurt of it was physical as well as emotional. He felt battered and unutterably tired. The door catch clicked and Bella's sharp ears caught the sound. She came bounding towards him down the wide hallway.

'Good girl, good girl. Down now. There's a good girl,' and he gently pushed Connie's black Labrador puppy away from him. The living room door opened and Flora stood, with pale face and tightly

50

clasped hands in front of her. She waited until Philip had taken off his coat and then motioned for him to follow her into the room.

'I told her this afternoon, after she got in from school,' she said quietly. Her voice was low and unusually soft, its normal confident and often imperious tones were absent.

'Where is she?' he murmured

'In her room.'

'I'll go to her straight away,' he said turning towards the door.

'Philip...Philip... could you come back here? I have to explain,' she looked straight at him and he realised that she had been crying. He had not seen Flora weep for a long time and he felt a pain shoot through his chest. For a moment he wanted to take her in his arms and tell her he loved her, but the moment was gone before his dulled brain could instruct his body to act. He left the room and climbed slowly up the stairs to Connie's room.

10

Diary

It's true! Daddy has told me. He says he's not my real father. He won't explain, he says he and mummy have to have a discussion. A discussion about what? I don't understand. I feel as though someone has punched a hole in my stomach and everything is leaking out. Granny! She'll help. She'll explain. She doesn't mince words, she'll tell me the truth.

***

Philip knocked gently on Connie's room door. There was no response and no sound within. He waited a moment and then knocked again and said quietly,

'Connie, it's Daddy. May I come in?' He waited and was ready to speak again when he heard a soft shuffling sound. The door opened slowly and his tousled-haired and swollen-eyed daughter peered cautiously through a narrow gap.

'Is it just you Daddy?' she whispered.

He nodded and Connie opened the door wider to let him in. He no sooner stepped through than she flung herself into his arms and began sobbing. He lifted her up as he used to do when she was just a small child. He sat on her bed and cradled her in his arms, rocking gently until her sobs slowly began to subside, too exhausted to cry any more. At last she spoke,

'Is it true Daddy? Tell me it isn't,' she pleaded looking up into his face. He gently eased her from his arms.

'Sit on the bed Connie, I'll pull up this chair. I want to face you, look at you as we talk.'

He paused, how was he to explain to this young, naïve girl that he was not her biological father?

52

'Well, it would seem that... that it is true, that I am not your *real* father,' he began. Connie gasped and reached out a hand.

'But how? I don't understand.' He took her hand in his and began again slowly.

'There are many things I don't understand either Connie, not yet, but your mother and I are going to have a long talk this evening. There's one thing I want to say now, regardless of any explanations that may come later, and that is that I love you, very much, and you must never forget that. I was there at your birth Connie though I didn't see much of you when you were a toddler. I had to rely on a few black and white photos that Mummy sent to me while I was away, taken with our old Brownie box camera.'

Philip tried to keep his voice steady and speak of normal things. Connie relaxed a little and gave a wan smile remembering the photos she had looked at time and again, now pasted into a black album.

'But remember this,' he went on, 'As far as I'm concerned you have been my daughter for over twelve years and whatever happens, in my eyes, you will always be my daughter. Promise me Connie that you will remember this.'

Philip heard the quaver in his own voice and could no longer trust himself to speak. They sat silently holding hands for a few moments.

'I'm sorry Connie, I can give you no more explanation until Mummy and I have discussed things a little more. I want you to be a brave girl and hang on until we can talk again.' Philip knew that in his present highly emotional state he lacked the ability to comfort his daughter and that he was, by postponing any further explanation, being feeble when he should have appeared strong and supportive.

'Garnet knows nothing of this yet I presume?' he asked.

'No, she's gone to her music lesson, straight from school. And then she's going to Vicky's for tea. Vicky's Daddy always brings her home after. What am I going to say to her Daddy? She'll go crazy when she finds out what's happening.' Connie's eyes began to fill with tears again at the thought of her sister's reaction.

'We shall tell her together, all of us, Mummy too. I'll arrange things with Mummy now before Garnet gets back. Now, you will you be all right for a little while, won't you? Why don't you go down to Annie. She will have got you some tea ready by now.'

'Does she know?' Connie asked.

'No, but look, I'll go down and tell her you've had an upset and then she won't be surprised to see you looking a little troubled. You know Annie, she doesn't ask questions. What do you say?'

'All right. Tell her I just want a sandwich. And a glass of milk, please.'

'Right. I'll see you later.' He gave Connie a hug and quickly left the room before his emotions began again to get the better of him.

Connie sat for some minutes trying to persuade herself that she could go down to the kitchen, act normally and eat some tea.

***

In 1940 Philip was already ensconced at Bletchley Park, highly hush-hush work that he couldn't speak about to anyone, including Flora. Flora had relied heavily on Amelia and Charles for support and comfort during the years that Philip was away.

He had had very little chance to go home and see his family, but just once, for a weekend, he was given permission to leave Bletchley Park. Connie was ten months old, making babbling sounds which Philip was sure included the word 'dada'. He left to return to Bletchley, thrilled with this child, his daughter, convinced that she would know him the next time she saw him.

It was January, exactly nine months later that he came home again, this time on compassionate grounds. Philip arrived at the doors of the delivery room in the maternity home just in time to hear his second daughter's first cries.

'What's her name?' he asked a sleepy Flora. 'Have you chosen?'

'Garnet,' she murmured. 'The birthstone for January. She is a gem, isn't she?' Philip nodded with tears in his eyes.

'And so are you, my love, for giving me two beautiful daughters.'

He didn't see much of his family during the years 1939 to 1945 and was grateful that Amelia and Charles lived close at hand.

***

It was 1942 that Annie received the yellow envelope, the dreaded telegram.

'We regret to inform you ....'

Frank was dead, killed in the Burma campaign; so many lost their lives due to repeated battles against the Japanese advance. The Japanese marched into the country like an unstoppable flood forcing the battered British army to pull back westward to India. It had taken a month for the report to filter through.

'I'm a war widow,' she said through her tears. Dipping into her apron pocket she pulled out a crumpled handkerchief. She mopped her tears, and carefully folding the telegram she put both back in the pocket. She sniffed and looking up at Philip and Flora she said,

'I've read about women who've lost their 'usbands but I never thought it'd 'appen to me. Thousands of 'em you know, all over the country, learning to turn their hands to any kind of work they can find, and more often than not trying to raise a family without a bread winner.'

Philip and Flora were at a loss for words, it was rare to hear Annie speak at length.

'Now I'm one of 'em,'she added. 'At least I don't 'ave any bairns to worry about.'

Philip took Annie's hand.

'Annie, you must stay with us. The children love you so much and you are such a great help to us. We'd be grateful, we would consider it a privilege if you would, that is – if you would like to,' Phililp told her.

'Well, I've got no 'ome to go to have I?' she said with a sniff. 'Anyroad, I can't think of anything I'd like better Mr H. Thank you. You're very good to me and I couldn't bear to think of leaving those bairns, they feel like – well, they feel like me own.'

The move to Harrogate in 1947, after Philip's demobilisation, had put Annie 'neither up nor down' as she said at the time.

'Where you lot go, I go, if that's all right with you Mrs H.' she had said. It was all right with all of them.

**

Connie and Garnet loved Annie. She teased them, she bossed them, she wiped their tears, rubbed Iglodine ointment on their bumps and through the years had given them their daily spoonful of malt extract. Even so, right now Connie couldn't face her and yet she couldn't stay in her room indefinitely. Suddenly she had an idea – Granny! Granny was full of common sense and always a source of comfort and advice. She would go to Granny and Gramps. She didn't stop to think about the consequences but took a small case from under her bed, and piled in a pair of clean socks, knickers, a vest and a thick woolly jumper, her favourite knitted rabbit (the one Granny had made for her when she was three years old) and a book. Connie was known never to go anywhere without a book. She didn't think she would feel like reading but it hinted at normality which comforted her. Finally she emptied her money box and put the contents in her school purse.

There was just one problem, she had to get out of the house without alerting her black Labrador, Bella. One could find a way to circumvent the adults but Bella was another matter. Then she remembered that Daddy had said he would speak to Annie. If she didn't turn up Annie might mention that she had not eaten. She left her case and school blazer on the bed and went down to the kitchen. She was lucky, she could hear Annie calling Bella to come in for her supper. Nothing would tempt a Labrador away from its food, no matter how loyal it may be. Now was her chance.

'Annie, you don't mind if I take my tea up to my room, do you?'

'Of course not, love. The sandwiches and your glass of milk are on the tray, ready.'

She managed a smile in thanks and quickly went back up the stairs. She poured the drink down the wash basin in her room and stuffed the sandwiches into a paper bag she found in her blazer pocket. She tiptoed back down the stairs again, she would have to be quick otherwise Bella would be waiting to come in.

Opening the back door only enough to squeeze through, to avoid it making a noise and disturbing Bella who was licking the last crumbs from her bowl, she fled across the grass patch at the back of the house. She forgot the clothes line which caught at her hair making her stumble. Her suitcase fell from her hand and she had to reach out for it, breathing heavily she ran on. A pain stabbed in her chest and her legs felt like jelly but she kept going. At the end of the road she turned into the avenue of modern, small bungalows. From there it was only a five minute walk to number 177.

Connie had been so glad that Granny and Gramps had agreed to move nearby shortly after their own move to Harrogate, she and Garnet spent happy evenings with them when Flora and Philip were entertaining.

As she reached her grandparents' house and stood outside their front door, she wondered what she was going to say to explain her arrival. They couldn't possibly know what had happened and she suddenly felt a slight betrayal of her parents arriving with such news. She hesitated, perhaps she should creep away before they saw her but it was too late, her grandfather, in his familiar diamond patterned cardigan, was opening the front door. There was the slightest pause and then, as though he had been expecting her, he said,

'Come in sweetheart, Granny's in the back,' and he led the way down the hallway into their cosy sitting room. Connie walked into the room, dropped her case on the floor and burst into tears.

11

Philip looked at his reflection in the hall mirror before going into the sitting room. He had changed out of his dark business suit and put on a light sweater and casual trousers. He looked drawn and his eyes were still moist from the tears that had not quite fallen in front of Connie but remained waiting to drop at the slightest hint of further emotional upheaval. He found Flora standing by the bay window gazing out, a habit of hers, looking and yet not seeing beyond the pane of glass.

'I've told Annie that we shall not be wanting dinner. I've asked her to bring us some sandwiches and a pot of coffee in about an hour. She's already made Connie some tea.'

He had done this without deferring to Flora, which he might have done under normal circumstances. There was a hint of his wartime behaviour coming into action, as it did in times of intense difficulty. He had the ability to remain composed and clear-headed. He had never been much good at coping with emotional situations; this way he could close off his mind on sensitive or painful issues, believing they would either diminish or even better disappear altogether. This hadn't happened with Connie, he had almost cried in her presence and he was afraid of losing control. This was a personal crisis, the like of which Philip had never had to face before. He was now making decisions speedily and calmly, and his switch to cool efficiency startled even himself. He knew it was the only way he was going to get through this highly emotional conversation with Flora.

She turned from the window, pale and distracted. Her short, springy brown hair was uncharacteristically flat against her head as though she had forgotten to brush it when she got up that morning.

'What have I done Philip?' she murmured.

'That is what you are going to tell me Flora. You are going to start at the beginning and explain everything, every little detail. Do you hear?'

Philip had never spoken to her in this commanding way. His tone was not unkind but it was firm and authoritative.

'I'm pouring myself a whisky. What about you?"

Flora waved a glass at him, a gin and tonic already half consumed.

'Come and sit down and let's get on with it,' and he signalled the comfortable suite set out in an arc in the large sitting room.

Flora moved away from the window and sat on the ample sofa. Her petite frame seemed to have shrunk even smaller as she sank into the feather cushions. She looked like a prematurely aged child, frail and vulnerable. Philip could feel a lump rising in his throat and he took a swig of the whisky. It was strong and the heat of it dissipated the tight feeling. He sat opposite her in a large matching armchair.

'I can't help you Flora. Just start at the beginning.

***

Flora Swinburne did well at school. Her parents, in the rag trade, spent little time with her. If not at the shop – "Ladies and Gentlemen's Outfitters" on the outskirts of London – then they were, one or both of them, off to the wholesalers' warehouses, or even better to the couturiers' personal showrooms both in England and in Paris, to inspect the latest and most desirable styles. The early nineteen-twenties saw an upsurge in the interest in women's clothes. There was money about, even so short a time after the deprivations of the 1914-1918 war. Indulgent husbands, lovers and rich consorts humoured their women in their efforts to emulate affluent Parisiennes. Ivy and Bob Swinburne loved their work and gave all their energies to it, at Flora's expense.

Flora knew that she was something of an encumbrance to her parents. Ivy told her that she and Bob had decided when they married that they didn't want a family. 'But then you came along,' she said and added jokingly,

'Quite an accident! We didn't know what to call you, you were such a surprise. But you were a happy accident dear,' she put in somewhat hastily.

Schoolwork and sporting activities kept Flora occupied. She liked the mental challenge and found learning and memorising relatively easy. Her parents' disinterest in her made her all the more gregarious at school. She was popular both with her peers and with staff. It was a difficult path to tread between being called a swot or teacher's pet, and being a friend who could have some fun, even get up to mischief from time to time. Such aberrations from her normally conscientious application were dismissed by those in authority as 'high spirits' and forgiven instantly when her next piece of work achieved a high mark.

59

In the summer of 1929 she passed her *Higher School Certificate* with top marks in all subjects, a distinction in French and no idea of what she was going to do with her life. It was her father who suggested that she take a two year course at the Secretarial College. It was the only time he took an interest in her future and the only piece of good advice he ever gave her. It was two years well spent equipping her with skills to earn her living and introducing her to the world of business and commerce.

After two years Flora realised that stuck in an office, glued to a desk, seeing the same colleagues day in day out, was not for her. But what next? She wanted something different; variety and perhaps a little glamour.

The catalyst for change was an advertisement in a magazine. Imperial Airways was looking for Ground Staff at their Croydon airbase. She applied and within days was called to an interview. She was an ideal candidate she was told; attractive, well spoken, a certain amount of confidence, and excellent French – the deciding factor. She loved the varied work; sorting out ticketing and baggage problems; but most of all the daily contact with travellers, answering their questions, comforting the nervous. She felt she was stepping out into the world. She enrolled at a class to learn Spanish, keen to add to her skills.

She worked for them for two years when one day it came quite clearly and suddenly into her mind that what she really wanted to do was to gain a proper qualification in languages. She was twenty three, a little late to take up university life, to become an undergraduate, and in any case the general expectation was that girls didn't need to go to university. Marriage and a family were their calling. But Flora's enthusiasm, her past record and her experience in the real world held her in good stead and she gained a place at London University (to the amazement of all her friends and colleagues) to study French and Spanish. It didn't matter that she was a little older than the other students. She was happy, in her element learning again, but this time of her own volition.

Flora met Ramon López visiting the Students' Bar of the university. It seems he met Rhonda there on several occasions. Flora learned from the chitchat that he was living and working in London, was studying some kind of management course and was preparing to take over, sometime in the future, his father's vineyards in northern Spain which produced Rioja wine.

No-one was aware of the true reason for his being in England in 1937, when throughout his country civil war raged. She and others were curious but their questions were ignored.

Flora sat her Finals in June and she and Ramon, with mutual friends, celebrated her success; a riotous party that went on all night and into the morning until finally Ramon and Flora fell into bed at six o'clock the next morning. They both slept through the day until three in the afternoon and woke to searingly bright June sunshine. Ramon turned over in bed and enfolding her in his strong, olive skinned arms said,

'I want to wake up with you beside me every day for the rest of my life.'

Being loved was a sensation Flora had never truly experienced or at first even recognised. She thought his behaviour was just the joy and excitement of her success and the end of his studies, spilling over into the next day. She thought he was joking.

'Don't be silly,' she said laughing. 'I bet you say that to all the girls.'

Ramon sat up in bed with a jerk.

'What do you mean, 'all the girls'? There are no girls. There is only you.'

He combed his fingers through her springy brown curls and gently smoothed her fine eyebrows, first one and then the other.

'Flora, I love you.'

She lay there looking up at him, disbelievingly.

'I love you too,' she whispered. 'And there are no boys. Only you.'

He clasped her in his arms and they rolled over and over making passionate love until finally they fell into a gentle sleep. At five o'clock Ramon woke and said,

'Get up sleepy head, we are going to make plans.'

The weeks sped by. They rented a studio flat with a bedroom, bathroom and galley kitchen. Flora became anxious about money and began to look for a job.

'Nonsense,' Ramon said. 'I have enough money for both of us. You can look for a job later. Let's enjoy ourselves before I go back home.'

Flora began to wonder why Ramon had never said anything before about one day having to return to Spain. She tried yet again to ask about his home and his family, she even mentioned the war.

'I've told you before, don't ask questions. Just enjoy our being together.'

It wasn't difficult to put it out of her mind; she was so sheltered in this wonderful experience of love. Her happiness, in the knowledge that someone cared for her, was a warm, comforting blanket which wrapped itself around her, blotting out her normally sound and sensible judgement in all things practical. Love was proverbially blind.

***

The weeks rushed by, boating on the Thames, trips to theatre and cinema, a taste of London life now that they were free from study. Little by little she did begin to think of what lay ahead. Where would she be when Ramon returned to his home? Would she go with him? There had been no discussion, they had made no plans.

Unbeknown to Ramon she found a job, just to be on the safe side she told herself, despite the fact that Ramon had said he had enough money for both of them. The post would not be available until early December, by which time, surely, she would know how things stood. She felt safer but her happiness was marred by the knowledge that Ramon would leave one day. His financial position remained a mystery and she was too afraid to bring up the subject of his departure. As yet he had said nothing more about waking up next to her for the rest of his life. Until that happened she resolved to enjoy their love and laughter, in the meantime she did not tell him about the job.

It was the last day in November when the break came, suddenly, in the form of a letter from Ramon's mother. The envelope was crumpled and smudged with dirty marks, it bore no stamp and had been pushed through the letter box by an unknown hand.

"Ramon come home. We are having a terrible time and your father has been wounded, he's desperately ill. We love you despite the quarrels. We miss you, and now we need you."

Ramon left the same day. Their leave-taking was short and Ramon was distracted. At Victoria Station, he gave Flora a perfunctory hug before disappearing through the ticket barrier to board the boat train.

Flora went back to their room and drank the best part of a bottle of red wine. She went to bed and cried herself to sleep. The next morning she had a thumping headache and was sick; a migraine, exacerbated by the wine.

'Drinking to excess doesn't ease anything,' she thought. 'I should know that by now.

The following week she started her job in the Foreign Department of a large insurance company. In the end she had never had the chance to tell Ramon about it. She had a lot to learn and remember which filled her mind and helped the days go by. A good helping of red wine with her evening meal dulled her brain and veiled the tedium of long, solitary evenings. Every day she waited for a letter. During the course of the next fortnight she felt more and more tired and depressed.

It wasn't until she had been sick on three consecutive mornings that she began to be suspicious. A visit to the doctor confirmed it – she was pregnant. She was stunned, why hadn't she realised it before? How naive she had been.

She was thrilled at the prospect of carrying Ramon's child but a cold fear crept into her belly.

She still had not a word from Ramon and it was only now that she became conscious of the fact that she had no way of contacting him. She did not even know where he lived, only that it was a *bodega* in northern Spain. All she could do was wait.

Flora dragged herself to work, feeling nauseous and miserable every morning and desperately tired by the evening. She got through each day in the hope that there would be a message from Ramon. If she could have seen how impossible it was for Ramon to send her a message she would have wept.

***

Ramon felt guilty, he knew he had been selfish in coming to England in the first place and he had stayed too long. He crossed the Channel by ferry and via Paris travelled through France and on to Bilbao by train. From Bilbao the rail system was all but destroyed. The land was ravaged, a wilderness, the people walked about as though in a daze, bedraggled and thin.

As he set out for his home in Haro, his guilt deepened as he saw the devastation and ruin. There was not much chance of a passing car to give him a lift, it would take him days to reach home. As he walked he thought of his father and the harsh words they had exchanged, their bitter quarrel over politics.

In theory they both called themselves Republicans, a centre right party, but under the umbrella of that name simmered a number of incompatible parties; Azan's Left Party, Radical Socialists, Centralists, Authoritarions, Communists, Regionalist and Libertarians. All equally suspicious of one another.

As he struggled across the now unfamiliar land his heart ached at what he had done; he knew he should have been home helping his father to run the business. From London, through France, to arriving on Spanish soil, and then onward, it was eighteen hours before he reached the bodega.

12

It took Flora the full hour to get through her story and Annie was tapping on the sitting room door.

'Come in. Thanks,' Philip said. 'Put the coffee on the table would you Annie? That's lovely.'

'Will you be wanting anythin' else Mr H? 'Cos if not I think I'll have an early night.'

'You do that Annie. And thank you again. Goodnight.'

Philip poured two cups of coffee and passed one to Flora as he spoke.

'That's where I came in, the skiing holiday?' He said. Flora nodded.

'So you knew you were pregnant?''

'Yes, a doctor confirmed it but I was only 8 weeks and I thought if I went skiing I might miscarry. I was convinced I was never going to hear from Ramon again. Then when I met you it seemed like an easy way out. I liked you, I liked you a lot and we laughed together. You were fun and then I really thought it would work.'

'And I, head over heels in love with you, in such a hurry to marry you, it suited you down to the ground.' Philip's tone was almost mocking. He had never felt like this in his life.

'It did work, didn't it Philip? I have loved you in my own way.'

Philip did not reply. He sat for a few moments, Flora's account of her life before he met her running through his mind like a series of animated pictures. He looked up and suddenly thought of Connie.

'Stay there, I'm going to see if Connie is all right, and then we'll talk some more. There's a lot more to be discussed.'

He glanced at Flora as he went out of the room. She sat with her head nestled in the crook of her arm, leaning on a huge cushion, visibly exhausted by her long narration.

Philip mounted the staircase slowly, deep in thought. He opened Connie's room door to see her counterpane still smooth. He had not expected her to be in bed but he was a little surprised not to find her in her room. He went back down to the kitchen. It was almost dark but he could see that Annie had tidied up for the night. There was no sign of crockery or Connie's tea. Connie's black Labrador puppy, Bella, her last birthday present, lay asleep in her bed next to the boiler, snoring contentedly. She merely opened an eye briefly, too comfortable to vacate her bed. Philip closed the door. Perhaps Connie was in the study doing some homework, though he doubted that she was in any fit state to concentrate on her schoolwork. There was no-one there and Philip began to feel uneasy. He leapt up the stairs now two at a time and gently rapped on Annie's door.

'Annie, I'm so sorry to disturb you but do you know where Connie is? She's not in her room.'

Annie came to the door in her comfortable dressing gown.

'She took her tea to her room Mr. H. She seemed a bit upset about something. I just let her go up, I thought it best. She didn't come down again.'

'Annie, I don't want to sound neurotic, but I can't find her in the house anywhere. She didn't go out did she?'

'Not that I know of. She couldn't 'ave, I was in the kitchen all the time and the front door never clicked, you know 'ow it does? I'd 've heard it.'

'All right Annie, I expect she's sitting quietly in a corner somewhere. I'm sorry to have disturbed you. Goodnight.'

'Mr H? You will call me if.... .if there's anything, won't you?'

'Yes, yes, rest assured I will. Thank you Annie.'

Philip went back to the sitting room. Flora was still sitting in the same position as though she had fallen asleep.

'Flora, I can't find Connie. Did you speak to her before she went upstairs? She couldn't have gone out, could she?'

Flora sat up. She no longer looked sleepy, just bewildered.

'No, she didn't say anything. In fact I haven't spoken to her since.....since I told her about... Oh Philip, you don't think she's gone off somewhere do you? She wouldn't do that, would she?'

'I don't know. There's no telling what she might have done. She was devastated, Flora. How do we know what she might do? Let's go round the house – no, you go round the house, I'll take the torch and look in the garden.'

They set off, arriving back in the kitchen at the same time. Philip was panting.

'Flora, I've found one of Connie's hairslides. Was she wearing this today.?'

'Yes, well probably. She wears such slides every day. Where was it?

'By the clothes line. It looks as if she might have been running across the back lawn.'

'My God, she's run away. Oh what have I done?'

66

'That's the second time you've said that tonight. And I still don't know the answer.' Philip ran his hand over his eyes and through his hair. 'We'd better call the Police,' he said, striding out into the hall to the telephone. He had barely reached the table on which the 'phone rested when it rang. He jumped involuntarily, its jangle sending a shiver of fear through him. He picked up the receiver but could not speak. There was a silence and then,

'Philip? Philip, are you there? It's mother.'

'I'm here. Mother, what is it we're in the middle of……of a problem…..is it important?'

'Yes, Philip, it is important,' she said firmly and then more softly, 'It's all right, she's here. She's going to stay the night, if that's all right with you and Flora. I think you should both come, not now, tomorrow morning. She's in no fit state to cope with anything more tonight. She's had some hot Ovaltine and gone to bed. Gramps is with her now. We've got the gist of the problem, between the tears, not that we understand one word of it. We need to hear the straight version, Philip. Come as soon as you can in the morning.'

Philip put down the receiver and faced Flora.

'She's at mother's,' he said. Flora was ashen and as he walked towards her he watched her, as though in slow motion, slip down the door jamb into a heap on the floor.

At that moment the front door bell rang. It was Garnet, accompanied by Victoria's father who had driven her home. Philip scooped Flora up in his arms and as he lifted her onto the sofa in the sitting room, she opened her eyes and sighed. He quickly pulled the door closed and went back into the hall. Garnet was already bursting her way through the front door, chattering and laughing.

'Oh Daddy, I've had such a nice time. It's kind of Vicky's Dad to bring me home, isn't it? Where's Connie? I must go and tell Mummy what my piano teacher said about my exam pieces. Where is she?'

'Garnet, wait a moment please.' He quickly fabricated a reason for keeping Garnet out of the sitting room. 'I think first we say our thank-you's, don't you?' Philip stretched out his hand to Mr Douglas, thanking him for his time and trouble.

'My pleasure, any time,' he replied. 'I'll be getting along straight away if you don't mind.'

Philip moved towards the hall door but turned to Garnet before opening it. 'Let's wave Mr Douglas off Garnet, then we'll go and see Mummy together.'

With renewed thanks they waved. Garnet shouted 'Thanks, bye,' and Philip closed the door quickly. He turned to his younger daughter,

'Darling, I want you to do something for me please, go up and knock on Annie's door. Tell her I'm sorry but I need her help. Please Garnet, do that first. Then go and take off your coat and put away your things.'

Garnet looked puzzled but did as she was bid. Philip immediately went into the sitting room. Flora was still lying where he had laid her, her eyes open. He knelt down and laid his hand on her forehead.

'Did I faint?' she asked thickly.

'I think so. I've asked Garnet to go up and fetch Annie,' but before he could continue Flora groaned,

'Oh my God, Garnet! I'd forgotten we have to go through all that yet. Poor Garnet. Philip help me!' Philip took her hand and said more softly,

'We have indeed to go through all that yet, but for the moment try to relax.' Annie arrived and came quietly into the room.

'Annie, Mrs H is not well, I think she fainted. Perhaps we'd better call the doctor. What do you think?' Annie looked down at Flora.

'She does look a bit pale. I think she's been overdoing it lately. Come Mrs H, can you sit up and let me 'ave a little look at you.' She helped Flora to sit up.

'I'll be all right Annie, in just a moment. Truly.'

'We'll see, but I think a little touch of brandy might help Mr H.' she said with a knowing wink. Philip went to the drinks cabinet and poured a small glass of Cognac, Annie taking it from his hand moved to beside Flora and lifted the glass to her lips.

'Sip slowly Mrs H. It'll bring a bit o' colour into those cheeks.' Flora coughed as the strong liquid caught in the back of her throat.

'Gently does it Mrs H. Now then, another little sip.'

'Annie, could you stay here for a few moments. I need to speak to Garnet,' Philip asked.

'Sure I can, no problem. You run along. She'll be all right,' she said nodding towards Flora.

Philip went in search of Garnet who was still in her room tidying away her things as requested. As he reached the top of the staircase Garnet heard his footfall and came out onto the landing.

'Daddy? You look worried - is everything all right? And where's Connie she's not in our room? I've got lots to tell her.'

'Garnet, actually everything isn't all right, Mummy's not well. It's OK, it's not serious, don't be upset. Annie is with Mummy now, we might call Dr MacCallister just to make sure, so don't be alarmed if you hear him come.'

'What's the matter Daddy, why is she ill? And where *is* Connie? There's something very funny going on, what is it?'

'Garnet, my darling. Always questions, questions, you funny girl. Look, I think Mummy has just been overdoing it a bit and Connie has gone to Granny and Gramps' for the night. All right?'

'But why? Why has Connie gone to Granny and Gramps'? There's school tomorrow. Is she poorly too? There *is* something funny going on Daddy, I can tell.'

Garnet's eyes were filling with tears. Philip gathered her up in his arms. For the second time that evening he felt the stab of pain at seeing first Connie and then Garnet deeply distressed, and he knew he was losing control again.

'Hush sweetheart. Don't get worried. Just be patient with us and in the morning we'll sort everything out. I promise. How about I send Annie up to help you get ready for bed. She could run you a bath.'

Garnet gave him an old-fashioned look.

'Daddy, I'm ten. I can get ready for bed by myself! I don't need Annie.'

'Of course you can. You get yourself organised but let Annie run your bath. And Garnet, tomorrow you can tell me all about your exam pieces. All right?'

She nodded and gave Philip a wan smile as he turned with a little wave to go back down the staircase.

13

Dr Macallister declared Flora 'just a bit under the weather'. He pulled down her lower eyelid and said, 'Perhaps a little anaemic but nothing to worry about. A careful watch on your diet, you know, plenty of greens and a steak or two – you can usually get hold of a nice piece these days. You'll be as right as rain, I don't think any pills are necessary,' he smiled.

After Philip had shown Dr Macallister out he went back upstairs to speak to Garnet. She was already in bed, looking very sleepy. He leaned down to kiss her forehead.

'Annie brought me some Ovaltine Daddy. It always makes me sleepy.' She smiled softly, 'See you in the morning,' he murmured and before Philip left the room her eyes had closed.

Philip went back down to Flora. She was sitting upright and the colour had indeed come back into her cheeks. Annie had returned after seeing to Garnet and was sitting next to Flora.

'Thanks so much Annie, I'm all right now'

'You call me now, if you need anything,' Annie said as she left to go back to her room.

Alone again Flora said,

'I'm sorry Philip. I'm not really ill, it was relief. I thought she'd run away.'

'I don't understand you Flora. It's you after all who are sending Connie away.'

Philip ran his hand through his hair holding on to a clump of it on the top of his head and pulled. The gesture expressed his exasperation and failure to understand Flora's twists and changes of mood.

'I'm sorry, I shouldn't have said that. But we're going to have to finish this discussion before morning. We have to talk to Garnet before we go to Mother's. Are you up to it? Talking now, I mean?' Flora nodded.

'Yes Philip, whether I am or not, it has, as you say, got to be done.' With a surprisingly brisk and acute return to the subject, as though nothing untoward had taken place, Flora picked up her story where she had left off.

'You swept me off my feet Philip but I couldn't tell you about the baby, I thought I would lose you. It may seem strange to you but I really did fall in love with you later - all the wrong way round - after our wedding. I didn't think it possible after.......after Ramon, to love someone again. I suddenly realised how lucky I was. And then everyone was so nice when they learned I was pregnant and so kind when the baby was born prematurely. She was premature, you know, well, early by a couple of weeks but that could have been a miscalculation. I think it must have been worrying that caused it, I don't know.

There were comments at the Maternity Hospital that she looked like a full-term baby.

"Happily for you this babe has arrived *now*," the midwife said. "She's a good weight. Any bigger and it would have been difficult for you." It went through my mind at the time that maybe she knew but I was too exhausted to care what she thought. It was your mother I thought might not be fooled but she never hinted at anything. Maybe she thought we had slept together on the skiing holiday and that's why we got married in such a hurry. As time went by it became impossible to tell you the truth. You loved that baby so much, even though you saw hardly anything of her for months at a time. I know I'm hard, but not entirely unfeeling and I just couldn't do that to you. I didn't think you would ever find out the truth. There was only one other person in my life who knew, that was Rhonda. I kept being sick on that holiday and she guessed. She swore she would never tell.'

'It was Rhonda blackmailing you, wasn't it?'

'Yes. She reneged on her promise made all that time ago. She wrote to me and said she would tell you and Ramon. I didn't know it but somehow she had started a spasmodic correspondence with Ramon. I don't know how she found out where he was. I think she fancied her chances with him. For the past three years she has demanded more and more money. I've never understand why she needed money, she came from a wealthy family. Finally I said I couldn't possibly give her any more. I didn't hear from her for four weeks and I thought she realised that she had bled me dry.

'Then the letter arrived from Ramon. He had known for a long time that I had married. Rhonda had told him in one of her letters. His letter was bitter, resentful and accusatory. He said I should have known he would come back for me. He wrote of another letter he had written, all those years ago, after he went back to Spain. The country was in a terrible state, the land all around was ransacked, and his father lay dying, it was a long and painful death. He had tried to be at his bedside

71

as much as possible, help his mother through her grief and take over the running of the business at the same time. This letter was written in the January, saying that thinking about me and the fact that I was waiting for him, sustained him through those terrible months. He could not leave his home to come to me but he wrote to tell me that he wanted me to go to him, in Spain, as soon as it was safe. But the situation in Spain was so bad there was no reliable postal service any more, his letter never arrived. Then quite a long time later he received Rhonda's letter telling him that I had married. In any case, rumblings of the Germans and their presence in Italy were already going on and that put paid to any plans he had.'

Philip listened silently. He felt as though he were reading a novel, it was all someone else's life and none of it had anything to do with him. He looked up at Flora and suddenly he felt the hurt and anger at having been deceived for thirteen years. At the same time, he felt an overwhelming compassion for her. He couldn't help but admire how she had held all this turmoil inside herself for so long, keeping it a secret from everyone.

'What was it Flora that made you tell Connie she had to go away? I don't understand how you could do this to her. To me, to any of us. She's a child. How do you expect her to cope? We must tell her it's all a mistake and that she doesn't have to go after all.'

'We can't, because Ramon made me sign a legal document. He said he would pay off Rhonda, once and for all, and pay my debts but I must sign the paper. It was all in Spanish of course, and I didn't pay enough attention to the legal jargon. I thought it was just to prove that he had paid me the money.

'He sent a letter to Rhonda to sign so that she couldn't demand any further payments. But mine was different, in fact it said that I agreed to give him his daughter, in return for his help and then...he...' Flora stopped and waved her hand in the air as though reluctant to say more.

'A condition Flora, was that it?'

'He said he would splash the story all over the British newspapers and that would ruin your career.'

'We'll fight it, this can't happen.'

'It's no good, it's a cast iron legal document. Added to that, there's her birth certificate. She's registered as Conchita Lopez, father - Ramon Lopez. Don't ask me why I did that at the time, it was stupid. I didn't think about the future; whether she would ever need a passport or that you would then see it.'

For the third time that evening she asked,

'What am I going to do Philip?'

'What are you going to do? What are we *all* going to do? The answer is - there is nothing we can do, I'm afraid you've already done it Flora.' Philip knew the words were unforgiving, he had never spoken to Flora like this before. He toned down the harshness of his voice,

'We can see a lawyer but I doubt if there is a way out.'

'There isn't, I've already seen a solicitor. He said it would be an almighty battle, costing the earth and Ramon would win anyway, I don't have a leg to stand on.'

Philip sighed. The prospect of giving up the child he had always known as his elder daughter was torment. He did not know the exact figures as yet but he already knew that the blackmailing had left them in an embarrassing position financially, even though Ramon had paid off the substantial sum owing.

In business Philip was decisive and resolute; where his emotions were involved he crumpled. At the best of times Philip did not like change, he was afraid of it, his strength lay in constancy. Only once in his life had he obeyed the pull of his emotions, that was when he had fallen in love with Flora and proposed to her within days of their meeting.

Philip was weak when it came to dealing with discord with those he loved. He hated emotional conflict and he also knew that a legal contest of this nature would indeed damage his standing in the financial world, which in turn would inevitably alter their family lifestyle as it stood. The thought of this affair becoming public knowledge was humiliating.

Besides, there was the question of all the shock and hurt to all of them, not least to Connie, which had already been inflicted. He had not forgotten that some of them were as yet unaware of the terrible situation. There was still Garnet to cope with and then of course his mother and father, and Connie's school must be informed. He sat on in silence, his thoughts churning, his heart heavy. Flora knew better than to break into his thoughts. She could contribute nothing to ease his anxiety. She lay back on the sofa, lost in the soft cushions, empty of all feeling after her outpouring.

They sat in silence for some time. Philip had begun to calculate, as though working with figures, how they would approach the situation. Listing the facts in his mind, working out practicalities; pushing his feelings to one side was the only way he could cope. At last he spoke.

'I have come to some decisions,' he said with firmness as though he were chairing a Board Meeting, and like an agenda he listed the actions they would take.

'First of all, we'll tell Garnet in the morning that Connie will be going away. She'll not go to school, she'll come with us to mother's.

73

Then we'll face mother and father and tell them the essence of the crisis, they are to be spared the details Flora, do you hear? Remember both Connie and Garnet will be listening, this time through me. I shall endeavour to give them some hope about their future happiness in an effort to soften the anguish they will both be feeling. That is something we all will have to work hard at to bring about. You don't need to say anything, unless you want to.' His matter-of-fact tone continued, as though still dealing with a crisis at the office.

Flora nodded. She was relieved that Philip had taken over. Now she could sit back and let him sort out all the problems. Even so, she whispered,

'I'm scared, and... and ashamed.'

Philip's firm, decisive manner fell away momentarily, the hurt was still there pressing against his ribs, the pain rising and falling with every breath. He rose and went over to Flora on the sofa. He realised he still loved her and wondered at the fact. How could he, knowing now what she had done? But his deep love got the better of him and he lifted his arm and tucked it around her shoulders. She leaned into his chest and sobbed. Philip could not now control his emotions and the trickle of tears running down his cheeks felt strange.

14

Flora woke early. She had slept fitfully and as she slipped out of bed her body felt weary and her head heavy. Without waking Philip she showered and dressed quietly and went downstairs. Annie had already laid the kitchen table for breakfast, including a place for herself. It was the one meal of the day that Annie shared with Philip Hampton and the girls. Annie was a little surprised to see Flora, she usually stayed in bed and came down for coffee at eight thirty, but then with her usual aplomb greeted her as though all was routine.

'Morning Mrs H. Are you feeling better?' Flora nodded.

'A little. Annie, I want you to sit down with me, I need to talk to you before ....before the others come down. Is there any coffee yet?'

'It's ready. Shall I pour?' and Annie poured her a cup, helping herself to a cup of tea. She sat opposite Flora at the table, who with her hands folded round the cup of steaming black coffee, gazed beyond Annie and out into the garden. She didn't speak.

'I know there's something wrong Mrs H, something pretty bad. I've known you all long enough to know when you're troubled. You're going to tell me aren't you? I need to know, you're my family after all. I'll 'elp, you know that.'

She spoke softly but matter of factly and looking straight at Flora she waited. Flora's gaze left the garden, and with her eyes full of tears said,

'I've made a terrible mistake Annie, several dreadful mistakes that go back a long time. You won't like me when you learn what I've done. I don't like myself. You'll think I'm cruel and you'll despise me.'

'That's for me to decide. There's no saying what I'll think until you tell me.'

Flora uncharacteristically put out a hand across the table. She was not one for gestures of affection but for once she acknowledged the need to make physical contact and she needed Annie's support. Annie gently took the hand in hers and there it remained as Flora told her the truth.

Annie sat silently, nodding now and then and even giving the hand a momentary squeeze. When it was all done Flora said,

'So now you know how foolish I have been and how much I have wronged my family.'

'We all make mistakes. I must say it's a pretty bad one but "There but for the grace of God go I", I alus say.'

'She'll never forgive me,'

'You mean Connie?'

'Yes. She disappeared last night and for a short while, I thought she had run away. I was terrified that something might happen to her. That's when I fainted and Philip called you.'

'I guessed it was something to do with Connie, Mr H 'ad come to ask me where she was. I felt bad, I should've known where she was. In any case, I 'eard her crying in 'er room earlier on. I thought she was in trouble at school or something. She didn't come to me as she usually does.'

'I know Annie, they both come to you – rather than me. I'm not a good mother. You have such patience with them.'

'Aye, I love them, like my own, well, if I'd 'ad any that is. So Connie isn't lost?'

'I'm sorry Annie, I should have told you straight away. She went to Amelia and Charles. She walked all that way by herself in the dark, I dread to think what might have happened. She's there now and we are going across there as soon as we've had breakfast. I couldn't go without telling you what's happened.'

'I'm glad you've told me. I wouldn't want to be shut out. As I said before, you're my family.'

'Annie, I have to ask you this – you won't leave us will you, because of what I've done? I couldn't manage without you and neither could Garnet.' This was the most warmhearted remark Flora had ever made to Annie.

'Wild 'orses wouldn't drag me away. Garnet'll need more lovin' than ever. Sorry Mrs H. I didn't mean anything by that.'

'I know. I'm not a demonstrative person, it's as though my feelings have been bundled up in a string bag for years, little bits of love only squeezing through the holes now and then. I can't help it, it's all I've been able to manage. I didn't have a very loving relationship with my own parents. I thought I could be different when I had children. But I haven't been. If only I could tear that bag apart and tell them I do love them but they'll not believe me. It's too late.'

'Perhaps if things had been different, I mean with … you know …'

'You mean Ramon, Connie's real father? You may be right.' Flora gave a deep sigh and looked down at their hands, still clasped, like lifetime friends. She pulled her hand away embarrassed at what she saw.

'I 'ope you don't mind me saying, but I always knew there was something about Connie but I couldn't quite put my finger on it. She was a new born when I came and as babies do she needed a lot of attention. Later when she was two and a bit, and Garnet was a little baby, I remember she used to try to dress 'erself, she was and still is an independent soul. Even so, fending for 'erself was one thing but it seemed as though you didn't 'ave time for 'er and as they grew you treated 'er different. I never knew why. I think I understand now, you were afraid, weren't you?'

'I suppose I was. Afraid that someone would guess, that I would be found out. Poor Connie. A real case of God visiting the sins of the fathers – in this case the mother – upon the children. She'll never forgive me.'

'Give 'er time.'

'All these years I thought I had dealt with my problem, that the deception was justified. I realise now that my guilt and shame are responsible for the way I have treated Connie. I've kept her at a distance, away from me because her very presence was like a finger pointing accusingly at me, a constant reminder of my cruel folly. How ironic that Philip should have chosen the name 'Constance'. What he didn't know was that when I registered her birth I gave her another name.'

'No! So what *is* she called?'

'It's Conchita, a Spanish name. I couldn't help it. It was almost a last defiant act. I thought it's so similar, no-one will ever know, and anyway the plan was always to call her Connie. I didn't think of the consequences; that the day would come when she would need her birth certificate, and a passport. It didn't occur to me that Connie herself would question it when she found out.'

'Does she know? About her name I mean, I suppose it was yesterday you told 'er the rest?'

'Yes, I told her – cruelly, I blurted out everything. I didn't know how else to do it. And now I have to tell Philip's parents - this morning. Garnet first, before we leave. I'm dreading telling her. She knows something terrible has happened. The poor child has had to wait in suspense until this morning. I don't know how I am going to face them all.'

'Aye, it'll be awful, for all of you, but you'll get through it. Mrs 'ampton's a wise lady with plenty of common sense. She'll not let you down.'

'Thank you Annie, for being so…. understanding. Why did I never realise that I had such a friend in you?'

'Aye well, we all need a friend at some time or other. It sounds like them Mrs H, we'd best get the breakfast on the table. I'll go upstairs and tidy up and make the beds. It'll be better just you three on your own. I'll be thinking about you 'til you get back.'

Annie left the kitchen, marveling to herself at the conversation she and Flora had just had.

'Whoever would've thought I could talk to 'er like that? But she invited it. I wasn't forward,' she thought, and as though pardoning herself she continued, 'It just came out naturally.'

***

Garnet's reaction to her parents' news was one of total disbelief. Her naturally buoyant character, propensity for asking questions and perpetually radiant smile all failed her. She sat with her mother and father at the breakfast table in the kitchen and received their explanation in total silence.

She looked at her mother's pale face and puffy eyes, which spoke of tears shed. Garnet had never seen her mother cry and did not know how to cope with it. She stared at her.

Flora found herself trembling under her younger daughter's penetrating gaze. Her guilt was such that she mistook it for reproof and disapproval.

'Garnet……I'm sorry. I'm sorry for everything.'

Garnet turned to look at her father. At last she spoke.

'Poor Connie, going away from us. She'll be lonely Daddy.' Her voice began to quaver. 'Does she have to go?' she croaked.

'I'm afraid so darling. But we'll work out something, I don't know what yet, but something to make it easier, for all of us.

The tears suddenly came and mingling with the sobs she cried out,

'How is Connie going to manage without us? What am I going to do without Connie?'

15

Diary

Granny was wonderful, I knew she would be. And Gramps – he must have been so surprised to see me on the doorstep but he just said 'hello sweetheart' like he always does. I tried to tell them what had happened but I cried like a baby and I know I didn't make much sense. How could I? It doesn't make sense to me anyway. I don't know what's going to happen now but I know they'll help me. IF they can, that is. Mummy was horrid and Daddy was...well, wet! Oh how can I say such a thing? I love him so much and I know he loves me but he didn't seem to want to do anything about the situation. He must, I can't leave them all.

***

As Annie Bates had predicted, Philip's parents took the news stoically. With sombre expressions, and some tears, they listened to their son. Occasionally Amelia Hampton glanced at Flora, who sat throughout with head lowered and hands in her lap. Connie sat beside her grandmother on the chintz sofa, her left arm linked through her grandmother's. Garnet sat on her grandfather's lap. He held her tightly. Neither of the girls spoke, occasionally each of them wiped a tear, or sniffed. When the story was told, as much of the detail as Philip was prepared to reveal in front of the two children, Amelia got up.

'Come to the kitchen with me girls. We'll make a cup of tea. Then we can talk together some more.'

As Garnet followed Connie and her grandmother, Charles Hampton got up and walked across the room to Flora. He leaned down, taking her hand in his he said,

'It's a sad business girl. I feel for you. You've had a terrible time carrying the burden of your secret for years. But that's over. We're all in this together now.'

Flora looked up. She found his sympathy and composed acceptance of what she had done more difficult to take than an outright denunciation of her deceit. With that she could have come back in self-defence, declaring her love for Philip despite what she had done appearing to be purely out of self-interest. Charles' words and affectionate action were unexpected and she wept.

Amelia returned with the tray of tea, Connie carrying biscuits.

'I've suggested to the girls that after our drink they should go into the front room. They need to talk to each other, to help each other. And we… well, we've got things to talk about too.'

They drank their tea; Connie and Garnet cleared the cups and saucers, took them to the kitchen and then went into the best sitting room, which normally was for Sundays or when Amelia had friends round for an afternoon.

Flora looked at her mother-in-law expecting some kind of judgmental comment. Instead she said quietly and with composure,

'Whatever we can do to help Flora, we will. You must tell us. Perhaps it might be a good thing if Connie doesn't go into school this week? In which case she can come here whilst you and Philip sort out what's to be done. It's only a suggestion,' she added.

'I haven't thought yet,' Flora said, 'but perhaps going back to school would be very difficult for her. Thank you Amelia, I think that might be a good idea. What do you think Philip?'

The discussion began and continued as though they were planning some kind of holiday, or family event. 'It's bizarre,' thought Amelia, 'it's like a strange film. It can't be happening to us. But it is. I've only to look at her. She weeps but she has no shame, they're crocodile tears, I know them when I see them.' She looked across at Charles, whom she knew was being more forgiving. Nevertheless, she held onto her own thoughts and felt he was being his usual soft, kind self. 'He's taken in,' she thought not unkindly. 'Just like Philip, a couple of softies, both, except Philip hides from the tender side of his character.'

For a while, without the children's presence, the two couples were able to be more forthright, though Philip still skirted round some of the details which he had no intentions of ever telling his parents. Their discussions were not without emotion, they all tried to face up to the task, intent on making the separation for Connie and Garnet the least painful as possible.

Amelia had prepared a salad lunch, having correctly assumed that this would be a protracted visit. They called Connie and Garnet in from the room next door. They appeared with smudged faces and red eyes. They had talked little, in truth they had sat beside one another on the carpet in front of the red brick fireplace, holding each other closely, crying and trying to work out what was going to happen.

It was a difficult meal, the conversation was stilted. The serious discussion of how Connie's departure was to be arranged and how Garnet was going to cope at school with the inevitable questions from her peers, were not aspects of the overall dilemma the adults could discuss in front of the two sisters. Flora spoke little. Amelia and Philip kept a desultory conversation going. Charles did his best to tease Connie and Garnet as was his wont with them. They smiled at his feeble jokes, pushed their food around on their plates and ate very little.

Connie and Garnet insisted on clearing the table and washing up. Normally Amelia would not have left them to it but it was another opportunity for the four adults to talk. She realised that it was an escape for them too, away from the frightening atmosphere of uncertainty and another chance for them to begin to work out together their own feelings.

After yet another cup of tea they left. The short drive home was a sad and quiet journey. Connie and Garnet sat huddled together in the back seat of the car, their hands entwined, though neither spoke, nor did they cry. They only looked at each other from time to time as though trying to memorise each other's features, afraid that the time would be arriving very soon when they would not be able to look at one another every day, as they did now and which they had naturally taken for granted.

Philip pulled the car smoothly into the driveway. Flora got out without speaking. Annie was at the front door as they entered. She put out her arms to Connie and Garnet, each one nestling into her soft ample figure, as the tears coursed down her cheeks.

'Annie, you help the girls get ready for bed.' Annie was momentarily taken aback. This was not the sad, remorseful woman who had, surprisingly, sat and confided in her only that morning. She was her former, cool, assertive self. Her remark wasn't a question or even a request. It was a statement.

'I'm exhausted, I need a drink,' she added as she made straight for the sitting room. Had Amelia seen and heard her at that moment she would have felt her earlier thoughts justified.

Annie nodded and quietly accompanied Connie and Garnet up the stairs. She held them in her arms, each in turn and said,

'Come now, you must have a nice warm bath and I'll give you supper in bed. I know, I know, it's a bit early to be going to bed but you've had a tiring day. And I know you're big girls now and you don't need my help but tonight is different. It's like a little treat, isn't it?

After, we can have a cosy chat. All right?' Normally they would have laughed at the suggestion that Annie 'look after them' but tonight they both nodded in response and went quietly with her.

As good as her word, Annie sat with them after their bath and they talked, with tears and some smiles.

'It's all right, I know all about it. I'm more sorry than I can say, you know that. But we 'ave to make the best of it. It's not the end of the world, although you might think so just now. My mother used to say "Things turn out best for the people who make the best of the way things turn out". I never quite understood when I was a child but I reckon there's some truth in it. You per'aps can't see it right now but something'll turn up, something nice. I know it. Just 'ang on and wait for it to come.'

Her words were not particularly wise but they were comforting and both Connie and Garnet knew that she loved them, as they did her. They settled in bed with a hug and a kiss from Annie and fell asleep without delay. The emotional strains of the day had taken their toll. Not even their father had time to kiss them goodnight, to his surprise they had fallen asleep quickly and soundly.

***

It was later, after the family had returned home, that Amelia and Charles Hampton yielded to the shock they had taken. They held each other closely and cried, each wiping the other's tears.

'I never suspected anything, did you?' Charles asked of his wife later that evening as they sat with a sandwich and a cup of tea. Amelia did not immediately reply and Charles turned his head sharply and stared at her.

'Don't tell me you knew? How could you?'

'No, I didn't *know*. But there's always been something strange about the way Flora treated that child, as though she didn't want her, didn't love her even. I couldn't understand why. It troubled me. When Garnet arrived I saw even more-so how different she was with her, more motherly and affectionate. Though I couldn't say she was ever the maternal type. Connie felt it, you know.'

'Do you really think as a little girl she would be aware of the difference in her mother's attitude between the two of them?' asked Charles.

'I'm sure she did, as young as she was. Little ones are very astute you know. I suppose Flora did love Connie in her own way but I can see how her very existence has been a daily reminder of her own terrible deceit. And yet she has managed to live her life playing golf and bridge, filling her time with pleasurable pursuits. I'll say this for her she's been a good hostess, supporting Philip in his work. She's played that role well and I'm sure it's been a challenging responsibility during all these years of rationing and food shortages. I'm sorry for her but I can't forgive her for what she has done to that child.'

'She's paying the price now though. Don't you think she's contrite?'

'Contrite? Not one drop of remorse – don't you believe it. Oh, I know, you think I'm hard. But I'm thinking of Connie, she is the one who is paying, and double the price for her mother's folly. She's never had her mother's true love and now she's to be banished to a strange land, a different language and what's more to leave her sister and father. Flora's a wicked woman. I'm sorry Charles, I can't forgive her.'

16

Diary

*'I used to love riding on trains but not this one, taking me away from
Nettie and everybody. Fancy, I've got a passport - but it's for someone
who's not me! I don't want to be this 'Conchita' – I hate her! Daddy is
sitting next to me, except he's not my 'Daddy' any more but I can't help
calling him that. He says he'll always be my father, always love me, but
how can he love me and let Mummy send me away? It's Mummy's
fault! I'm scared of meeting Ramon – sorry, 'Daddy' in whatever it is
in Spanish. If where I'm going weren't so hateful I would be quite
enjoying the journey; the scenery is lovely. The steward on the train
keeps smiling at me, he says we can go into the dining carriage and
have lunch soon. When we get to Bilbao we are not even there, we have
to travel on by road to Haro, wherever that is. HE is coming to pick us
up at the station, I don't know how long in the car to this place, and
then...oh help, I'm scared!*

***

Ramon arrived at the station too early. He had been anxious to be there
in good time, to be waiting, to catch sight of Conchita before having to
greet her. He was worried that so young a girl was making this long
journey alone and he wondered what contingencies had been made for
her safe passage. He felt a twinge of guilt that he had not asked nor had
he offered to do anything about it. He moved away from the waiting
area and other eager, excited people looking forward to the return of
loved ones. He walked towards a small café near the exit, sat down on a
high stool, and ordered an espresso. It was coffee of indeterminate
origin, nevertheless he drank two cups of the strong bitter liquid. What
else was he to do for forty-five minutes? He began to pace about,

restless. Is it the coffee pumping adrenalin around my body, or am I nervous? he thought. He didn't want to admit it. He moved back nearer to the waiting area. He so wanted to catch a glimpse of Conchita before she saw him. He had a photograph of her in his pocket, by now well fingered and curling at one corner. He fiddled with it now though he did not need to look at it again. The smiling dark eyes shone out at him – they were his mother's. He would know her instantly.

The announcement came,

"The train now arriving at Platform 3 is the train from Biarritz..."

Ramon's excitement and apprehension rose in those few last seconds. He edged closer to the barrier as the passengers began to push their way out. He grew impatient with them for blocking his view and his heart began to thump against his ribs. Then the crowd began to thin out. This was the moment – *'venganza'*! Revenge, revenge on Flora; the feeling almost overwhelmed him. He pushed forward, his height giving him some advantage of being able to see over the heads of the few people remaining to greet the arrivals. Ramon caught sight of a tall man of about his own age amongst the stragglers making their way along the platform. He recognised instantly that he was English. His blond hair, his tailored clothes even down to his highly polished shoes. Ramon smiled to himself. He knew this type; conservative, traditional, the epitome of an Englishman. He noticed a girl beside him, with head down she clung to his arm. The man spoke and she raised her eyes. It was Conchita! There was no doubt about it. He began to tremble. The blond man, who was he? Why did she cling to him? Ramon suddenly understood, my God it was Philip Hampton. He had brought Conchita himself. He should have guessed that no rational parent would allow a young girl to travel so many hundreds of miles alone.

What could *he,* who had never set eyes on this daughter of his, say to this man, the man she had known as her father for twelve years and who so obviously loved this girl? It was evident in the closely linked arms, even though the look that the girl gave him was melancholy. Ramon, the confidant, revengeful man shrank back. The fleeting sweetness of revenge turned bitter in his mouth and he became conscious of his cruel act. He had torn this girl away from all she loved, he had used her in his fury and need for retaliation. His excitement should have been out of love for this girl, not revenge. In that moment he asked himself how could she be expected to love someone she had never seen and never even knew existed until a matter of only a month ago. In the melée of conflicting thoughts and doubts he found he could not move. Emotions the like of which he had not felt since his father died, paralysed him.

It was Philip, with Connie still hanging on his arm, who saw a lone man standing behind the barrier. Coming alongside him Philip touched his sleeve. Ramon was startled out of his thoughts and turned to face Philip Hampton and *their* daughter. Their eyes met. They should have hated one another on sight but a look passed between them, an unspoken recognition that they had both been cruelly fooled and hurt by the same woman, the woman they both had loved. Ramon gave a slight bow. Philip put out his hand.

'I see no reason,' Philip began, 'to be discourteous. I'm Philip Hampton.' So English, was the thought that went through Ramon's mind, but he took the proffered hand and they clasped in a firm handshake.

'Ramon López,' he replied.

Connie watched in wonder as these two men who, apart from their build and stature, could not have been more different. They were both charismatic men, not handsome, but fine-looking. At that moment she saw her father as an Englishman, his blond hair flopping forward on his forehead - reminiscent of his schooldays - making him look younger than his years. His fair skin and blue-eyes seemed all the more Anglo-Saxon in comparison with the Spaniard's dark smooth hair brushed back, whose gleaming deep set eyes searched for some indication of how this cool reserved Englishman might be judging him. Yet there was an empathy immediately felt and seen by each of them, a totally unexpected connection between them.

'I have two fathers,' Connie thought suddenly, as she looked first at one then at the other. For the first time she acknowledged to herself that the link between these two men was her, and yet not her; it was her mother.

'This is …..' Philip stopped himself just in time from saying 'my daughter'.

'This is Connie.'

Ramon looked straight at her. He did not offer her his hand and he did not trust himself to speak directly to her. His usual eloquence failed him. He smiled gently inclining his head in a slight bow and instead addressed Philip,

'I have a car waiting,' he said. 'Let's go home.'

Throughout the meeting Connie had hung onto Philip's arm and uttered not a word.

Ramon turned and led the way across the station out to the car park. He was still trembling. He did not speak to Philip or Connie as they walked and he smiled as he pointed to his vehicle. They got in and

Ramon drove smoothly away, travelling eastwards in the direction of the Cantabrian mountains and Haro.

'It's nearly 90 kilometres to Haro I'm afraid. I expect you are tired so I shall take it steadily to make it as comfortable as possible for you. It'll be about two hours' drive. Please, I don't intend to talk to you, I prefer to concentrate on the driving. If you feel like closing your eyes and relaxing I shall quite understand. There will be plenty of time to talk later.'

Ramon was a skillful driver and obviously knew the road well, nevertheless he was indeed concentrating on the road in an effort partly to give them a smooth ride but mostly to calm his own thoughts.

Philip became aware of Ramon stealing glimpses of Connie in the rearview mirror and was grateful that they did not have to make conversation. Both he and Connie gazed out of the car windows at the scenery. Connie still held Philip's arm but her grip lessened and though she did not smile, her dour expression relaxed into one of interest as she gazed out of the car window. She even gave out an involuntarily gasp as they saw the white craggy mountains in the distance. On their tops were patches, dark against the white, and she thought of a picture she had seen at the dentist warning of the dangers of too much sugar. Despite the grandeur of these mountains she saw them not as glorious scenery but in her unhappiness as enormous decaying teeth.

Ramon heard the intake of breath and misunderstood her reaction. His was a different view.

'It's beautiful, isn't it? The roads are quite winding in parts but keep a lookout, you can catch glimpses of medieval hilltop villages, with their church steeples and towers rising up out of the centre of the villages. Don't worry, I know this route well. You are quite safe.'

Philip acknowledged the remark with a respectful wave of his hand, a gesture of recognition of his competence. Connie began to relax with the rhythmic swaying of the car and despite her obvious curiosity she fell asleep.

'Is everything all right for you in the back there?' Ramon asked, having seen Connie's head nestle into Philip's arm.

'We're fine. Somewhat reluctantly she's fallen asleep. It'll do her good. We left Harrogate late yesterday evening, continuing on the night train through France. She is tired from the travelling to say nothing of the excitement of it all and I have to say a good deal of apprehension. I'm surprised she has managed to stay alert for so long.'

'I understand. You and I must talk Philip, I can call you Philip? But first we must help Conchita to settle in a little. Then later, over a glass of wine perhaps, we can discuss things.'

They drove on in silence and Philip too closed his eyes for a while. It was not the journey they had made which had tired him but the emotional gymnastics which he had already been through at home, and the stirrings of more, which he knew were to come and would surface when he returned alone, without his beloved daughter.

As they drew nearer their destination the land fell away into a valley, neat rows of thousands of vines spread out before them, their dark brown trunks clear against the chalk rich clay, with the dazzling green of the first leaves. The late afternoon sun washed over them; the thin glistening stems moving gently in the breeze gave life to the otherwise still countryside.

They arrived in Haro but Ramon drove through the small town and out to the other side. At last he turned through two stone pillars and followed a track for about a quarter of a mile. Then Philip saw the cream edifice rising above the surrounding trees. Through an archway they entered a large courtyard, the house behind the entrance glowing pink in the late afternoon sun. The car slowed down and the change of speed and break in the rhythm of the movement woke Connie. She looked up to see the archway as they drove into the beautiful courtyard filled with huge terra cotta pots planted with oleander, lemons and bougainvillea. She sat up and without thinking said,

'Oh Daddy, look isn't it beautiful. Where are we?'

Ramon got out of the car and opened the door for Connie.

'This is our home,' he said.

17

May 1951

Diary

What a lovely house; it's got lots of tiles everywhere quite unlike houses in Yorkshire. It's strange how I'm fascinated by everything but it's like a dream, and I don't want to wake up because then I'll remember why I'm here. I'm so unhappy I wonder how I can see the charm of the place.

I can't believe how Daddy and...Ramon, get on well together. Why aren't they daggers drawn? I thought they would hate each other but they don't. Ramon's English is fantastic – thank goodness! But I'm going to have to learn Spanish, I can see that.

Ramon took us out today to show us a bit of the countryside. It's rugged and striking with mountains in the background with high rocky points; I think they are called the Cantabrian mountains. There are just miles and miles of vines. The earth is very light coloured almost white, not brown, and it shines through the stark brown vine stumps and stems. They don't seem to have many leaves yet but they shine bright green in the sunlight, and I wonder how on earth they are going to produce grapes in time to make wine in the autumn. That's what Ramon said they would do.

I'm dreading Daddy leaving. How can he do it? Doesn't he realise that he's leaving me with people I don't know? It's horrid!

***

The first evening Philip and Ramon talked into the early hours; the war years, their work, even their mutual love of Flora. And finally Connie's reaction to the separation from the life she had known.

'She's a tough little lass,' Philip had said. 'She keeps her thoughts to herself. She's a very independent child. It's always been something of a worry to me, but she seems to cope. I was never there when she was a baby you know. It was the early years of the war. I was working on secret work and I wasn't allowed home. I was a stranger to that young child, and she to me, and it was a long time before I felt she was my child. Ironic isn't it? She wasn't my child. Sorry, Ramon. I'm not bitter, I'm sad that I have had her for only a few years. I missed the beginning of her life and it looks as though I'm going to miss….'

'No, don't say any more. Now that I have met you I am feeling bad about how this situation has come about. There's no denying that I'm exhilarated at the thought of having a daughter but it is marred knowing that I have come by her only by causing others pain and sadness. I didn't think it through, I was blinded by my emotions. My mother accepted everything I explained to her without demur, until I told her that Conchita would be coming here to my home.

My mother wouldn't speak to me for three days. You've no idea what that meant to me, there has never been a cross word between the two of us all my life, unlike my relationship with my father. But my mother and I have always been close. She told me I couldn't do it, it wasn't right, but I would not listen. I tell you my judgement was totally without reason. I'm going to confess to you Philip that my hold over Flora was simply to reap revenge. I was so angry and of course deeply hurt. But it's no good, is it? We can't turn the clock back and pretend none of this has happened. Your whole family has gone through enough as it is. Crazy isn't it? You should be hating my guts – is that a coarse English expression? I think so. I learned many such expressions during my time in London. Let me be honest, I find you, as they say in English, a jolly good fellow. No, I mean it. I'm not making fun – I wish so much we had met under different circumstances.'

'You're right, we can't change anything now. But we don't have to be enemies just because fate dealt us a disagreeable hand. How we handle this between the two of us could mean the difference between Connie being happy with you here or not. I have no war to wage with you Ramon. All I ask is that you look after her, that you love my……….' Philip could not finish his sentence.

'Your daughter, you were going to say. She *is* your daughter and always will be, whereas she is not yet 'mine' but I hope she will one day see me as a father.

'Before you leave Philip I have to tell you something about myself. In such a short time we seem to have struck up a rapport but there is one more thing about which I am ashamed and then… perhaps the rapport will shrivel up.'

'I agree we seem to be able to be honest with one another but there is no need to tell me anything……'

'Yes, selfishly, I have to tell you this. Something that Flora never knew. It might explain why I left so abruptly.' Ramon began his story.

'I left home in late 1936. Of course you will know about the Civil War which raged through our country, leaving it devastated, ruined, thousands of people killed. In July of that year General Franco had attacked the mainland from Morocco, at the same time a force from Navarre under General José Sanjurjo moved south. There was resistance by Republicans in Madrid, Barcelona,Valencia, and the Basque country and Franco's move to seize power was not successful. The people of my country were at war with one another.

'You will be wondering how I could possibly have left my home at such a time. My father and I disagreed on a question of politics. My father claimed he was a Republican, which was an unstable coalition of left and right constantly disagreeing.

'My father believed in regional independence, freedom of the individual, he was determined to protect his ownership and hold over the family *bodega*. He and his father before him had always treated his workers well; he said they were as much a part of the life of the *bodega* as the family. The workers respected him and were loyal hard working people.

'In theory we were both Republicans, a centre right party, but under the umbrella of that name simmered a number of incompatible parties. All equally suspicious of one another.

'I was not a Nationalist - they had no pretence of democracy, the Fascists believed in dictatorship of the extreme right, and the merging of state and business leadership. But it was not as simple as that. I couldn't call myself a Republican, believing in political power exercised by the whole community, with the production and distribution of goods owned collectively; an absence of class, and common ownership. The Republicans were a terrible mixture of Communist, anti-fascists and socialists. I tell you this war was not a clash between left and right, it was a cauldron of incompatibilities.

'Enough of the lecture on Spanish politics. We had a terrible argument, and in a fury I told him I couldn't work with him unless he saw sense. My father had an equally fiery temper, we were so alike in this respect and he said if that's how I felt then I had better find somewhere else to work. I left home in a wild fit of temper, my mother wept and begged me not to go but I ignored her.

'In the autumn of 1936 I went to London and found a study course that I thought would give me some standing and then I could say to my father, 'You see, I know better than you.' What a fool I was.

'I turned my back on the news and reports of what was happening at home; cruelty, degradation, barbarism, and the slaughter of innocent people. I read of the bombing at Guernica in April 1937, by the Nazi German Condor Legion, killing 1,654 people and wounding nearly 900. I remember those figures, I will remember them all my life, because I continued to stand aside and do nothing. Franco denied the raid ever took place.

'Then I met Flora; and I fell in love with her. I rebuffed her questions about my family and I refused to acknowledge the truth. I was incredibly selfish and took cover in my love for Flora. I assure you Philip my love was sincere, I had never felt anything like that before.

'It took the news of my father's involvement and injury to bring me to my senses. Someone carried that message from my mother out of the country, there were no postal services, the whole infrastructure of our country had broken down. I never discovered who brought me that news.

'My father died three months after my return.'

Neither Ramon nor Philip could speak for several moments. Then Philip said,

'Thank you for telling me that. It helps me to understand your situation but I would like you to know, that I think no less of you for what wrong you think you did. I believe human beings are allotted an existence on this earth for a period of time and we have to make the best of whatever life throws at us.'

'Thank you Philip.'

'Had I had to fight during the Second World War I don't know how I would have coped; I know I could not have killed a man. But I was not tested; I was selected to work on secret work, I'm sorry I'm still not at liberty to talk about it. I didn't even wear a uniform. I considered myself fortunate, I did not face death and danger as so many men did. I missed my family, I rarely saw my wife and daughters during a period of six years but I never suffered as you and your family has done.'

'Yes, we suffered Philip, but it's over twelve years ago now and though the scars are still visible throughout the land, the Spanish people are slowly pushing the horrors of the war to one side and we are building our lives again. Here, we are developing the *bodega* and beginning to produce some good wine. So many men were killed but a few came back to work for us. Most importantly to me, my mother and I are at peace with one another and for that I am grateful.'

'Come, we have been serious for too long. Let's have a glass of wine. It's time you tasted a good Rioja.'

Ramon rose and went to a nearby table. Two bottles stood already opened and he chose one of them.

'Before we taste, perhaps you would like to look in on Conchita, put your mind at rest that she has fallen asleep.'

'I'm a little reluctant to disturb her if she is asleep. I think she was just so tired after the long journey, to say nothing of the emotional turmoil she has been going through that she was probably relieved to climb into bed.'

'I'll call my mother, she is staying here with me for a few days to help Conchita settle in. She can listen at the door. In any case, I think you should meet my mother sooner rather than later.'

Ramon left the room returning with his mother.

Isabella Garcia López , a slender, graceful woman stood barely to the height of her son's shoulder. Her silver hair was pulled back into a tight coil at the back of her neck, her smile and bright eyes softening the harshness of the style. She stepped towards Philip with her hand outstretched.

'I'm so pleased to meet you, not a moment too soon I think.'

'Thank you. It would seem that I already owe you some thanks for being willing to help Connie...' Philip searched for the right words '...in her new life.'

'It starts now; I'm going to check on her but I don't think you need fret. I'm fairly sure she is sound asleep and I shan't disturb her if that is so. That's all for now Ramon, I shall see you both tomorrow morning.'

Isabella smiled at each of them and left.

'She's a wonderful woman Philip, she'll do her utmost to help Conchita.'

Ramon was silent for a moment and then raising his head said,

'Now, where were we? Yes, a little introduction to our wine.

'Our vines are mainly in Rioja Alavesa, an area extending from the Sierra de Cantabria to the steep north bank of the River Ebro with predominantly limestone soil. This particular wine is made from Tempranillo from vines that are at least sixty years old. Not much fruit from such old vines but what they do produce is incredibly concentrated.

Philip nodded and raised the glass to his lips.

'This is a Reserva' Ramon continued; 'the wine is released after four years with a minimum of one year in cask. This is a good choice I think for your first taste of Rioja wine.

'In 1902 a Royal Decree was given to La Rioja, this defined the area of origin for Rioja wines and gave the winemakers the right to label their wine *denominacion de origen.* So what do you think?'

They drank together and discussed the aroma, and flavours of redcurrant and creamy, smoky, blackberry fruit.

'It's very good Ramon. If this is the kind of wine you produce no wonder you are doing well.'

'So you can see Philip, we are fortunate to have a good living already after those terrible years, so you need have no fear that Conchita will be well provided for. I'll do whatever is possible to make things easier for her, and also for Garnet.'

'Thank you. We must both try to make the best of the situation we find ourselves in.'

Plans were made for Garnet to visit sometime in the near future and their grandparents and Philip himself of course. No mention was made of Flora.

There was a pause in their deliberations when a deep sigh broke from Philip.

'I'm going to miss her, so much,' and he closed his eyes as though trying to block any tears that might show themselves.

'My home will always be open to any of you Philip,' Ramon said with sincerity.

'Thank you,' he replied hoarsely and then with a twisted smile added,

'But I don't think you realise what you might be letting yourself in for. Flights are becoming less expensive and more frequent, I can quite see my parents booking their seats the minute I get home.' He laughed softly as he spoke, imagining his mother Amelia already at the Travel Agents.

On the night before Philip's departure Ana Maria served a simple but delicious dinner to the three of them.

'It's not too spicy,' she whispered to Ramon. 'The English are not used to our spicy food, I think,' and she winked at him. She smiled warmly at Connie as she put her plate in front of her.

'*Come, mi pequeña*, eat little one, you will like it. I make it especially for you.'

Ramon translated for her and Connie still not trusting her voice to be steady just smiled her thanks. Throughout dinner Connie was quiet but calm.

The next morning they said goodbye. Ramon waited by the car as Philip and Connie parted in the tiled hallway of the house. Philip wrapped his arms around Connie in an enormous hug and wept openly.

94

Connie trembling in his embrace, stretched up her arms around his neck, a great sob shaking her shoulders. Neither could speak.

Philip pulled himself away and went out to the waiting car. He climbed in beside Ramon and turned to Connie still standing in the entrance.

'Write to me Connie,' he called out through the open window.

She nodded, waved briefly and turned away.

Ramon had spoken to his mother, Isabella, the night before, to ask if she would look after Conchita when he drove Philip to Bilbao. She was standing in the hallway when Connie turned into the house. Isabella Garcia Lopez spoke excellent English and had a natural and easy manner with children. It had been her life's sadness that she had only one son. Once she had come to terms with this young girl's arrival she determined to be a true '*abuela*' to her.

'Come Conchita, we are going to get to know one another. You can call me 'nana'. You have two English grandmothers haven't you? Tell me about them. What do you call them?'

What was to become a lasting and loving relationship began.

The next morning Connie wrote to Garnet.

July 1951

Dear Nettie,

I have been here a week now and it seems like a year. I am missing you all so much. I'm sorry I didn't write straight away but we were taken round the vineyard and introduced to people and then I was so tired. Daddy left yesterday and now that he has gone I feel really lonely. I feel bad writing that because Ramon is very kind and tries to make me feel welcome.

There's a housekeeper, Ana. Isn't that funny – we have Annie at our house . But this one's called Ana Maria. Well she's a bit more than a housekeeper, she was Ramon's nanny when he was little. She's a lot like Annie, but bossy. She does the cooking and keeps everything and everyone in order. But she has lots of help in the house too.

Ramon is going to find a teacher to teach me Spanish but I don't need to go to school yet – not until I can speak good Spanish he says. I think that will be ages but he says he just knows I will pick it up quickly

How is Bella? I miss her so! Yesterday I felt something brush past my leg and just for a moment I thought it was Bella's tail, of course I knew it wasn't but it felt just like it. Please look after her for me. I know you are not a doggy person like me but Mummy doesn't like her,

Annie's too busy and Daddy is at work all day. You understand her and she loves you too. I know I can trust you.

I haven't written to Daddy yet but I saw him just two days ago so don't tell him I'm sad. It will upset him. I've not written to Mummy either, I don't know what to say. I still don't really understand why I had to come.

It's certainly a beautiful place and it's obvious I shall have to make the best of it. I hope you can come and see me soon.

I hope you are getting on all right at school and your music exam went well. Of course it did – you're a whiz at the piano!

Give my love to Granny and Gramps and Daddy and tell them I'll write soon.

Lots and lots of love
Connie.

***

For several nights after Philip's departure Connie cried herself to sleep, sobbing into her pillow as she had at times at home in England, of which Philip had never been aware. When Ramon mounted the curved staircase at midnight, the first night after Philip's departure, he became aware of an unfamiliar sound coming from Connie's bedroom. He did not know what to do, whether to approach her, try to comfort her or to leave her to cope by herself. He thought of waking his mother but then he remembered Philip's words and his remark that 'Connie rarely cries, certainly not in front of any of us though I suspect Annie, our housekeeper, has had occasion to comfort her from time to time. She seems to think she is being a trouble to us if she comes crying with her problems.'

He went to his mother's room and was not surprised to find that she was still awake, reading in bed.

'Conchita is crying *Madre*. What do you think I should do?' He related his conversation with Philip and watched his mother's expression as she listened.

'I should leave her Ramon. She needs to cry sometime and the sooner the better. If you go to her now she may well feel that she is being troublesome, as you said, and that may cause her more pain. She will fall asleep soon and in the morning things will be a little better, we

96

shall see to that. Every morning things will be better.' She looked at Ramon closely.

'She is a lovely child Ramon. You are very lucky. She is a precious gift which you must treasure.'

He took his mother's hands in his and kissed them.

'Thank you *Madre*. I know it will not be easy but I will make her happy. Goodnight and thank you for today.' He left her and went to his own bedroom but could not sleep for some time, his mind turning over his conversation with Philip.

Ramon heeding his mother's early advice, had the foresight to make sure that Connie's ensuing days were full. He took her for tours around the vineyard in his horse and trap, explaining what he did and how he ran his business. He described how the wine was made. He showed her the vats, and told her how the grapes were harvested and placed in these huge containers, watched over and finally the rich red liquid drawn off; wine at last but not yet ready to drink.

He explained that normally he rode round the *bodega* on his favourite horse Cesar, and that he was planning riding lessons for her to start straight away.

'Riding on horseback over the land is so much more pleasurable and one can see much more,' he told her. 'I learned the business from my father as we rode, listening and observing as he pointed out the way of the vines. How they grew so much in a season, producing, from a dead-like dark brown stump, the rosy pink shoots that burst forth with bright green leaves and bear bunches and bunches of grapes, all in a matter of weeks. My father's enthusiasm was infectious, I couldn't help but learn.

'I hope you will learn about vines and winemaking in the same way that I did,' he told her.

The full days tired Connie and usually she fell asleep quite quickly. At first this bothered her, she felt guilty. She missed her family and Garnet's company, particularly at bedtime when they used to whisper to each other in bed before they went to sleep.

Garnet only a year and a half younger than Connie went to bed first. In theory it was assumed she would be asleep by the time Connie got into bed, but she never was. They were allowed to read in bed for a little while and during their reading time their father usually came up to wish them goodnight. After this they were left alone. Their mother never came up, she said her 'goodnights' before they climbed the stairs. Sometimes their enthusiasm got the better of them and they would chatter and giggle. It was always Annie who came in to speak to them, not to reprimand but to chat for a moment, tuck them in once again firmly and put out their light. No-one came to tuck Connie up in bed in her new home. Ana Maria gave her hug before seeing her into bed and closing the bedroom door. Ramon not sure of what was expected of him, kissed her on each cheek and wished her *buenos noches*, sometimes with the promise of an outing or event the next day as though he were trying to leave her with something pleasant to think about.

18

Diary

I'm going to learn Spanish. Ramon has found me a teacher. Oh dear, I really must stop calling him Ramon – not that I do to his face! Ana Maria calls him 'Papa' when she's talking to me about him. I certainly don't think of him as my father, not yet anyway. I wonder what my teacher will be like. I hope it's not some grumpy old man or, worse still, a strict, bossy old woman.

Ramon's mother, my grandmother! is a real sweety. She's called Isabella but I can't call her that. Granny in Spanish is 'abuela' – what a mouthful. She says I can call her 'Nana Isabella'' if I like. She speaks fantastic English and comes to talk to me and we have been for a walk together. She told me about the vineyard and how it's been in the family for four generations. She's very calm and gentle but I can tell she's quite a strong lady.

***

Carmen Ramirez Flores was twenty-eight years old. It was six weeks since her mother had died; Carmen having nursed her for the last two years through cancer. Her letter to Ramon López Garcia told him little of her personal life other than that she was a teacher wishing to come back to teaching after her mother's death.

Carmen knew of the López family and their reputation as the owners of one of the up and coming vincyards in northern Spain. By her standards, they were well off and the house was grand compared to her own. She also knew of them through her mother's long and faithful friend Ana Maria, who had been with the López family since she was nineteen years old. Ana Maria did not gossip but talked of the family with deep affection. Carmen and her mother had learned of the family's history; the death of Ramon's father, Luis López Galvez, their kindness to their employees and despite the terrible war years their success in producing some good Rioja wine. In return Ana Maria knew all about Carmen and her sadness. She had persuaded her to write to Ramon and apply for the post of teaching the young English girl and Carmen had agreed on condition that Ana Maria would say nothing to pre-empt her letter. Carmen wanted this job on her own merits, not out of sympathy.

She was nervous. Carmen had not had to go through anything like this for a long time. Unbeknown to her she need not have worried for Ramon had more or less made up his mind to employ this young woman, of whom Ana Maria had spoken so highly, even before she had ridden through the archway into the courtyard. He watched her lean her old bicycle against the stone wall and walk across the neatly paved enclosure with its terracotta pots of oleander, hibiscus and burgeoning bougainvillea. She stopped momentarily and put the open palm of her hand under a particularly fine apricot-coloured bloom. She cupped it in her hand, she spoke and he read the movement of her soft red lips as she murmured,

'Beautiful. Like a baby's skin.'

She was a tall slender young woman and moved gracefully towards the house with long purposeful strides, smiling to herself as though she had some amusing secret.

Ana Maria opened the heavy oak door before Carmen had time to clang the bell. She welcomed her with a huge warm embrace.

'*Mi muchacha pequeña*, my little girl, how are you? You look good, better than the last time I saw you. You are eating properly I hope.'

'Yes Ana Maria, I'm eating properly. Don't fuss now, you sound like my mother.'

'And so I should, who is to look after you now that your dear mother is gone, God rest her soul,' and Ana Maria crossed herself hastily. Carmen hid a wry smile. Her mother had not had occasion to look after her for a long time; these last two years had seen the roles reversed. She continued to hold her arms around her mother's lifelong friend and hug her. They swayed together for a moment or two, taking comfort in each other's embrace.

'And I'm not such a little girl any more, see I'm taller than you,' she teased the older woman. Ana Maria gave her an affectionate push towards one of the kitchen chairs.

'Sit,' she commanded and went on, 'Now this little one, she's a lovely girl, you'll like her. She needs a young woman like you, with energy and fresh, modern ideas. I'm too old fashioned and set in my ways. Be kind to her my dear, she has been pulled out of the bosom of her family, poor little wretch.' Ana Maria knew a litttle of the truth and did much speculating.

'Ana Maria, what are you talking about? I haven't got the job yet,'

'You will, I know him. Go now, he's waiting.'

Ramon was relaxed and his naturally friendly manner began to dispel Carmen's fears of him as an autocratic landowner. Ana Maria brought them coffee and *almendrados*, small almond cakes, which she laid on the wooden table in front of Carmen. With her back to Ramon she winked quickly at her. Carmen had difficulty in keeping her smile under control.

'Perhaps Señorita Ramirez will pour the coffee. I've work to do.'

'Of course Ana Maria, thank you.' He looked towards Carmen, 'Do you mind?' he asked her.

Carmen was grateful for the small task which freed the tension in her posture and she found herself explaining quite naturally that she had not taught in school for three years.

'I left my job in the Secondary School after four years of teaching, in order to spend a year travelling.'

'That's very commendable,' Ramon said, nodding, and thinking to himself, so she's not a provincial young woman. She's had some experience, that's good.'

Carmen's thoughts were quite different; not so commendable, if you knew why, and she swallowed hastily as she felt the old constriction in her throat as the memories began to filter back into her mind and fill her head with painful images. She quickly pushed them down and did not enlighten him as to her very personal and tragic reason for running away. For that is how she had thought of it at the time.

It was still a closed book the contents of which no one spoke, to each other or to Carmen herself. Many in the village where she lived knew that Carmen could lose the soft look in those almond shaped eyes and lose her temper once in a while, like a summer storm that raged suddenly and forcefully. Even Ana Maria was forbidden to speak of it though she knew every little detail.

Friendship with Juanita Ramirez had brought Ana Maria into Carmen's life as a small child. She was more like an aunt to Carmen than just her mother's friend. She had watched her grow from a quick witted, delightful girl into an attractive but not a happy, young woman. She had witnessed Carmen's guilt at the death of her fiancé, just three months before their planned wedding.

She had sensed that Carmen did not love Pedro but the marriage was the wish of the two fathers. Like Ana Maria and Juanita's friendship these two men had grown up together and on marriage had each made a solemn promise that if one had a son and the other a daughter they would be pledged in marriage. Such a pledge was sacrosanct and Carmen knew she could never break it. She thought for a brief time that the marriage promise might be annulled when her father died but Pedro's father gravely reminded her that it was her duty to the memory of her father to keep the promise.

Pedro loved Carmen with a fierce and desperate passion. He could not remember a time when he had not loved her. At six years old he had declared that he would marry Carmen. Their respective fathers had smiled and nodded.

Neither of the children was aware of the sworn agreement and Carmen had just laughed, too young to take Pedro's declaration seriously. She had gone on laughing as she grew up, thinking it a joke. But Pedro's love for her increased as he grew older. He had cried with joy when his father told him of the marriage pledge knowing that this would secure him the bride of his dreams. He was a sensitive young man and aware that Carmen's feelings did not match his own but this pledge meant that when, at twenty-seven years old, he asked her to marry him, he knew she could not refuse. The formal question was not obligatory, after all it had all been settled many years before, but Pedro was a romanticist. After the betrothal, he openly paid court to her, proud to be able to touch her to show the world that she was his. At every opportunity he stroked her straight shining hair and later he kissed her full red lips and traced the curve of her infectious smile with his finger-tips. He loved the way she walked, swaying on her long legs. After the betrothal he had said to Carmen as they planned the wedding day,

'I have enough love for both of us.' Carmen had gasped never realising that Pedro knew she did not return the passion he felt for her. She had tried to say the words, 'I love you,' but could not, only the word 'I...' had escaped her lips then he had pressed his fingers on her soft mouth saying,

'Don't. You will say it later, I know you will.' Carmen lowering her gaze had held his hand and remained silent.

His suicide was a horrendous shock. The letter he left behind said only that he could not go on. No explanation, no apology, no reason for his action. Only his doctor knew of the unexplained depression he had been suffering and had signed the death certificate citing it as the reason for taking his own life. Pedro had hinted at worries but did not reveal the cause of them.

Juanita told Ana Maria of Carmen's self-imposed seclusion after the funeral.

'She has shut herself away in her room, lying on her bed every day. She believes it is her fault because she did not love him and that he could not go on loving her without something in return. Her guilt is so great and her sorrow deep, believing that she has caused Pedro to die. She does not weep but her eyes, wide open, stare at the ceiling. The sun rises in the morning and shines through her white lace curtains and I see her watching the moving patterns on the walls. She watches the changing shapes and shades until evening, only when they fade does she falls asleep.'

Ana Maria comforted her friend.

'The whole village thinks her self-imposed confinement a sign of the depth of her mourning, they admire it, respect it and grieve with her. Let them do so. She will return to us soon, you will see.'

'It is five days now that I have taken her meals and left them on a small table beside her bed. I do not speak to her but I gently lay my hand on her arm to tell her I love her. When I go back more often than not the food has hardly been disturbed.' Juanita sobbed.

'Five days is enough. It is time you spoke to her,' Ana Maria said. 'You cannot go on like this; it is hard on you also.'

Juanita heeded her friend's words. Sitting beside her daughter that evening she began to speak.

'The grieving is over *mi querida hija,* now my dear daughter you must get up and go out into the world. Begin again.'

It was as though her mother's words had broken the spell which had befallen her daughter; and Carmen sat up.

'Thank you mother,' she whispered, 'for your patience and understanding. You're right, I can't stay here forever. It will not mend what I have done.'

'You have done nothing. Nothing, I tell you. Do you hear me? It would have happened, someday. It was written.'

Carmen looked up with a question on her lips but her mother hushed her.

'Come, now we make plans.'

***

Ramon placed his coffee cup on the tray and the clink of the china brought Carmen back to the large crescent shaped salon, with its tiled floor and grand arched window. She had been gazing out and beyond the vineyards which stretched, row upon row, into the far distance. Her memories had risen unbidden and the strength of them had held her so tightly as she sat in Ramon's elegant sitting room that it was difficult for her to pull her gaze away from the sight. She heard his voice and she turned her face to look directly at him.

'You know of course, that I am looking for a teacher for my daughter.'

'Yes, Ana Maria told me. What exactly do you want me to teach her?'

'To speak Spanish,' he said.

Carmen looked at him with a puzzled expression and he smiled,

'Yes, I know, it does sound odd. I can see that you are wondering why my daughter does not speak Spanish naturally. Suffice it to say that she has been brought up in England but...' he hesitated. Carmen was aware of his struggle to explain how suddenly this daughter had appeared in his life. Of course Ana Maria had told her what she thought she knew about the English daughter. Ramon continued,

'....circumstances have changed and she is to live here with me now.'

Carmen nodded.

'If you are in agreement I'll ask Conchita to come down and meet you now. We can sort out the details later. She is a little shy, so....' he tailed off, pursing his lips and waggling his fingers in the air he asked,

'You'll speak English, of course?' Carmen nodded.

He moved over to the wall beside the great stone fireplace and tugged at a long embroidered bell pull. Almost immediately Ana Maria appeared at the door and ushered Conchita into the room. Ramon smiled to himself. That woman read his mind. One of these days she'll read something she shouldn't, he thought. Carmen saw the smile and having caught Ana Maria's eye, conspiratorially winking at her again, correctly interpreted Ramon's mixed expression of amusement and bewilderment.

'Come in, Conchita. I want you to meet Señorita Carmen Ramirez Flores. She is going to teach you Spanish.'

Conchita stepped forward and with well remembered good-manners shook hands with Carmen. There was an instantaneous, magical current between them. Carmen smiled.

'I hope we are going to have fun together,' she said.

'I do too,' replied Conchita and the sad expression which had lingered since her arrival was for a moment transformed into a soft smile.

Ramon watched in admiration and joy. This looked as though it might work. That damned Ana Maria was right again, he thought. She'll gloat all day when she finds out. But it's a small price to pay if it begins to make my daughter happy.

Gradually Conchita settled into a busy routine of two hours study with Carmen every morning, riding some afternoons and homework in the early evening to be presented for correction the next day. She wrote letters home to Garnet and her grandparents and joint letters to her mother and father. Ana Maria welcomed her into her kitchen and chattered as she cooked, knowing that most of what she said was beyond Conchita's comprehension, but also knowing that what was important was the company and that Conchita was kept busy.

The nights came, Conchita, physically and mentally tired, fell asleep instantly her head touched her pillow. It became a pattern and as the days went by the dark circles under her young eyes faded and the furrowed brow began to relax.

Ana Maria spoke not one word of English but she and Conchita began to understand one another. Ana Maria gesticulated, pointed, patted, propelled by the arm and even hugged Conchita and it was with Ana Maria that Conchita voluntarily uttered her first words of Spanish. *'No comprende'.*

'Bravo, mi muchacha pequeña inglesa,' my little English girl, she called, pulling Conchita round the kitchen in a skipping dance, even though Conchita's words were saying that she did not understand. Conchita grinned. But the short tentative utterance was like a magic charm. From then on she began to try out what she had begun to learn with Carmen. Ana Maria was wily. She went to Carmen and said,

'What is she learning? Then I can use it, speak it to her – it will give her confidence to hear it and understand.'

'What a wise old bird you are Ana Maria,' Carmen said. So between them Conchita made rapid progress.

***

It was after a month of Carmen coming to see Conchita every morning that Ramon decided that having her around was of real benefit. He could see how Conchita was blossoming, losing her shyness and beginning to relax. It was quite obvious to him that it was Carmen's doing. She was not just teaching her Spanish, she was becoming a friend, almost an elder sister. Ana Maria saw it too but she was astute enough to know that Ramon's enjoyment of Carmen's visits went beyond what he saw her doing for his daughter. She saw him looking at Carmen with appreciative eyes. Without his knowing it she watched him looking out for Carmen's arrival each morning; riding into the courtyard, striding across the stone paving, as she had that first day. As the days went by she became more relaxed, swinging her shoulder bag, her shapely legs revealed as her light summer skirt wafted in the air.

Ana Maria was ready for Ramon's visit to her kitchen. She knew he would come, not calling her to come to him in the salon or his study, as he did when it was a matter of business. When he was unsure of himself he came to her, as he would now. He arrived with a pseudo-casual manner, which did not fool her for one moment.

'Ana Maria, a word of advice,' he began.

'Since when did I need your advice?' she said looking askance at him, knowing full well what he meant but resolved not to help him.

'No, no. I wouldn't dare. *I* want *your* advice.' He hesitated and then went on,

'I'm thinking of asking Carmen to stay with us, live in I mean, for a few weeks. I think she is bringing Conchita out of her shell. After all cycling here every day is quite difficult and time consuming. She can have those rooms in the wing which have just been renovated. What do you say?' The words rushed out revealing his apprehension at Ana Maria's reception of his idea.

Ana Maria was careful not to agree too hastily, she knew the right tactics to play with this boy. She still thought of him from time to time as the boy who came to her when he wanted something and his parents had refused. She was longing to throw back at him, 'I wonder you didn't think of it earlier,' but instead she said,

'I think Conchita would like that. Perhaps you might like to discuss it with her.'

Ramon had failed to consider Conchita's feelings on the matter and felt duly ashamed of his lack of sensitivity though he made a good show of not revealing this fact to Ana Maria, she read his thoughts, learning to be a father is a difficult process.

'Yes, yes I intend doing that but I thought I would seek your feelings on the matter first.' Ana Maria took the flattery knowing it for what it was.

'Of course if she is happy about it then I will approach Carmen,' he added.

'The sooner the better,' she replied and turned back to the cooking where she vigorously stirred a pan of chicken and vegetables, smiling to herself.

'Do I take that remark as approval of my idea then?'

Ana Maria offered him her profile and nodded quickly turning back to her stirring. Ramon took his cue and left Maria reigning in her domain. Perhaps it was fortunate for him that he could not go straight to Conchita to speak of his idea. She was out having a riding lesson, as she did on alternate days. Ramon had already explained that to oversee and enjoy his vineyards one had to ride, he hoped that Conchita would accompany him in the near future. As he walked back to his study he felt elated and in that moment he recognised his feelings were not entirely altruistic. It was a long time since any intense passions had been aroused, as far back as the time of his father's death when his emotions were in turmoil, more precisely just prior to Rhonda's letter telling him Flora had married. He stopped in mid-step and with a scowl on his brow faced the fact that he had an underlying motive in his actions. He realised that he found Carmen attractive and for a bachelor, though still living with his mother, he began to see that he lacked female company. He didn't count Ana Maria, even though he had known her almost all his life, which was perhaps a little unfair. Thus he began to see how sterile his personal life had become. The beautiful house in which they lived had been and still was his mother's home. She was fully aware of her son's lack of young and female company and frequently made clear to him her opinion of the situation.

'It's time you married, Ramon. Who is going to inherit the vineyard if you don't have an heir?'

His recollection of his mother's words startled him and he muttered to himself,

'Don't be stupid! Who's talking about marriage? And she's probably not the least bit attracted to me anyway.'

With that he pushed open the door of his study, slamming it behind him and settled down to deal with some enquiries from a new English wine buyer, consciously thrusting such thoughts out of his mind.

19

The next morning Ramon received a 'phone call from Philip. They greeted one another like friends of some long standing.

'Philip, good to hear from you. How are things? I will tell you before you ask that Conchita is doing well.' Before Philip could respond he continued, 'She is riding quite well and her Spanish is coming along nicely. I presume that is why you are telephoning, to make sure I am looking after her?'

'Of course I want to know how Connie is, but I'm sure Ramon that you are doing everything possible to help her settle into her new home. Actually, what I'm also 'phoning about is to ask you a favour.'

'Please, fire away. Forgive me, I love using your strange English expressions. Please, go on.'

'Well, I'm ringing to ask if Garnet could possibly come to visit Connie. It's a long story but suffice it to say she has been ill. We none of us realised, it's terrible that we didn't see what was happening to her. She needs to see Connie.'

'But of course. We shall be delighted and I think I can say Conchita will be more than happy to have her sister.'

'There is one more thing. It's Garnet who has pointed out to us that maybe Connie would like to have her dog Bella, with her. How do you feel about that?'

'That is fantastic. She talks about Bella all the time. I think that would be most wonderful. Her sister and her dog would really help her I think. Thank you so much.'

'Don't thank me, as I said, it's Garnet who suggested it. Despite her problems she has been thinking about Connie's needs. We are all feeling a little ashamed of ourselves.'

'So, when will she come? And the dog?'

'I'm making travel arrangements now. I think it would be better if we travelled by 'plane. Train travel takes so long and is not so comfortable. Bella too, of course. I'm in the process of finding out what papers we need for transporting a dog. And if it's all right with you I shall accompany them.'

'My dear Philip, I shall be delighted to see you again. As soon as you have the date and the time of arrival I shall be at the airport to meet you. Just 'phone me.'

'I can't tell you how grateful I am Ramon. I'll 'phone in a couple of days, so I won't speak to Connie now, not until everything is definite. Until then give my love to Connie and tell her the good news.'

'Of course, straight away. Goodbye for now.'

'Oh Ramon, one small thing, Garnet says please don't tell about Bella. She wants to give Connie a surprise.'

'It will be a wonderful early birthday present.'

They each put down the receiver with a smile on their faces. It was odd that both felt that out of this tragic mess they had made of their earlier lives something good might be growing. Ramon certainly felt that he was gaining a valuable and sincere friend. He wondered at the probability of two men coming together in the way that they had, and their relationship developing into one of friendship and trust, as theirs seemed to be doing.

Philip sat with his hand still on the receiver, his head lowered on his chest, a smile playing on his lips. Suddenly the significance of Ramon's reference to a birthday present struck him - Connie's birthday on the 2nd of August. My God, he had almost forgotten. He leapt up almost knocking the receiver off its cradle.

'Flora? Flora? Where are you?' He hurried out of the study calling for Flora in the hall and in the sitting room. There was no reply and he pushed open the kitchen door,

'Annie, have you seen......?' but before he had finished his question he saw Flora standing at the sink, looking into the blackness beyond the kitchen window. It was the last place he would expect to find her, in her view that was Annie's domain.

'Flora? What are you doing? Where's Annie?'

'I've no idea.'

'Flora, what are you doing in here? Are you all right?'

'Fine.'

'I need to speak to you. Could you come into the sitting room.'

Flora followed Philip with an abstracted look as though in a dream. He looked back over his shoulder to see her behind him scuffing her feet on the tiles of the hall and she seemed to move reluctantly towards the sitting room. He held the door open for her but she stopped just inside blocking the area, and he couldn't close it.

'Please Flora, come right in. I want to speak to you.' She moved forward a pace or two and stood as though in a daze. Philip looked hard at her. He began to wonder if she were not feeling well.

'Flora? Are you all right?' She nodded and then moved forward and sank onto the large comfortable sofa and curled up as she had that day when she had told Philip her long involved story. Philip looked at her and not for the first time felt a deep compassion for her and though he thought it strange, he also felt the old feeling of love. He wondered how he could still love her but he did, and he was afraid of the fact. Her face was pale. He strode over to the sofa, knelt and took her hand.

'Flora, have you remembered, it's Connie's birthday in two weeks' time? I have to admit it had slipped my mind.'

'What? Whose birthday?'

Philip got up from his knees and sat on the edge of the sofa, still holding her hand. Flora definitely looked unwell. He did not repeat his question about Connie's birthday but immediately made up his mind to call Dr MacAllister the next morning. It was obvious to him that Flora was suffering from some kind of exhaustion. He thought perhaps he had not given due weight to how much pain Flora would feel at Connie's departure. He had been blinded with regard to both Flora and Garnet, by his concern for Connie. He resolved to be more attentive and caring to help Flora. His brow began to pucker with the slight worry of remembering to make the 'phone call, family matters tended to slip his memory once he arrived in his office. At least he had set the ball rolling with regard to helping Garnet and Connie too. His frown deepened as he realised he had yet to tell Flora that he would be going away again.

Flora had put her head back and sunk deeper into the cushions. She had closed her eyes and though Philip was still holding her hand it was limp and unresponsive. He rose gently, placed her hand on her lap and tiptoed out of the room.

Garnet was already in bed but he knew she would be reading before settling down to sleep. He climbed the staircase with less of his usual springy step and rapped once on her bedroom door and without waiting for a reply slowly opened the door.

'Hello Daddy. I hoped you would come. I was just going to put out my light but I was hoping you might have some news.'

'Yes my love. I have some news. I have spoken to Ramon and he will be delighted to have you to stay.'

'And what about Bella? You did ask about Bella, didn't you Daddy?'

'I did, I did. Yes, Bella can come too and he promised not to tell Connie so that it would be a surprise as you requested.'

'Daddy, I'm just a bit....' she stopped and cast down her eyes.

'The journey? You needn't worry, I'm coming too, you know. Did you think I would let my little girl travel all that way alone? Besides I look forward to seeing Ramon again, to say nothing of our darling Connie.'

'Daddy?'

'Yes, what? Lots of questions, that means my girl is feeling better. Is that true Garnet?'

'A little, but what I wanted to ask is, well.....do you like him?'

'You mean Ramon?'

Philip tucked Garnet down into her bed and placed his arms around her shoulders.

'Garnet, it's very difficult to explain but, yes I do. I didn't think I would. I think you'll like him too. You're not nervous or worried about going, are you?'

'Never! I want to see Connie. Oh Daddy I really want to see Connie.' Tears welled up in her eyes and she covered them with her hand. She stifled a sob and muttered,

'Sorry Daddy, but I do miss her.'

Philip clasped his arms around her as much to hide his own welling emotions as to comfort his daughter.

'We all miss her darling. Now go to sleep and think about the lovely times you are going to have with Connie.'

'Daddy, just.......'

'Now what Garnet? Another question?'

'Well, what about school?

'Don't worry about that. Mrs Cole thinks you should have some time off. She's sure you will be able to catch up later. You won't worry about that will you?'

Garnet rocked her head on the pillow and smiled.

'Night-night Daddy. Thank you for coming. I love you.'

'And I you sweetheart. Goodnight.'

20

Diary

Nettie's coming! Oh gosh, I can't believe it. It'll be fantastic. I've missed her so much. Ramon says that she's been poorly – I don't know what with, I hope it's not bad. But it can't be too bad if she is able to travel. She and Daddy are arriving here the day after Ramon's birthday, and then in August it's MY birthday! We're going to have such a good time, I know it.

Conchita could not believe her ears when Ramon greeted her the next day with the news that Garnet would be arriving in two weeks' time.

'How? Why? Oh Carmen, Garnet's coming.'

'Yes, my sweet I heard. I'm very pleased for you. We shall have lots of fun together.'

'To answer your questions my dear,' Ramon smiled at her, 'She and your father are flying to Bilbao. I have to tell you that Garnet has not been well and a little holiday with you I am sure will make her better. Don't you think so?'

'Not well? What do you mean? Why is she not well?'

'Now don't worry, I am sure your ....I am sure it will all be explained. Aren't you pleased?'

'Oh yes, I'm thrilled. Oh Carmen, what shall we do? There is so much to show Garnet isn't there?' Conchita paused for a moment and then said with a slight frown,

'But what about her practising?'

'Practising? What is that?'

'Her piano. Didn't you know? Oh no, I don't suppose you do. Garnet plays the piano. She's an absolute *chispa brillante, es fenomenal*. Her teacher says she's the best pupil she's ever had. She practises every day for hours. Garnet just loves music and she sings too. I think she'll be a professional pianist when she grows up, or maybe a singer.'

'So, if we have – what is it you say? - a *chispa brillante* coming to stay with us, perhaps we had better have a piano here for her to practise, to make her feel at home. What do you say to that Conchita?'

'You have a piano, I've never seen it. Where is it?'

'We don't have a piano - yet. I think perhaps we can make a telephone call and arrange something, fairly quickly. Carmen can you help us make this little surprise?'

'I can and I will do it straight away. Come Conchita you can help me.'

As Conchita skipped her way out of the room Ramon winked at Carmen and whispered,

'Did you hear her Spanish? She is making such good progress. Thanks to you. By the way, what's this phrase *chispa brillante*?'

Carmen coloured slightly 'I just translated Conchita's English word - 'whiz', it's slang for genius, expert, it's all I could think of. It means a bright spark, that's all,' she said and hurried after Conchita so that Ramon would not see her self-consciousness. She laughed and closed the door without replying. They went to Ramon's study to use the telephone and as they walked down the long tiled corridor, Conchita asked,

'Carmen? Is he...is....I mean, Ramon, oh dear, what shall I call him? It's not polite to call him that, is it?'

'Why don't you call him Papa? He is after all your father. He would be so happy if you did. Do you think you could?'

'I think so. Is he, is....Papa rich? I mean, how can he buy a piano just like that? They are so expensive.'

'He has enough money my love, don't worry about that. He loves you already and he will do almost anything to make you happy, did you know that? I guess he thinks buying a piano to help your sister will also make *you* happy. So it's wonderful because he is making you both happy at the same time.'

'Garnet will be thrilled. I do hope she will sing for you as well, she has such a beautiful voice. Oh Carmen, I am so looking forward to her arriving.'

Conchita sat in a great leather chair beside her father's desk, swivelling it round and round, as Carmen speedily made some enquiries on the telephone.

'Done!' she said brightly as she put down the receiver. 'Now shall we do some work? It's time you did a little grammar.'

Conchita placed her hand through Carmen's arm as they left Ramon's office and they made their way to a small room where they worked every day on language, geography and the history of Spain. Conchita was an able and willing pupil.

'Carmen, Papa liked that word 'whiz' in Spanish, didn't he?'

'He did, I was a little afraid when you said it that he might be cross with me for letting you use slang. After all you're going to hear these things when you go to school so the sooner you understand them the better. That's my feeling.'

'When *am* I going to go to school Carmen? I'm not sure that I want to go. I love our days together here.'

'So do I. I shall miss you. But you need to learn far more than I can teach you and it will be good for you to be with other young people. Your father is arranging to visit some schools soon and then he will decide.'

'Will you come with us? Will you help him to decide?'

'If your father invites me along, yes.'

Two days later the piano arrived. It was a Steinway, a rosewood boudoir grand. How on earth Carmen had managed to secure such a beautiful instrument was a mystery. It was not brand new but had come from the home of a former professional pianist and was in excellent condition. It was placed at one end of the long sitting room, the room curved round forming the shape of a crescent moon with rounded ends. One end looked out onto the garden through full length windows and at the other the piano fit neatly into the half-circle, away from the direct sunlight. It was wheeled in on a platform with small wheels, they carefully fixed its sturdy but elegant legs and pushed it smoothly into position. The piano tuner had travelled with them and no sooner had they placed the piano at the right angle, than he set to work. Conchita heard the familiar tinkling and strange combination of tones as the man strove to create euphony. She crept into the sitting room and stood by the door listening. She was so entranced, though she had heard it many times before in her home in England, that she did not hear Ramon walk up behind her.

'Why don't you go in?' he asked her quietly. She jumped almost guiltily.

'I...I didn't want to disturb him,' she whispered.

'Come, we'll both go in and watch and listen.'

'I think he's nearly finished anyway,' she added knowingly. He had indeed just finished but he continued, playing the first movement of Beethoven's Moonlight Sonata. He caressed the keys in appreciation of the instrument and its singing tone. He did not stop when he saw Ramon and Conchita enter the room. They sat down and listened attentively until the movement came to an end.

114

'That was beautiful,' Conchita said in Spanish.

'Do you play young lady?' he asked her smiling.

'Yes, but not as well as my sister. She can play like you. Sorry, I don't mean to be rude but she is very, very good, even though she is only ten.'

The tuner smiled and said,

'Thank you my dear. You can play too, I think. How about your playing a little something for us so that you can tell us what you think of the piano?'

For a second Conchita hesitated, she had understood but she was nervous, unlike Garnet who loved performing and did so with confidence, loving her music so much that she forgot the people sitting there and became lost in the magic of the music.

Ramon touched her on the arm,

'Go on,' he said, 'I would really like to know what you think of it, try it out for me and see if you think Garnet will like it.'

The piano tuner got up, smiling he gave a little bow and pointed to the stool. Conchita sat and pulling it a little nearer, began to play.

At that moment Isabella walked silently into the room. Conchita played well though she knew that her rendering of Beethoven's 'Fur Elise' did not measure up to Garnet's. Surprisingly she found she was not so nervous after all but was enjoying herself. She rose from the piano and turning saw Isabella standing beside Ramon.

'Oh why didn't you stop me? I can't play in front of lots of people.'

'You just did my dear, well, not 'lots', just family. It was beautiful. I can see we are going to have some delightful concerts over the coming weeks.'

'So, what do you think young lady?' Ramon asked.

'Papa, it's just wonderful. Garnet will be so happy. Thank you, thank you a million times.'

Ramon stood stock still. She had called him 'Papa'. He could not speak but stretched out his arms. Conchita went toward him and they hugged. Over Conchita's head he looked at his mother, and gave an emotional smile.

'Thank you,' he said, turning to the piano tuner. 'Thank you for responding so quickly to my request. It is important, you see, that we have a piano; the younger sister of … this young lady, is a very good musician and whilst she is here she will need to keep up her – what is that word Conchita?' he asked grinning.

'Practising,' she said with a smile. The tuner bowed.

'It has been my pleasure sir. Have a happy time with your sister and I hope she enjoys the piano.' He went out of the room leaving Ramon,

Isabella and Conchita smiling down on the piano. Conchita's hand was still in his and she turned,

'Thank you so much. I just know Garnet will have the biggest surprise and be so happy. It's very, very kind of you.'

Ramon did not trust himself to speak but he held onto that small hand. Taking his mother's arm in his the three of them went out into the garden.

21

Philip Hampton was feeling guilty. He was looking forward with enthusiasm to going to Spain for a second time. The decision to take Garnet on a visit was a double pleasure; it would help her recovery to normal health and he would see his beloved Connie sooner than he could have hoped. What he hardly dare admit to himself was that he was looking forward to meeting Ramon again.

Compounding his sense of guilt was the fact that he would be leaving Flora knowing that she was not entirely well. She had been behaving oddly, she had lost her confident manner and it worried him. He had not yet contacted Dr MacAllister, when it came to describing Flora's behaviour as 'strange' it seemed as though he was making a fuss over minor symptoms. But he knew Flora, and he felt that her behaviour of late *was* strange. There wasn't much he could do for the time being except ask Annie to keep an eye on her.

Philip, for all his ability these days in directing a major branch of a large bank he was, like many a highly intelligent person, never at ease with emotionally charged decisions involving his family. Of course he loved his daughters and he loved Flora still, despite what had happened. He did not have the faculty of forming ideas to be creative or resourceful where his emotions were involved. His mind was logical, rational, deductive but with flashes of intuition which had made him so successful in his war work. He had been a hero of sorts, instrumental in helping to crack the German code through the amazing machine the Enigma, giving the British the upper hand which led to the end of the Second World War.

Now, in an emotionally charged atmosphere, he was out of his depth. All he could do was rely on his mother and right there in their home, Annie. He spoke to her the evening before he left with Garnet.

'Annie, would you keep your eye on Flora? I think she's not as well as she might be. If by any chance you have cause to worry then 'phone my mother. I wish in a way that I were not going away, I don't think it's the best time to be leaving her.'

'Don't worry Mr H. You know I'll look after 'er. But as you say, she's not 'er usual self. She seems sort of... distracted. She's taken to gardening of late. I alus thought she didn't like it but maybe she finds it soothing. You know, quiet and peaceful like. I gather she's told the gardener not to come so often.'

'Really? I didn't know that.'

'Oh dear, have I spoken out of turn Mr H?'

'No, no. I'm glad you've mentioned it. Flora must have forgotten to tell me. Perhaps being outside in the fresh air, having time to think, will help her to come to terms with……..well, all that's happened.'

'I know, I know what you mean. I'll keep my eye on 'er anyway. Enjoy the trip Mr H and let's 'ope this visit will put Garnet to rights as well. Be sure to give my love to Connie, won't you? Ee, I do miss that face and 'er cheerfulness.'

'We all do Annie. We all do. We're off early in the morning but no doubt we'll see you before we leave.'

'Indeed you will, I'll be there to see Garnet's got all she needs. I've already checked 'er packing.'

'Thank you Annie, you're a treasure. I don't know what we'd do without you.'

'Aye well, it works both ways Mr H. But thanks anyway. See you at breakfast.'

Philip left the kitchen and went to the 'phone in the hall.

'Mother? Just thought I'd have a word before we leave in the morning.'

'I'd have telephoned you myself, but you beat me to it. I was just settling Dad with a glass of ……….' She stopped, realising that Philip would pick up any hint of his father not being his usual bright self.

'What did you say?'

'Oh, he just felt like a little drop of Scotch, for a change.'

'Is everything all right? He's not ill, is he?'

'No, no,' said Amelia with feeling, 'you know Dad, he just likes a wee tot from time to time.' Amelia was convincing, despite the fact that she knew her husband was unwell. He was wheezing more often and his breathing was becoming more laboured. She also knew that the family 'upset', as she and Charles called it had taken its toll on him. Charles had appeared to accept it all with such equanimity and understanding but underneath he had been deeply disturbed, perceiving the possible repercussions for all of them. He had said little to Amelia, nothing to Philip and offered only comfort and consolation to Flora. He had behaved normally with Connie and Garnet, told them he loved them, as he always did every time they visited, and continued to do so in his letters to Connie. The shock, his sadness and his fear for the future for his two dear grand-daughters was kept within his heart and it

118

was beginning to reveal itself in his demeanor and reduced energy. Amelia recognised the symptoms.

She told Philip nothing of her thoughts and worries but bade him 'au revoir', a safe journey and be sure to give the two girls much love from both of them.

Philip had intended mentioning his worries about Flora but he thought better of it. He admired his parents so much for the way they had taken the shattering news. He was afraid of adding to the load and after all he had not even mentioned anything to Dr McAllister. If he voiced his concerns to anyone it should be to their own doctor first. He would have to rely on Annie's common sense.

22

Diary

Tomorrow is the 9th of August, Papa's birthday. We are having a surprise dinner party that night and Nana Isabella will be with us. I couldn't think of anything I could give him. I haven't any money and I can hardly ask for some to buy him a birthday present. In any case I could never ask him for money, after all he does for me. I asked yesterday if I could 'phone Granny, he didn't mind that at all, he's always saying I can speak to any of them, any time I want.

It's going to be such an exciting week; Nettie and Daddy are arriving the day after Papa's birthday. Nettie's going to stay for a whole month. No studying, just fun. Perhaps I can persuade Nettie to learn to ride. And then....it's my birthday! Wow whee!

Two days before Philip's arrival with Garnet, Conchita showed Ana Maria how to make marmalade. Conchita had asked Ramon's permission to telephone Granny Hampton to ask for the recipe. There had been a discussion that morning with Carmen and Ramon, about what the English ate for breakfast.

Conchita admitted that she missed toast and marmalade and that her father loved it too.

'And so do I,' Ramon had added, with enthusiasm.

The 'phone call was made. Conchita had not yet grown used to the unrestrained use of the telephone and she began to feel a little guilty. Unbeknown to her they were privileged to have a private telephone. It seemed to Conchita that Ramon would do anything to please her. Had she not been such a practical and unselfish child she might well have taken advantage of Ramon's generosity. Carmen too had a hand in guiding Ramon's extravagancies.

That evening Carmen spoke out. She and Ramon were dining alone, Conchita was tired after a day out riding and had her supper early and went to bed. Without Conchita Ramon had chosen to dine later than usual and Carmen had dressed in an elegant and stylish dress of blue

120

silk. It emphasised her slim figure and showed to advantage her mildly tanned skin and dark hair. She knew she looked attractive which gave her the confidence to speak.

'I hope I don't offend you Ramon when I say that you must not always give Conchita what she wants. She is a lovely child but like all children she must learn that........' she stopped as she saw his dark expression.

Suddenly she was afraid that she had overstepped the mark and interfered between father and daughter. She silently chastised herself, remembering that she was after all in his employ only to *teach* Conchita. Ramon frowned.

'You are quite right Carmen, as you so often are. How is it you know these things - for one who has no children of one's own and, as far as I know, no experience of raising them?' His sarcastic tone stung Carmen and tears welled in her eyes. For a second she thought she would bend under his gaze and then the courage of her convictions rose and she retorted,

'You seem to forget that I do have experience of children, that I have been a teacher and observed children for some years. In any case, I ......' she faltered and added defiantly, 'I find... I love this child. She means a great deal to me. Perhaps it should not be so, but it is. I am sorry if I offend you. If you are not happy..........'

Ramon put out his hand towards hers.

'Carmen. Stop! I'm sorry, my words and tone were unforgiveable. I don't know how to thank you for what you have done for Conchita. I should have realised that only such progress both in her school work and in settling into a new life, could have been achieved only with dedication and... and love.' He moved his hand nearer and touched her fingers. She rectracted her hand, his words had hurt and though he apologised Carmen could not immediately look at him. There was silence for a moment or two and then Ramon said,

'Am I forgiven? I am truly sorry. I do admire you so much Carmen. Have you not noticed?' His hand crept forward and took hold of hers and this time she did not move her hand away. To her annoyance she blushed. She felt the glow rising from below the line of her low cut dress, suffusing her slender neck, and rising to her face. Blaming her anger on bringing colour to her cheeks, she said rather formally,

'I apologise, if I spoke out of turn.'

'No, it is I who should be sorry. I am grateful to you for guiding me,' he smiled ruefully. You see, I've never had a daughter before, I do need your help. And I'm envious of your skill in the way you deal with her. It's obvious that you have grown very fond of her.'

Their hands stayed intertwined as they drank their wine. Although Carmen liked the feel of Ramon's hand in hers, she was afraid of giving too much meaning to the gesture. Her mind flew back to Pedro and how he had held onto her hand wherever they went, possessively, flamboyantly, declaring his love for her openly; 'This is my wife to be,' he had been saying and it had embarrassed and frightened Carmen. Ramon was an attractive man, she admired him, she liked him and she loved his daughter. She realised that she was becoming inextricably entangled within this household and her emotions were in turmoil.

Carmen thought about the morning she had spent with Ana Maria and Conchita in the kitchen, Ana Maria exclaiming at such a use of bitter oranges.

'Ah Seville oranges! No good at all, except for cooking,' she added with a grin.

'But that's exactly what we are doing with them Ana Maria,' Conchita declared laughing brightly. 'You'll see. Papa loves marmalade, and so does Daddy, and I do too.' Ana Maria and Carmen had grown used to Conchita's use of the term Daddy and understood that she could no more stop calling him that than she could forget him.

In speaking to Carmen privately she had called Ramon 'Papa' several times but only in her excitement over the piano had she said it to his face. Now she was happily using both names with Ana Maria.

'You know why Papa likes it? He ate it in England you know, when he was working in London. And.......well, I thought...maybe...' Conchita hesitated.

'Sí mi pequeña, yes little one, you thought what?' Ana Maria said encouragingly. 'Perhaps I could, I mean we could give him some for his birthday. I can't think of anything else. He has every....' Again she stopped, embarrassed by the fact that she knew there was nothing she could buy or give to him that he didn't already have, not that she had any money of her own anyway. The question of money for Conchita's own personal use had never been raised.

Suddenly, this thought hit Carmen and she made a mental note to bring up the subject with Ramon.

'He has everything, you were going to say. You're right, almost everything he needs - if money can buy it. He is very fortunate. But he can't buy kind thoughts and special presents from his daughter. It's a lovely idea Conchita. What do you think Ana Maria?'

Carmen and Ana Maria exchanged glances and smiles, their looks saying: this child is looking better, eating well, having plenty of exercise and now beginning to chatter in Spanish. It was obvious much of the stress had left her and her shoulders were no longer hunched up under her ears. Carmen wondered if Ramon was aware of the physical change in her in so short a time; she was no longer a child, she was growing up.

Carmen came back to the moment,

'By the way,' she asked Ramon suddenly, 'do you really like marmalade?'

'Marmalade? Yes, I do. Why do you ask?'

She began to tell him about the marmalade making and the chatter and laughter, the fact that Conchita thought she had taught Ana Maria something new in the kitchen and that nothing had been said about the fact that marmalade was a Spanish recipe of old, even though not served here in his home.

'You must be sure to thank Conchita, it was all her doing. You know she telephoned her grandmother in Yorkshire for the recipe?'

'Of course I know she telephoned, I dialled the number for her but I had no idea why she so urgently needed to speak to her. I thought she was just having a fit of homesickness. I didn't stay to listen to the conversation.'

'Well, be ready to say thank you, because....well, I'm not supposed to tell you this, but it's your birthday present. She didn't know what else to give you, in any case she doesn't get any pocket money, money to call her own, and she so desperately wanted to give you a present.'

The reference to pocket money had been made, but it was lost in the ensuing conversation and Carmen let it lie for the time being.

'Birthday? How does she know it's my birthday? I never celebrate my birthday, it's just another day to me. I don't like a fuss. You mustn't let her make anything out of it.'

His voice was sharp again almost angry and once more Carmen was startled and she pulled her hand away from his. She was sorry that she had told him, both because she realised that she had given away Conchita's surprise and also because her remark had induced this change of mood.

'I think Ana Maria let it slip. Apparently in Conchita's family they celebrate birthdays with a cake and candles and presents. She was upset because she had nothing to give you.' Carmen paused and made ready to leave the table, looking directly at Ramon she said,

'Please don't spoil it for her, she wants to please you and in her mind she has so few ways of doing so. You must try very hard for once to ...' Carmen's courage dried up.

'Go on, tell me,' he charged rather aggressively.

123

Carmen sat up straight, her old strength coming back, she was not going to be bullied again by this man, even if he was handsome and he had held her hand. He was her employer after all!

'No,' she said. 'I will not tell you anymore. You must wait and see. And what's more you will accept whatever Conchita does for you tomorrow, it means a great deal to her. If you wish to create a bond between the two of you, you must learn to give of your feelings. Riding lessons, a piano for her sister, new clothes, all these things are very nice but they are not enough! They are only money. You must give a little of yourself to her.'

By this time Carmen was standing and her face was bright pink. This was the second time she had spoken her mind that evening.

'Thank you for dinner. I must go and prepare a few things for Conchita for tomorrow's work.' She stiffly left the room. Ramon was taken by surprise by her sudden outburst and just stared at her with open mouth and wide eyes. His expression had been amusing and despite her anger, Carmen had wanted to laugh but she had managed to hold back the rising chuckle in her throat until she left the room. It was only as she closed the door that she let go and laughed. She laughed until tears began to trickle down her cheeks, then she realised that she was no longer laughing but crying.

'I've done it this time,' she thought. 'I really have said too much. No doubt he will tell me in the morning that I am dismissed and that will be the end of it.' She slowly undressed and before getting into bed took from the dressing table drawer, the small parcel she had prepared, and laid it on her bedside table. It was Ramon's birthday present which she had carefully selected just two days before, nothing extravagant, just a simple carved olive wood paper knife with his initials on the handle.

***

Conchita woke early, excited at the prospect of surprising Ramon with her special present. She crept downstairs into the kitchen to find Ana Maria already busy, coffee brewing but no breakfast table laid in the annexe next to the kitchen, as it usually was. Conchita looked at her questioningly.

'Ssh, breakfast is in the dining room this morning. It's my surprise,' and she winked conspiratorially. At that moment Ramon walked into the kitchen.

124

'Good morning Conchita, Ana Maria.' He looked around at the empty table and his smile faded. 'Where.....?' he began.

'In the dining room this morning Ramon,' Ana Maria said casually.

'The dining room? Whatever for?'

Carmen came into the kitchen and saw Ramon's expression of incredulity.

'Good morning Ramon, I believe we are having breakfast all together in the dining room today, aren't we?' she said calmly.

For a moment Ramon looked as though they were all mad and then he caught Carmen's determined nod of the head.

'Yes, yes, of course we are. Well what are we waiting for? Coffee please, Ana Maria.'

Ana Maria tossed her head indignantly. 'Patience,' she called, 'it's coming.'

They all trouped into the dining room in single file to find Isabella already seated at the table. Ramon felt foolish but realised that something was afoot and bearing Carmen's warning in mind, fell in with what was obviously a plan. On the table was a large bouquet of flowers with a small card attached.

Ramon put out his hand and turned over the card. It read,

'To Ramon:
Happy Birthday and Best wishes,
from Philip and Garnet
Looking forward to seeing you all.'

Ramon was touched. He had never received flowers in his life, for a birthday or any other event. He looked up to see Conchita watching him closely, her eyes twinkling and a tentative smile on her lips.

'This is wonderful Conchita. Thank you so much.' He moved round the table to her and kissed her gently on each cheek.

'It's from Garnet and Daddy, not me,' she said, smilingly.

'Yes, I see that, and how lucky I am that I shall be able to thank them in person tomorrow.'

Carmen looked on, smiling at Ramon and nodding her approval of his behaviour.

As Ramon sat down he became aware of an envelope on the table in front of him. He also noticed, to his credit, that he was being closely observed.

'What is this?' he pretended to be surprised. 'Another bill I expect,' and he opened it with a sigh. Conchita looked at Carmen out of the corner of her eye and waited.

'It's a beautiful picture,' Ramon exclaimed, 'I wonder where it came from?'

Conchita could contain her excitement no longer.

'It opens up, open it and you'll see,' she said breathlessly. Ramon slowly opened the card to read the words:

'A Papa, el dia de su cumpleaños. Con amor de Conchita.'

She had asked Carmen for the word for 'birthday', *'cumpleaños'* she told her but the rest she had composed herself.

Ramon could not lift his eyes from the card, to his amazement they were full of tears. Thickly, from behind the shelter of the card he said,

'This is the best card I have ever had, I didn't know you could draw so well. Thank you Conchita.' She smiled contentedly and watched him rise from the table and place the card on the long mantel shelf over the open stone fire place. It gave him a moment to compose himself before he returned to the table, passing behind Conchita's chair he placed his hand on her shoulder and gave it a gentle squeeze. She hunched her shoulders with pleasure and turning her head to Carmen, screwed up her eyes and grinned. Carmen laughed out loud.

'What are you two laughing at?' Ramon said as he sat down again. 'I think there is some kind of conspiracy between you two. Let me into the secret.'

'Shall I give it now Carmen?' Conchita half whispered.

'Well, I think you must, otherwise what is he going to eat on his toast?'

'Toast? Toast? What are you talking about? We are not in England where they eat toast, and marmalade too.' He looked meaningfully at Carmen who smiled gratefully and nodded.

She felt like she used to do in class when a pupil responded to her teaching and produced the correct answers. Ramon was doing just that. Conchita stood up.

'Excuse me, Papa,' she said as she moved in the direction of the kitchen door. She was heard to say in a loud whisper,

'Now!' and Ana Maria came into the dining room on the pretext of bringing in the coffee. Conchita reached over to a small table and lifted up a small parcel. She walked round the table and with ceremony handed it to Ramon.

'Que aproveche. Enjoy your meal,' she said brightly. Ramon's grin was wide and genuine as he carefully tore off the wrapping.

'Marmalade!' he yelled. 'Wonderful marmalade. But we need toast to do it justice.'

'And what do you think this is?' Ana Maria said as she placed in front of him, a platter with a white linen napkin folded upon it, inside piled with crisp toast.

'Ana Maria made it really,' Conchita said 'but it was my idea. Wasn't it Ana Maria?'

'I could never have made it without you, you are the expert Conchita,' she responded, a happy smile on her face. 'Whatever next? Making jam out of oranges! Some people like some strange things.'

'Have you ever tasted it, Ana Maria?'

'Of course I have, when I was ….. when we were making it. Isn't that so Conchita?'

'Ah yes, but now you must eat it on toast,' Ramon said.

Isabella sat smiling, watching the faces of her son and granddaughter as the scene unfolded.

'Come, join us Ana Marie', she said. 'After all, this is a special day, is it not?'

Ana Maria hid her smug smile and sat down. Not for a very long time had she witnessed Ramon acknowledging his birthday. Normally she would not have complied with Ramon's request to sit at his breakfast table. She had been his nanny, become his housekeeper, and then the much esteemed cook, but this was different; she was now a self-appointed *abuela,* another grandmother to Conchita. The appearance of this girl in their midst had changed their lives; Ramon's, Carmen's and hers. In practice they had become a family and Ana Maria was revelling in it. In time it would become a reality, she was sure.

23

Annie Bates rose at six thirty the morning after Philip's departure. She had not slept well, aware of movement in the house, which unnerved her knowing that there was no-one but herself and Flora. She thought about Philip's words, that Flora was not her usual self, and wondered if she should get up and check that she was all right but each time she put one foot out of bed with the intention of investigating, the sounds stopped and the house seemed to settle down peacefully again.

Annie went down and quietly set about the ironing whilst waiting for Flora to arrive for her breakfast cup of coffee at eight thirty. Lost in her thoughts for a while she then looked at the clock; it was nine o'clock and Flora still had not appeared.

Perhaps she's slept in, she thought. It'll do her good, she's been under some strain, like the rest of us, she added. She didn't worry, but had her own breakfast and left the coffee things ready. She was surprised when Flora still didn't appear but felt she couldn't go chasing after her, like one of the children on a school morning. She went to the bottom of the staircase to listen. All was quiet.

It was eleven fifteeen when Flora wandered into the kitchen fully dressed but looking dishevelled.

'Morning Mrs H. Everything all right? Can I get you some coffee?' Flora didn't immediately answer but looked at Annie with a puzzled frown.

'Where is everybody Annie? Have they all gone out? Why didn't they tell me? I might have gone with them.'

For a moment Annie was non-plussed. Then she noticed Flora's hands which were grubby and her shoes were caked with soft mud. Before she could reply Flora began again,

'It's a lovely morning Annie. I've weeded the rose bed. That's a good job done isn't it? Is there any coffee?'

'Right away, Mrs H.' Annie said, wondering about 'the job done' and whether to respond but decided to leave well alone. They both sat down to a cup of coffee and biscuits and Flora continued to tell her how she intended to start growing vegetables.

'You know, growing vegetables is very therapeutic. It's also very economical. We did it during the war remember? 'Dig for Victory' and all that. I'm sure I can grow enough for the whole family.'

'Well that'll be nice Mrs. H. but you mustn't do too much you know. Perhaps you ought to let Mr Tubbs help you out.'

'Mr Tubbs? Oh yes, the odd job man. What happened to him? He doesn't seem to come anymore.' Annie did not reply, remembering quite clearly hearing Flora tell Mr Tubbs, a fully qualified horticulturist (odd job man indeed!) that she would not be needing him anymore. Annie had told Philip that Mr Tubbs had been most upset and that he felt he deserved some sort of explanation. Philip had diplomatically put the matter right with him.

Annie changed tack.

'You got cracking nice and early today, Mrs H. Did you sleep all right?'

'Like a log Annie, thank you.' Flora got up from the table. 'I must 'phone Sarah Shaw, we might play golf this afternoon,' she said and walked into the hall. Annie heard her talking quite normally to Sarah on the phone and pondered about the strange conversation they had just had.

The next day passed uneventfully, Flora came down for her coffee at eight-thirty and then spent her time in the normal way for a Wednesday; golf in the morning and Bridge in the afternoon. Annie was grateful for the fact that Flora was busy. All Annie needed to do was provide the coffee and sandwiches for the Bridge session. The rest of the time she got on with her normal daily routine.

With Philip and Garnet away she had fewer household chores to do than usual and she took the opportunity to enjoy doing some patchwork. It was all hand sewing, a slow and painstaking business, piecing together the shapes, creating the colourful designs. Her current project was a quilt for Garnet. She had hurried to finish Connie's quilt in time for her to take with her to Spain. She always imagined Spain to be a hot country and wondered whether Connie would ever need its warmth and comfort. Little did she know how much comfort it had given Connie in some of her lonelier moments, even though she had not needed its warmth.

Annie thought about how a quilt made up of pieces of fabric sewn together, was like life itself. Good times, thin times, happy events, sad happenings, dark or bright weather, colourful or drab like the pieces of fabric, all forming a patterned and harmonised whole. Life was a pattern, events and occasions strung together through time, conforming to some kind of design. Annie called it Fate. Intermingled in the design of Connie's quilt were pieces from all her cotton dresses through the years, even some from her school uniform. It was a memory quilt consisting of her childhood years that Annie had hoped would give Connie something to hold on to, her English background to give her a sense of belonging. She wanted to do the same for Garnet.

On the Thursday morning Flora came down into the kitchen very promptly. She was dressed in a smart beige suit with a pale blue silk knitted top beneath the jacket. She was wearing the string of pearls that Philip had given her for her thirtieth birthday and the matching drop earrings. Her shoes and handbag were matching light brown leather and she was carrying a pair of ecru fine leather gloves. Her brown springy hair was well brushed and shining.

Annie hadn't seen Flora dressed up for some time, since Connie's departure in fact. She appeared to have lost all interest in her appearance and even for her golf and Bridge sessions had made little effort to make herself presentable. All the more surprising therefore to see Flora appear early and looking more like her old self.

'My, Mrs H, you look smart. Going to something special?'

'No, no, Annie, just going into Bradford.'

'To Bradford, Mrs H? 'Ow will you get there?'

'I'll take the train, it'll make a nice change I haven't been there for a while. I'll probably have lunch there. I might meet Sarah but I've left it a bit late to make an arrangement, she might be busy. Anyway it doesn't matter, I've a few things to get. Coffee ready, Annie?'

'Didn't you play golf with her yesterday?' Annie said as she poured the steaming hot coffee.

Flora looked blank and without replying began to sip her coffee.

'Be careful you don't burn yourself Mrs H,' she said, 'Will you be needing anything else?'

'No nothing, thank you. And by the way, don't make dinner for me. I'm sure I'll have a good lunch in town. Why don't you take the day off Annie? Perhaps you might like to visit a friend, or something. With all the others away there's not a great deal for you to do, and in any case what there is can wait. I think you deserve some time off. Look, don't be offended but I'd like to give you some money, to take a taxi if you like. Relax and do something different.' With this long speech Flora handed Annie a five pound note. Annie gasped.

'I can't take that Mrs H.! It's very good of you, but no, I can't, it wouldn't be right.'

'Annie! You do so much for me, and particularly lately. Don't think I'm unaware of how helpful and loyal you've been. Let me do something for *you*, please.' She pressed the note into Annie's hand, curling her fingers around it and holding them there. She smiled, 'All right? Just to please me.' She gulped her hot coffee and stood up.

'I must dash, or I'll miss the train. Have a nice time and don't hurry back. I might even go to the cinema in the afternoon, or even the Alhambra. I haven't been to the theatre or a show for such a long time. I don't know what's playing but there'll be something interesting I'm sure. So don't worry about me.'

Before Annie could respond, Flora strode out of the kitchen and into the hall. As she reached the front door she called, 'Bye, see you later,' and banged the door as she went out.

Annie was stunned by the speed with which this whole episode had taken place. Left sitting in the kitchen by herself, Flora's cup of steaming coffee only half drunk, and her own still in front of her, she said,

'Well, what a turn up for the books. She hasn't been as chirpy as that for a long time. I suppose I should be pleased, well I am pleased, that she's finally picked herself up and got going again. Mr H. you're going to have a nice surprise when you arrive home tomorrow. She's just about her old self again.' Annie sighed and remembered the scrunched up five pound note, still tightly held in her fist. She uncurled her fingers.

'Well, she's never done that afore! Then everything's been a bit strange lately, to put it mildly. I'd better get meself moving and decide what to do. She'll be a bit disappointed if I don't take up 'er offer, meant in all kindness, I'm sure.'

***

Annie had left behind her few friends in Bradford after the move, now she had acquaintances, as she called them, not quite friends. She did though have her cousin Beatrice. They were close in age and Annie kept in touch through Christmas and birthday cards and occasional visits.

'Not a bad idea,' she thought to herself. 'I'll call Beatrice and see if she's free.'

It wasn't long before she was on her way to Shipley, in a taxi. What a luxury! She smiled to herself and looked forward to telling Beatrice how the trip had come about. By the time she arrived Beatrice had prepared a picnic and they walked to the park just half a mile away.

131

It was one of those fine, unexpectedly sunny days and the two sat on the tufty grass and talked, just as though they had seen one another the day before, picking up where they left off, as close friends always do.

It was seven o'clock before Annie returned home to find that Flora had not yet returned. Nothing strange in that, she thought. She's obviously gone to the cinema, as she said she might.

Annie settled down to watch her favourite television programme. Philip had given her a small television for her room – 'So that you can watch whatever you like, whenever you want Annie. It's a small thing I can do for you.' Annie had been thrilled and felt privileged. She knew no-one else amongst her acquaintances who had a television set. Becoming drowsy after her day in the sun and fresh air, she decided to climb into bed and watch the rest in comfort with her feet up. Flora had still not arrived at ten thirty but that wasn't late, Annie thought, after all many films went on until eleven o'clock these days.

It was the persistent ringing of the phone that roused Annie at a quarter to midnight. She felt a pang of guilt as she realised she had dozed off. For a moment she panicked. Why would anyone phone at this time of night? There must have been an accident. Flora's calm voice was something of an anticlimax and at first Annie could not take in what she was saying.

'I'm going to stay with Sarah. Annie, are you there? I've decided to stay the night with Sarah. Don't wait up. I'll see you in the morning.'

Annie nodded, forgetting that she couldn't be seen but it didn't seem to matter, Flora had already put down the receiver.

Annie rose early the next morning but it was some moments before she remembered the late night phone call and the fact that Flora was not home. She got on with her own breakfast and thought about Philip's impending arrival on the train from London in the afternoon.

By noon Annie began to wonder whether Sarah would drive Flora home or whether she would come back again by train. By early afternoon she began to feel anxious and decided to phone Sarah even though she had never met her. 'It doesn't matter, needs must when the devil drives,' she muttered to herself. If only she could find her phone number.

The entry in the family book, in Flora's handwriting, was indistinct. The first name had been scratched out and the name 'Sarah' scribbled over it, but the surname clearly said 'Shaw'. She dialled the number a little nervously. It was with some anxiety that Annie heard Sarah disclaim all knowledge of Flora's visit to Bradford and certainly had not had her as a guest the night before.

'I'm so sorry to have troubled you, I've obviously got Mrs H.'s arrangements all mixed up,' she said.

'Sure. No problem. Let me know if you want me to..........well, you know do anything,' Sarah tailed off. Annie had tried not to give anything away but she felt that something in the tone of Sarah's response had shown that she knew that all was not well.

Annie was now in a near state of panic, the nearest she had ever been in all the years with the Hampton family, a feeling of overwhelming anxiety. She sat beside the telephone in the hall for several minutes, trying to calm her racing pulse. As her thoughts cleared she remembered Philip's words. 'If you have any worries, phone my mother.' Annie leaned over to the phone again and dialled Amelia Hampton.

'I'm really sorry to bother you Mrs 'ampton, but I.........' Annie didn't know how to explain her doubts about whether Flora would turn up at the station to meet Philip Hampton. She explained the events of the day before and the 'phone call from Flora and her own subsequent call to Sarah and her denial that she had seen Flora at all.

'There's obviously been some awful mix-up, a misunderstanding Annie. Now don't you worry, Charles and I will go and collect Philip. If Flora is there, we'll say nothing, we wouldn't like her to think that we don't trust her or anything, would we? We'll just pretend that we took it into our heads to meet him too. Do we understand each other Annie?'

'Yes, Mrs 'ampton, I think we do. Thanks so much. I'll look forward to 'earing from you later.'

This news was not the best kind that Amelia Hampton could have received at that time. She had said nothing to Annie about the fact that Charles was not well, only telling her 'You stay home Annie, just in case Flora should ring.'

Philip's train arrived on time and greeted with hugs and smiles was told that Flora had been delayed in town and was sorry but she would see him at home soon. Philip accepted the apology but soon became anxious when they arrived back at the house to find that Flora had still not returned. Annie had received no messages.

At this point, Annie felt she should say something to Philip about Flora's strange and erratic change of moods but she didn't know where to begin. As she went into the kitchen Philip followed her.

'What's bothering you Annie? I know there's something.' At first Annie was hesitant and then after a pause, she said,

'It's no good Mr H, I think I'd better start at the beginning.'

133

She described the morning when she discovered Flora had been out in the garden, not sleeping in as Annie had thought. She went on to tell of the strange questions and Flora's rapid change of moods. She finally told him of her setting off to Bradford looking like her old self, you know really smart and bright.

Despite their move to Harrogate, they still made frequent visits to Brown, Muffs in Bradford. Philip knew Stephen Robertson, the Managing Director, through business, but he and Flora also knew Stephen and his wife Helen, socially. They played Bridge together and Flora played golf with Helen from time to time. Philip telephoned Stephen immediately. He seemed to understand that it was a 'delicate matter' without Philip having to spell it out.

'Don't worry, Philip. She may have come in to meet Helen for coffee or something. I shall be discreet and if Flora was in the store yesterday I shall be able to find out. I'll phone as soon as I have any news.'

It was only twenty minutes later that Stephen 'phoned back to say that Flora had made several purchases in the store during the course of the morning, with instructions for them to be delivered, and had had lunch in the restaurant alone. Philip related the news to his mother and father and Annie.

'I want to go into town and look around. Perhaps go to the store. You never know she might be there again today.'

Amelia was on the verge of saying that she didn't think that would serve much of a purpose but held her tongue. She realised that Philip had to get up and go out, do something, no matter how futile the action might seem to be. Instead she said,

'All right, we'll stay here with Annie and if Flora comes in we'll just say........we'll say that you were delayed. Phone us, if you can, so that we can keep you posted.'

As Philip made to leave the house, barely having closed the door, the 'phone rang. He leaped back inside. Annie jumped up and then hung back,

'You answer, in case it's Flora,' Amelia said. It wasn't Flora. It was Sarah.

'Are you the housekeeper? This is... Sarah. I'm with Flora. We're having a coffee in town. I think I ought to accompany her home, she doesn't seem well. I just wanted to make sure someone was there.'

'Yes, we....I'm here. That would be very kind of you. About three quarters of an hour you say. Thank you. See you then.' Annie put down the receiver. Her hand was trembling and she was pale.

'It was Sarah. I don't know how she comes to be with Mrs H. but apparently she is. She's bringing 'er 'ome right away, she's not too well.'

'Thank goodness you didn't leave Philip. Annie put the kettle on, there's a dear. We'll sit in the front room and wait for them.'

Philip 'phoned Stephen to tell him that Flora was on her way home and that he would speak to him later when they had sorted out the mystery.

'Anything we can do Philip, let us know.'

'Will do. Thanks Stephen,' Philip responded.

When Sarah and Flora arrived, the Hamptons and Annie were sitting round the occasional table in the sitting room, having drunk their tea. It all looked homely and casual. Two more cups and saucers were brought in, and Annie went to put the kettle on again. Flora and Sarah sat down as though they had been expected. Flora, kissed Philip when she came into the room and said,

'Hello, darling.' From then on she said not another word.

Philip went into the kitchen to fetch the fresh pot of tea and was surprised to see that Sarah followed him.

'Mr Hampton, I hope you don't mind but......well I think I should say......'

'Yes Sarah, I would be grateful for any light you can throw on what has been happening this last day or two. We're very anxious about Flora.'

'It was sheer coincidence that I happened to come across her in Market Street this afternoon, just opposite Brown, Muff's. She looked tired, poorly even and she didn't at first recognise me. I'm not sure that she knows who I am even now, which is ridiculous because...'

'Sarah, I don't know how much you know of what's been going on in our family. Flora has probably filled you in a bit.' Sarah coloured deeply and turned her head in the hope that Philip wouldn't notice, she felt not only some embarrassment but also shame. She took little comfort in the fact that he could not possibly know how she had been involved with Flora and to what extent she was responsible for Flora's state of mind. There was nothing to connect her to the happenings and nothing to be gained at this stage by divulging the truth. In a small way she felt that what she was now doing would make some reparation for her action in the past. She kept thinking of Connie and how she must have felt being banished without explanation. She gave a slight shudder but her courage failed her, now was not the time to make a confession.

'Yes, well, as I said she looked as though she didn't know where she was, almost as though she had lost her memory, so I took her off to

135

Brown, Muffs for a coffee, we go there from time to time. She went to the Powder Room and it was while she was there I managed to telephone your home. I thought it best to get her home. I had my car in town so I drove her back here. I hope I did the right thing.'

'You did exactly the right thing Sarah. I don't know how to thank you. I have been concerned about Flora just recently. She seems to be a bit confused. We shall get the doctor to look at her straight away. I don't know how to thank you.'

'No, no really it was nothing...I...'

At that point the front door bell rang. Annie came to open the door and she greeted Dr MacAllister. Sarah took the moment as an opportunity to leave.

'I'll go now, Mr Hampton. Your family's all together and that'll be good for Flora. I'll phone sometime soon I need to talk to you. It's important and... well, I'll 'phone to see how Flora is.'

Philip put out his hand to thank her but she turned and was out of the door in seconds, pushing past Dr MacAllister. Philip felt very uneasy at Sarah's mystifying comments but this was not something he could deal with right now.

Unbeknown to Philip, Amelia had phoned the doctor immediately after receiving Sarah's call. At the time she had no idea how she would explain his arrival, but she felt she could devise some excuse when the time came. In fact the explanation proved not to be necessary. Dr MacAllister saw fairly quickly how the land lay.

'I do hope you don't mind my dropping in unannounced like this. I see you are having almost a family gathering. I was just passing and I thought I would call and see how you all are and ask about Garnet.' He looked directly at Amelia who met his gaze with a smile.

'That's very kind of you Doctor. Well Philip can tell you about Garnet, he's just come back from Spain, after taking her out there to stay with Connie for a few weeks.'

Flora's scream came like an electric shock coursing through their bodies. She leapt up, flinging her arms in the air, and then slumped to the floor. Charles Hampton jumped with the suddenness of it and turned pale. Amelia's attention was immediately on him and she took his hand.

'Charles, Charles, are you all right?' He nodded slowly and held her hand tightly. Dr MacAllister glanced at him and saw that he had only been startled, then he was on his knees beside Flora.

'My bag is in the hall,' he said to Philip calmly. 'Please fetch it.' Philip did as he was bid quickly. They lifted Flora onto the sofa and as he examined her, he nodded slowly and looking up at them said,

'As far as I can tell she's all right, nothing serious. She just passed out.' Slowly Flora came to and turned her head toward Philip. Her eyes were glazed and vacant.

'Flora, I'm Dr MacAllister. You've not been very well. I'm here to help you. Do you understand?' Flora frowned and turned her eyes on the doctor.

'I want you to tell me if you have any pain, or feel dizzy or anything unusual, all right?'

Flora shook her head. She looked hard at him.

'Who are they?' she said, indicating with a glance of her eyes towards the others in the room. 'What are they doing here? I want to go home.'

'Of course, you shall very shortly,' he said in a comforting tone. 'I'm just going to listen to your heart for a moment. All right?' Over the next few minutes he examined Flora carefully. He looked up and turning away so that Flora could not hear him, he said quietly

'Could you sit with her for a few minutes please Mrs Bates. She doesn't appear to be recognizing where she is for the moment but I know she knows you well and I would rather not leave her alone. I would like to take a look at Mr Hampton senior.' He turned to Philip.

'Could we move into another room? I'd like to see if Charles has been behaving himself, and I'd like a word with you too.'

It was in the study that Dr MacAllister told them that he felt Flora was experiencing what he hoped was only a mild nervous breakdown.

'It would not surprise me. Remember she has been living with a great deal on her conscience for some time. Forgive me Philip if I speak plainly. The effect of that guilty secret burning inside her, and being unable to reveal anything to the people she loved the most, has taken a toll on her emotions and more importantly on her mind. This kind of suppression of emotions over a long period can be very dangerous.' He paused to give weight to his words.

'As far as I can see there's nothing physically wrong. I think the best course of action is to admit her to a private clinic for a few days where she can rest and be quiet. The medical staff will also be able to observe her whilst she is not under any stress, and assess her condition. I feel this may not be a temporary state of affairs.'

He turned to Charles Hampton with the comment,

'Now then young man, how've you been? No more pain?'

'What do you mean, no *more* pain?' Philip broke in. 'Is there something you haven't been telling me?' he faced his mother as he spoke.

137

'Well, Dad wasn't too well. But we didn't like to worry you just before you went away with Garnet. He's been all right these last few days, until now.'

Dr MacAllister checked Charles' pulse and listened to his breathing and his heart.

'You're fine,' he declared. 'A bit of a shock that scream, wasn't it? But your ticker is coping just fine. Don't worry. Just follow my earlier instructions and you'll be all right.'

'So what do we do now Doctor?' Philip asked.

'Well, it might seem a bit odd getting Flora into a Clinic late in the evening like this, but I think the sooner she's in a quiet atmosphere with a mild sedative and is under observation the better. Perhaps I could make a phone call to see if it can be arranged straight away?'

It was an hour later that the private ambulance arrived to take Flora to the Clinic. Philip accompanied her having seen his parents safely away to their own home. When he finally returned home at 2 a.m. Annie was waiting up for him.

'Kettle's on Mr H. Cuppa in just two minutes. Or is it a whisky you're needing?'

'No, tea would be just lovely. Thanks.'

'Is she a'right?'

'In good hands now Annie. We just have to wait and see.'

Flora stayed in the Clinic for five days. She returned home as though from some outing, bright and cheerful. It seemed she had no idea where she had stayed that night and remembered nothing of her wanderings in Bradford and being brought back by Sarah. Philip told her she had been unwell and fainted and that Dr MacAllister had recommended a checkup and rest. No mention was made of any other problem.

***

It was some days later that Flora said to Annie,

'Why don't you go and do the shopping Annie? It'll do you good to get out. I think I'll do some gardening today'

Annie thought the suggestion was a bit odd and wasn't sure about leaving Flora alone but going just to the local shops she could be back in less than an hour. Flora couldn't come to much harm in so short a time, especially if she got lost in her gardening which she tended to do these days.

Flora got lost all right, but not in the way that Annie had imagined. Minutes before Annie's return Flora walked out of the house without her coat or handbag, her keys were left in the bowl on the table in the hall, where she usually placed them.

'Oh Mr H. I feel terrible. I'm so sorry. I should never have left 'er. Y' know, I reckon she waited for me to go out. That's a terrible thing to say, it sounds as though she did it a' purpose.'

'It's not your fault Annie. If she hadn't done it today she'd have done it another day. Fortunately she followed exactly the same pattern as before, took the train to Bradford and went to Brown, Muffs. It was lucky for us that Stephen Robertson saw her and recognized that something was wrong. He took her straight to a private room next to his office and gave her coffee on the pretext of having a chat. Then he 'phoned me at the bank. But she's in a safe place now, so don't worry. Dr MacAllister says they will take great care of her in the Clinic. It's definitely a nervous breakdown. I think we've all seen it coming but didn't recognize it for what it was. If anyone should feel guilty I should. I should not have gone away but I couldn't let Garnet travel all by herself. Perhaps in the long run it's best that Flora is where she is. We at least *know* where she is.'

'What flummoxes me Mr H. is how did she pay her train fare? Mebbe she had some money in her pocket 'cos she left her 'andbag behind, I saw it on the chair.'

'As you say, she must have had some money in a pocket but we'll not worry about that now. My next concern is whether to tell this to the girls. I think for the moment, if you should be writing to either of them Annie, it would be better if you didn't mention it.'

'I think that's right Mr H. They'd only worry. In any case, Mrs H. might be 'ome and better by the time Garnet comes back and then we can explain what's necessary.'

'Exactly. I'm going to my parents now to tell them what's going on but I'll be back for dinner if that's all right with you Annie.'

'Oh Mr H, anything's all right with me I just can't say 'ow sorry I am that all this 'as 'happened. Y' know I'll do anything to 'elp.'

'I do know that Annie. Now, I must go. See you about seven.'

***

Just before Philip left for the office the next morning he called Sarah.

It was agreed that they needed to talk, coffee at ten thirty on neutral ground, in the lounge of the Grand Hotel. Sarah took the lead.

'Before you say anything Mr Hampton, I think I should tell you something. My name is not actually Sarah, it's what Flora has been calling me in order not to reveal the truth. I'm ... I'm Rhonda Shaw.'

Philip nodded. 'I guessed as much. I think it's time we spoke about the whole situation, don't you? Get it all out in the open between us.'

Their talk lasted until lunchtime when Philip left for the office and later to his parents.

That evening in discussion with his parents Philip told them he had decided not to speak to Flora of any of the details of the episode, in case it upset her and trigger unpleasant repercussions.

'I've also decided not to tell the girls for the time being. They were so happy to be together I don't want to put a cloud over everything. So, don't mention it in your letters will you?'

The Clinician's report was cautious but Dr MacAllister told Philip that Flora's recovery was likely to take some time. The severe stress Flora had suffered for a protracted period of time followed by the unusual circumstances of her daughter's departure, precipitated her collapse and breakdown. Dr MacAllister had imparted information on the family background, Philip was sure of that.

For the time being Flora was to stay in the Clinic until her confused state decreased and she no longer needed the help of a sedative.

After three weeks Flora came home for a day, to be amongst familiar things for a while and to spend time with Philip away from a hospital environment. She didn't seem at all perturbed about being taken back again at five o'clock. This seemingly successful trial visit was repeated over the next few weeks until finally Flora came home, a subdued and fragile likeness of her former self.

Philip felt bad about leaving Annie to keep an eye on her on a day to day basis. 'She's no trouble, Mr H, she's very quiet,' Annie responded, 'and anyway it's the least I can do.'

Flora rose later in the mornings having her breakfast coffee at nine thirty, read or watched a little television, and occasionally did short bouts of gardening. She seemed to enjoy the fresh air though she tired quickly and needed to rest. Helen Robertson came to visit a few afternoons but Flora did not go out other than with Philip to visit Amelia and Charles.

24

September 1951

Garnet's stay with Conchita over-ran the allotted school holiday, a possibility Philip had discussed with Garnet's Headmistress, but it was worth the delayed return to school; it brought her back to full health. She seemed to forget within a few days that she could not eat and though the food was different she took to it, gradually at first and later with enthusiasm. Conchita took the greatest delight in introducing her to Ana Maria, proud to be able to translate. She found it was fun and that, in its turn, gave a boost to Conchita's morale and confidence.

Philip was able to stay for only three days; he was still worried about Flora. Leaving his darling Connie this time was nothing like the wrench it had been last time, for one thing he could see that she was well and seemed happy. For another he was leaving Garnet with her, and Bella, who obviously suffered no ill effects from being shipped in a crate in the hold of the aeroplane. She attached herself to her mistress from the moment of her arrival and followed her everywhere. In fact his return home this time was one without deep concern for either of his daughters, knowing that they had each other. By now Philip had full confidence in Ramon and he was enchanted with Carmen. He could see that Carmen and Connie had formed a strong relationship. It was obvious, in the way that she relaxed and laughed in her company that Connie liked her.

Philip was grateful to her though he could not find a way of telling her of the debt he felt he already owed her. All in good time, he thought.

Garnet was elated to find that Ramon had such a beautiful piano and without invitation began to play, even before Philip departed. This gladdened his heart too, to see that his younger daughter had at last broken out of her depression. He could not believe how quickly she responded to the change of atmosphere but most of all to Connie's company. It was at Carmen's instigation that the conspiracy, between

141

the three of them, not to tell Garnet that the piano had been bought especially for her visit, led rise to the myth that Ramon could play the piano. Why else would he have a piano in the house? Garnet remarked. It was amusing but a mystery to her that he would not play for them and so she was called upon to play every evening after dinner and sometimes to sing, Connie accompanying her, as she had in England from time to time. It became a ritual, the after-dinner concert, Carmen called it. The bond created by the secret between Conchita, Carmen and Ramon, and of course Nana Isaabella, along with the music drawing in Garnet, engendered a relaxed family atmosphere to which both Garnet and Conchita responded. During the course of the weeks the two girls flourished. Conchita spoke less Spanish now that she spent much of her days chattering to Garnet. Nevertheless Carmen kept up the daily lessons and whilst Conchita worked it was agreed that Garnet should do her piano practice.

All too soon, as far as Connie and Garnet were concerned, it was time for Garnet to return to England. The extended holiday had given Garnet plenty of time to recover and build up her strength. A late return in September proved to be the right decision. She was a different child. Tanned, back to her normal weight, eating well and smiling, but the most important thing of all to Garnet was that she was once more playing the piano. She wanted to sing again and was looking forward to her lessons when she returned to England.

***

September 1951

Though Conchita was sad at Garnet's departure both of them were now ready for a new start. Garnet having regained her strength was yearning for her music. Conchita had a new life at the Colegio Sagrado Corazoni to look forward to. Conchita was excited and looked forward to meeting other Spanish girls. Her language was now fluent and her confidence much improved thanks to Carmen and Ana Maria. Ramon's input with the language had been minimal. 'I don't want to frighten her,' he declared 'until she feels at ease.' The irony of this was that she was the one who led the Spanish-speaking conversations and he the one who lapsed into English, more often than not.

142

The one worry for Conchita was Bella, who would look after her whilst she was at school? She had settled so well, as though she had always lived there, no doubt because she was beside her beloved mistress. During Garnet's stay a second bed had been put in Conchita's room so that they could be together as much as possible. Bella was given the special privilege of being allowed to sleep in a small side-room with a connecting door. After Garnet's departure Conchita left the intervening door open at night and kept up a whispered one-sided conversation with her dog. Ana Maria turned a blind eye to the open door, in her opinion dogs should sleep outside.

Conchita knew that she had Garnet to thank for having Bella here with her in Spain. Garnet's unselfish insight into what her sister would need, despite her own sad state at the time, was the sole reason for Bella's arrival. It had not occurred to any one of the adults that it would be a good idea, if even feasible. She knew friends at school whose fathers had been posted abroad, almost always took their pets with them when the family went to join them. Conchita realised how lucky she was to have a sister who pressed home the point until it was agreed and the reunion was made possible.

***

Conchita soon realised that making friends was easier than she had thought. She was a novelty; English but speaking near perfect Spanish, clever but not conceited, and ever ready for fun. As she confided to Carmen,

'I'm really enjoying school and I'm making friends. Papa says if I have a particular friend she can come to visit.'

Ramon's unexpectedly good idea, to encourage Conchita to invite a friend sometime, appealed to and gained approval from Carmen. Conchita was surprised by it, she knew that many of the suggestions which arose were inspired by Carmen. For those, and for many other reasons, Conchita loved Carmen. Carmen also eased Conchita's worries about the fact that *Colegio Sagrado Corazón* was a Catholic school and that the teachers were nuns. She wrote to Philip;

'They float around in their dark blue robes, with plain white cotton triangles pinned on their heads. I thought I wouldn't like this Daddy, but they talk to me just like my teachers in England. I didn't know that nuns could be such ordinary people.' Philip had smiled when he read this.

'But there's no uniform,' she had added. 'I can't believe it!'

Conchita was pleased about not having a uniform but at the same time had a slight twinge of regret knowing that she had been proud to wear the mauve and white striped school blouse, amethyst coloured skirt and even the blazer. She had worked hard at her Primary School and had not only achieved a place but a scholarship also. She confided this to Carmen.

'I got a scholarship to the school,' she said. 'It's not bragging is it, I mean, if I say that?' Conchita was modest about her achievement but at the same she recognized her ability and this had given her a certain amount of confidence.

'Mummy used to say I was 'sensible' but she made it sound as though I was a boring person when she said it. Perhaps it'll stand me in good stead in my new school, even though it's all in Spanish.'

'You should have no qualms at all about speaking Spanish Conchita. You have made amazing progress and have hardly a trace of an accent. I predict in three months no-one will know you were not born here in Spain.'

Conchita thought about what she had just said and was struck by her own unintentional use of the past tense when she thought about her mother's remarks. She suddenly realized that she had relegated her mother to her other life, the life in England, the one that she tried not to think about too often.

By the action of their visit, Philip and Garnet had become part of her new life. She longed for Granny and Grandpa Hampton to come too, she so much wanted them to be included in her Spanish life and see how she had taken to it. She wrote to them begging them to come and stay, and explained when would be a good time to visit, but she knew nothing of her grandfather's declining health. She had already asked Ramon if they might come and his response, as for every request she made of him, was 'of course, whenever you wish'.

***

Garnet's return to school was greeted, to her surprise, with congratulations. Despite her illness and inability to sit her end of year school examinations she received a good report. Her absence and illness was taken into account of course, nevertheless the term's work before the upheaval had shown that she was making excellent progress. To her music teacher's surprise and delight Garnet's piano playing did not seem to have suffered. Not until Garnet explained about the beautiful piano in the house where she had stayed, could Miss Woodhead understand why Garnet's playing was as brilliant as ever.

At ten years old Garnet had just one term in which to prepare for the entrance examination to Donnington High School for Girls. The exam would be held in the following February. She did not dare to hope for a scholarship like Connie, she knew that she put more than a fair share of her time and energy into her music and that her other studies were less important to her. Even so, after her return from Spain, full of enthusiasm not only for her music but for school life in general, she felt that she could at least achieve a place. It came as something of a shock when her father spoke to her about the possibility of applying to another school instead.

'It's a school specializing in music Garnet. You have, according to Miss Woodhead, an amazing talent which she feels would stand a greater chance of reaching its potential in a school where music would have a more important place in the curriculum. You would, of course have all the normal lessons too but your music would take precedence. What do you think?'

Garnet was dismayed and at first unenthusiastic. She had been looking forward to moving on to senior school with all her pals. Going off on her own to a strange place did not appeal to her at all.

Miss Woodhead said she had exceptional talent; Granny and Gramps said it was a wonderful opportunity; Mummy said 'Whatever you want Garnet, it's up to you'. Annie said 'You'll be famous, mark my words.' Daddy said, 'It's for you to decide but we want you to be happy and you are always happy when you have music. Think about it.'

Everyone seemed to think it would be a good thing. She wrote to Connie immediately.

25

Dear Con

I do hope you like your school. I am so glad you've got Bella now to welcome you back and to play with.

I might not be going to Donnington's next year Daddy says. Miss Woodhead says I ought to go to a special music school and she has asked Mummy and Daddy to think about it. I would have to board because there would be practices and rehearsals at weekends for concerts and performances at the school.

I don't know what to do. I think I would miss all my friends but I would get the chance to do more singing. Miss Woodhead says I could have proper singing lessons and develop my voice. She says I'll be an opera singer some day! I don't know about that. Doing lots of music every day certainly sounds very nice so I've promised Daddy I'll think about it. I don't have to make up my mind until Christmas. Then if I want to go Miss Woodhead will make the application and I can go for an interview. What do you think?

Mummy is getting better. It was horrid when Carmen told us she was ill, wasn't it? Even so, I felt cross with her, Mummy I mean, not Carmen! I know it was beastly of me but I really thought she had done it on purpose, you know, so that she wouldn't be here when I came home. I keep feeling that she's not interested in me either, though I used to think she loved us both. I do wonder if she really does love us. Daddy has tried to explain it to me and he tells me she couldn't help it. She's going to come home for a day this week to see how she gets on. Annie has been a brick; she has looked after me most of the time because Daddy spends all the time he can at the Clinic with mummy. I miss him.

Daddy does go to see Granny and Gramps every weekend and most visits I go with him. By the way, Gramps has not been well but I don't know what's wrong with him.

Annie sends her love. Write to me soon,

Love Nettie

***

Dear Nettie,

You've been having a tough time. I'm really sorry. But, hey, the special school sounds a fantastic idea. You really are a whiz at music you know. We all think so. You would be doing more of what you really like doing and would much rather do most of the time. What luck! But I know how you feel about leaving home. It's hard at first, I should know! At least you wouldn't have to learn another language. But I think you would soon get used to it. I can see that things would go on at weekends and you would miss out, anyway you have to practise every day whether you have rehearsals for concerts or not. That was never a problem for you - practising that is – it's just fun for you, not like me, I hated the practising bit.

Mummy and Daddy and Granny and Gramps will want to come to the concerts, I know, and may be even Annie too, so you would see everybody some of the weekends. Except me. You never know, even I might come one day! I think Papa would let me. He is so kind. I really like him now and he's not the least bit scary any more. Anyway, you know that, now that you've been here and seen him.

It's still a bit strange having two fathers. Daddy in England is still my father to me. It was so awful at first, leaving you all. I still miss you even though I have lots of wonderful things to do. Carmen is like a big sister to, she's not just my Spanish teacher. She's really funny when Papa is being difficult, she can persuade him to do things that at first he doesn't want to do. And she tells him off sometimes, in a nice way of course. Then he's just like a naughty boy. Carmen has told me not to let him see me laughing but it's very difficult, he is so funny when he sulks. I've never seen a grown up sulk before. Carmen says it's the Mediterranean temperament coming out but she doesn't seem to have it.

Well, here I am going on and on but I have to tidy up now ready for evening prayers. We go to chapel at half past four on a Friday, for evening prayers before we go home. We sit lined up in the pews and all the girls – except me – go to confession, one by one. Because I'm not a

147

Catholic I'm allowed to just sit and pray. Tonight we have to practice something ready for Christmas after the prayers. We have strict rules but they are quite good ones, I don't mind them really. My friend Elena thinks they are a pain, but once you know them they make things easier, they have helped me to settle in.

Here I go again! Write soon and tell me what happens. I really think you would be all right. Just think, doing all that music – you'll love it.

Lots of love
Con

***

March 1952

Dear Con

I'm here! But I expect you know that by now, Daddy will have told you. Sorry it's taken me so long to write and tell you but it all happened so quickly. We've never left such a big gap between our letters but it has been so hectic.

The school's right out in the country. It's like a fairy castle, all turrets and long windows. Inside there are loads of corridors with lots of rooms for people to practise in. And guess what, there's the most beautiful concert grand piano in the main hall. The older pupils play our walking-in music for assembly and sometimes the hymns.

I haven't made any special friends yet, because I was a late entrant, most of the other pupils who have been in the school for ages have already made friends. But it seems there are new ones all the time, they just appear; there will be some after Easter, then I won't be a new girl! So I'm not worrying about it.

I keep talking about pupils don't I? That's because I didn't want to tell you straight away. Here comes the bombshell – there are boys in the school! It seemed odd at first but it's actually quite fun. We all get on very well and it's great having some boys to play things like the double bass and the bassoon. I think a girl looks silly playing the bassoon. There are about one hundred pupils and we have two houses, one with dormitories for the boys and one for the girls. Then there is a main building with the assembly hall, dining hall and the practice rooms. We all do our homework in our own rooms. I'm really busy and - oh, I nearly forgot, I'm starting singing lessons this week. Got to go – the tea bell has rung.

Write soon. Hope Bella is fine.

Love to everybody.

Nettie

PS. Mummy has been coming home regularly for a day at a time and seems much better Daddy says. All being well, she's coming home for good very soon. She'll be home and I won't! Funny!

Lots of love

Nettie

***

June 1952

Dear Nettie

Now it's my turn to say sorry for not writing sooner. School work and riding round the bodega with Papa keeps me busy.

What a super letter, you are obviously happy there in your new school. I'm so glad. I hope Mummy and Daddy and Granny and Gramps are visiting you. Have you had a concert yet? I wish I could come and see you in your new school and hear you play of course. How is the singing? Do you like it?

I can't wait another second; I have something special to tell you. Papa and Carmen are getting married! I am so excited and really happy for them. They told me last weekend and said they were sorry if it was a bit of a shock. 'Bit of a shock'? It's been obvious for quite a while that they really like each other. Do they think I can't see? They must think I'm still a little girl, they've forgotten I'm fourteen this summer. Ana Maria is thrilled to bits and is already planning the food for the wedding. She doesn't know that Papa is arranging for caterers to make everything. He will have to tell her gently, she will be very cross. Papa says she is not so young and it will be too much work for her but that's not what she'll think. I think she will be disappointed. Papa is right – he's got lots of friends and though it's going to be just family and close friends at the ceremony it looks like being a huge reception. I'm looking forward to finding out about all the plans. I think the wedding is going to be in late October.

If that isn't enough, I have some more super news. Bella is going to have puppies. One of the estate workers José, (I don't think you met him) has a gorgeous Labrador – well actually he's got three. They often walk beside him when he rides round the estate and especially when Papa goes too. José thought it would be good for Bella to have a family

149

whilst she is still quite young. The puppies will arrive in las vacaciones escolares – my school holiday! thank goodness. I don't want to miss that. September andOctober look like being a busy time!

Now I've been talking all about myself and happenings here which is very selfish. I hope you don't mind but I'm sure you can see why I'm so excited.

Please write as soon as you can, I know you work terribly hard, what with all your ordinary school work and your practising. I'm longing to hear you sing. What are you learning?

I write to Mummy now and again but she doesn't reply. Is she all right now? Perhaps she is busy. Does she play golf anymore? I write to Granny and Gramps and they always write back. Gramps makes jokes all the time and Granny tells me what they have been doing. She tells it so well I can see them in their bungalow just as if I were there. They haven't said anything about Gramps being poorly. How is he?

Sorry - bell for chapel! Bells, bells; they tell us what to do all the time. I expect you know what I mean. Actually I quite like them.

Lots of love
Con

***

September 1952

Dear Con

I wish I could come to the wedding but I can't. Daddy says if it had been in the half term holiday he would have taken me with him but I shall be working for a concert in October, I'm singing a solo, nothing classical but I really love it; it's 'Over the Rainbow' from 'The Wizard of Oz' I think that will be fun. Plenty of time for the real classical stuff later Miss Grey said. Daddy says I've not to be disappointed, there will be other chances for me to visit you again and this will be my first real performance so it's special. I'm quite nervous at the moment but my teacher says that will go away when I'm more confident about my singing. She says it's good to have butterflies on the night, it makes the adrenalin flow, whatever that might mean!

By the way, did you know that Ramon is going to invite Daddy to the wedding? I expect so. The invitation arrived just when I got home from school for the summer holidays. He was really pleased. Mummy smiled

150

when Daddy told her and said 'Good, I'm glad about that.' And do you know what? Mummy got hold of Daddy's hand and they sat like that for quite a long time. I suppose they love each other, so I shouldn't be surprised at something like that but I've never seen them kiss, or anything, before.

Coming to stay with you again in the summer was great. Fancy me travelling on an aeroplane all by myself. I must say I thought having to wear that dreadful notice round my neck 'Unaccompanied Minor' – at my age - was a bit off! Still, it was worth it. Please thank Ramon and Carmen again for having me. I had a great time. I did write my bread and butter letter, not that we ate much bread and butter, ha ha! That sounds like one of Gramps' jokes.

I can still remember the Spanish words you taught me. My singing teacher says I'm going to have to improve at languages if I want to sing in opera. She seems to think that's what I ought to do, I'm not sure yet. I spent quite a bit of time with Granny and Gramps after I got back. I asked about Gramps, he just has to take it steady Granny says. He takes pills when he doesn't feel well but he's still funny, makes me laugh all the time even if his jokes are a bit old fashioned.

Hey lucky you! I like the name you've chosen for the puppy – Pablo, very Spanish, then I suppose it would have to be wouldn't it? Fancy having eight babies all at once, well - I know - one after the other. I bet Bella was exhausted. It's nice that José will train Pablo whilst you are at school. I hope all the puppies find as nice a home as Bella and Pablo have. What a long letter. Must go.

Lots of love, as always.
Nettie

**

April 1953

Dear Nettie

Guess what? Carmen's going to have a baby! It'll be my half-brother, or sister, nearly fifteen years younger than me! I suppose it was

151

inevitable but it'll be a bit funny having a baby in the house. I can just imagine what Papa will be like with a crying baby! Hopeless!

I'm not sure I'm looking forward to it. Listen to me, anyone would think I was going to have the thing.

Sorry this is so short but I'm revising for exams. Got to go.

Lots of love
Con

***

Dear Con

Terrific news! Or is it? You don't sound too thrilled at the prospect. Watch out they might have you babysitting! (Only joking!)

Hope the exams went well. Did I tell you? I passed my Grade VII piano with distinction. I'm really pleased about that. I still don't know whether to stick with the piano or not. I think it's too early to decide. My singing teacher says my voice is still developing and who knows it might not be good enough. Anyway, I'm in another concert. I'm singing a German Lied, only piano accompaniment, it's terribly difficult.

Write soon, I love your letters.

Lots of love
Nettie

***

October 1953

Dear Nettie

It's good news – Carmen's baby arrived yesterday. It's a boy.

They are going to call him Juan Luis after Papa's father. Everybody is so excited and Ana Maria is bustling around trying to take charge. She says she is his Nanny just as she was for Papa. I saw Papa whisper something to Carmen but she shook her head and just said, 'Leave it be, for now.' So I think something is going on to do with Ana Maria. We shall see.

The baby arrived on Friday morning so I got time at the weekend to see and hold him. It felt very strange holding a baby, he was so still in my arms. I sat and talked to Carmen quite a lot, she looks really well. She asked me if I was happy to have a brother. I said it seemed a bit strange at first and that he is a half-brother really. I told her that so many things in my life seem to come in halves. It turned out even you are a half-sister, (but I never think of you as a half – you are more than a whole to me!) I'm half English and half Spanish and I've lived half my life in England and half in Spain. I said I often wondered if I will ever get the whole of anything. She said I was too young to be cynical like that, and had I forgotten that in one way I had got double the normal share. I suddenly saw what she meant – I've got Daddy and Papa. Sorry Nettie, for all this drivel. I suppose having a baby around has unsettled me a bit. Dwelling on such things doesn't do one much good I know and I can see this baby is going to take centre stage.

By the way, I found out what all the fuss was with Ana Maria. She thought she was going to be nanny to Juan Luis, just like she was to Papa. But Papa said to Carmen, 'No she's too old.' Carmen told him to be kind to her and he was much more diplomatic than usual. He said;

'That would be wonderful Ana Maria but with one condition. We have engaged a young girl from the village to help you.' Ana Maria went very red and threw up her arms, I have never seen her so cross.

'Me, Nanny to his very own father, need help? Bah, and this young girl - she can't tell me anything.'

'Of course not, she will be learning from you.'

Ana Maria was flattered and seems to have fallen for it. I do hope so. There's enough tension in the house at the moment.

All for now,

Lots of love
Con

***

December 1953

My dear Nettie

I know I just wrote to you not long ago but it was a load of rubbish. Sorry! Your visit this year seems such a long time ago and it was too short! Oh, I know you had lots of concerts and therefore lots of work. At least you came, I really would complain if you didn't come at all. I'd love to come to Yorkshire sometime. The last time I wrote to Mummy I suggested it but I haven't heard a word. I really think she could write to me, just once! I mentioned it to Daddy when he came to the wedding. That was ages ago, I expect he's terribly busy and has forgotten. He did say that his work at the bank seemed to grow every year, I don't understand what he does really.

You'll laugh when I tell you that I'm going to be singing in the school Christmas concert this year. Don't worry, I'm only in the choir, no solos for me! Can you imagine it – me singing a solo? We started rehearsing four weeks ago and some of us – Elena and me and a couple of others – were getting a bit fed up with the repetition. I'm afraid we were a bit giggly at the last rehearsal and we all had to suffer a serious telling-off. No great shakes, but with very solemn faces (and some sincerity) we apologized to Sister Hermana Angelita, who's the 'Producer'! She's very sweet really and patient though she does take her title of 'Producer' rather seriously. I have to admit we were a bit of a nuisance.

Elena came to stay recently and Papa said he thinks she's going to be a bit of a handful when she gets older. I think that's why I like her so much, she's got a spark. Papa thinks she will lead me astray but I'm beginning to think I don't need much leading! I think Papa is a bit worried I won't work and get my Bachillerato. I'll get it, but a fat lot of use it will be. Papa has been giving me a pep talk about my future, he wants me to go to university but I don't! Heaven knows what I'm going to do - I certainly don't want to go to university. Sorry Nettie, I'm not enjoying school very much anymore and I don't enjoy the weekends either. It's all baby talk and about how much weight he's put on and what a lovely smile he's got. It makes me sick. I might as well not be there.

Write and tell me all about the concert.

Lots of love
Con

154

***

Dear Nettie

It's me again, moaning! I'm in trouble. I've been a real pain at school. I know it, but I'm fed up. Life at home is boring and I hate the weekends. Carmen has changed. She doesn't seem to have any time for me anymore, only for that podgy Juan Luis. I hate him! I was in a terrible mood last weekend and very rude to everybody. Even abuela Isabella was a bit cross with me, I could see. She, at least, has time for me normally.

I was almost glad to get back to school. And then I was stupid, I didn't bother to do my prep. I missed morning assembly, and then Elena and I skipped lessons and went into town. We mooched about and had coffee but we were seen by one of the school governors who reported us. What's worse we were smoking! We were up before the Directora, the Headmistress, that is Mother Superior. I have to tell you it's not the first time I've had to go and see her (Papa doesn't know) but this time she gave me a warning. One more time and I might be asked to leave! Papa would go wild.

I haven't told you anything about Christmas but you know what goes on by now. I didn't enjoy it very much; there was so much fuss about Juan Luis opening his presents. I ask you, at fifteen months old did they really expect him to be able to open presents?

I haven't been so unhappy since I was sent away. Please don't tell anybody about this, will you? I'm sorry to burden you with my worries. I love you lots.

Con

***

April 1954

Dear Con

I cried when I got your letter. I don't know what to say except I'm terribly sad that you are so unhappy. It seemed as though you had made the best of everything in your new life and were having a good

155

time. *If you can't talk to Carmen why don't you talk to Nana Isabella? You've always said how she has helped you in the past, even if she was cross with you a little while ago.*

I'm sorry this is short. Please write soon and tell me how you are.

Lots of love
Nettie

***

Dear Nettie

I'm out! I'll be lucky if I pass my Secunda etapa – my next set of exams. This time I've done it! I couldn't help it. The Directora has written to Papa and told him I can't come back next September. She's going to allow me to sit my year-end exams, in a room, all by myself, and then I must leave straight after. I'm not allowed even to finish the term which means I shall miss all the fun and the school concert, and the presentation of prizes, not that I shall have won any! Papa is absolutely furious about it.

OK, you want to know what I did? I'm not a bit ashamed (but I expect you'll think I should be!) I'm so fed up with everything I had to let off steam somehow. I was in charge of prep for Year 1 girls and I just sat and told them jokes. I said it didn't matter if they didn't do their work today, there was more to life than working all the time. One or two of them were a bit worried but in the end they all joined in the fun. It became quite riotous and there was so much noise one of the teaching Sisters, Sister Hermana Maria, came in to see what was going on. She sat down and said quietly, but with a face like thunder,

'Get on with your work girls, immediately,' then she turned to me and said, 'Go to my room and wait.'

It went deadly quiet and I crept out. It doesn't sound all that bad, does it? But along with all the other things I've been getting up to lately I suppose this is the straw that broke the camel's back! I've had four years of this miserable place, with its pious teachers and dutiful pupils, I'm sick of it. I'll soon be shot of it and staying home. Did I say 'home'? It's no more home to me these days than an orphanage! That's it, I'm like an orphan.

156

Neither Daddy nor Papa care anymore and Carmen is besotted with the brat. As for Mummy, she might as well not exist; she never writes to me.

Oh Nettie, what a terrible letter to write to you, you who I love more than any one else. But that's just it, I have no one else I can talk to.

Please write soon.

All my love
Con

26

Diary

I'm going to leave school. I'm being expelled. 'Expelled' - would you believe? Mother Superior called it being 'asked to leave' – what's the difference? It's all so stupid. I wish I'd never come to Spain. Well that's silly, as if I ever had any choice! I've written the most awful letter to Nettie and I know it will upset her. Nettie, you're the only one who still loves me. I'm scared now that you won't any more, when you read about this fiasco. Oh God, what am I going to do at home all day? Everybody will be horrid to me, I just know it. Well, I'll be horrid to them and we'll see who cracks first.

The interview with Mother Superior, the *Directora* of the school, was not as unpleasant as Conchita had expected. She had been sad, rather than angry, and expressed her disappointment that Conchita would be finishing her time at the school in such an ignominious way.

'I'm going to be rather less severe with you than I might. You may not think it so, for being asked to leave the school is a serious matter.'

She looked at Conchita as though waiting for her to agree but she did not reply.

'I am going to allow you to sit your exams next week. Until then you will not mix with the other girls and you will be in a separate room for each of your papers. That may seem like harsh treatment but I cannot afford to let the rest of the school see any kind of tolerance on my part, or on that of the staff, for your reprehensible behaviour over the past twelve months. Do you understand my position?' Conchita nodded.

'You are an intelligent girl, Conchita. You speak beautiful Spanish, you have so successfully become a young Spanish girl, integrated into this school and in your community at home. No-one would know that you had not been born in this country. But something has gone wrong, hasn't it? I know you have had a difficult time in the past but I thought you had overcome those difficulties. I'm sorry that your time in this school has to end before it should but you have repeatedly broken our rules, refused to study, and become a bad example to other girls. We cannot have that.'

Mother Superior sighed and with a softening of her expression, said to Conchita,

'So, what has happened? Are you going to confide in me? Maybe I can help you.' Conchita shook her head again.

'Nobody can help me,' she replied rather curtly, and then more softly, she said, 'I'm sorry for upsetting you, Thank you for letting me sit the exams but I don't think they'll be much use to me.'

'Despite your unwillingness to study of late, I have no doubt the exams will not prove beyond you. You never know Conchita, you may well decide to go to university when your present problems are ironed out. And I'm sure that they will be. If you decide to apply I will do my best to help you.' She stood up and walking round her desk approached Conchita with her arms held out. She took Conchita's hands and held them.

'You said "nobody can help me"'. But have you asked the one person who can?'

'I don't know what you mean....'

'Think about it. *He* will not help if you don't ask, and when asked He listens. The Lord God listens Conchita. Have faith, trust Him and ask.' She let go of Conchita's hands and turned away. Conchita felt sure that she saw tears in her eyes and for a moment she felt a stab of guilt and shame. Mother Superior did not turn round, with her back to her, she said in a whisper.

'Go now.'

Conchita left her study, closing the door quietly behind her. She stood for a moment unsure of what to do next. She was to be segregated – no contact with other pupils. Where was she to go? At that moment Sister Hermana Maria appeared from the room next door.

'Come with me,' she said kindly. She led her to a small study in a side corridor, not far from the *Directora*'s room. It was sparsely furnished ; a desk, a chair and to her surprise a low bed. The walls were unadorned, save for the crucifix above the desk. But it was light and cool.

'All your belongings and books will be brought here for you in about half an hour. If you need help of any kind, you are to ask me. No-one else, Mother Superior expressly wishes it so. I will bring your meals and tidy the room each day. If you wish to go outside for fresh air, or a walk, I will accompany you. I hope you will... find peace here. We pray for you.'

Sister Hermana Maria paused for a moment and then quietly left the room, the only sound her blue skirts swishing against the door as she closed it behind her.

Conchita lay down on the bed and wept silently. The tears ran down her cheeks, dripping onto the thin pillow, as they had done so many years before back in the twin room where she had slept with Garnet, in that other life.

***

August 1955

Diary

Not a very nice birthday celebration, though I have to admit Papa and Carmen did make some effort for me but I wasn't in the mood to enjoy it. I didn't show much pleasure or gratitude. I can't help it. I'm so bored! Papa is making me ride round the vineyard with him on daily inspections of the vines. He's says I must learn to be a winemaker. What rot! What's the point? Juan Luis will inherit the place when he grows up. After all he is a true Spanish-born son and boys always inherit their father's business don't they? Who ever heard of a female winemaker? Thank goodness for Miguel, I'd go mad without him. But nobody knows about him. What luck I met him just before everything blew up.

Ramon Lopéz was a disappointed man. He had been so proud of his attractive daughter, boasting at every opportunity of her charm, her intelligence and, within the family, of her reconciliation to a new life. Never at any time had he felt it necessary to explain to anyone exactly how her arrival had come about. He had been so confident that he could pull it off, make the acquisition of a thirteen year old daughter appear quite normal and unremarkable. 'It's none of their business anyway,' he had told Carmen.

Now privately, he was ashamed of her but, as before, he saw no need to give explanations to anyone with regard to Conchita's unexpected daily presence at home.

He was also an angry man, though he began to recognise that both he and Carmen had been so wrapped up in their son, they had closed their eyes to the needs of Conchita. Carmen had cautioned him several times in the past, not to spoil Conchita 'for her own good' but he had

160

disregarded her advice, mistaking his attention and desire to fulfil all her wishes, for love. Then, when that special treatment was diverted to Juan Luis, the lack of it was all the more palpable to an impressionable teenager who had been the centre of his attention since her arrival in that household.

Then his anger began to turn into a fierce determination to pull Conchita back into the fold, and to give her an opportunity to redeem herself. His plan was to teach her the business of winemaking, as he had been taught by his own father. Day by day, out in the vineyards, he was trying to instil a love of the land and reveal the mystery of the vines as they produced the miraculous fruit that had provided the Lopez family with a living for a hundred and fifty years. They had lost so much during the civil war and it had been a struggle to pull the business back to its present standing. Every day he and Conchita rode and he lectured her.

'You see Conchita, over there? Those vines are over sixty years old. But they are not spent yet. They might produce only a tiny quantity of fruit but what they produce is excellent quality. These grapes are then carefully fermented and the wine then transferred to French oak casks for eighteen months, sometimes more.'

Conchita was not looking at where Ramon was pointing, she was not even listening. Despite her sullen expression, lack of enthusiasm, and downright hostility to Ramon's instruction, he would not let up.

'You're wasting your time, my love,' Carmen told him.

'I am not. I am determined that she shall learn and eventually make herself useful.'

'I understand how you feel, but.........'

'But what, Carmen? Why are you not working with me on this? All of a sudden I do not have your support. I don't understand you. You said yourself that you also felt partly to blame for Conchita's change of attitude. You too abandoned her remember.'

Carmen was vexed and her colour rose. Ramon saw the signs of a retort looming.

'You are not handling the situation well, Ramon. No, let me speak. I will have my say on the subject, this once, and if you don't like my advice then heaven help you with the ensuing problems.'

'Very well, say what you must.'

'Thank you Ramon, but not very graciously put. You're understandably concerned about Conchita's attitude and recent behaviour but have you considered *her* feelings? Have you taken a moment to find out why she's like this? I could speak to her but that wouldn't do. It's got to be you, her father, who sits her down and talks -

and *listens*. I see rather late in the day, that she is jealous of Juan Luis, and I'm sorry that we allowed that to happen. Make time for her on your own. Be firm but be kind.'

'I *am* finding time for her, I'm taking her out every day around the vineyard, time I can barely afford. You seem to forget that I run this place. I'm trying to tell her the history of it, talk about the vines and explain how everything happens.'

'But that's just it, Ramon. You're lecturing her but avoiding the subject of *her*. She needs some words of kindness and encouragement. In any case, if you want her to learn the business, riding around for an hour every morning is not the way to do it.' Ramon sighed.

'Then I don't know what is.' He turned and left the room.

'Ramon? Where are you going?' Never before had he walked out on a conversation with her and she was annoyed. From the window she watched him walk away with hunched shoulders and measured step. She knew him well enough to recognise that he was aware of his failure to handle the situation sensitively but as yet could not openly acknowledge it. She felt her annoyance subside as her compassion for him rose.

27

Diary

I don't know how much longer I can go on meeting Miguel in secret. It's getting more and more difficult. Papa keeps asking me about where I'm going. I had to lie the other day; I told him I was going to spend some time with Nana. Now that she has moved into her own house I go there from time to time. I shall have to see her much more often because if Papa asks her I'll be found out. I don't want to involve Nana in any kind of a lie, she at least is patient and kind with me.

Miguel is getting ratty with me as well. He says he's fed up with all this hole in the corner stuff. 'Why don't you tell your father and be done with it,' he said. That's just it – I think we would be done with it! I just know Papa won't like Miguel. He hasn't got a job and he looks...well, a bit rough. I must say he never seems to do anything but ride around on his motorbike all day. Last night I asked him where he worked.

'Me, work?' he said.

'You mean you haven't got a job? Why?' I asked him.

He laughed and said, 'What! Get a job you mean. I don't need one, do I? You've got plenty of money, you can pay for both of us.'

I was a bit shocked. I didn't tell him that all I get is a small allowance. It made me think a bit.

Nettie didn't come this summer, she's far too busy working and singing. She has to attend rehearsals for concerts, even in what are supposed to be summer holidays. That's hard! Perhaps it's a good thing she didn't come; I can't tell her about Miguel.

Conchita had written few letters to Garnet since leaving school, and was resentful that Garnet had not kept writing to her as often as in the past. Yet another day went by with no letter from her; she became petulant and reckless. She sneaked out of the house, grabbing her bicycle to ride down to the bar in the town, where Miguel would be waiting for her. She didn't dare pretend to be with Nana again. But Miguel was not there. She waited for an hour tucked in a gloomy corner, afraid that some local might come in and recognise her, until finally she left, cross but afraid. It was the first time he had stood her up.

Two days later Miguel telephoned. Conchita had pleaded with him never to 'phone the house, and up until then he had reluctantly obeyed. Fortunately Conchita answered the 'phone.

'Tomorrow night, in the bar. 8 o'clock,' he said briefly, in a low voice. She had been so cross with him but now when she heard his seductive voice her heart thumped at the thought of their meeting. She smiled to herself remembering his good looks and his dark hair, which fell to one side in a deep wave just waiting to be flicked back by a hand such as hers.

Ana Maria, who had come scurrying out of the kitchen to answer the 'phone, gave her a questioning glance.

'Wrong number,' Conchita said, turning away to hide the smile on her face.

'Bah!' Ana Maria responded and waddled off, back to her kitchen.

This time she would have to spend some time with Nana.

'May I come in Nana, for half an hour or so? I'm going to meet a friend but I thought I could come and see you first. Is that all right?'

'It's always "all right" my darling. I'll be delighted to see you. But only for half an hour? We can't say much in so short a time. But never mind, come in.'

Conchita felt a little guilty. Nana Isabella was a true *abuela* – a grandmother of the same calibre as Granny Hampton; affectionate, wise and fair. Conchita knew that Nana had believed in her, had always had the time to listen, and had offered her sound advice swathed in words of encouragement. Of late, Conchita had not given her the opportunity to listen, or give advice. Miguel was her big secret, she could not tell either Nana or Garnet.

He was waiting for her.

'Where were you on Tuesday? I waited an hour.'

'Since when do I have to tell you all my business and where I'm going?'

Conchita's stomach churned. Miguel's occasional smooth charm was again absent, with his hands slotted into the narrow top pockets of his denims, he struck an arrogant pose.

'Sorry, I didn't mean to be rude,' she said. 'I was worried about you.'

'Well don't. I can look after myself.' He lifted a hand to attract a passing waiter and ordered himself a double whisky, but nothing for her. The waiter turned to Conchita and gave her a languid look.

'I'll have a coffee please,' she said quietly. Miguel's demeanour exuded self-satisfaction and confidence, a new posture. It unnerved her.

'Well,' he said loudly. 'Things are going to change a bit round here. I'm not taking any more of these encounters in sleazy bars I'm coming up to your place – I want to see for myself this grand bodega which has won a medal, and made your family so rich.'

'Ssh,' Conchita said, putting her finger to her lips. 'We are not rich, and people will hear you and it'll get back to my father.'

'I don't care about that. It'll get to your father sooner than you think.' He swigged the last drop of his whisky, stood up and pulled out a handful of money, slapping a large note on the table.

'Where did you get all that money?' Conchita asked in amazement.

'I told you, business. Not that it's anything to do with you.' He turned. 'I'm going, I've got more *business* to see to.'

'Already? When will I see you?'Conchita said, in shock at his sudden departure, wondering why he had bothered to meet her. Perhaps to show her that he had some money at last. He left her there without replying, her cold, untouched coffee, sitting in front of her.

***

It was ironic that her earlier than usual return home, on her bicycle, made her visit to Nana all the more credible. She had neither the courage nor the spirit to face her father and Carmen. They were still at dinner which gave her a pretext for not joining them.

'I've eaten,' she lied. 'I'm a bit tired so I'll go to bed if you don't mind.'

Carmen and Ramon stared at each other in disbelief.

'That's the most polite remark she's made in weeks,' declared Ramon. 'She must be ill!'

'Don't be unkind Ramon. Perhaps we....' She corrected herself, '*she* - has turned a corner. I do hope so.'

***

A week later Conchita and Miguel went to the cinema. Despite the fact that Miguel had shown her that he had money, he expected her to fund their evening's entertainment.

'I've no change,' he said, but flashing a very large note.

It was the latest film featuring James Dean, 'Rebel without a Cause', the last one he made before his death in a car crash just a month ago. It was a strange feeling looking at the posters, and then watching the film, of a glitzy young man who was no longer alive. He was only twenty-four, younger than Miguel. The newspapers, the wireless and the television continued to talk about the tragedy. He was mourned by Hollywood stars, film directors, and thousands and thousands of young people, but Conchita had perceived him as a conceited and selfish individual. He was known to be callous and to forget friends who had been loyal or useful to him in the past. Nevertheless she was pleased to have the opportunity to see the film, which was in English, a pleasant change for her to hear her mother tongue, even if it was Americanised English. Miguel complained.

'I didn't understand a word,' he grumbled as they came out of the cinema.

'But there were sub-titles. Didn't you read them?'

'Couldn't be bothered,' he snarled.

Conchita was bewildered by his attitude; he was sullen again. It had been quite obvious to her that he was revelling in the character played by Dean. She was now convinced he had taken the young actor as a role model, perhaps because he appeared to have suddenly acquired a lot of money, he saw himself as a kind of rebel.

'Come on, let's go to my place,' he said grabbing her arm. She had been to his room only once before and remembered how very small, unkempt even grubby it was. His rumpled bed in one corner, had an air of not having seen clean linen for a long time. She had been glad they had stayed for only a matter of minutes. Now she climbed reluctantly on to the back of his motor bike. She realised if she wanted to get back home from the town tonight, travelling on Miguel's bike was the only option.

Her eyes travelled unwittingly to the bed as she entered the poky room. To her surprise she saw that it was neatly made. Miguel followed her look, and a grin replaced his previously surly expression. He moved towards her and gently pulled her arms out of her jacket.

'Warm, isn't it?' he smirked, beginning to unfasten the buttons of her blouse.

'What are you doing?' she protested, yanking his hand away from her breast.

'Now, now, you're not going to be difficult, are you?' and he propelled her towards the bed.

'Miguel, what are you doing?' she said again.

166

'Oh come on, Conchita, don't pretend to be naive. I don't believe for a minute you haven't done this before. I told you things were going to change, I'm not waiting any longer.' Conchita began to panic, the more she resisted his pushing the more aggressive he became, forcing her backwards. As she felt the edge of the bed against her legs she overbalanced and fell onto the bed. His weight, as he threw himself on top of her, knocked the breath out of her.

'Get off,' she shrieked. 'You're hurting me.'

Conchita wriggled and grabbed his ear but he gripped her arm and held it above her head. She could see contempt mixed with desire in his eyes as his other hand began tearing at her blouse.

'Not yet I'm not, but I will if you don't behave.'

A blouse button flew off, Conchita heard it roll onto the floor and a vision of how she must look flashed through her mind. It was dispelled in an instant by the harsh feel of his rough hand, groping for her breast. He grasped it and squeezed hard.

'Oh God, that hurts, please stop.'

'Even remember your manners do you? 'Please' indeed!' He pushed his head down and sucked her nipple hard. Conchita shrieked and with her free hand grabbed his hair, pulling as fiercely as she could.

'So, we're going to fight, are we? Well the sooner we get on with it the better.' With one knee pressed firmly against her thigh, he reached down and yanked up her skirt. Conchita writhed but his weight pinned her to the bed. Suddenly she felt his rough hand exploring, pulling, deep into her underwear. For a brief moment his weight shifted, and she thought she might throw him off but he came down again, this time what she felt was not his hand. He plunged into her and thrust upwards with such force that Conchita screamed. He rhythmically rammed into her again and again, the pain searing through her with each push, until her body went limp.

Suddenly he stopped and rolled sideways.

'Next time, will be much better,' he said.

Conchita could barely speak but whispered 'There will never be a next time.

'Of course there will, my fighting angel. What a laugh, when I tell my mates that I'm laying the daughter of Ramon Lopez, the great Rioja wine maker.'

'No, no. You can't,' she cried hoarsely.

He stood up arranged his jeans with one hand, and then leaned over her. With a hand on each side of her, he pinned her down on the bed.

'You don't want them to know uh? Then there will be many more 'next times' won't there? Get my meaning?' As he moved away he gave a harsh laugh.

Slowly she sat up and pulled down her skirt. She whispered,

'Take me home please.'

'Pretty please. Still minding your manners. Well, seeing you asked so nicely. Let's go.'

Conchita stood up unsteadily. There was a cold, sticky feeling between her legs and she hurt horribly. She walked gingerly towards the door, wondering how she was going to climb onto that bike, but she had no option.

28

Diary

I haven't written in my diary for several days. How can I write about what has happened? I'm so ashamed. I can't believe I ever liked that creature. I thought he was trendy, he was certainly good looking. But looks don't mean a thing, I can see that now. He was so beastly to me and he hurt me dreadfully. I've been such a fool; I should have known what was coming. I've had to lie again, I just couldn't go riding the next day with Papa so I asked Carmen to tell him I was having a bad monthly. There was blood on my pants but I knew it wasn't my period, it was far worse than any period pain. My God, if that's sex you can keep it! Fortunately for me, Papa has been extremely busy because of the recent medal, meeting wine merchants from all over the place, and I haven't had to make any more excuses.

***

Conchita was in fear and dread that Miguel would 'phone or even turn up as he had threatened to do. It was with surprise that she received a note from him a week later. It was brief.

'I'm going away on business, for some time. Don't go meeting anybody else – I'll know if you do, I have my informants. Keep that cosy little place warm for me, I shall be needing it when I get back!'

Conchita was horrified. What insolence. How uncouth. She was appalled to think that this note might have got into her father's hands. She burned it immediately. She was unsure what Miguel had meant by his words 'some time'. She desperately hoped it meant a long time.

***

The buzz and growing excitement of Christmas was infectious and Conchita managed from time to time, to push thoughts of the ordeal to the back of her mind. She was subdued but found herself wanting to join Carmen and Ramon for dinner, a routine she had shunned for a long time. They couldn't help but notice her change of manner but her presence at the table precluded any discussion they might have had about her. She was quiet during the meals though she was not unresponsive. They exchanged looks but their comments to one another had to wait until after a particularly pleasant conversation at dinner that night, about the arrangements for the family gathering on Christmas day. It was Carmen who broached the subject.

'How do you think Conchita looks?' she asked.

'She was quite animated this evening I thought. It's so good to have her joining in again. It looks as though she's coming out of this phase of teenage hostility.'

'Yes, but how do you think she *looks*? Carmen said again.

'She looks all right to me. Why?'

'I don't think she looks well. She's very pale and lacklustre. I just wonder what meals she's had all the weeks she hasn't eaten dinner with us. I wonder if she's anaemic.'

'Well, the Christmas feasting should put that to rights, don't you think?'

'Perhaps, I hope so. We should keep our eye on her,' she added with feeling.

***

Preparations for the Christmas festivities were well under way. The Christmas lights were now strung across the streets in Haro and the Christmas market was set up; stalls piled high with fruits, flowers, marzipan and sweets. The children in the streets swarmed round them every day with their pocket money clutched in their cold hands; a favourite was the Turron, a nougat made of toasted sweet almonds. Candles, decorations and hand-made gifts abounded. Conchita felt herself being swept into the joyfulness of the forthcoming celebrations and began to look forward to the Christmas Eve meal when the whole family would come together, along with the longest-serving of Ramon's estate workers. This year Juan Luis, as a two year old, would be joining the family for the Christmas Eve dinner.

170

The Christmas tree arrived and Conchita asked Carmen if she could help her decorate it.

'Of course, we usually do it together. I would hate to do it without you.'

Conchita smiled and said,

'I'll go and get the box of decorations from the store cupboard, shall I?'

They trimmed the tree in companionable silence for a while, except for ponderings on where to hang a particular decoration.

'You hang these little angels Conchita. They're the ones your father brought for you from England.'

'So they are,' she said smiling. 'Do you know, I've hung these on the tree since I was three years old. Or so Daddy told me. It was really sweet of him. But I was worried that Nettie might mind.'

'Nettie?'

'Yes, oh sorry, I mean Garnet. We have special names for each other when we're on our own together, or when we write to each other. We don't usually use them when talking to other people because we don't like anyone else to use them. We've always done it.'

'You still miss her dreadfully, don't you Conchita?'

Conchita nodded and moved around to the side of the tree and went on hanging the angels, out of sight of Carmen.

'You know don't you? you can 'phone her any time you want. We are very lucky to have a telephone but you may use it any time you wish.'

'Yes, thank you. But it's a bit difficult. You see she's at boarding school and she can't come to the 'phone very easily. Besides, I never know when she is practising, or in a concert, or something or other. She's always busy and works terribly hard.'

Carmen was astounded at the natural and confiding way in which Conchita talked of her sister. She casually edged closer to her, feigning to reach a particular branch for the wooden toy she held up. It was with dismay that she then saw tears slipping silently down Conchita's cheeks. Carmen kept silent for a moment to give her time to recover.

'So, what's your special name,' she asked lightly.

'Oh, I'm just Con. Funny isn't it? It fits for both Constance and Conchita.'

'Sorry. I don't understand. What is Constance?'

Conchita stopped dressing the tree and turned her sad face to Carmen.

'I'm not surprised you don't understand Carmen. I'm still trying to understand it myself.' To Carmen's surprise she gave a little chuckle.

'You see, in my other life,' and she chuckled again, 'I was called Connie and I always thought it was short for Constance. And so did everybody else. But it wasn't. Apparently, my birth certificate said Conchita. It was quite a shock. Poor Daddy. I don't know how he coped.'

For the second time Carmen was stunned by these revelations. She couldn't wait to tell Ramon about this encounter. She knew he would be pleased that such a conversation had taken place. Surely it meant that Conchita was at last coming to terms with her dual life. It was Conchita who broke the silence that ensued.

'Carmen, I've already got a few gifts ready. Is it all right if I put them under the tree now? Or do you think Juan Luis might take a liking to them?'

'Even though he's only two he certainly understands the word 'No!' so I think we might manage to keep him away from them. He's so much easier to control now he's walking. That crawling nearly drove me mad; he got into everything.'

They laughed together as they finished the tree, and then Conchita cleared up the pine needles that had fallen as they worked.

'I'm going to get my parcels,' she said. 'Then I'm going to write to Nettie. See you later.'

***

December 1955

Dear Nettie

One week to go till Christmas! There's so much going on here at the moment that I haven't had time to write to you properly. I'm really sorry, we used to write to each other all the time, didn't we? But I know how busy you are with your studies. I haven't got that excuse, just the opposite - I've got time on my hands, though Papa is still trying to teach me all about wine! To tell the truth, I've not been feeling too well lately. I just feel so tired all the time. I think it's all the fuss and commotion after I left school and maybe my guilty conscience wearing me down! Things are getting better though. I've been trying really hard to be nice and be what I think is normal; the atmosphere is certainly more peaceful, except for all the activity preparing for the festivities! It's such a palaver but lots of fun.

172

Yesterday I went down to the town in the afternoon. Everywhere there were Belén, that's nativity scenes to you, not just in the church but in the streets and the shops too. Some of them were absolute works of art. I prefer the simple one we've got at home. It reminds me of the wooden figures you and I used to arrange on the hall table. Mummy hated it when we put straw in the little stable, do you remember? She used to say it was messy. By the time I got back it was getting dark and everyone was lighting the little oil lamps in their windows. It all looked so pretty and...well, Christmassy. I lit ours too as soon as I got back.

On Nochebuena, hey that's Christmas Eve I'll have you know! we all get together and sing carols round the tree and party until midnight when the church bells ring. Then we go to church for a candlelit Mass. It's really quite beautiful. Most people go to church again on Christmas Day when the church is absolutely packed. But Papa says we've been up so late after dinner the night before that we don't need to go. He says once is enough. We don't have the Christmas dinner until after midnight. It's tradition to wait until the midnight bells ring to call everyone to church, then we eat after the service. Crazy isn't it? But I'm getting used to it, after all, this is my fourth Spanish Christmas. After dinner the grown-ups open their gifts but the children, if there are any still up at that time in the morning, only get a small gift, they have to wait for the night before Epiphany when they place their shoes on the doorstep in the hope that the Three Wise Men will leave them some presents. They don't have Father Christmas here, delivering presents on Christmas Eve, but I expect I've told you this before. It's all quite different. One day, when you have finished all your serious studies, you must come and have Christmas with us. And Daddy too perhaps.

Well, that's all for now. I think I'll go and see if I can help Ana Maria in the kitchen.

Give everyone my love, lots to Granny and Gramps and to Daddy, even to Mummy if you think she's interested. I've already written to everybody but tell them anyway.

My love to you,
Con

***

More gifts began to appear under the tree. The kitchen was a hive of activity with Ana Maria baking and cooking; making soup, cleaning crab, preparing cold meats, all to be served as part of the midnight

173

festive dinner. Ana Maria, normally independent and noisily efficient, was beginning to feel her age. It was a lot of work, even with the help of a young girl who now came up from the village to do Ana Maria's bidding. Conchita saw Ana Maria huffing and puffing as she bustled around the kitchen. It would be like old times if I help, she thought. Ana Maria was taken aback at her offer but was grateful, not just for her quiet assistance but also for her company. It wasn't long before they were both teasing each other and laughing, like those early days when Conchita had learned her first Spanish words.

29

December 1955

Conchita's letter crossed in the post with one from Garnet. She was home from school for four weeks, though not all of that was free time. Inevitably she had a lot of work to do, including a concert on Christmas Eve which, conveniently, was to be performed in the Concert Halls in Harrogate. She was both singing and playing the piano, which her singing teacher had declared was too much. Miss Grey wanted her to concentrate all her energy and time on singing, but Garnet was loathe to sacrifice her piano work, to which she continued to be so dedicated.

'Please let me play this time, Miss Grey. I promise I'll still work hard on my songs,' she pleaded. 'I think after this year, I'll be able to decide which I'm going to specialise in.' Miss Grey reluctantly agreed but warned her;

'You certainly will have to decide soon. It's a gruelling life Garnet, being a singer. You have such talent and you must begin to focus on it before long if you want it to be your career. You have the potential to be a great opera singer, famous, you know.'

Garnet had nodded gravely, not too happy at Miss Grey's words. They scared her. She wasn't sure if she wanted to be 'great' or 'famous'. Garnet was still extraordinarily modest about her musical talent. All she was sure about was that she loved music and couldn't live without it.

The concert was an unqualified success. Garnet played Träumeri from Schumann's Scenes from Childhood, and later the Humoreske, in Bflat Major. The audience obviously appreciated her playing with such grace and technical skill for a girl of her age. Along with Miss Grey as accompanist she sang Josephine's song; 'Oh joy, oh rapture unforeseen', from Gilbert and Sullivan's 'HMS Pinafore'. The Headmistress had insisted in adding some 'fun' to the programme and had instructed the staff to make this a concert to suit all preferences. It was not to be too serious but at the same time, it must show off not only the pupils' aptitude but also their pleasure in creating music. Philip and Flora, Amelia and Charles Hampton, and Annie, all attended the concert.

Garnet, though tired out, was thankful that everything had gone so well, particularly her own performances. Though she was pleased to have everyone's congratulations, it was the praise from her mother that took her by surprise.

'Garnet, I didn't know you could sing so beautifully,' Flora said as they all walked out to the car. 'Why have I never heard you before?'

Garnet looked at her father, but before he could say anything, she replied,

'Oh I suppose it's because I didn't really sing much at home Mummy, before I went to this school. I used to sing at Donnington's Prep School, in the choir. Anyway, I'm glad you enjoyed it.'

Charles and Amelia were walking slowly behind them, Charles' arm in Amelia's for support and Annie on the other side of him, ready with a steadying hand.

'How about all coming back to us for a cup of tea before you go home?' Charles called out.

'Aren't you too tired, dear?' Amelia said.

'Even if I am, I want to celebrate Garnet's success. Besides it's Christmas Eve. In fact I think it should be a noggin, never mind the tea.'

They all laughed and Garnet looked up at her father.

'He's still funny, isn't he Daddy?' she whispered. 'Even though he's not very well these days. I'm just so thrilled that he could come. You don't think it will have been too much for him do you?'

'I think he'll be just fine. Don't worry your little head.'

'Daddy?'

'Oh here we go, it wouldn't be you if there wasn't a question or two.'

'I've been thinking…'

Philip pretended to groan, but smiled as she continued,

'I've wondered whether we should tell Connie about Gramps. About his not being very well I mean.'

'I have mentioned it, but not in any detail. You see, Connie has been having a difficult time and I didn't want to add to any problems.'

'I know, Daddy, she wrote and told me about having to leave school early. She also said she wasn't happy any more. But I didn't say anything to you because I didn't want to tell, in case she hadn't said anything.'

176

'She hasn't, Garnet. It was Ramon who told me. In fact I've been very worried and I was considering whether to pay them a visit in the New Year. Now that's a big secret, I haven't mentioned this to anyone. So mum's the word please Garnet, until I've thought about it a bit more. I didn't intend telling you this just yet, but your questioning, you see, brings all sorts of things to light,' he said grinning at her, trying to take any reproach from his voice.

'I promise. You will tell me, as soon as you know though, won't you Daddy?'

'Yes my pet. Now, let's curtail this serious conversation for the time being and go and celebrate as Gramps suggested.'

***

Christmas Day was yet another happy day with all the family together. Philip had persuaded Annie to invite her cousin Beatrice over from Shipley and had arranged for her to be collected in a taxi.

'How on earth did you manage to get a taxi on Christmas Day, Mr Hampton?' she had asked him.

'Magic, Beatrice. And don't you worry, it'll be taking you home again this evening.'

She was overwhelmed and could but fluster her thanks for their kindness. They had a happy day and Annie did them proud with the traditional Christmas dinner.

Later in the afternoon, Annie cut the iced cake, taking the Father Christmas model off the top, and the little robin. Garnet picked them up and held them in her hand for a while. When no-one was looking she put them in a pocket. She had plans for those.

Amelia and Charles stayed overnight on Christmas night, so that they could completely relax, go to bed when they felt like it but not miss out on the evening's enjoyment. It also meant that Philip would not have to drive after indulging in a glass of wine or two with dinner and later his favourite whisky. Flora was looking well and joined in their traditional Christmas day games, playing Monopoly and cards. Philip looked round at each of them, the worry and responsibility of Flora's illness alleviated she now seemed happy and relaxed. He looked for signs of stress in his mother, due to dealing with his father's deteriorating health, each day not knowing what it would bring, but she seemed to be coping. He remembered Dr MacAllister's words at the last check-up;

177

'We've got to keep an eye on that heart of his'. Watching them all, relaxed and having fun, he thought, if it were not for Connie's absence, this would be the happiest Christmas we have had for some time. That brought his thoughts round to what he had told Garnet earlier. Before he broached the subject to any of them he decided to look into the availability of flights over the New Year.

Garnet relaxed but she soon took up her books again. It was a demanding time for her, with 'O' levels looming in the following June. That's one reason why she had wanted so much to be at home before Christmas, to be able to revise for her mock exams, in peace and quiet, before her return to school in mid-January.

Flora continued to be relaxed and contented and so Philip decided he could arrange a trip to Spain. He spoke to Flora that night.

'Flora, how would you feel if I went away for two or three days?'

'That's fine darling. Is it business? Surely not at New Year?'

Still unsure of her reaction if he spoke of Connie, he hesitated, then said,

'No it's not business. As a matter of fact, I was thinking of going to see Connie. She hasn't been well and I'd like to see for myself how she is.' Philip waited and was then taken aback by her response.

'Oh Philip, why didn't you tell me? Nobody tells me anything these days – do they? Just like my not knowing that Garnet could sing so beautifully.' Philip paused again before asking,

'So how would you feel, if I went?'

'Of course you must go. I'm absolutely fine, I've got Annie, and Garnet. Unless you'd like to take Garnet with you? She'd absolutely love that Philip. Why don't you?'

Philip was bowled over by her obvious consideration for both Garnet and Connie.

'To tell you the truth, I didn't think of it. How clever and thoughtful of you. It would be wonderful for both of them. But Garnet's got a lot of revision to do. I don't know how she'll feel having time away. She won't be doing revision if she's with Connie!'

'Ask her Philip. In any case, she's been working so hard, I think it will do her good.'

Once again, Philip was stunned by her remarks. His Flora was coming back. No, this was a new Flora, a kinder, gentler Flora. He hugged her and said,

'Yes, I will. Thank you Flora.'

30

Diary

¿Feliz Navidad! Happy Christmas.

Papa gave me the most beautiful necklace last night. It's a drop pearl, set in a gold claw, hanging on a gold chain. It's absolutely gorgeous. I was quite overcome and made a fool of myself by bursting into tears. We hugged for ages. I could see Nana Isabella watching us and as I turned she nodded and smiled at me. She gave me some new riding boots. Everyone is being so kind and patient with me, I'm feeling a bit guilty as I begin to see what a dreadful person I've been the last few months, probably even years! I told Nettie, I really am trying to change.

We had the most fabulous dinner last night. There were twenty-one round the table! All of us – our family I mean, that includes Juan Luis who really is still a bit young to sit at dinner at that time of night, but we couldn't leave him out. Then there was Rodrigo de Silva and his wife, and Catarina their six year old daughter. Rodrigo is a wine merchant in Logrono, that is he buys and sells wine, he doesn't produce it like Papa does. Rodrigo is quite a bit younger than Papa but they are good friends, they have known each other for years. Then there was Luca, he's not married, he's a good neighbour and owns the bordering vineyard. Then there was José and his wife and three children, he works in the vineyard, he's in charge of some of the other workers. Then there were three other couples; the husbands are now retired but they used to work here when Papa's father was alive. They're quite a lot older than Papa but he is terribly caring and keeps an eye on those who loyally served his father.

The food was fantastic. We had shellfish, cold meats, soup and baked besugo – I think it's called bream in English. And then, more to come! We had roast lamb. I just couldn't eat the caramel custard, I was absolutely bursting. Juan Luis soon got tired and Carmen had to take him off to bed, but it was nice that he was there for a little while. It made the family complete.

Thank goodness we went to church before dinner. I couldn't possibly have gone this morning, I'm feeling quite nauseous. I obviously ate far too much. I should never have eaten that cake covered in rich marzipan. I used to love Christmas cake at home – I mean in my previous life! Fruity, coated with marzipan and thickly iced, with a little Father Christmas figure standing on the top and a robin beside him. Annie made fantastic cakes. Oh, I must stop, I feel queasy at the thought of it. There's no way I'm going out to swing on that contraption Papa has had put up in the courtyard. I know the tradition by now, we swing and we sing! But not me, not today! It's supposed to be for children anyway so I can claim I'm not a child anymore. I hope they think I've stopped behaving like one! I'll have to make a fuss of Juan Luis and give him a turn or two, if I can stand it. Goodness, I haven't written so much in my diary for ages. I've got so much more to tell Nettie. And we haven't even had New Year's Eve yet!

***

The celebrating continued right through to the New Year. On New Year's Eve there was the traditional street party in the town, people dressed in fancy outfits, music and dancing, entertainment and a firework display. Ramon's father and mother had always attended the party. They were popular with their neighbours, known to be generous and considerate employers. After Ramon's father died, Isabella was adamant that she would continue the tradition of being at that party and serving the wine, as they had always done. Now, they were a family again; Isabella, her son and daughter in law, her grand-daughter and grandson. They were welcomed with applause and given a good viewing place at the long table, in readiness for the fireworks. Though the party was likely to go on until the small hours, and the fireworks continue to the enthrallment of the children, until almost dawn, Ramon and family left by midnight. Juan Luis was just too young to cope with any more excitement and lack of sleep.

Yet more rejoicing and fun was to come. Presents for Juan Luis were secretly being wrapped and hidden away for the Eve of Epiphany.

'He's really too young to understand what's going on,' Carmen had said to Conchita. 'Even so, we have to follow the tradition and let him put his shoes on the doorstep, to be filled with gifts by the morning, gifts from the Three Wise Men.'

'You did that with me the New Year after I arrived. I felt a bit silly, waiting for presents like a child. But I was a child, wasn't I? If I'd been in Yorkshire Garnet and I would still have put out our stockings at the end of our beds on Christmas Eve, waiting to be filled with little gifts from Father Christmas. We used to get chocolate pennies and an orange. It was such fun.'

'You know, I think we're doing this as much for ourselves, as for Juan Luis. Ramon is so excited about it. He's still a child himself in many ways!'

'Perhaps we should put Papa's shoes out as well,' Conchita joked, and they giggled together at the thought of it.

***

Conchita didn't have to write to Garnet to tell her all the news of Christmas. She was able to tell her in person. Philip and Garnet arrived in the late afternoon of the fifth. That morning Ramon and Carmen had said to her,

'We have a surprise for you.'

Conchita looked at them, frowning slightly, unsure of what might constitute a surprise now that all gifts and secret parcels had been opened.

'Go on, you tell,' Carmen said laughing.

'Philip, I mean, your Father is arriving this evening. And Garnet is coming with him.'

On hearing their words Conchita went pale and to their alarm they saw her sink slowly to the floor.

'My God, she's fainted,' Carmen said hurrying to Conchita's side.

Ramon lifted her up and placed her on the chaise longue.

'What's wrong with her? Do you think it was the shock of the news? I should have told her more gently.'

Conchita stirred and opened her eyes to see both Ramon and Carmen peering down at her with anxious expressions.

'Oh dear, what happened?' she mumbled. 'I suddenly felt funny.' She sat up slowly and as her head began to clear she smiled and asked,

'Weren't you telling me something, or did I just dream that brilliant news?'

'It was no dream, my dear. I'm so sorry I blurted it out, it was meant to be a surprise, but obviously it was more of a shock.'

181

Carmen was looking closely at Conchita, seeing the dark rings under her eyes and the paleness of her complexion.

'You know, young lady, I think you've been partying just a little too much. I think you need a good deal of sleep and also maybe a pick-me-up to boost your general health. You're looking quite pasty Conchita. There's nothing wrong, is there?'

Conchita fidgeted to get away from their gaze. She couldn't tell them at this stage, perhaps never, of the ghastly episode with Miguel. Over the Christmas festival she had managed to block out the memory but the horror of it seeped back into her thoughts from time to time. She stood up.

'I'm sorry, it's my own fault; I didn't have any breakfast. Silly me. But I'm thrilled to bits with the news. And…it's the fifth… so that means they'll be able to join in the fun of Epiphany. Thanks Papa, thanks Carmen. Hey Carmen, how about we make Garnet put her shoes on the doorstep too?'

'We could, but she might object. After all she's sixteen this January, older than when you came here and remember how you felt?'

'True, but Garnet's always ready to enter into the fun of anything. She's a great sport. I bet she does it. In which case, I'll have to think of something to put in the shoes.'

'First, go and make yourself a tasty enchilada, with plenty of chicken in it! But no eating the Rosca de Reyes, not until the sixth remember. Then we'll think of something for a gift,' Carmen said.

Ramon turned to Carmen, after Conchita left the room.

'That scared me,' he said. Do you think she's all right?'

'I'm not sure, I told you before that I thought she hadn't been eating properly. I think we might get her to have a health check.'

'I don't know how you'll persuade her to do that. She'll think it rather odd.'

'We'll wait until Philip and Garnet's visit is over, then we'll put our minds to it.'

***

Philip and Garnet arrived in good time to join the family in watching the Eve of Epiphany procession through the town. Thousands of sweets were thrown from the brightly coloured passing floats, cakes and candies galore, supposedly for the children, but the adults joined in the scramble to catch as many as they could. When they returned home it

182

was time to eat the Rosca de Reyes, the ring-shaped pastry baked on Los Reyes Day – the Three Kings' Day.

'It's delicious,' Garnet said munching away. 'It's a bit like our hot-cross buns, but much more exciting with all this sugar and fruity jellies all over it. Yum, yum.'

Philip smiled to himself, remembering all too clearly, how not very long ago Garnet had gone through that dreadful phase of barely eating at all.

'Be careful as you crunch,' warned Conchita. 'You might get one of the charms hidden inside. If you do it means you will be blessed with good luck for the rest of the year.'

She had no sooner said the words than she yelped.

'What's the matter, have you bitten your tongue?' joked Garnet.

'No, I've got one, a charm I mean.' She spat it out onto her hand and stared at it for a moment. Then she burst into tears.

Everyone sat staring at her, puzzled by her sudden outburst of emotion. Garnet jumped up and sat beside her, putting her arm around her she said,

'Con, what is it? I thought you said it's lucky to find one. Why are you crying?'

Conchita put her face in her younger sister's shoulder and sniffed. After a moment she murmured,

'You should have it, not me. You've got exams coming up. I want you to have lots of luck.' Lifting her face she said, 'But knowing you, you won't need it, you'll do really well without it, I just know you will.' She smiled, 'Sorry about that,' she said. 'What a softy.'

Carmen watched the whole scene with concern. 'There's more to Conchita's pale face than tiredness,' she thought. 'We really must get to the bottom of this.'

***

Later that evening everyone put their shoes on the doorstep, with much laughter and teasing about what they would find in them the next morning.

It was Conchita who helped Juan Luis fill his shoes with straw. It was a strange tradition Conchita felt and it reminded her of the straw she and Garnet used to place inside the little wooden stable of their nativity scene. Only tonight, it got everywhere, except in Juan Luis' shoes, which gave more cause for merriment. Conchita wondered what her mother would have thought of this.

'You see, it's the Three Kings, travelling on horses overnight and leaving presents for the children,' Conchita explained to Garnet, as they all trooped inside again, Conchita leading Juan Luis by the hand.

'In that case, if it's horses who arrive on the doorstep, I hope I shan't get a nasty surprise when I look in my shoes!' Everyone laughed not only at Philip's mischievous remark but also at Garnet's shocked expression.

As they came in, Conchita picked Juan Luis up in her arms. He was beginning to get tired and she sat him on her knee saying, in musical Spanish,

'.......so, presents for you tomorrow, my little one........'

She turned back to Garnet, cuddling Juan Luis as she continued;

'Tomorrow is Los Reyes, the day when the Kings supposedly arrived in Bethlehem. So tonight is what we used to call 'Twelfth Night'.

Garnet listened attentively, admiring the way her sister switched from English to Spanish and back again. Even though Conchita had told her some of this in her many letters, she sat entranced at her animated explanations. It was entertaining and it was good to see Conchita in a happy mood.

The following morning presents were opened, amid much gaiety. Small, fun items for the adults, but a handsome fountain pen and pencil set, nestling in its own satin lined case, was given to Garnet.

'We hope you will find them useful at exam time,' Ramon said.

Garnet was overcome but delighted and kissed both Carmen and Ramon in thanks.

Juan Luis' gifts were all expectedly much too large to go in his tiny shoes. Carmen had been right, the whole pretense of his opening presents was for the benefit of herself and Ramon.

It all came to an end after four days. It was the longest Philip could be away, both because of work and his concern of leaving Annie for too long with the responsibility of Flora, to say nothing of Garnet's need to get back to her studies. Ramon and Carmen managed to have a quiet talk with Philip, before his departure, about Conchita's state of health.

'I hope my letter, speaking of our worries about Conchita, didn't upset you, but we felt you should know that she's been going through a very bad phase. You may feel you've come on a wild goose chase now when you see her, almost her normal, happy self. It's ironic that this last fortnight she's seemed to be better, on the other hand she's not

184

looking well, pale and tired, but we have plans to address that in the very near future.'

'No visit could ever be a wild goose chase, it's always a great pleasure to come. You make us so welcome. No, I really must thank you for writing the way you did. And now I've seen her I feel reassured that you're keeping an eye on her. There's obviously been an improvement in her behaviour from what you have told me.'

'Don't thank us, Philip. I feel quite at fault. Ramon and I should have foreseen what might happen. It does happen in families occasionally, you know, when a new baby arrives. And I think that's when it all began. All I can say is we'll do our best to make sure that she knows how much we love her.' Carmen's eyes filled with tears.

'I know that by now. Don't feel blameworthy in any way. God knows, I felt it when Flora had her breakdown, and I rebuked myself time and again for not noticing that something was wrong with Garnet. But our trusty, family doctor persuaded me eventually that we can't hold ourselves totally responsible for everything that happens in life. So I pass on his philosophy to you, for what it's worth. I hope you find it comforting as I did.'

The goodbyes were tearful, especially from Conchita, but with the promise of a long visit from Garnet in the summer, she cheered up.

'Exams will be all over Con, then I can come and spend time with you, and everybody,' she said smiling and looking round.

'Nettie,' Conchita said quietly. 'I've written a letter to Mummy. Would you give it to her. I'm rather hoping she'll write back one day. Do you think she might?'

'Yes, I do. You know, she's quite changed. She's.....well, much nicer. I don't think anybody realised she was actually ill, growing ill, obviously for quite a long time. Even I can see that now. It looks as though she's recovered, she's certainly much happier. I'll tell her lots about this visit and maybe that will help.' They smiled and hugged and Conchita and Carmen waved them away, as Ramon drove them to the airport.

31

Late January 1956

Miguel's return was without warning. It was the sound of his motor bike that alerted Conchita as she rode Alvaro early one evening. To her surprise he didn't stop at the house but continued along the track down the hillside towards her between the blocks of vines. He revved the engine as he zoomed past her, swerved round and skidded to a stop right in front of her. Alvaro neighed in fright, and shifted nervously from one foot to the other. Miguel laughed.

'Poor little horsy frightened then?' he mocked. 'That's nothing. Watch this.'

Conchita trembled in the saddle unsure what to do as Miguel sped away in the opposite direction. She looked behind her and in the near distance saw him turn, and gathering speed head straight for her. She kicked Alvaro into action and bursting into a gallop racing to the bottom of the hill. There the wide path narrowed and snaked left, curving round the next plot of vines, the great swathe of dark trunks, with their long spindly branches waiting for their late winter pruning, stretched out in front of her. She felt sure Miguel would not attempt to round that sharp corner, he would have to stop. The increasing noise of the engine catching up with them was terrifying Alvaro. Conchita was straining to rein him in and then it happened.

She was right. Miguel could not swerve round that corner at speed. He slammed into the horse, Conchita was thrown over his head as he lurched to the ground with a great whinnying scream of pain. Miguel was hurled in the air, landing amidst a tangle of vines and cordons. The engine of his bike continued to throb in what was otherwise a silent scene.

It was the worker, checking a nearby block of vines, who heard the screaming engine descending on Conchita and Alvaro. He looked up and witnessed Miguel hurtle into them. The shock was such that he stood for a moment disbelieving the sight. Then he ran.

186

***

Ramon sat beside the bed throughout the night. Carmen reluctantly left to go home to tend to Juan Luis. The doctor warned them it could be some time before Conchita regained consciousness, they were not yet sure of the extent of her injuries. Ramon held her right hand very gently in his own, the left was immobilised on the bed to secure a drip in her arm which lay limp. Suddenly there was a mild twitch in Conchita's hand and Ramon's drooping eyelids came wide open. He leaned forward slightly to look into her face, completely drained of all colour. Her eyelids flickered and she moaned. At that moment the doctor returned.

'She moved a little,' whispered Ramon. 'She must be regaining consciousness.'

'It's a good sign but I'm afraid you must be patient. It'll will be a little while yet before you'll be able to speak to her, or more to the point, she to you. In the meantime, I'd like to talk to you for a few minutes.'

He called a nurse to the bedside.

'Stay and watch over this young lady, please, whilst I speak to Segñor López. I'll be in my private office, if you need me. Call me immediately if there is any change, no matter how slight.' They moved away from the bed to a small side room.

'Please sit down Segñor López. Now, straight to the point; I will give you the good news first. As she fell from the horse, she obviously hit the ground on her right side and sustained a broken shoulder and some fractured ribs. We would like to take another x-ray of the neck area but we don't suspect any further injury there. I have to say she is extremely lucky not to have come off worse. The healing will take time but all will be well in due course.'

'That's a great relief. But she looks terrible, she's so pale.'

'That's shock I'm afraid, and loss of blood of course. There again she will get over that with rest and good nursing.'

'You said good news first. Does that mean there's something you haven't told me yet?'

'Yes,' the doctor hesitated and then continued, 'I'm afraid she has lost the baby.'

Ramon's jaw dropped in shock.

'The baby,' he said numbly. He was quiet for a moment and then said,

187

'The loss of blood, yes, now I understand.'

'I think it would be kinder if you and your wife were to break that news to her, not straight away, but in a few days' time when she has regained some strength. I'm not evading any responsibility here I assure you, but you will be able to comfort her, whereas it may seem rather clinical and unfeeling coming from me at this stage. Do you agree on that?'

Ramon had blanched at the doctor's earlier words. He merely nodded.

'Are you all right Segñor López?'

'Yes, yes. What you just told me is...of course... a shock.' Ramon paused and then continued in a stilted formal tone, 'I am reassured by your words but am still feeling rather stunned at my daughter's... accident. I've been trying to stay awake beside her all night, so forgive me if I seem to be taking this impassively.'

'Not at all. Shock knocks the stuffing out of you. That and no sleep are enough to exhaust anyone. Now, if you wish you may go and sit beside Conchita again. But I would seriously advise you to get some sleep.

You want to be there when she is awake and able to talk to you, don't you?' he said smiling.

Ramon was beside Conchita when she opened her eyes.

'Papa?' she murmured.

'Yes, I'm here. Now don't worry. All is going to be well. The doctor tells me you may come home in two or three days.'

'Papa, there are things...I need... things I have to tell you.'

'I know, but not now Conchita. We just want you to get better as soon as possible so that we can all be together, and then we'll talk. But you're not to worry about anything. Understood?'

'Yes, Papa,' she murmured with tears running down her cheeks.

'Now, no tears, they won't help you to recover. I'm so happy to see you awake and talking, but you mustn't do too much of that either. You must rest and we will see you every day, until your return home. All right?'

'Papa?'

'Yes, what is it darling?'

'I love you.'

'And I love you too Conchita. We all love you. Carmen and Nana Isabella send their love to you. Juan Luis wants to know where you are. He keeps saying; 'Conchita come?' and we say, yes soon, and he smiles. So you see we are all waiting for you. I'm going to leave you now and let you sleep. I'll be back very soon but I need some sleep too,' he added with a smile.

Ramon leaned down and gently kissed her forehead. Looking over his shoulder as he left the room, he raised his hand in a little wave but Conchita had already drifted off to sleep, still under the effects of the sedation.

February 1956

Diary

I'm propped up in my bed and trying to write in my diary. I don't know where to begin and it's terribly hard to write. My shoulder is stiff and all strapped up but it's my side that's painful. When I breathe in it hurts, like a sharp knife jabbing me. That's my broken ribs Papa says. They're going to take some time to get better. That means I won't be able to ride for a while. But I can't anyway – Papa told me yesterday, Alvaro is dead. I cried and cried but it hurt so terribly when I sobbed that they gave me some painkillers and I fell asleep. They had to shoot him, his back legs were broken, smashed to pieces by that idiot. He's dead too. I should feel sorry but I don't, and now I'm feeling guilty because I'm not sorry. Everybody knows everything now, well Papa and Carmen anyway. We had a long talk last night and I told them about Miguel. I even told them about what he did to me. Both Papa and Carmen cried – we all cried. It was ghastly. But they held my hands and stroked my head. They couldn't hug me it hurt too much.

Daddy is coming over in a few days' time. Papa 'phoned him – poor Daddy, hearing bad news by telephone must be horrid. This is the second time Papa has asked Daddy to come over. It's only a month since he was here, but I didn't know that Papa had suggested he should come. I was so worried about what Papa would tell Daddy but he says he has explained about the accident. He told him it was a shady character, known to the police, who resented people with money and position because he had neither, and that he went around menacing and threatening people against whom he had a grudge.

He told him he thought we were prime targets because the vineyard was doing well and we had been in the news recently for winning a gold medal in an international wine competition. He said 'this man'

189

had been caught once, stealing, but the police didn't have enough evidence to convict him. They had known for some time that he was involved in crooked deals, even drugs. I didn't know any of this, I was shocked. But it explains first the lack and then the sudden appearance of money. I didn't know about the vineyard's award either, which just shows how disinterested I've been regarding what's been happening, right here under my nose!

He didn't tell him about the baby. I'm so relieved. He said Daddy didn't need to know that, it was between the three of us. He said it was all over, all that mattered now was that I had to try to forget the dreadful ordeal, get better and start a new life. I cried again, a lot.

I told them I hadn't realised at first that I was pregnant. I didn't notice when I missed my first monthly; it was all the excitement of Christmas and New Year and Daddy and Nettie coming —it took my mind off that terrible night and the fact that I didn't feel well. I just thought I had overindulged in all the Christmas fare. I wasn't ever sick so I didn't suspect anything until I realised I missed a second time. Carmen said she never suspected, which means that she never thought anything bad about me. Nevertheless, she had been worried about me and she and Papa had agreed to arrange for a health check-up for me. Well I've had one – but not quite the one they had in mind!

I've had a letter from Mummy. After all these years! I couldn't believe it, I didn't recognise her handwriting. She said how sorry she was to hear that I'd had an accident and she hoped I would get better soon. She said she'd started playing golf again and was enjoying the fresh air and exercise. She and Daddy had been on a golfing weekend at Blackpool and they had had a great time. Annie seems to have become more of a companion and friend to Mummy from what she tells me, though apparently she still calls her Mrs H. which I think is funny. They've got a girl to come in two days a week to help Annie with what Mummy calls the rough work, but she still does all the cooking and just recently made Mummy a lovely birthday cake. I had forgotten it was Mummy's birthday in February. I've had rather a lot on my plate, as they say! No, that's an excuse – I've just been so selfish and thoughtless these last few months. I did remember Nettie's birthday and have written to her but no special card or present from me, not yet anyway.

She's working terribly hard – as usual. Mummy says Nettie sends her love, lots of it, and promises to write as soon as she can. I shall write to her again – but not today, my hand is getting so tired and beginning to ache.

It was a super letter from Mummy with so much news. I never realised that Mummy could write so interestingly. There was just one thing she told me which is a bit worrying. Gramps is not at all well; he has heart trouble. It appears he's has had it for some time but nobody's ever mentioned it before. Granny is looking after him, she copes really well Mummy says, but Granny always did cope with things. I'll never forget that day I turned up at their house. Gramps didn't bat an eyelid when he saw me standing on their doorstep, like 'little orphan Annie' he told me later. He just handed me over to Granny knowing that she would be the one to sort out whatever it was that had brought me there. She was wonderful, she listened patiently as I tried to tell her through my tears that I was being sent away. She hadn't the foggiest notion of what I was talking about but she stayed calm and wasn't the least bit cross that I had turned up with a suitcase full of troubles so to speak. Gramps gave me Ovaltine in bed and told me a joke, which wasn't very funny, his jokes never are; it's the way he tells them that makes us laugh. I wish I could see them. I know Papa has often said I can go to Yorkshire for a visit if I want to. Perhaps when I'm better I'll go. I'm going to rest now and tomorrow I'll try to write some letters home. To Yorkshire I mean. .

32

Dear Con,

I'll begin with my good news, and that is that I have gained As in all three of my exams, I'm so relieved. This means that my place at Music College is assured. Aren't I lucky? I am really looking forward to the start in late September.

Now I'm afraid my next news is not so good. Gramps is quite poorly. He had a mild heart attack three days ago. At least, they tell me it was mild but I suspect it's worse than they're saying. He's only seventy-three. He's now very fragile and it's very hard for Granny to look after him. They're talking about Granny and Gramps coming to live with us. Daddy says they could convert the study into a downstairs bedroom so that the stairs wouldn't be a problem. There's lots of discussion going on. Granny doesn't want to leave their bungalow but she realises that she can't go on like this, it's taking too much out of her. Gramps is as amenable as ever and will do anything to reduce what he calls the burden on his 'darling Amelia'. They are so sweet, still in love after fifty years! I don't think I'll manage that.

By the way Mummy and Daddy are planning a surprise Golden Wedding Anniversary party for them but that's a secret. In any case, it's going to have to be a much quieter affair than they at first envisaged. Gramps couldn't cope with a crowd of people. Wouldn't it be fantastic if you could come? I know Daddy is going to write soon and tell you all about their plans but I'm telling you now to forewarn you, because I do so want you to come. You'll have time to make arrangements well in advance and in any case, I know you'll want to discuss it with Ramon and Carmen. But please don't tell Daddy I let the cat out of the bag – he would be disappointed not to be the one to tell you.

How are the studies going? Are you a fully fledged 'viniculturist' by now? You sounded so terribly knowledgeable when we last spoke on the 'phone. I think you're amazing to have thrown yourself into the family business after your terrible accident. I admire you for taking the wine-

192

tasting training course in the way that you did. All those men and just you! I bet you beat them into a cocked hat. I know you're good – Ramon told Daddy! He says you have a naturally discerning palate. I don't know one wine from the next, except one's red and the other's white! Next time I come you can start teaching me how to appreciate your Rioja. Ramon must be thrilled to have you working beside him.

I was really sorry to hear that you had lost Bella. You must still be feeling rather sad, she was such a good friend to you. I know – dogs can't talk! Well, some people think they can't anyway, but I know you used to have conversations with Bella after I left, that summer I came to stay with you when I had been ill. Gosh that seems such a long time ago. It is! Thank goodness you have Pablo, but no puppies for him.

Annie's banging the gong, that means dinner but I don't need to tell you that! Anyway, keep well. Give my love to everyone and lots for you,

Nettie
P.S. Pl...ea....se, do come to the party!

***

September 1958

Diary

I'm going to Yorkshire – at last. Ramon and Carmen were darlings and said I must on no account miss this special occasion. I feel a bit guilty because it will very soon be grape picking time and all hell is let loose here. I'm not putting on airs when I say that I'm needed; I know that I'm useful. They told me to stay as long as I like but I've arranged for just a week. I haven't seen Mummy for seven years and I'm rather apprehensive about how we'll get on. I know I've changed such a lot, and I don't just mean my looks! Nettie says I mustn't worry, Mummy told her she's looking forward to my arrival, in fact she even said she was excited. Wow! Yes, I'm excited too.

Daddy's going to meet me at the train station. He offered to drive to Heathrow but I reminded him that I'm twenty one, not a child anymore,

193

and I can manage perfectly well to catch a train. It was generous of him nonetheless.

Of course I haven't seen Granny and Gramps for years either. I expect I shall see a great change in them, and they in me.

I'm not taking any wine with me, just some Turrón, that delicious almond nougat. Carmen has given me some almonds and a chunk of Manchego cheese. I hope it doesn't smell – it's all wrapped up in one of my sweaters! I told them I can't carry any more. It's so kind of them all to want to send presents. Of course I've got lots of photos too. There's an absolute beauty of Juan Luis astride his pony, looking very important. At five years old he's already a good looking boy, he's going to knock the girls flat in just a few years' time. How could I have ever hated him? He's a darling.

I've packed, following Nettie's instructions about making sure I take some warm clothes. 'Don't forget late September can be chilly here, not like in Haro', she said. I don't care what the weather is like. I just want to see everybody again.

***

'Connie, you look wonderful. How that green dress suits you. You are positively radiant. Come and sit next to me, I want to hug you and not let go.'

Conchita laughed at Amelia Hampton's enthusiasm, happy at the use of her childhood name.

'You hugged me lots yesterday, Granny, but it will never be enough. Isn't it wonderful to be all together again? You know, I was a little afraid about how it would all work out. I wasn't sure if…well, I think you know what I'm trying to say.'

'I do and there's no harm in saying it. Mummy does look well doesn't she? And she has hugged you lots too, I saw her. She's happy again, happier than I've ever seen her. Heartbreaks need time to mend, you know that, and I do think your mother's heart was broken, long ago. You've both been through the most terrible anguish but you have come through it.'

'You know Granny, I still don't know the ins and outs of the whole thing. I'm hoping that one day Mummy might be able to tell me. I have got over it now, you're right, but sometimes there's a little niggle at the back of my mind. One day, perhaps it will all come clear. But for now, I want to hear about Gramps, tell me if you can.'

'There's not much to tell my dear. His heart is weak but providing he doesn't over exert himself he...well to put not too fine a point on it... he'll last a bit longer.'

'I'm so glad you're going to live with Mummy and Daddy. I know it's sad for you to leave your lovely little bungalow but you'd get exhausted if you went on coping by yourself for much longer.'

'Yes, it's the sensible thing to do. As soon as we've had a little respite after the party we're going to move in, but I'll be glad when it's all over. Everything is ready; the bedroom, a new bathroom and even a small sitting area with our own television. Mummy and Daddy have been so generous to us.'

'Of course, why wouldn't they be? You're treasures you two, did you know that? I've missed you so Granny, though I have to say I've been very lucky to find I have another very nice grandmother. Nana Isabella is very good to me and has been a real help throughout my – shall we call them – difficulties? Anyway, you know from my letters that I'm now very happy. I really could talk to you for hours Granny and I shall when you move in, because I'm going to be here for a few days. I'm so glad of that; I shall be able to help you. But now I must go and find Gramps.'

'Off you go. I'm going to talk to Annie, bless her. She's a godsend.'

Charles Hampton was in a wheelchair which Garnet kept pushing around so that he could talk to the guests one by one. He was dressed in a smart suit and colourful tie. Connie couldn't remember if she had ever seen him dressed like this before. She always visualised him wearing his favourite clothes, a soft woolly cardigan and corduroy trousers. Despite his illness he sat upright in the chair with his military bearing from long ago. He had kept his neatly clipped moustache, it still gave him that air of authority which he had always had despite his casual clothes. His face was thinner which aged him, and there was less of his wavy grey hair than the last time Connie had seen him. His gentleness was still there and very soon Connie discovered his jokes were just as amusing as they had always been, but not in quite the way he intended.

Indeed, Flora did look well. Relaxed and smiling happily, she was being the most attentive hostess, moving round amongst the twenty-five guests, making sure everyone had eaten well and was enjoying a glass of wine. Connie was thrilled that the week before her departure Ramon had arranged for three cases of a Gran Reserva to be despatched by special courier. 'It's a little something of your life here for you to give for the celebration.' She smiled to herself; she could hear Ramon telling her; 'Now Conchita, an excellent vintage; having spent two years in

195

barrel, then three years in bottle, eventually released after six years.'
Now she listened and what's more remembered.

Flora had greeted Connie on the day of her arrival, with a smile and
her arms outstretched. Connie could not remember when her mother
had ever approached her in such a friendly even loving manner; it
momentarily startled Connie.

'It's been a long time Connie. I'm so glad you've come. Until
Granny and Gramps' party is over we're not going to have much time
to talk, but after...shall we get together?'

Connie was bowled over by the warmth of her mother's welcome
and said,

'I'd like that.' It would seem that Nettie's comment was right, her
mother was a different person. Connie thought she was going to like
this one much more.

Amelia and Charles' move into their new 'apartment', as it became
known, took place two days later. They retired to bed early soon after
the family dinner and the special wine. They were tired after all the
exertion and excitement of the day's proceedings. As they settled down
in bed Connie went in to say goodnight and then returned to the sitting
room where Philip, Flora and Garnet were enjoying a glass of Bodega
Lopez Rioja. They too were tired after all their hard work, even though
the bulk of the furniture removing and the emptying of the packing
cases had been carried out by a professional removal firm.

'Come in Connie and sit down. How about a glass of wine? Connie
nodded. It was strange sitting there with her sister and parents just as
though nothing had ever happened between them. Connie thought it
must be rather like the experience of someone having lost their memory
for the last eight years, and then suddenly remembering who these
people were. Lost years, she wondered what she would have done
during that time if she had never gone to Spain.

Her thoughts were interrupted as Garnet stood up and moved
towards the piano.

'What would you like?' she asked.

'Chopin,' came Connie's immediate reply. The Nocturne in E flat
was the piece she always thought of when she visualised Nettie playing.
It was one of the pieces she had played for Ramon and Carmen on that
first visit to Haro. They sat in silence enjoying the music and each
other's company. Garnet rose,

'That's all for tonight. I think I'll go to bed. I'm really quite tired
and I have to get up early tomorrow. It's the first of my auditions
tomorrow.'

'My gosh, Garnet. I'd forgotten. And you've done nothing but work these past few days. Will you be all right?'

'I hope so,' she said laughing.' She kissed Flora and then Philip.

'Might be awake when you come up Connie. But if not, we can talk tomorrow.'

Philip rose as Garnet wished them goodnight.

'I'll just go and check that Mother and Father are settled,' he said following Garnet out of the room.

Connie looked across at her Mother and wondered how they were going to begin to talk to one another after all these years. She waited, after all it was Flora who had suggested the get-together to talk. But with a faint smile Flora just looked at Connie without speaking.

'How are you Ma? Are you quite well now?' Connie began nervously.

'Yes, I've been well for some time now,' she said and was silent again, still looking at Connie with the smile.

'I wrote to you Ma,' she said and then suddenly realised how she had addressed her Mother.

'Oh I'm sorry, I forgot, I mean Mummy. You never liked me to call you Ma did you?'

To Connie's amazement Flora laughed.

'How silly of me,' she said. 'I did a lot of silly things didn't I?' she paused, 'And some very unkind things too.'

Connie didn't know what to say or if Flora was even expecting a reply, for she looked away towards the window and even though the curtains were drawn against the dark night, she fixed her eyes on them. Connie was reminded of how she used to stand in the bay window and gaze out but never seeming to see anything beyond the glass.

'I'm sorry Connie, for those times,' she said continuing to stare at the curtains. 'I've been hoping that one day I could say that to you. I can never make it up to you but – well, do you think it would be possible for us to start a new relationship?' She turned back to Connie. 'Is it possible for an estranged mother and daughter to start again? Could we pretend we have only just met and begin, perhaps, to like each other?'

Flora said all this almost in one breath and leaned forward with her last question as though asking a great favour of Connie.

'I think we might Ma…Mummy.'

'Oh forget the Ma thing,' she said quickly. 'You know, I think I quite like it. It's become special, it's you. What do you think anyway?'

'I think – we could try. I expect Daddy's told you I was a rebel teenager and gave Papa and Carmen a lot of trouble. But I've improved

197

a lot since then,' she said laughing. 'I think the accident had something to do with it. I've certainly grown up you might say. Yes, we've got to try, both of us, from now on. It might take a little time, we've a few years to catch up on, but this is a good time to start, isn't it?

Connie was near to tears but as Philip strode into the room with a wide grin, she was able to recover her self-control. She had desperately not wanted the conversation to turn into an emotional scene. Nevertheless, she was thankful that the first tentative rapprochement with her Mother was over.

***

Connie spent the whole morning with her grandparents the next day, fulfilling her promise to help them arrange their belongings. Connie unwrapped, Amelia put things away in cupboards and drawers, finding appropriate places for their precious ornaments, and Charles gave them instructions! It was a happy interlude.

Garnet returned in the late afternoon, just in time for tea and fairy cakes.

'I'll get fat, living here,' Charles joked. 'All these cakes every day.'

'Well Mr 'ampton, you don't have to eat them,' Annie said, winking at Amelia. It was clear that the two women were already settling into an easy relationship, developing a rapport that would be pleasant for both of them.

***

October 1958

Diary

I can't believe how quickly that week passed. It's like a dream. So many wonderful things happened; Nettie launched on her music studies; Granny and Gramps settled in a safe haven and I saw for myself how changed Mummy is. I can't help it but I have to say that I feel, one day, I shall love her, but not just yet. Am I going to discover the real Mother I didn't have as a child? As we said to each other it's going to take time. I think I have to learn to like her first. She seemed happy and loving towards Daddy and I liked her for that. She was patient and kind to Granny and Gramps too, they deserve it, they stood by her through her illness. They were so saddened by the crumbling of our family, but not once in their letters to me, did they blame her. They came to terms with it, as time went by, and in so doing showed her that it was possible to overcome the unhappiness that had enveloped the whole family.

We are a family again. Granny and Gramps' Golden Wedding Anniversary was more than a celebration for them; it brought about the reconciliation between Mummy and me. I am grateful for that. From now on I shall write to Mummy more naturally and with much more sincerity. I'm hoping that we shall get to know one another through our letters. I'm looking forward to hearing from her.

33

Diary

The years seem to go by so quickly, I can't believe we're organising Christmas already. Papa and Carmen have decided to have the usual dinner on Christmas Eve, as if there was any decision to be made! We're all frantically dressing up the house and the tree. Juan Luis is as keen to trim the tree as ever. There'll be no problem of his trying to reach up to put the star on the topmost branch this year; he has grown so much in the last few months. I remember Carmen and I dressing the tree together when Juan Luis was only two years old, and worrying about his enquiring little fingers getting into all the boxes of ornaments. He thinks he's quite grown up now at nearly ten, and is absolutely certain he's going to be allowed to stay up 'all night'. If he does he'll be alone, not one of us manages to stay awake until dawn!

I must go and help Ana Maria in the kitchen.

***

The activity in the kitchen was hectic. Ana Maria was bustling around giving instructions to Carmen. It said something for Ana Maria's acceptance that she could no longer manage to cater for such a large gathering, that she had allowed Carmen into the kitchen in the first place.

'*Hola*, Conchita. Where've you been? We need you in here. Now get over there and stir this whilst I show Carmen how to make this sauce.'

Carmen raised her eyebrows and gave a sideways glance at Conchita who caught the look and smiled back. Carmen knew well enough how to cook but throughout the eleven years that she and Ramon had been married she was only allowed in the kitchen when Ana Maria had a day off, or when Carmen absolutely insisted in making something for a special occasion. But things were changing; Ana Maria herself and the whole family knew that it wouldn't be long before she was kindly established in a small house in the village, where she could meet her friends and enjoy a well-deserved retirement.

'So, I need to know, how many at the table tomorrow?' Ana Maria asked.

'The usual,' Carmen replied. 'Well no, there's a sad exception; Rodrigo's wife, Adelita. But you all know about that tragedy, Rodrigo losing not only a second child but also his wife'.

'What happened exactly?' Conchita said.

'The baby was premature and there were complications at the birth. Catarina was heartbroken, she'd been looking forward to having a brother or sister. Rodrigo couldn't bring himself to join us without Adelita. We are all so thrilled that he is coming this year and bringing Catarina with him.'

It was some time since Conchita had seen Rodrigo and family but she did remember their excitement at the prospect of another child. They had so wanted a large family but Rodrigo's wife Adelita was not in the best of health and had almost died when Catarina was born. Their doctor had advised that she may not conceive again and so what seemed like a miracle turned into a tragedy. Rodrigo was such a gentle and kind man and the loss of his wife and child had all but broken him. Although Ramon and Carmen had nursed him back from a depression and included him and Catarina in all their family events, he had found it too much to join them for the Christmas dinner. Now three years later his sense of humour and sparkling eyes had returned and he was once more joining the Christmas Eve dinner.

Conchita was quiet for a moment, remembering that she too had briefly carried a child. She pushed the thought aside.

'How old is Catarina? She must be what – about twelve now?'

'Yes, she lives with her grandparents, in Logrono. It was too difficult for Rodrigo to look after her, travelling so much on business as he does. Along with Catarina there will be Luisa and Xavier, Rodrigo's parents.'

'I just love these events, the enormous table seating so many people. It's such fun. It happens in England too, everybody getting together at Christmas and New Year, following the traditions, eating mince pies and Christmas pudding.'

'What on earth are 'min- spies'? Carmen said frowning.

'M-I-N-C-E pies' laughed Conchita. It's a kind of sweet tart with…'

'Yes, yes, this is all very well, talking, talking. Never mind this 'spies'. You haven't answered my question! How many people will be sitting down at this enormous table?'

Ana Maria was not as tolerant as she used to be. Some of the joy of cooking and serving had left her in worrying about whether it would be as good as it ought to be. She was so proud it was difficult to give her help, in her eyes the kitchen was still her domain and she ruled.

'Conchita, go and write down everyone's name. Your Papa will be wanting to make a seating plan so it'll come in handy. *Rapido*!' Ana Maria called after her, scowling. 'Then come back here and do some more mixing. I told you, we need you.'

Conchita scurried away laughing but was back within five minutes with the list drawn up.

'*Vale*, OK – the number is…..twenty-two!'

'*Oh mi Dios*! It gets more every year,' Ana Maria exclaimed.

Conchita and Carmen burst out laughing but Ana Maria couldn't see the funny side of it. To her this was no joke, it meant a lot of work.

However, she was not left with all the chores, nor all the responsibility, Carmen and Conchita saw to that, they worked alongside her and at one point even Juan Luis arrived to give a helping hand.

***

Then came Los Reyes, The Three Kings' Day, when Juan Luis as a small boy had traditionally placed his shoes on the doorstep. This year he felt he was quite old enough to dine with the adults on Christmas Eve and stay up into the small hours of the morning, but he was not too old to expect his shoes to be filled with gifts at Epiphany!

Ramon, Carmen, Conchita and Juan Luis were dining one evening, happy to be the small family cosily seated round the table. There had been so much feasting and excitement after the Christmas and New Year events it was a pleasant change to dine calmly and quietly together. It was Juan Luis who upset the composure of their meal.

'Do you like Rodrigo Conchita?'

'What? What do you mean? I – well, yes I like him. He's a very nice person, isn't he Papa?' Ramon nodded and looking at Carmen, he smiled.

'I mean, do you like him a lot? You seemed to be talking to him all the time at the Christmas dinner.'

Conchita was ruffled by the young but observant Juan Luis' words. She squared her shoulders, and sitting up straight, she said rather defensively,

'Well, of course I talked to him. I was only being polite. What are you smiling at Papa?' Conchita's unusually brusque tone gave away some feelings which she had barely acknowledged herself.

'Nothing at all, my dear. One can smile, can't one?'

Carmen touched Juan Luis on the arm and said, 'Just be quiet and eat your dinner darling. You must go to bed early tonight, you've had very little sleep these last two weeks and you'll be back at school in a few days' time. We don't want you falling asleep at your desk.'

Juan Luis was a little annoyed that the conversation had turned away from Conchita and had focussed on him. He finished his meal without another word and asked to be excused from the table.

No sooner had he left than Ramon took up the subject of Rodrigo.

'It's true, he is a very nice person Conchita. I like him enormously, always have. We've been good friends for a long time.'

'Who are we talking about now?' Conchita said with an affected indifference.

'Why, Rodrigo of course. Don't you agree my dear?'

Conchita was flustered again and pretended not to understand his question.

'Agree with what Papa?'

'Rodrigo, we're talking about Rodrigo and what a dependable and honourable person he is. Quite charismatic too, and now that he is eligible again you might say, he's much in demand at dinners and parties. All the single ladies in the area have fixed their eyes on him.'

Conchita turned her head, trying to hide the rising colour in her cheeks, which revealed her feelings better than any words. She was embarrassed that at twenty-four years old she found herself responding to her father's deliberate teasing and evident matchmaking. She recovered her composure slightly by turning her embarrassment into attack.

'What are you doing Papa, trying to sell him to me?

'Well you have to admit he's a good catch. Don't you agree?'

'Yes, of course. He's very nice,'

'That's good, because he has a soft spot for you.'

'Well, let's hope Conchita has a soft spot for him,' laughed Carmen.

'When you two have finished your matchmaking,' Conchita began in an agitated tone, 'I'll.......'

'Yes?' Ramon said, laughing at Conchita. 'Darling, we're teasing you. Juan Luis was right, you did spend most of the evening talking to him. But it's true, he does like you, you know. Rather a lot, I think.'

'Well, to tell you the truth I actually like him, rather a lot!'

***

January 1964

Diary

It's to be a spring wedding. It should be warm and bright with plenty of blossom out. Rodrigo wanted us to marry shortly after our engagement, which we haven't actually announced - only immediate family know as yet. I haven't even told Ma and Daddy and now Papa says he has already sent them an invitation! I wish he had let me speak to them first, but it's done now, I hope it's a nice surprise rather than a shock.

We're supposed to be having a quiet wedding. At least that's the plan but Papa and Carmen's ideas are running away with them, again! I've asked Catarina if she will be my bridesmaid and she is delighted. Juan Luis wants to play a part too, he says can he be an attendant. I'm sure he'll figure in the proceedings somewhere.

Papa says the rest of the invitations are being been sent out this week and I'm already looking forward to the replies arriving, it's really exciting. I'm so happy!

***

Flora picked up the post from the door mat and recognising the Spanish stamp on the envelope, she called out to Philip.

'There's a letter from Connie. It looks rather exciting.'

She walked through the hall into the kitchen and sat down at the pine kitchen table with Philip and Annie. She no longer had breakfast in bed, but joined them for coffee and toast every morning. She handed over the envelope to Philip who laid it beside his plate.

'Go on, open it now, it looks exciting,' she said again.

'It's not from Connie,' he said pulling out the silver edged card. 'It's from Ramon and Carmen.' He paused and waved the contents teasingly.

'It's an invitation.'

'Invitation? Goodness, could they be inviting us for a holiday? That would be nice.'

'No; they are inviting us to a wedding on the 26th of April,' he said with a wide smile.

'A wedding?'

'Are you ready?' Philip asked Flora with an ever widening grin. Flora nodded but looked perplexed.

'Connie's,' he said simply. Flora lifted her hands in exclamation, forgetting she had a cup in her hand she sent the coffee in all directions.

'Flora, what are you doing?' he demanded, laughing at her.

'Never mind that, it's only coffee. Let me see, let me see. Oh Connie, to be married. I told you it was exciting news. I just knew it.'

'Well, that's wonderful,' Annie said. 'I'm right pleased for 'er.'

'When, where, oh Philip, we will go, won't we?'

'Yes, I think so. Though we need to think about......'

'Excuse me Mr H. but I think I know what you're going to say.' Annie interrupted.

'It's your mother and father your thinking about, isn't it? Well there's no need to worry on that account. I'm 'ere and can perfectly well keep an eye on things. You know Amelia and I – excuse me Mr H but she insisted I call her Amelia- we get on really well and we can cope with... well, with whatever comes along. So you mustn't think twice about it. You must accept right away.'

'Annie, you're a godsend. Thank you for that. I know we couldn't leave them in more capable hands.'

'Well between you, you seem to have made the decision. As Annie says, I must accept right away.'

'Eh Mr H. you know I didn't mean that rudely. I'm that excited for you and for Connie. My little Connie getting married, I can't believe it.'

'Not so little anymore Annie, a grown woman.'

'I must get down to Brown, Muffs and look for an outfit. April, it should be quite warm, don't you think?'

'Here we go, you and your Brown, Muffs. Any excuse for new clothes,' Philip said giving Annie a mock doleful look. Annie laughed but in Flora's defence said,

'Nay Mr H. this is one time Mrs H has to have something really special I'd say.'

'Mm, enough of you ladies ganging up on me. I'm off to work.' He rose to leave the kitchen.

'Philip, you will reply immediately, won't you?' Flora asked anxiously.

'Immediately,' he said, 'never fear.' He gave Flora a light kiss on the cheek and with a wave he left her and Annie to launch into what he knew would be a discussion about wedding outfits and hats.

34

May 1964

Garnet gave the operator the number of her parents' house in Yorkshire. She was holding the folded pamphlet in her left hand, a little crumpled but still in one piece. She replaced the receiver and waited for the operator to call back with the connection.

'I shall keep this,' she whispered to herself, 'for the rest of my life, to remind me of this wonderful night and my first major role.'

She read again 'La Scala, Milan'. Underneath in bold text was the title of the opera; 'The Marriage of Figaro'. Her eyes sought her own name in the list of performers;

'Garnet Hampton as Susanna'

She paused and smiled to herself letting her eyes drop to the last, but for her the most important name;

'With the celebrated English Conductor
Jonathan Birch'

All the hard work was over, the singing practices, the rehearsals, and now the excitement of this last performance. She could at last look forward to two whole weeks of unwinding, relaxing, a little sight-seeing, but more than anything -spending time with Jonathan. First the call home, as promised.

***

It was after midnight when the telephone rang. Philip had stayed up in anticipation of the call. He felt sure Garnet would ring as soon as the performance was over.

'Daddy? It's me.'

'Garnet, we've thinking about you all day and especially this evening. How did it go?'

'Oh Daddy, it was wonderful. The applause was non-stop, we had six curtain calls. They just wouldn't let us go. It was so exciting.'

'I'm so glad. I'd have given anything to hear you in your first major role. If only it had been broadcast we could have listened to it on the wireless. Next time Garnet, we are coming to hear you, no matter where it is.'

'None of the last night performances I've been in over the last three years have been like this one. The audience went crazy, they called us back again and again and the applause went on forever. In the end the producer gave a little speech and politely reminded everyone that we were tired after six weeks and twenty four performances. More applause broke out until he raised his hands and said,

'So sadly, ladies and gentlemen, now you must let them go.'

It was terribly emotional. So I'm really ready for my two weeks' break. I shall start rehearsing soon after that for La Cenereltera, it sticks quite well to the fairy story Cinderella that we used to ask Annie to read to us. But you'll never guess where it's to be performed. Covent Garden! That means that the whole family will be able to come to that.'

'My words, they don't give you much of a respite do they?'

'It's not much of a holiday, I know, but I'm rising up the ladder Daddy so I must accept what comes along. I'm terribly lucky to have got this next part. But don't worry, Jonathan...our conductor, and I, are going to Paris for a few days. He's going to the States soon so we shan't see much of one another for a while. He's very nice, you'd like him Daddy.'

'That sounds … er… interesting sweetheart. When did you meet him?'

'When we started the rehearsals for this production, about four months ago. But we've had to keep the relationship hush-hush. The producer doesn't like members of the company hobnobbing, as he calls it.'

'Tell me, this sounds serious. Is it?'

'I think … yes, I think it is. But don't tell anybody just yet, will you? I'd like you all to meet him first, sometime soon I hope.'

'Count on it, not a word to man nor beast!' Philip said in a stage whisper. Garnet laughed.

208

'I must go now, Jonathan is waiting for me. We're going to have a late supper with everyone, and a glass of champagne. I'll drink to your health. Give my love to everyone.'

'Mummy said to tell you she's sorry she couldn't stay up to speak to you but she sends her love. Granny and Gramps are asleep but I'll tell them in the morning. Have a good time. Goodnight and God bless.'

***

It was midday when Garnet and Jonathan disembarked from the aeroplane on the Sunday morning at Le Bourget airport. It was a surprisingly warm and sunny day in late April. They held hands tightly as they walked from the plane to the main building, as though afraid of losing one another in the melée of passengers pushing forward to Passport Control.

Jonathan's surprise waiting for Garnet was that he had already booked a charming hotel just outside the city. On arrival she gasped with pleasure, it was a romantic location and suited their mood perfectly.

'How did you know about this place?' she asked Jonathan as they settled into their beautifully appointed room.

'Oh, I have my informants,' he teased her, smiling.

'You haven't been here before, have you? Perhaps you bring all your lovers here?'

'I do not!' he said indignantly. 'I haven't had a 'lover' as you call it, for three years.'

'Jonathan - I'm sorry. I was only kidding. I didn't mean anything by it. Oh gosh what a dreadful thing to say! Please forgive me?'

'Don't be so dramatic darling, you're not on the stage now,' he mocked. 'It's all right. I just want you to know that you are special,' Jonathan said taking her in his arms.

'And you to me. I love you Jonathan, very much.'

'Good, that settles that,' he said. Garnet was taken aback by his change of tone, she frowned. 'Now, we are going to make the most of these few days; the three R's! You know what they are, of course? Rest, relax, and read.'

'Oh my God, is that all?' Garnet said still rather bewildered by the sudden switch from the romantic moment to this practical approach.

'Yes absolutely all. It goes like this: the 'resting' is in bed, in between any ...er activity! The 'relaxing' is talking in bed, to each other, about each other. The 'reading' is studying the dinner menu lying on, or in, the bed in each other's arms. How does that suit you?'

'You idiot! It sounds wonderful. When do we start?'

'Now!' he said. 'We need to rest!'

Four days passed blissfully with trips to the Left Bank, the Eiffel Tower, dinner on a Bateau Mouche and plenty of the three R's routine. It was on the fifth day, lying on the bed before changing for dinner, that Jonathan produced something other than the menu to read.

'What have you got there?' Garnet asked.

'I'm not sure I should let you read it, at least not until I've asked you a question,' he said holding back the official looking envelope.

'Ooh, it sounds mighty serious,' Garnet said trying to look solemn.

'It is serious, very serious. I'm serious,' he said taking her left hand in his and kissing each of her fingers. 'Will you marry me?'

Garnet sat up. 'You can't…..I mean, we can't. We haven't known one another very long. How can you be sure?'

'Answer my question first and then I'll answer yours,' he said sitting up beside her.

'The answer is…,' she began and then whispered, 'Yes.'

'And my answer is, how long we've known one another is irrelevant. How much we love one another is the important factor. And I love you more than I've ever loved anyone. What about you?'

'The same,' she whispered again.

'Then we should get married straight away, don't you think?'

'Yes, oh yes. But these things take time, darling.'

'Not if you are in possession of this,' he said, passing her the envelope he had held back. She tore it open. 'Steady, don't rip it open. We can't get another one in a hurry.'

She gasped. In her hand was a Special Marriage Licence. Garnet sat absolutely still staring at the piece of paper.

'I'm a wretch, I've sprung it on you, haven't I? I've had the Licence in my case all the time but I couldn't pluck up the courage to ask you until I realised time was running out. I've been so afraid you would say no.'

Garnet sat very still holding up the Licence in front of her, as though reading a book. She looked up at Jonathan.

'When?' was all she said.

'It's dated for the day after tomorrow. It's all arranged at the British Embassy, here in Paris,' he went on hurriedly. 'I've had the licence for over a week, it's been burning a hole in my case. I made the bookings as soon as it was organised. It was presumptuous of me, I know, but I love you so. Whatever would I have done if you had said no? I'm sorry, I should have given you time to think, and to get ready.'

'What is there for me to do to get ready? No white dress, no cake, no guests….. not like Connie's wedding. Oh I'm so longing to hear all about that. You know how beside myself I was when I realised I couldn't be there.'

Garnet found herself filling the moments between Jonathan's bolt from the blue and the need for her to say it was fine, she didn't need all the trimmings, she didn't mind. But the words, any words, didn't come immediately. Jonathan felt the uncertainty.

'I realise you will have to forego such a lot to marry like this and I'm worried that in the future you will wish you had had a day like your sister's. I'm afraid that you might feel you're missing out on, you know, the frothy white wedding dress and the bridesmaids and, and... all the trappings. Do you think you will?'

'No, my love. All I want is to be your wife. That's enough for me. Perhaps my family might be disappointed at not being present but I think they won't mind too much when they see how happy I am. We'll make it up to them - perhaps at some later date, when you come back from New York, we can have a quiet family gathering and a church blessing so that they...we, all of us together, will have been a part of our coming together.'

'You're right darling. You are so thoughtful and generous. You're a gem, true to your name.'

'But Jonathan, how did you know what to do, how to make all the arrangements?'

'I did my homework,' he said smiling. 'And no, I've not been married there before,' he couldn't help teasing.

'Oh Jonathan, please don't tease me about that.'

'So, one more day and though you will be Garnet Hampton, the celebrated soprano, you will also be Mrs Jonathan Birch, my wife.' They waltzed around the room with their arms around each other.

***

The final day of their stay in Paris as Garnet Hampton and Jonathan Birch, was spent in the morning checking the formalities and in the afternoon out walking through the Bois de Boulogne where they sat and enjoyed the fresh greenery and the flowers of the early spring, and watched the Parisians walking by.

'I hate to be a wet blanket,' Jonathan began, breaking the companionable silence that reigned between them. 'But, we have to start planning ahead.'

'I know. We have to come down to earth. Not just yet though, a few more hours, I'm living in Paradise and I don't want to return to earthly matters.'

'It's more than that, it's not just our careers I had in mind. We haven't got much time left together and I've been thinking…'

'Mmm, very dangerous stuff!' she said lying back on the grass with her hands behind her head. She closed her eyes and felt the warm sun on her face. Jonathan ignored her facetious remark and continued;

'I wondered - if, instead of staying here another two or three days after the ceremony, and before we each have to present ourselves at appointed places; we might fly to England together. We could go and visit your parents, that way I would meet them before I go off to the States. Would you like that?'

'Oh why didn't I think of that?' Garnet said, her serene mood leaving her in a flash.

'I'm being incredibly selfish, I'm just so happy I can't think of anything or anyone else but myself. But you're right. It's a wonderful idea. Oh, and I'll be able to hear all about the wedding, sooner than I thought and I expect there are heaps of photographs. So, practical husband to be, ground me! What do we do now?'

'Let's make our way back to the hotel and find out when there's a flight. As soon as we've organised something, you'd better telephone your mother and father and tell them we'll be on our way sometime during Tuesday. It wouldn't be fair just to turn up; too much of a shock.'

'I think the news that we're married is going to be something of a shock, without turning up on their doorstep unannounced. Two daughters married within the month is a bit much,' she mused.

'Is it going to be difficult, I mean, do you think they'll be angry?'

'Angry? Good heavens no! My father will be….well, I gave him a little hint that there was love in the air, but of course I didn't tell him I was going to get married. How could I? I didn't know myself, did I?'

'Do you always ask so many questions?' he said smiling up at her.

'Yes. When you meet Daddy, he'll tell you that I used to ask questions all the time. He teases me and says it's the one flaw in my otherwise perfect character. He's wrong about the perfect character and I'm afraid I've never got rid of the flaw.'

'I'm glad, I like you this way. It's not much of a flaw, and so far I can believe the perfect character bit.'

212

'You'll find out, I can be a demon.'

'Mmm, I like demons too,' he said laughing. 'Seriously, what about your mother what will she think about our haste?''

'Mummy will be delighted. On the other hand, neither of them have met you yet, have they? So maybe they won't be delighted,' she said laughing at his expression of unease. Jonathan jumped up and grabbed her round the waist.

'It's high time, I took you in hand, and gave you a wifely spanking,' he said.

'Ooh, yes please,' was her giggly response, accompanied by a long and ardent kiss.

***

It seemed to them that fate was being kind to them; the last two seats were available on a flight to Manchester on Tuesday late afternoon.

The evening before their departure Garnet telephoned home.

'Daddy, it's me again. I've got a surprise for you.'

'Well, this call is a surprise. Are you having a good time?'

'Yes, very good, you can't know how good. But Daddy, listen, I really do mean a surprise,' she hesitated and heard Philip draw in his breath.

'Go on,' he said.

'We're coming to visit you – I mean both of us. Jonathan wants to meet you as soon as possible, and before he goes off to the States on his tour. Is that all right?'

'Wonderful! The best surprise. When?'

'We leave Paris at sixteen thirty tomorrow afternoon and should arrive at Ringway at four fifteen local time. We'll make our own way to Harrogate on the train. I'm so looking forward to seeing you all. Granny and Gramps are all right, aren't they? I have more to tell which I hope won't be too much more of a surprise for everyone.'

'We're all fine and we'll look forward to whatever surprise you have in store for us. Take care. See you tomorrow.'

Garnet rang off to see Jonathan staring at her.

'You didn't tell him!' he said anxiously. 'That we're married, I mean. Were you scared that they would react badly?'

'Not at all,' she said smiling. 'I'm being selfish again, I just want to be with my family when we tell them. I want to see their faces and feel their kisses and hugs.'

The Hamptons were not given the opportunity the next day, to hear of Garnet's surprise and congratulate the happy couple, nor were they able to give them kisses and hugs. Fate had run out of kindness. The plane crashed on landing at Ringway airport in severe gale force winds. Pilot error was initially deemed to be the cause of the crash but no official opinion was being given until the black box was recovered and the investigation was complete.

Jonathan was dead, along with seventy three other passengers and the flying crew.

Shortly after the news reached Philip and Flora, that Garnet was in Manchester Royal Infirmary, Philip left Harrogate to drive to Manchester. Despite the fact that Garnet and Jonathan had been sitting together, she had escaped death.

Her injuries were grave but she was not in a critical condition. Philip arrived at the hospital and was taken to meet a doctor who took him into his office.

'Your daughter's right leg has compound fractures and some damage of the ankle joint in her left foot. She also has a deep gash on the forehead. Although these injuries are in themselves major, they are not life threatening and should, in time, heal without future complications. However, there is another matter which concerns me.' He looked hard at Philip as he spoke.

'As yet, she has not spoken a single word since the disaster. Of course, it's obvious that she is in shock and as she's in considerable pain she is sedated. But as far as we can tell she doesn't yet know that her husband was killed. It has never been mentioned. Under the circumstances we feel we cannot give her this news at the moment.'

'Husband? I didn't know…I mean….I'm sorry, I too am suffering from shock. I'm a little confused.'

'Of course. I think you should see her and I hope she will recognise you, it will comfort her. I would ask you though not to excite her. She is conscious but as I said sedated in order to prevent her disturbing the injured leg. If you are ready I will call a nurse to take you into the ward.'

***

Philip was not prepared for the sight of his daughter swathed in bandages across her forehead, a pulley system holding her right leg in a splint, and a drip tube into her left arm. He stopped before reaching the bed and took a deep breath. As he approached he could see Garnet was asleep. His eyes went straight to her hand and there he saw, on the fourth finger, the gold band glistening in its newness. He gently touched the finger.

As he sat down to wait Ramon came into his thoughts. He too had kept vigil beside a critically ill daughter, 'their' daughter, waiting for her to open her eyes with a glimmer of recognition. What a strange twist of fate that they should both go through the same painful experience. What Philip never knew was how similar were the cases of each of the two sisters.

Philip closed his eyes and for the first time in years he prayed.

35

Diary

The most ghastly thing has happened. Nettie is in hospital with awful injuries. Daddy 'phoned to tell me the news. He also told me that Jonathan was killed. Poor Nettie, she must be devastated.

Daddy says they will send her to Harrogate District Hospital as soon as her leg is out of traction. Then she can go home to convalesce.

It was sad enough that she couldn't come to our wedding, I know she was bitterly disappointed – we all were, but now this has to happen to her - just when she is becoming recognised as one of the best British sopranos. I know Mummy and Daddy will help her to recover from her injuries but what about losing Jonathan? How on earth is she going to come to terms with that?

I must stop this, it's making me cry. I must write to her straight away.

June 1964

My dearest Nettie

I was shocked when I heard the news from Mummy and Daddy. I can't tell you how I feel for you though I'm sure you'll think I can't possibly understand how much pain you are suffering to say nothing of grief. But I am suffering for you. We have always been so close that we feel for one another deeply. I'll never forget how you understood what it was like for me when I was sent to Spain and you suggested sending Bella for me. That was the most unselfish and caring deed. How can I do something like that for you? I want to help you but I am far away. Darling Rodrigo has said he doesn't mind if I go home to Harrogate – he is so unselfish – but when I suggested it to Daddy he thought it would be better to wait a while. Perhaps he's right, I'll come when you are out of hospital.

My dear Nettie, I know you can't write to me yet, but I do hope to hear from you soon. I only want to hear that you are beginning to get well. I will write again soon. In the meantime, all my love

Con

June 1964

Dear Connie

I have read your letter to Garnet, several times and I know she would thank you if she could. I'm sorry to tell you that she is still not speaking. When we ask her if she would like something she closes her eyes to tell us no or gives a slight nod if she means yes. Her head injury has now healed but she has a bright pink scar which we are told will fade in time. She holds my hand from time to time, but she does not smile and no tears fall. It's heart breaking to see our vibrant, happy daughter, always so full of the joys of living, unable to respond. The Consultant doesn't think there is any physical reason for her inability to speak, he puts it down to the trauma she has suffered. He's sure that in time she will recover but it could take months. We have to be patient.

Now that she is at home we are able to sit and talk to her every day, tell her what is going on, although there's not much to tell. We are very quiet here these days. Granny or Gramps, just the other side of the hallway, pop in to her room for ten minutes each day just to say hello and Annie is wonderful keeping her comfortable, gently helping her into a chair whilst she makes her bed, and then unobtrusively tidies the room. We have flowers in there all the time, you know how she loves bright colours. I often cut roses from my rose bed; red, deep apricot or bright yellow. By the way I planted some new ones – they have a special name – they are called 'Constance', what do you think of that?

Last week Vicky called, you probably remember her from school. She brought some photographs of them both when they were at Donnington's Prep. School, she thought it might stimulate Garnet a little but there was no response, not even a smile. Vicky was quite upset and I had to explain to her that Garnet is like this with all of us and that she most definitely would have enjoyed seeing her. Vicky's a sweety and has promised to come again.

I'm sorry this is such a depressing letter for you but I know that you are desperate for news of any kind. There is one good thing I can say; Garnet is eating well, thanks to Annie who goes to a lot of trouble to make delicious and tempting dishes. Daddy and I will 'phone you later this week to have a chat and let you know how she is progressing.

Thank goodness we were with you last month for your beautiful wedding. We talk about it often and the memories keep us going when we get a bit down. We really liked Rodrigo and he obviously adores you!

Why, oh why, have I never been to visit you before? After I recovered from my breakdown I could have come with Daddy, but I didn't. It was silly of me, but do you understand that I was a little afraid? I needn't have been. Ramon and Carmen were so kind and there was no resentment between us. And do you know when I started speaking Spanish again, just like that, I felt quite proud of myself. It was wonderful to feel that it had never left me, even if I was a bit rusty. Carmen was terribly impressed.

I felt so close to you when we had a little joke together, speaking Spanish quite naturally, and Daddy couldn't understand us. It was naughty of me but I actually enjoyed it.

We were never close Connie, as we should have been, were we? It was all my fault, I didn't allow myself to get close to you as a child because deep down I knew that I had committed the most cruel deception. Daddy was stunned when the truth came out and I allowed Ramon to force us into sending you to Spain. Never think that Daddy was weak for allowing this to happen, he was bewildered and at the time we both honestly believed there was nothing we could do to redress the legal complications. The realisation of what I had done to him and to you was what made me ill; guilt and remorse after years of holding onto the lie finally tipped me over the brink and into the breakdown.

Why am I telling you all this now? Perhaps it's because I lost you – for a while – and am so grateful to have you now. As I sit beside Garnet each day I realise we nearly lost her.

Granny is quite well but Gramps is not so good these days. He leads a very quiet life though he still manages to make one of his quaint jokes from time to time.

They all send their love, Annie too. I look forward to talking to you later this week.

Love Ma

July 1964

Dear Ma

Your letter made me cry, but I was so glad to have it. Thank you for all the things you said. And thank you both for the 'phone call. I will call you sometime soon, by which time I'm hoping you will have some positive news.

I have some nice news, our house is nearly ready. You know, the old stone house on the edge of the vineyard which Papa said he would have renovated for us? Rodrigo wanted to pay for it himself, he said it was only right and proper! But Papa said it could be our wedding present. I must say it's looking rather grand. It's bigger than I had envisaged - it has four bedrooms - I think we two are going to rattle around inside it! We shall have to fill it with large Spanish furniture to absorb the echoes! Rodrigo has some lovely pieces which belonged to his parents. Living in Rodrigo's small apartment has been useful in the short term, but we are really looking forward to moving in, arranging everything and having a bit more space. So you can see Ma, there'll be plenty of room for visitors!

When Nettie is well again it would be wonderful if all of you could come. I'll hope and pray for that. Back to work!

Hope you and Daddy are looking after yourselves too.

Lots of love
Connie

36

November 1964

Flora was waiting for Philip to come home from the bank. She had very nearly telephoned him and then decided it would be selfish to break sad news to him in the office. Instead she sought out Annie in the kitchen.

'Annie, are you busy? Sorry, that's a silly question, you're always busy.'

'Only doing a bit of ironing Mrs H. You look a bit bothered, is anything wrong?'

'Yes, I'm afraid so.'

Annie stopped pushing the iron up and down the sheet that was on the board, and stood the iron on its rest. She turned, picked up the kettle and filled it with water.

'Let's have a cuppa. We'll sit in the kitchen then we can have a little chat without being interrupted.'

By that, she meant they would not be overheard. Annie rightly presumed that whatever was troubling Flora, she had not yet mentioned to Philip's parents.

'Would you get the cups Mrs H while I mash the tea?' Annie asked more to cover the silence of the moments before they sat down at the pine table, than the need of help. Annie took a sip of her tea and waited.

'It's Connie,' Flora began. Annie looked up sharply.

'It's not...?' Annie began.

Flora nodded and her eyes filled with tears. 'She's lost the baby.'

'Eh, Mrs H. 'ow sad. When did you 'ear?'

'Rodrigo telephoned – that was him, just half an hour ago. I expect you heard the phone ring. I've been thinking of 'phoning Philip but decided that it's not fair to tell him whilst he's at work. I know he'll be upset.'

'Do you know what 'appened? I mean, she didn't fall, or anything like that?'

'No, she just started to haemorrhage yesterday evening. They called the doctor but he said he thought she'd lost too much blood and didn't hold out too much hope for the baby. They had to call him back again this morning and she's gone to hospital for a check-up.'

'That's a real shame. Poor lamb.'

'I shall have to go and tell Amelia and Charles, but I think I'll wait for Philip first.' As she spoke she heard Philip's keys turn in the lock and the front door open and then click closed.

'He's here, thank goodness,' sighed Flora.

Flora got up and opened the kitchen door, stepping into the hallway she signalled to Philip. He came straight through without taking off his coat.

'Darling, you look tearful. What is it?' Flora put a handkerchief to her face and gave a little sob.

'Oh Philip! Annie tell... I can't say it,' she said.

'Mr H. it's Connie, she's lost the baby I'm afraid.'

Philip stepped forward and took Flora in his arms, she was now crying openly. Annie turned away, not from embarrassment, she was now quite used to seeing the affection that existed between Flora and Philip. Tears were trickling down her cheeks too. Philip saw the cups on the table and said,

'I'll join you in a cup, please Annie.'

Flora stopped crying and in a shaky voice said,

'Rodrigo telephoned and he's going to ring again later this evening after he's seen Connie. She's in the hospital – just to make sure everything is all right, he said.'

'In that case, we'll wait until we've heard from him before we say anything to mother and father.'

'What about Garnet? Should we tell her?'

'All in good time, I think not tonight though. You know she finds it difficult to get to sleep sometimes; the news might upset her and she would lie worrying through the night. She'll feel for Connie.'

It was as Philip said these words that the kitchen door slowly opened. Garnet was standing on the other side swaying on her crutches. She was frowning as though with concentration as she made to move into the kitchen. Flora jumped up and came round the table towards her as though to help her.

'We're just having a cup of tea Garnet. Would you like one?'

Garnet manoeuvred towards a chair and sat down, one of her crutches clattered to the floor. Annie took another cup and poured her some tea. Garnet looked from one to the other of them. Her expression was quite obviously a question but she made no sound.

'I think we should tell Garnet the news Flora,' Philip said quietly. Flora nodded. Garnet turned and looked directly at her father.

'We've had some rather upsetting news Garnet, from Rodrigo.' He paused and then went on, 'I'm sorry to tell you that Connie has lost the baby.'

There was silence for a moment and then Garnet slowly dropping her head, lay on her arm across the table. Flora stroked her hair gently, each one of them still not speaking. After a few moments Garnet raised her head, the tears shone on her cheeks. She slowly sat up.

'Con. My poor Con,' she said in a hoarse voice.

Annie gasped. Flora's hand flew to her mouth in shock as she heard the words; the first words Garnet had spoken since that dreadful day in May.

37

Diary

My God, what is Fate doing to this family? Nettie desperately ill and now I've lost the baby. I'm scared that what happened to me ages ago has done me some harm and I will never have a baby. I'm waiting for the doctor to come, he knows the full story and won't give away my secret, so I can ask him in all confidence. I think Carmen may be thinking on those lines too but she hasn't said a word.

Rodrigo is so comforting but I know he is sad and troubled. He's had more than enough of loss and grief. Thank goodness we are in our own house now and it's clean and tidy. What am I worrying about housework for? Rodrigo has taken on a young girl to help – I'm going to be spoiled!

Nana Isabella came to see me this morning. She has always been kind and supportive even when I was a brat. I asked her once why she had never reproached me for my behaviour, but she said 'We all make mistakes and we all have our little secrets'. For a second I wondered if she knew more than I thought but she wasn't looking at me when she said it, she was looking beyond me with a faraway look.

***

The knock on the door was barely audible. Conchita turned her head and saw the door slowly opening.

'Come in, whoever it is. I'm wide awake and longing for company.'

A large bunch of carnations made its appearance round the door followed closely by the smiling face of Isabella.

'I don't want to disturb you if you are resting.'

'I'm feeling fine and I want to get up but Rodrigo is being very strict. Only after the doctor's visit he said, that is providing I'm declared fit enough. Sit down next to me Nana.' Isabella laid the flowers on a table and sat beside the bed.

'Quite right too. You know a miscarriage is not exceptional, there's nothing to be unduly worried about but that doesn't meant to say you shouldn't take care.'

Isabella took Conchita's hand and began to stroke her fingers. She said,

'It wasn't meant to be this time Conchita. I have great faith in providence you know, the care and guardianship of God, or perhaps we could say that Nature takes care of things in her own way.'

'You're always so kind Nana, so wise in your advice. I don't understand how you put up with me during those awful years. I was such a monster. I don't know what happened, I still haven't worked it out. Why did I behave like that?'

'Don't try to analyse it my dear. It's in the past and you have come out of it all, the better person for it. We all have a past you know.'

Conchita looked at her and smiled.

'Not you Nana, you're a paragon of virtue. I mean it, I'm not mocking you.'

'Oh but you're wrong. Would you like to hear what a naughty girl I was?'

Isabella leaned back in her chair, her voice grew quieter and she turned her gaze again as though looking into the distance.

'I wasn't in love with my husband when I married him. That surprises you doesn't it Conchita? I know Papa has told you what a devoted couple we always were. When I was young, girls did not marry for love, their parents arranged a suitable match and woe betide any young lady who disobeyed. My parents had chosen a very eligible young man; he was handsome, intelligent and quite wealthy. He was also heir to a large bodega! What more could a girl ask for?

'My two sisters had married young and were not at all worried about whether they loved their husbands or not. 'That's life,' they said. 'You've just got to get on with it. And who cares as long as we've got money and position?' Their attitude horrified me.

'I have to admit I was a bit spoiled, coming several years after my sisters, I had had a lot of attention and at nineteen I thought I could do as I pleased. On this particular point my parents thought otherwise and we had a battle. Everything had been agreed with Luis' parents and, according to my mother and father, he was besotted with me. I didn't believe them, I thought how could he? he hardly knows me.

'For a whole year I resisted. What my parents didn't know was that I was in love with a young worker on the bodega, at least I thought I was! What brought me to my senses was seeing him with a girl from the village in a somewhat brazen embrace. That may sound harmless enough, but you see, he had told me he loved me, I was the only girl for him and of course I believed him. I realised how immature, how naive I was. I felt very stupid.'

Isabella turned her gaze and looked hard at Conchita.

'You see my dear, how similar we are. During your 'difficult' time I knew you were infatuated with someone, someone 'unsuitable', as I was once. No, don't worry, no-one has spoken to me about anything but I have eyes that see!' Tears began to run down Conchita's cheeks.

'But Nana, that's nothing, you don't know everything about what happened.'

'No, and I don't want to know. I say again, it's all in the past. And here you are happily married. And you will have children, all in good time. It's quite obvious you are in love with your husband whereas I, on the day I married Luis, did not love him.'

Isabella paused and smiled, she shook her head as though surprised at her own behaviour at that time.

'We had been married a year when one day I tripped and fell in the house. The doctor was called immediately and diagnosed a sprained ankle. Nothing serious at all, but oh dear me, Luis made such a fuss of me. I grew angry with him continually asking me all the time if I was in pain, what could he do to help? would I like something to eat or drink? I shouted at him – 'Go away, and leave me alone!'

'He did, for three days he didn't come near me. I had hurt him deeply. By this time I could walk and I hobbled my way to his office one morning to find him leaning on his desk with his head in his hands. He turned his face towards me and I was shocked. I had never seen such despair in a man's face. I felt ashamed.'

'He stood up and came towards me and then stopped. I was a little weak after my days of doing nothing and I began to sway. I thought I was going to fall and I cried out. Luis put out his arms and took hold of me. He cried, I could feel his tears against my ear, and running down my face. Oh dear, I think I'm going to cry now with the memory of it!'

'Oh Nana, it did all turn out all right didn't it? You did love him in the end?'

'Indeed I did, that was the turning point when I almost fell into his arms. Actually I fell in love.'

'I do wish I had known him. I think he would have been a wonderful *abuelo.* '

'He would have loved you Conchita, I know that.'

'I do have an English grandfather you know, Daddy's father, he's great fun, but not very well these days. I never knew my mother's parents. They never kept in touch with Mummy once she was married, I don't know why. There are quite a few things about our family that I don't understand.'

'We never understand everything in our lives Conchita. One has to learn to let go and enjoy the present.'

'Nana, you have been a tower of strength to me. I thank you for it. Like you, my Granny in Yorkshire listened and gave good advice. On the night I learned that Daddy was not my 'real' father, which I didn't understand at all, I ran away to Granny and Gramps. My disappearance caused some concern for a while but I didn't think of that at the time, all I could think of was my own misery and fear. Granny and Gramps, whatever they might have thought about the situation, just got on with supporting the whole family. They took it on the chin, as we say in English.'

'As you have with your life Conchita. All is going to be well, I have prayed for it and I will continue to do so. Now my dear, I'll leave you. You'll soon be up and about again. Come and see me when you can.'

As Isabella walked to the door there was another tentative knock. She opened it to find *Doctor Giraldez Cervera* waiting to come in.

'Conchita is waiting for you *Doctor Giraldez*, impatiently I have to say. She is longing to be up and bustling about again.'

'We'll see what we can do, *Señora Garcia de López*. Good day to you.'

November 1964

Diary

Doctor Giraldez has been to see me. I'm fine, I can get up and carry on – slowly for a day or two he says. I plucked up the courage to ask him if this has anything to do with the 'accident' I had. He shook his head and smiled. 'Not at all,' he said. 'This is yet another of life's little knocks.' He looked at me closely and said some people seem to get more than their fair share of knocks in life, but I am resilient and courageous he said. His words made me cry. Anyway, he says I need have no fears for the next time.

I'm longing to ride out and see the vines burgeoning with this season's fruit, if I don't get out immediately I'll miss it; they will be harvesting any day now. But no riding for a few weeks either. What's happened is sad, but in the end not serious.

226

Nettie is improving Ma says, she 'phones me frequently and keeps me up to date with news on Granny and Gramps as well. Ma and Daddy are hoping to pay us a visit in the New Year and bring Nettie too. Whoopee!

38

January 1965

The arrival of Philip, with Flora and Garnet was causing some excitement. Juan Luis kept asking questions about Flora and whether Garnet would be able to talk now and ride out with him.

Juan Luis knew that Flora was Conchita's mother and that Conchita had come to live with his father and mother in Spain when she was very young, before he was born. He had never questioned the situation, he had accepted that she was his sister but had never pondered over the fact that they had different mothers. Ramon and Carmen had not exactly concealed the truth from Juan Luis but had cloaked the explanation that his father was also Connie's father, in obscure terms. At the time it hadn't mattered to him; Conchita was his elder sister and he loved her. Now at twelve years old it still didn't seem important to him.

He soon found out that Garnet could talk and though he was encouraged to speak to her in English Carmen warned him not to overwhelm her.

'Now remember Juan Luis, you are not to tire Garnet, she has been very ill.'

'But Mama, you said I must speak English, so that I can become fluent. You said it will be good for me.'

'Indeed it will, but too much of *you* will not be good for *her*.'

Juan Luis spoke English quite well but he was determined to 'perfect' it, as he put it, as soon as possible, ready for the day when he could go to England and represent the bodega.

'I doubt if you are quite ready just yet to represent the family company in Britain, Juan Luis, but your enthusiasm does you credit,' his father had said kindly.

As for Flora, Juan Luis was swept away by her charm. She treated him as though he were a sensible young man whom she had known all

228

his life but not seen for some time. She asked him questions, listened to him attentively and flattered him.

'You speak very good English Juan Luis.'

Juan Luis was gracious and smiling, 'Ah but I *am* lucky, aren't I? My father speaks English like an Englishman,' he said proudly, 'and I do my homework otherwise he gets cross and won't let me work on the vines.'

'Quite right too,' she responded smiling. 'And I understand you know quite a lot about wine already, isn't that so?'

'Yes, but not enough yet, you see Fl...,' he hesitated, suddenly realising that he couldn't address this lady by her first name; it wouldn't be correct. He didn't remember even speaking to her at Conchita's wedding.

It was as though Flora had read his thoughts as she said,

'You know Juan Luis even though I am Connie's...I'm sorry, Conchita's mother, and she is your half sister, I am not really related to you. So let's decide between us how you should address me, shall we?'

'Yes please, but I don't really understand these relationships. Perhaps sometime you can explain it to me because I did ask Mama once and she just told me I don't need to understand it at my age. What's my age got to do with it?'

'One day, you will. In the meantime why don't you call me Flora and enjoy an extended family. What do you think?'

Juan Luis accepted Flora's words with the equanimity of an untroubled child, just as he had accepted the non-explanation of many things in his young life.

'Will Papa mind do you think, I mean, won't he think it a bit disrespectful?'

'Leave it to me, I'll tell him it was my choice. I'm sure he'll think it's a good idea. Now you were going to tell me something.'

Juan Luis launched into an explanation of his latest learning with regard to the making of their esteemed *Grand Reserva*. He spoke confidently, asking her for English words and phraseology when he grappled with the syntax. Not once did it strike the ingenuous, young Juan Luis as odd, that Flora was understanding everything when *he* spoke Spanish but at the same time was offering him translations in English with ease.

Diary

I can't believe Ma and Daddy have been and gone, their visit flew by, it really was too short. Listen to me, I sound ungrateful, when in fact I should be thrilled, indeed I am, because Nettie has stayed! Now Nettie has experienced her second New Year with us. I'm just so delighted that they came, it was all a wonderful surprise. There was such a lot of discussion as to whether Nettie would need medical care; her leg is weak though she doesn't have to lug that plaster around more, they took that off ages ago, but she still needs her crutches to get around. I think it will do her good to have some sunshine and warm weather, and young company. Of course Ma and Daddy are very caring but I think they realise that we two will have such a good time together. I'm hoping that being together Nettie might talk about – well everything.

Ma told me the doctors have said that she needs to talk about what happened and about Jonathan. She still finds it physically difficult to speak, her voice is still a bit croaky. I know she is desperately afraid she will not sing again even though the doctors have told her she will, it will just take time.

I'm quite well again now but I'm not riding, in any case Nettie can't and I want to spend as much time with her as possible. She is staying with us, in our home. It was Rodrigo's idea to have a bed put in the downstairs room. There is a bathroom next door so Nettie will not have to negotiate stairs. Outside is a terrace so she can sit outdoors to read or snooze undisturbed. She does seem to need to sleep quite a bit. That too, they say, is healing.

Nana Isabella is coming to have lunch with us today. It's wonderful that Nana speaks such good English so that she and Nettie have already struck up a rapport with one another. Nana is wise; don't I know it! One's often afraid to tell the hurtful and upsetting things to those one loves for fear of distressing them, but Nana is sufficiently removed from Nettie that she might be able to draw her out and I'm hoping Nettie will respond. Nana understands that talking, and listening which she does so well, is part of the healing process. Oh my, here I am pontificating again!

Papa had the piano moved into our house shortly after we moved in. He said I would find more use for it than he would! Carmen wanted Juan Luis to learn to play but he didn't like it; he thinks it's a girl's instrument. He wanted to play the guitar, in fact he's coming along quite well and sings rather nicely too. When Nettie feels better perhaps we can have a musical evening.

April 1965

'Con, Con, are you there? I want to show you something,' Nettie called from the small terrace outside her room.

Connie hurried across the hallway to find Nettie standing with her arms outstretched on each side of her.

'What is it? Are you all right? You haven't fallen have you?'

'Calm down big sister. Look, no hands! Or more precisely no sticks.'

'Nettie, that's fantastic. How long...?'

'I've been practising, little by little over the past four weeks but I didn't want you to see until I could manage really well. Now we can go for little strolls like two normal people.'

'Nettie, are you implying I am not a normal person at all times? Because if you are...' Connie stepped forward, 'Can I hug you? You won't fall over will you?'

The two sisters put their arms around each other, and tears trickled down their cheeks.

At was at this moment that Nana Isabella stepped through the door.

'I'm so sorry my dears, I didn't knock, how discourteous of me. I'll come back.'

'No you won't Nana Isabella.' Nettie called out. She had taken to calling her Nana Isabella within hours of their first meeting. 'Come right in, I mean out – out here on the terrace. Come and see what I can do.'

'My dear, show me.'

Nettie stepped out with firm and steady steps.

'What a girl, and with a straight back and head up high, just what I expected of you. I think you are as good as new. What do you say Conchita?'

'Every bit as good as new, Nana. Isn't she just so...brave.'

'I think this is where I might use an English expression; 'the pot calling the kettle black', if I may say so.'

Both Nettie and Con burst out laughing at the not entirely appropriate expression.

'I think I'd like to be the pot. You Nettie can be the kettle. After all it's the kettle that sings, isn't it?' Nettie's smile faded.

'Well, perhaps one day, we'll see,' she murmured.

231

'What I meant was,' said Nana 'that each of you seems to see a virtue in the other, without recognising it as one of your own. In my view, you are two of the bravest girls I have ever known. Come to me.'

The tears not yet dry on their cheeks despite their laughter, they each clasped one of her hands.

'And you *will* sing Nettie. Do you not realise how the timbre of your voice has gradually been changing? I predict that you will be singing very soon.'

'Well what's going on in here?' came Rodrigo's deep voice from the hallway. 'May I join you, it looks like secrets and I want to be in on them.'

'No secrets, just laughter and tears, and lots of love flowing around out here. Come through and see Nettie's amazing progress.'

'Good heavens! You've thrown the sticks away! But you stand so beautifully and straight, no wobbling. First the crutches and now the sticks – we must burn them - have a bonfire! What do you say? No, a better idea - we shall have a barbecue this evening.'

He turned to Conchita. 'In fact that's why I came in. I just suddenly decided, it's such beautiful weather, we should be eating outside.'

'Good thinking Rodrigo, I'll bring one of my salads.'

'Thank you Nana. I'll prepare a few things and you, Rodrigo can cook the lamb.'

'And what about me?' Nettie asked. 'Can't I do something? I've been pretty useless around here for weeks and weeks.'

'Pretty, yes. But useless no,' chimed in Rodrigo.

'It's time you left Rodrigo, before the romantic side of your nature gets out of hand,' Conchita teased him.

'I'm gone,' he called, as he leapt through the doorway and out of the house.

***

Garnet's walking improved daily and the soulful expression on her face gave way to smiles.

It was at another barbecue evening that the second breakthrough occurred.The whole family had assembled, the meal was over and everyone was sitting relaxed in the warm evening air.

Juan Luis had come with his guitar and was quietly strumming away against the background of the conversation. At twelve years old he was growing into an affectionate and considerate young man, and his playing was proving the affinity he felt with this musical instrument. He had been right to choose the guitar over the piano. He loved both the traditional Spanish music, fast and vibrant, and the classical, and he gently picked out an aria from the opera La Bohème.

Conchita, leaning against Rodrigo on a comfortable garden sofa, suddenly stiffened. She took his hand and held it tightly as she heard a soft voice join in with Juan Luis. No-one moved, Juan Luis played on as Garnet sang stronger and louder. Conchita couldn't bring herself to look up at anyone, she felt she might cry and break the spell and she did not want this magic moment to end. The music faded; Juan Luis laid down his guitar and moved towards Garnet. He took her hand and in the manner in which he had seen his father take a lady's hand, with great composure he lifted it to his lips.

'Thank you Garnet. You sing beautifully. Please may we play and sing together again soon.'

There was an audible gasp from Ramon as he watched his son's behaviour. All were taken by surprise by the boy's self-possession and charmed by his evident pleasure in making music, but he did not seem to understand that it was he who had freed Garnet's imprisoned voice. Garnet smiled at him.

'Thank you Juan Luis. I shall never forget this evening and your beautiful music.'

It was too much for him, he was suddenly embarrassed and turning to his mother and father, he said goodnight. He waved briefly to the group and quietly walked back to the house with his guitar in his arms.

Quiet conversation began, yet no-one mentioned the singing. Perhaps all were afraid it was an illusion; they had imagined the gentle voice, the kiss of the hand but a fantasy.

Isabella was the first to rise. She moved towards Garnet and took both her hands.

'Goodnight, my brave girl. Sleep well.'

It seemed to be the cue for everyone to make their way to bed. Conchita kissed Garnet on each cheek. They smiled at one another but neither spoke.

Later in their room, Rodrigo held Conchita in his arms. He had felt that terrible tension in her, the grip of her hand in his, and he had placed his arm around her shoulder to comfort her.

'It has happened. Like a miracle. Who could have known that it would be Juan Luis and his music that would bring it about.'

Conchita nodded. 'You know, years ago I hated that child. I was so jealous of him. Did you know that?'

'There are many things from your childhood that I do not know. If you tell me them then I take it as a compliment that you wish to confide such things in me. But I do know that you do not hate him now, do you?'

'No, I love him dearly – my half- brother. He is so much more than a 'half' and he has always accepted me as his sister, without question, so that I find it rather a strange thought when I remember, now and then, that *my* mother is not *his* mother.

'How beautifully he behaved this evening towards Garnet, so grown-up, and how kind and thoughtful he is. No rebel teenager there, like me. He'll never give his parents heart ache as I did.'

'Leave the past Conchita, look to the future, the two of us together, and be happy in it.'

***

The following morning Conchita found Garnet sitting in front of the piano, the lid raised but her hands in her lap. She was staring at the keyboard.

'Shall I play?' she asked simply, as though needing permission.

'That would be ... nice. I will sit and listen.'

It was Chopin, always Chopin for Connie – Garnet's gift to her whenever she played just for her. It was Waltz No 9, Opus 69, No 1, one of her favourites.

Conchita closed her eyes against the tears that she felt welling up. It would be a shame to spoil this wonderful interlude by crying. She wanted to accept Garnet's gift, sit and listen and enjoy it like old times. It ended and Garnet paused for a moment or two then she burst into the Mozart 'Sonate Facile'. It belies its name, it is simple in its composition but it's not an '*easy*' sonata at all if it's to be played well. They had had such fun as girls competing as to which one of them could play it the faster. Surprisingly Conchita always won, timed against the second hand on Garnet's watch. But it was Garnet who played it with skill and feeling and they both knew it.

She began Beethoven's 'Fur Elise', another of the pieces she had played so often at home when they were girls. It was almost as though she were rehearsing the early years of learning and playing, as though trying to climb back into the present and her changed life. It was the piece Conchita played when the piano arrived at Ramon's house, just before Garnet's first visit.

Conchita could see again the piano tuner standing beside the piano, Papa and Nana Isabella sitting nearby and their applause when she had finished. She had assured them that Garnet could play it so much better then she could, 'You will see' she had told them. In the intervening years there had been happiness and also so much sadness. Conchita felt deeply that this piece played now by Garnet heralded a new phase in life.

'Do you remember when I used to play that all the time?' she said at the close of the piece. 'I think Mummy got tired of it. But I still love the haunting melody, those climbing arpeggios as though they are reaching for something, and that rather sombre bit in the middle that drums along in the base. When I was about nine I found that rather exciting.' She paused and looked across at Conchita who was still sitting with her head leaning back in the chair and her eyes closed.

'Oh dear, I'm being frightfully technical and boring.'

'It's the most wonderful thing you have said for some time Nettie. It's almost as though your soul has reawakened. Has it?'

Nettie rose and left the piano. She came and knelt on the floor in front of Conchita.

'Con? Con, I think it's time I went home. It's nearly a year since…the accident. Do you mind terribly?'

'No, I think the time is right. I'll miss you horribly.'

'And I you. Everyone, but especially you. The generosity of time, patience, and understanding throughout the months has been beyond measure. You have all been so kind and caring; you have brought me back. Now I want to start again, do you understand?'

'It's what we all hoped for.'

'Before I go, I want to talk, tell you… about Jonathan.'

'Don't if it hurts too much.'

'Yes it hurts, I think it always will, but if I can tell you first, then later perhaps I can tell Mummy and Daddy about it too. Facing up to something, talking about it for the first time is always the most difficult, isn't it?'

The two rose and walked arm in arm to Garnet's room and took a chair out onto the terrace.

Garnet began, telling of the immediate attraction between herself and Jonathan.

'He was a really good conductor, you know. I had only met him once before, briefly, when he had come to Covent Garden to look in on what was going on, some months prior to his next engagement there. We, I mean the orchestra and cast, were so lucky to have him.

'When he came in...it seems like a lifetime ago...' Nettie stopped and lifted her gaze out across the vines, for a moment she was far away. She gave a deep sigh, then continued, 'when he came in to meet everyone, before rehearsals began, he came up to me and said, "I know you don't I?" I think I must have looked a little taken aback and I didn't reply.

"Yes I do, Covent Garden, last year, wasn't it?" he said. I nodded. "Nice to see you again, looking forward to working with you." I was dumbstruck. He, looking forward to working with me? Wow! I didn't know what to say. He said something to one or two others, then I thought, ah yes, he'll say nice flattering things to everyone . He was nice to all of us and encouraging but oh, he worked us hard. He was very strict about arriving at rehearsals on time, tea breaks and so on. He kept us going, making us go over and over again on some small detail. One or two of the cast got a bit fed up, they thought he was too exacting.

But he was a fabulous musician and by the time we were ready for the first performance, everyone recognised his genius.'

'What a loss to the world of music Nettie. How brave you are to think of that alongside your own personal grief.'

'Everyone will miss him. Most of all me.' Tears filled her eyes but she shook her head and almost threw the tears away from her, before they could run down her face.

'I'll be all right Con, I'm determined to get back to where I was. At least this time I'm not starting at the bottom of the ladder. I know I was good, and I'm going to be again. I'm not being funny when I say does that sound like 'singing' my own praises?'

'You've never been one to boast and Nana is right. She recognised in you the ability to come back.'

'She helped me you know. I talked about what music meant to me in my life and she... she talked and talked; about life, relationships, marriage, running away, facing up to things, the choices we have to make as we go along. She never once asked me any questions. It was all very soothing.'

'You know Ma and Daddy will be thrilled to hear you're going back. They have waited patiently and with great hopes that your stay here would help you. They have quite a responsibility with Granny and Gramps. I think the fact that you could stay here was a tremendous weight off their minds. We shall 'phone them tonight – you can tell them the good news.'

'Yes, then perhaps Rodrigo would help me make the bookings?'

'I'm sure he will. Nettie - will you fly?'

'Of course, it would be silly not to. Remember what Nana said, one must face up to things and this is one of them.' She shook her head, the fair curls which had grown quite long during her stay, swung from side to side. She put her hands up to push them back behind her ears.

'And I *must* get my haircut!' She laughed. Connie smiled and then with a more serious expression said,

'Nettie, before we get caught up in preparations and perhaps don't get a chance to sit and chat like this before you go, well, I have some news. No-one knows but me, not even Rodrigo. You know what you said about telling someone something for the first time, and it's important who it is you tell? I'm actually quite frightened of saying this because of what happened last year.'

'Con, you're not...?'

'Yes, I'm pregnant.'

'My God, what terrific news, but why doesn't Rodrigo know? How could you keep it from him?'

'He's a worrier and I wanted to wait a couple of months. I've seen the doctor, and that's not all.'

'What else?'

'It's twins!'

39

Diary

No birthday party for me this year, just a quiet dinner. I'm tired out and Rodrigo knows it. I'm wondering how I am going to continue coping with these two rascals. At not quite a year old they are walking and full of energy. But there is a reason why I'm tired, other than that, I'm pregnant again! I've not kept the news to myself this time, I couldn't, he saw for himself how wishy-washy I'm looking. I shall give in to his persistent offers of help.

Conchita was feeling the weight of the baby, bending was becoming more difficult and as for chasing Luis and Carlos and rescuing them from their pursuit of some adventure or their next bout of curiosity, she could not now reach them in time before they caused disarray.

It was only in the last few weeks prior to the birth of Luis, named for his Spanish grandfather, and Carlos, named for his English grandfather, that she had given up working. If the truth be known, she had missed it. Now another baby. Going back into the business would be postponed again, and Conchita was feeling just a little bit resentful.

This mood was quite unlike Conchita. Since Garnet's wonderful recovery and recent news that she had again been offered a good singing part, she had been cheerful and happy, initially pleased that there was to be another baby. As she walked back to the house, after a little stroll with Luis on one hand and Carlos on the other, watching their unsteady feet pick their way along the path, she saw Catarina coming towards her.

Conchita suddenly felt ashamed of herself. Here was this delightful girl who had blended into her new family with undemanding graciousness. She had continued to live with her grandparents for a while after her father had married Conchita but it was apparent that they were finding the task of caring for a fourteen year old granddaughter a heavy responsibility. Catarina began to spend more and more time with her father and Conchita, and to stay with them at weekends. It was Conchita who suggested to Rodrigo that she come to live with them permanently. Typically, Catarina asked her grandparents if they would be hurt if she accepted the invitation. They knew it was much more natural for her to live with her father, and younger ones, and they were grateful for the offer.

'Luis, Carlos, come to Catarina,' she called out as the trio neared the house. It was Luis who fell first with Carlos tumbling on top of him. Catarina was there in a flash.

'Oh my fault, I shouldn't have called them,' she wailed.

But they were laughing and rolling around, not hurt at all. Catarina picked up one and then the other, one under each arm despite their roly poly size. They wriggled and squealed until she put them down.

'May I help bath them this evening?' she asked.

'Of course, but you must do your homework first,' Conchita said. Secretly she would be more than glad of the help.

'You look tired Conchita,' Catarina said. 'Go and sit down, I'll stay with the boys and Manuela will help, won't you?' The young woman nodded in agreement, smiling broadly, she adored these two *diablillos* as she called them. Conchita's emotional state during the recent few weeks had been unpredictable and she felt herself ready to cry at Catarina's thoughtful offer. She handed over the twins and went to her small day room where she lay down on the couch.

It was hot and stuffy and she thought of what a mistake it was to be heavily pregnant at this time of year. As she lay breathing deeply in order to control the tears, it came to her that she must confess to Rodrigo tonight that he had been right. She needed help.

'So, at last you have come down off your high horse,' Rodrigo had said with some laughter. At first Conchita was offended by his remark but soon realised it was only a tease.

'What a good thing I have already made some enquiries,' he added. 'I was not prepared to see you getting more and more tired Conchita. I can't bear to see you worn-out, with a pale face and no smile.'

'My goodness, am I really like that? I'm sorry darling, have I really been a misery?'

'Not quite a misery, but you were getting there. Now, don't be upset, plans are afoot for a nice young girl to come and look after those two sons of mine.'

'Er...and mine, I think!' She smiled, 'so where did you find this 'nice young girl'?

'She is the niece of a friend of mine. I have known the family for some time. She is the eldest of a large family, seven children I think. With a repeatedly pregnant and exhausted mother she has had plenty of experience of looking after younger siblings. I have already spoken to the family. They suggested that I approach the young lady straight away. She was delighted with the proposal and....well, she will be coming to stay next week.'

'You have been busy! And all without telling me.'

'But you would have argued with me Conchita. No, not argued, you don't argue, you would have resisted my suggestion. This way...it is settled.'

'But what about her family and the poor exhausted mother? And how old is she?'

'She is sixteen, and as for her family, there will be one mouth fewer to feed and the younger sisters will take over the care of the little ones. The parents are pleased for her and, I gather, the mother will not be having any more babies after complications with the last one, which is a blessing I think. Nina herself is delighted at the prospect of having only two children to look after. So, it is settled''

'As you said it's settled, it seems to everyone's satisfaction. You're right I do need help, I'm very tired. I was going to come to you this evening and admit it but as always you are one jump ahead Rodrigo, with your caring and thoughtful planning. All for our benefit. What would I do without you?'

***

Rosita Isabella arrived on the 15th of September with a mop of thick brown hair, and large eyes the colour of bitter chocolate. There was no denying whose child she was. Rodrigo was charmed by this dainty child, with pink cheeks and a ready smile.

'It's not a smile, Rodrigo. Don't you know all babies do that, it's wind!'

'Nonsense, she recognises me and she knows I am her father, and she is pleased about that.'

'What vanity, Rodrigo!'

'I know and I am not ashamed of it. I am proud of my family – my wife and my children. He leaned over the baby's cot, murmuring unintelligible sounds.

'I am blessed, thank you my love for such a wonderful family.'

'I join you Papa, in those thanks.' Catarina had come quietly into the room with a cup of English tea for Conchita. 'Am I not the luckiest girl to have a *madre* after all, and two brothers and a sister?' She handed the tea to Conchita and sat on the end of the bed.

'I hardly remember my mother now, I was only three when she died. And all the time I was growing up with my grandparents I longed for a mother like other girls at school. It took a long time to find one – but I did. So I say thank you too, *Mama*, for you and my family.'

'Excuse me! Do you think perhaps I had anything to do with your finding a mother? I rather feel I found her first, don't you think?'

'Of course you did Papa. I knew you would, but you did take a long time about it, didn't you?' Conchita began to giggle and her tea spilled in the saucer.

'Now look here, are you ladies ganging up on me. I hope this one,' he said taking Rosita's tiny little finger in his hand, 'is going to be on my side in the future.'

'No such luck, Papa. Don't you know by now, we women are liberated!'

'You are a mere fourteen Catarina, you are not yet liberated!'

By this time Conchita was laughing openly and couldn't hold the cup and saucer any longer. Rodrigo took it from her and marched out of the room.

'Oh dear, was that a bit cheeky?' Catarina said looking concerned.

'I don't think so, you were so funny. Don't worry he'll get over it.'

'Funny? But I'm serious *Mama*. I want to be a modern woman, you know - independent.'

'You are a clever girl Catarina. Have no fears you will make your way in life quite independently.'

'You see *Mama*, I don't want to learn about the wine industry. I don't want to be absorbed into the family business. I want to be an artist. I haven't told Papa yet, he'll have a fit. I know he'll think it's not a good choice. No jobs, no money, that's what he'll say.'

'You know Papa, he can be a little bit pompous sometimes, and likes to state his opinion. We have to handle him gently, let him think it's his idea. We'll do it Catarina, if it's an artist you want to be, you shall. But remember this, he loves you very much and he will do anything to help you.'

'You said "we" *Mama*, does that mean you will help me too?'

'Of course I will help you, we girls must stick together. But truthfully, the reason I will help you is because I believe you have a special talent. Soon we must start thinking about your studies to get you on the right path.'

Catarina leaned forward and gave Conchita a gentle kiss on her cheek.

241

'You do know that I love you don't you *Mama*?'

'And I you, my dear. Now how about another cup of tea, the last one disappeared.'

40

Diary

I've had a distressing letter from Ma. Gramps is very poorly and they are all worried about him, about Granny too, who apparently confided to Ma that she thinks he won't pull through this latest heart attack. I so want to go and see them, dare I say it - before it is too late. Of course I don't want to leave the children, but I also want Gramps to see them and they to meet him. I suppose in years to come they won't remember such a meeting, after all the twins are not yet four and Rosita is just two. Just imagine, what a handful on a journey to Yorkshire! I have spoken to Rodrigo and he thinks we could do it. The awful thing is he can't come, he is desperately busy just now and couldn't possibly take time away from business. We are going to discuss it with Nina and see how she feels about going with me and the children.

Nina, little girl, an appropriate name for her; small and slender but wiry. When she first arrived to live with the family, Conchita was afraid this girl would not cope with two strong bouncy boys. But Luis and Carlos at the tender age of two years old fell in love with her and even with their high spirits they would do almost anything for her. She took no nonsense from them, fair and affectionate though she was she disciplined them. Conchita was full of admiration for her. The household calmed down and Conchita's physical and emotional health soon returned after Rosita's birth.

It was the news from Flora that unsettled this happy state. Charles Hampton's recent heart attack was, this time, more severe. Flora had written the news, Philip had wanted to telephone Conchita but Flora felt hearing their own sad voices would distress her even more.

Rodrigo came in from his morning's work to find Conchita in her day room with the letter in her hand. There were tears glistening in her eyes.

'What is it, my love?'

'It's Gramps, he's very ill. Rodrigo what would you say...?'

'You don't have to ask, you must go. Nina can manage the children for a few days and Catarina will help out.'

'But I thought... well I thought I might take the children with me. Everyone would love to see them, it might be good for them.'

'On the other hand, it might be too much. It depends on how ill your grandfather is and whether your mother and father can cope with three young children in the house. I'm not sure it's a good idea.'

'Maybe not. Could we ask Nina how she would feel about going with us? No, perhaps I had better speak to Ma first and see how things are with them. I'll phone them tonight.'

'I agree. I'm so sorry my love, it is sad for you.'

'Sadder for Granny I think. She'll be lost without him.'

***

The phone call to Harrogate that evening was a tearful one. Conchita had only once seen her father cry and that was when they parted after her arrival at Bodega López. She could not see him now but the crack in his otherwise steady tone of voice revealed his sadness. It was the final sob before he handed her over to Flora that broke Conchita's composure.

'Ma? Are you all right?'

'We're all right darling, but as you can tell Daddy is distraught.'

'And what about Granny, is she coping?'

'You know Granny, she's a rock on which we have all leaned over the years; she is keeping calm. She is managing to comfort all of us when she must be in anguish herself, I don't know how she does it.'

'Ma, I don't know whether to ask you this, I want to bring the children. Rodrigo says he thinks it would be too much for you and I'm inclined to agree in a way. I so want Luis and Carlos to have met Gramps just once. They each have a photo of their grandfathers in their bedroom, knowing that they are named after them and it would be so nice if Carlos, at least, could have met his namesake. I know he's very young but maybe he'll have a memory of him in the future. Am I being horribly selfish?'

'Darling, I'd like nothing better but...well it's a question of fitting you all in. I think I need to discuss it with Daddy and Annie. By the way she sends her love.'

'Thank you, give mine to her, and to everyone. Will you phone me when you've had time to think about it? And Ma, if you decide it's too much, I'll understand, but I'll come anyway.'

'I'll phone tomorrow. Connie, if it's possible we'll do it. Don't forget, I haven't met my grandchildren yet!'

'I know, I'm sorry. Thanks for considering it Ma. Love you. Bye.'

***

Conchita had never seen Nina flustered. Normally nothing perturbed this good-natured, capable girl. The news that she might go to England with Conchita and the children set her in a spin. There was a genuine obstacle, she thought, she had no passport. But she was wrong.

With great aforethought Rodrigo had applied for a passport for her three months earlier; he had foreseen the possibility of her accompanying Conchita one day on a trip to family in England. He had told Conchita what he had done, with the advice not to mention it to Nina for the time being. It was yet another of Rodrigo's considerate pieces of planning. When he presented Nina with the document, she shrieked,

'But how did you get this photo of me?'

'Remember the photographer who came for the day of Nana Isabella's birthday? He took many photographs, including yours. So now, you can go abroad whenever you wish.'

'I don't wish,' she whispered.

Conchita gasped. This unexpected turn was a jolt. Neither she nor Rodrigo had considered that Nina might not want to go away with the family.

'Oh Nina, I'm so sorry, we assumed... it was thoughtless of us, but we thought you would like to...well, to come with me, and the children.'

Tears came to Nina's eyes, she dropped her head and ran from the room.

'Now what do we do? We have really upset her Rodrigo'

'Leave her for a while, let her compose herself, she is a very proud little person.'

***

That afternoon, as soon as Conchita knew that the children were having their nap, she knocked on Nina's door. It was Nina's quiet time, the

245

family recognizing that she needed not only a rest but some private time.

'I'm really sorry to disturb you Nina. But I would like to talk to you.'

Nina rose from her comfortable chair dropping her magazine on the floor.

'I've come to say I'm sorry we upset you this morning. We should never have taken it for granted that you would want to come to England. You are so wonderful with the children that we naturally felt you would be the best person to help me. If you feel that you cannot, then I understand, and I hope you will forgive me for being a little selfish.'

'No, no, I'm sorry Señora da Silva, it is I who must say sorry. But I cannot go with you, I cannot leave my country, not for anything. Besides I don't understand English and I am frightened of aeroplanes. I am now so unhappy because I think you won't want me to live with you anymore, and care for my boys and little Rosita.'

'That will never happen Nina. There is no question of your leaving us. How could Luis and Carlos bear it? And little Rosita loves you so much. We all do, you know that, don't you?' Nina nodded and with the back of her hand wiped a tear from her cheek. Conchita handed her a small white handkerchief.

'We could not manage without you Nina, please tell me that you want to stay.'

'Oh yes, more than anything. I live in heaven here with all of you. You are so kind and...and I love the children.' The tears began to roll down her cheeks again.

'Please dry your eyes and do not worry anymore. You want to stay and we want you to stay, so it's settled.' The words reminded Conchita of Rodrigo's favourite expression; and she smiled to herself.

'Now, I'm going to tell Señor Rodrigo that all is well. It is, isn't it?'

'Yes, but I worry, how will you manage?'

'We shall find a solution.' Nina made to give back the handkerchief but Conchita said,

'No, it's a new one, I've never used it. It's pretty, keep it, to remind you that we all love you very much.'

***

Nina, with a somewhat quieter manner than usual, fed the children their evening meal, bathed them and put them to bed, first Rosita and after the reading of the customary story, tucked Luis and Carlos up in bed too. She ate with the children in the early evening, preferring the more informal meal than dinner with the adults. Even becoming good friends with Catarina did not tempt her to join them in the evening. She was used to the buzz of non-stop childish chatter at a mealtime and was not comfortable with adults discussing more serious matters.

Catarina had tried to chat to Nina as she ate with the children but the conversation was half-hearted and Catarina saw she had been crying.

'What's the matter with Nina, *Mama*? She's been crying, but she didn't seem to want to talk about anything,' she asked at dinner.

'We rather upset her this morning, which I feel guilty about. You see, I'm trying to plan the trip to England...no, I'd better begin at the beginning.

'My grandfather is very ill and we have been discussing the possibility of my taking the children with me on a visit to my parents' home. It's not a journey it would be wise to try and cope with alone, so we assumed that Nina would come with me. Your father, with anticipation applied for a passport for Nina, ready for the day when she might want, or we might like, to take her abroad. We presented her with this information this morning and she was stunned. She actually said she didn't want to go.'

'I can believe it, she's such a simple soul *Mama*. She has no ambitions. She feels she has reached the best she could have hoped for in her life, living with us. She told me so one day when we were having a quiet chat. I was flattered, she doesn't offer much insight into her feelings. But what about me? Can I go instead?'

'It's a lovely idea Catarina, but you've got to put your education first.'

'I agree,' said Rodrigo. 'And I think a trip to England would be very educational.' Both Conchita and Catarina looked at him, with their mouths open.

'You mean you would let me go, with *Mama*?'

'I do. I think it's a marvellous idea, but of course I had just thought of it myself when you spoke.'

'But I was only... *Mama*, what do you say?'

247

'What a solution, I told Nina we would find one. But *we* didn't, you did, I mean Papa did really.' Conchita's eyes slid sideways and caught the grin on Catarina's face.

'I will be absolutely thrilled to have you with me. You will love my grandparents, they are so....well, English!'

'Fine, so we know what we have to do first thing tomorrow morning. I'll do the difficult job and make the bookings, and you two can organise the simple job of packing!'

This time Conchita and Catarina openly exchanged glances and smiled but neither of them said a word.

'I will tell Nina the plans in the morning and I think I shall suggest she has a little holiday.'

'You don't mean go home to her family, do you *Mama*? That won't be a holiday at all.'

'You're right. You know I have a better idea. I'm going to suggest that she helps Ana Maria a little each day. They will both enjoy that. At seventy-six Ana Marie is a little slower than she used to be but she won't give up. Papa and Carmen are going to have a struggle eventually persuading her to retire.'

'Brilliant, and in between Nina can do her embroidery, pay little visits to her family, have chats with Manuela, do whatever she likes.'

'Oh Harrogate, here we come!'

41

Diary

Gramps has died. Only three weeks since I was there. He was still making his feeble jokes, bless him. There won't be any anymore. What a time we had despite the cloud of sadness. Ma was amazing; she had changed round all the bedrooms so that we could fit in. Catarina slept in the spare room with Luis and Carlos, Annie had Rosita with her – they took to each other within minutes of our arrival, Nettie and I slept in our old twin room which meant we had little sleep; reminiscing, talking of sad things as well as happy times. It was wonderful. She has told me a secret, I hardly dare write it down. She has met a very nice man, his name is David Chang and he lives in Hong Kong and works in the export business. His mother was English and his father was Chinese, they both died some time ago. How on earth did you meet him? I asked straight away. He travels all over Europe and loves opera. He knows a lot of musicians and one of them took him backstage and introduced him to Nettie. They meet whenever he is on business where Nettie is singing. It sounds like a lot of his business visits coincide with opera performances! I suspect he engineers a few trips but I didn't dare say that to Nettie, she's keeping a lot of things to herself at the moment. She did at least tell me she had spent ten days in

Hong Kong with him. I'm so happy for her but I can't share it, not even with Rodrigo, I'm sworn to secrecy.

I've already 'phoned Daddy to say that I can't really make a second trip so soon to attend the funeral, but they didn't expect me to. Nettie will be there, which is a comfort to know that at least one of his grandchildren will be there to say goodbye.

Ma says they will try to visit early next year and persuade Granny to come with them. She hasn't ever been out of the country! She'll take some persuading.

***

Diary

*It's taken a while but at last they are coming! I think my call to Granny
helped to persuade her to come. No time to write, lots to do.*

The two were sitting on the small terrace where Garnet had learned
to walk again nearly five years ago. Since then Conchita had decorated
the room which led to it; white painted walls showed to good effect
Catarina's colourful paintings of the surrounding countryside. Over the
bed was spread a much loved but rather old light-weight quilt. Without
a doubt Granny Hampton would recognise Annie's handiwork. The
colours were a little faded now but it sat easily here beside this simple
decor. The fine white cotton curtains framed the double doors onto the
terrace. Conchita had given Amelia this room, knowing that she would
like the idea that Garnet had spent so much time in here.

'Well, what do you think of your Granny coming all this way at my
age? I'm eighty you know.'

'Granny you'd better not speak of your age like that in front of Nana
Isabella. She'll wonder what you're so in awe of, she's soon eighty, but
she thinks she is still young. You are young, both of you. Despite
everything sad and your difficult times, you've both moved with the
times retaining a modern outlook. Lots of older people don't do that.
They live in the past, grumbling about the present.'

'There's no point in doing that. I've taken each year as it came, and
now I'm taking each day. Every single one is a bonus.'

'I wish I had had longer with you before I was sent...no, let's not say
that, before I came here. There's so much I don't know about you, such
as I never knew about Gramps being in the war. It's only now that I'm
hearing what happened to him. Can you talk about him.'

'I can talk about him, sometimes I talk *to* him. Does that sound
silly?'

'No, when I was first here I missed you all so much that I used to
talk to all of you in bed at night. I used to ask questions but of course I
never got any answers.'

'No, and I'm not going to get any answers either, but that's not the
point of the talking, is it? It's just the feeling that you are keeping in
touch.'

250

'Tell me about those years Granny.'

'I'm sure you know all about the First World War, you must have learnt it at school. We were married in 1909 and your Daddy was born in 1910, we didn't waste any time! So he was four when Gramps joined the army. It was going to be all over in no time they said, but we all know that it wasn't.

'Gramps spent a lot of time in knee deep water in trenches; what a ghastly time they had. Pals were being killed all around him, so many wounded, some soldiers lost their minds; the exhaustion, the dying, the wounded, the noise and mud eventually sent them crazy. One day Gramps was shot, the bullet lodged in a lung. He was lucky, they got him to a field hospital but then the wound became infected. They shipped him home as soon as they could because they couldn't treat it, and they needed the bed. No penicillin in those days.

'He nearly died, but as sure as can be, I reckon he would have died if he had gone back to those terrible conditions. Either he would have been killed by enemy fire or he would have been ill again. That infection in a way saved his life. But it left him with a weakness.'

'So that's why he had such wheezy laughter. It used to make us laugh as children, he sounded so funny.'

'Yes, his breathing was affected for the rest of his life.'

'Poor Gramps, we never knew anything about it. Do you remember he used to say "here comes the steam train, puffing along," when he laughed and we girls thought it was just another of his little jokes.'

Amelia paused as though she were remembering his voice.

'I would have liked more children but times were hard and Gramps was worried that one day he might not be able to work because of his health. He said we had to content ourselves with our one son and be glad of him.'

'Do you know Granny, Gramps not once ever mentioned the war.'

'No, he wouldn't - couldn't talk about it. He said it brought back horrible pictures in his mind and so we promised each other never to discuss it. Some people said we were silly to try to hide from it, that we should face up to it and the memories would fade. What some people didn't understand was that there was no hiding from it, he had been there, and the memories never did fade he said.'

'Thank you for telling me this. One day I want to tell the boys about him.'

Amelia leaned down to retrieve the handbag that she had put beside her chair. She opened the bag and took out a small square box. It was dark blue, still shiny as though new.

'I thought you might like to have this,' she said, 'as a keepsake. And perhaps give it to Carlos one day.' She handed the box to Conchita. As she pressed the tiny button in the front of the box the lid sprang up to reveal a white satin lining. Nestling in the lower half was a medal; on the face of which was an effigy of King George V, attached to a blue, white and red striped ribbon. Conchita gasped.

'Was it Gramps?' she whispered.

'Yes, he was awarded it for bravery.' Amelia turned the medal over. 'You see it says 'For Bravery in the Field.' He saved the lives of seven of his men. They were wounded in an attack and they couldn't get back to safety. Your Gramps crawled out to them through the mud and brought them back one by one.'

'But I've never seen it before. Why don't we know about it?'

'You know Gramps, ever modest. Not even your father knew about it. You see I had to promise never to tell anyone about it. That made it all the harder to bear the not so kind comments from people who told him to 'snap out of it' when he was unwell.'

'But you must tell Daddy about this, you must show him the medal. In fact, don't you think he ought to have it, rather than me?'

'I have, and I told him I wanted to give it to you. He was quite happy about that. "Who better", he said, "she has little else from her life in England."'

'You know Granny, the older I get the more I realise how little we all know of each other. I'm not just talking about big things like this, but the little things in life that we tend to gloss over. Secrets are dangerous things aren't they? Even when they are meant to be for our own good.'

'You were never a talker when you were a youngster, always the quiet one, keeping your own counsel. Have you learned to talk, Connie, to share your thoughts and feelings?'

'Indeed I have. Don't forget I live in a Spanish family now, everybody talks all the time, at speed I tell you! And unlike the British, they show their feelings, they express them with both laughter and tears. It was one of the things I found difficult to adjust to.'

'And now you can talk to Flora, your mother. I'm glad about that.'

'We are reconciled, I've forgiven her. No, that's too righteous of me to say that. I felt sad for her when she went through that terrible illness. She did an awful thing but she paid for it, didn't she? You and Gramps were marvellous, you didn't abandon her, which you might easily have done.'

252

'Gramps was not judgemental, but I was. I said at the time that I could never forgive her. I was so angry, on your behalf. You see I had been aware of how she treated you and never understood it.'

'That makes two of us!' Conchita said laughing. 'And now?'

'Now? I don't know what I would have done without her, strange isn't it?'

'I do love her now Granny. I never stopped loving Daddy and I grew to love Papa. Looking back, I might well say, 'All's well that ends well.'

'But it hasn't ended Conchita, it's going to go on and on, look.'

They both turned and saw Nina walking across the garden with Luis and Carlos leading a pony with Rosita sitting confidently .

'My great grandchildren!' she whispered.

42

Diary

This month has held both sadness and joy.

Juan Luis is twenty-one on the 15th and Nana Isabella will be eighty-four the day after. It was Juan Luis' idea that they share a party. Nana didn't think that fair. She thought it should be a celebration day for Juan Luis, after all 21 is rather special. She had already declared on her 80th that she would never have another party, which I have to say was a very grand affair. Relatives and friends came from everywhere and it was one of the happiest occasions we have ever had.

'You will be inviting all your young friends Juan Luis and they won't appreciate having an old lady like me around.'

'Nana! You are fishing for compliments. So I'll give you one. They'll never believe you are my abuela. We are going to share this day.'

Papa is so pleased with the way in which Juan Luis has launched himself into the business. He works really hard. He didn't want to go to university, he said he could learn from Papa and the enólogo but he is studying too. We are all very proud of him.

Papa gave him a holding in the company for his birthday gift; and has renamed the company 'López and Son' to make him feel proud of being part of this family concern. Juan Luis was rather shy about it when he told me, wondering if I might be a little hurt about the change of name. "You work here too, and very hard, and you are his daughter after all. Perhaps he should have named it 'son and daughter'."

Dear Juan Luis; ever thoughtful of others' feelings. I assured him it was fine with me, he deserves it.

Now for the sadness. I have been postponing writing about it. It's six weeks since dear Granny died. We all knew it was coming, after months of sickness and suffering she slipped away under heavy sedation. Even when one knows it's coming, the sorrow is not lessened when it finally happens. Now there's only Ma and Daddy and faithful Annie in that large house. Daddy asked Annie if she would like to retire, she is 65 this year. "Not really," she replied, "providing you can put up with me for a bit longer." Typical Annie, always so self-effacing! Apparently they all laughed and then she added "Besides, those bairns might come a-visiting and I want to be 'ere." Dear Annie, she's a member of the family now, has been for a long time.

I've sandwiched these sad memories between two lots of good news. That way I can cope with them a little better.

Nettie is coming to stay! I invited her ages ago and told her to bring David, we want to meet him. They have been – well, as Ma put it – having an affair for over four years now. It seems he'll not be coming, I am disappointed but more than that I'm a little concerned about Nettie. She didn't sound too buoyant. She'll be here in time for the big party, that might cheer her up.

Garnet arrived looking very slim and a little pale.

'You look as though you need some sunshine and a few good meals inside you. Look at you, so slim! You've been working too hard.'

'When the work is there, one doesn't say no. It's a cut throat world.'

'I hope not!' Conchita giggled, 'otherwise there wouldn't be much singing going on.' But Garnet didn't laugh, not even a smile.

'Nettie, are you all right, you're not ill or anything are you?'

'No. I'm fine. So many questions Con.'

'Mmm, that's your prerogative isn't it? Or it used to be.'

'Yes, well then, when is this party?'

'The day after tomorrow. Nettie, I know you've just arrived so forgive the question but how long can you stay?'

'I'm not sure. I'll see how I get on.'

'That's a funny thing to say. Are you sure you're all right?'

'Can I help? There must be something I can do, make jellies, ice buns, whatever.'

'He's twenty-one Nettie, not five! In any case they don't eat jelly here, nor buns!' Garnet turned away.

'I think I'll just go and sort out a few things. I expect I'm in the room I had before?'

'You'll be comfortable there, won't you?'

Garnet walked away without answering. Conchita watched her go, frowning at her sister's silent departure.

***

The party was a 'ball', as the young ones described it the next day; the dancing wasn't exactly the waltz or the valeta, more a case of Rock and a little Tango. Juan Luis was never without a partner, whirling around on the wooden dance floor specially set up in the garden. The band was a local pop-group made up of his ex-school friends who were making quite a name for themselves.

Supper was an enormous barbecue served with their own Rioja wine. Just before midnight Juan Luis stopped the music. He walked across the floor to an area set out with tables and chairs. Sitting in a comfortable lounger was Nana Isabella.

'Nana, may I have the pleasure of the next dance?' he asked.

She looked up at her grandson with signs of slight panic in her eyes, but she took his hand and rose out of her chair. Her heart fluttered, how on earth would she cope with this dreadful music? It was the one thing that she had not managed to adjust to in her advancing years. She held on to his hand and as he led her towards the floor the band struck up with the soft gentle music of an old fashioned waltz. The whole assembly went silent and Isabella found herself trembling.

'Come Nana, you can dance. You told me so. Let's show them how to do it.'

They waltzed round the floor several times, Isabella found herself relaxing and as she looked up at her grandson she could almost believe she was in the arms of her beloved Luis, sixty years ago.

The music stopped. Juan Luis bowed. The whole assembly broke into spontaneous applause. He took her arm and led her back to her chair.

'It's midnight, Happy Birthday Nana,' he said kissing her gently on the cheek.

'And to you too, my handsome grandson. I had no idea you could dance so gracefully. Now go out there and show me how it's done the modern way.'

Juan Luis walked back into the middle of the floor but before he could say or do anything, the singing and the shouting began. Happy Birthday, Congratulations, Good Luck.

Gradually everyone joined him on the dance floor and a final energetic bout of rocking and rolling erupted. It was a grand finale to a wonderful evening.

***

Quite a few members of the family emerged later than usual the next morning, except Garnet. Conchita had a late breakfast, after the children, and then helped Manuela clear the table.

'We don't need any shopping Manuela, there's loads of food left from last night. I think Carmen and Papa thought we were feeding the world.'

'Oh, it was lovely food, Señora. I had a lovely time.'

'Yes, I noticed you dancing. Who's the young man Manuela?'

She blushed and lowered her head. 'I hope it was all right that he came. You said I could invite a friend.'

'I did indeed. Tell me, is this a boyfriend?'

'Yes. Señora...I have been wishing to tell you. You see, we would like to get married, but I have my job here. I am very lucky, I love it, I can't give it up. We don't know what to do,' she added breathlessly.

'I'm sure Señor Rodrigo and I can sort something out. So stop worrying now. I'm very happy to hear your news.'

Conchita left the kitchen and walked out onto the main terrace. She could see Garnet in the distance. She had obviously been for a walk. It was puzzling, not like Nettie at all to go off on her own. She waited for her to come back.

'Hi. Had a nice walk?'

'Yes,' was all she said.

'Like a coffee? On your little terrace?' Conchita had deliberately suggested the secluded place, where miracles happened. Before Nettie could refuse she went back into the kitchen to switch on the espresso machine.

'I'll bring it through,' she called out.

As she walked through Nettie's room she caught sight of her already sitting on the terrace, partly concealed by the floating white curtains, but she saw her with her head in her hands. Conchita put the coffee on the table without a sound and laid her hand on Nettie's head.

'Come now. Drink first, then you are going to tell me what's wrong.'

Garnet dropped her hands and obediently drank the coffee. Conchita waited.

'It's David. I think I've ruined everything. He says he loves me and wants to get married.' She stopped speaking and began to pick at her fingernails.

'And you don't, want to get married I mean, is that it?'

'Yes.'

'Why don't you Nettie? Don't you love him?'

257

'Yes, I do but I can't marry him now, I've done the most terrible thing. He wouldn't have me if he knew.'

'If he loves you he's not going to let whatever it is you think you've done, make any difference.'

'It's not *think*, Con, it's a fact. You see, David wants to have children.'

'Don't you? Or do you think it will interfere with your singing career? Is that it?'

'Yes, and no. Con...' Nettie again put her head in her hands and began to sob. Conchita laid her hand one her arm and waited.

'Oh Con, I don't know how to tell you this. You, who have dealt with one blow after another and come through. When you lost the baby I was so broken hearted for you, it made me see that others were suffering too, that's when I spoke for the first time after months of not being able to utter a sound.'

'Yes, Ma told me how it happened. Losing the baby was sad, but some good came out of it, didn't it?'

'That's what I mean, you always see the good that comes out of things.'

'I haven't always.'

'Con... I lost a baby too.' Connie gasped.

'Oh Nettie, how awful. When, how? David's I presume? You said he wanted children, was he terribly upset?'

'He doesn't know anything about it. Con, I haven't told you the truth. I didn't *lose* the baby, I had an abortion two years ago.'

Connie gasped for a second time. She couldn't speak, she didn't know what to say.

'You'll hate me now. You lost a baby you wanted, and I got rid of a baby I didn't want. How ironic is that?'

'Why Nettie? Why did you get rid of it?'

'I was so scared of being trapped. I thought once I told David about it he would insist that we get married. I couldn't, I thought I would be marrying him because of the baby. I still wasn't sure that I loved him enough to marry him.'

'And now?'

'I do love him, desperately. He's such a nice kind person and he loves me to bits. But I've left it too late to tell him so.'

'Where is he now?'

'He's in London on business. He wanted to come with me but I persuaded him not to.'

Connie stood up. She walked to edge of the terrace and gazed across the land. After a couple of minutes she turned to Garnet.

'Drastic situations require drastic measures. Go to the telephone, tell him you are missing him and you want him to join us here as soon as possible.'

'I can't face him. I won't be able to hide my shame from him any longer.'

'Exactly, and you are not going to. You are going to tell him the truth. He loves you – he'll not desert you.' Connie spoke with confidence. She didn't quite understand how she could feel so convinced that this was the right thing to do. What she did know was that Garnet could not go on living in torment. It must be resolved one way or the other.

She accompanied Garnet to the telephone and stood over her while she dialled the number. It wasn't until she heard her say,

'David? It's Garnet,' that Conchita walked away.

It was half an hour before Garnet sought her out. After the telephone call she had returned to her room and Conchita had heard her crying, but had waited in fear that her confident prediction of David's response was not as she had promised her.

'Let's walk,' Garnet had said as she approached her sister.

They set off down a path that led to the vines and then veered off along the hillside. Conchita pointed out the remains of square stone shapes cut into the hills.

'What are they?' Garnet asked.

'This is where the Romans made wine. The wine presses were made of wood, but those are long gone of course. The wine ran into these stone baths and out through these holes.' Garnet looked at them with interest and then Conchita said,

'Come, it's too hot to be out walking at this time of day. Let's sit down here close to these bushes, in what little shade there is.' They sat and stared at each other for a few moments, Conchita's stomach churning with misgivings.

'He's coming, he'll catch a plane tomorrow.'

Conchita heaved a great sigh.

'Thank God,' she said. 'I was so afraid I had forced you into something which was none of my business.'

'Everything that has happened in each of our lives has always been the concern of the other. We have told each other everything, until now. I'm only sorry that I didn't tell you earlier, I should have known you would tell me the right thing to do.'

'Did you tell him anything...anything about...?'

'No, I didn't think it right to blurt it out over the telephone. I just said I was very unhappy about something which concerned him deeply and I needed to tell him.'

'You're very brave Nettie. That call needed real mettle, I admire you. That's the first step and the worst. It can only get better.'

'Con? Thanks... for everything, I love you so.'

They stood up and walked arm in arm back to the house.

43

Autumn 1976

Philip's retirement was well overdue. Flora longed for him to be home; she had plans.

Annie was sixty-seven and at last had decided that perhaps she should call it a day. She was sorry to leave Philip and Flora who had given her a home and a family. She had weathered the ups and down with them and had come to love them as though they were of her own flesh and blood. Her one and only relative was Beatrice, in Shipley.

When Annie had broached the subject of retirement, Beatrice had been the first to suggest that Annie should come and live with her. Annie wouldn't have asked but secretly she had hoped it might prove to be a solution.

Philip, in his true generous way, organised the removal of Annie's belongings. She had accumulated over the years a few small pieces of furniture for her own room and Philip insisted that she take the television.

'I think Beatrice has got one,' Annie had said.

'Probably, but you can have this in your own room. You never know you each might like to watch something different and you can watch it in bed,' he added, knowing that that is just what Annie liked to do.

On the day of the removal, Philip and Flora went with her to Shipley. After the furniture had been installed in what was to be her room in Beatrice's bungalow, Philip took them all out to lunch.

'We shall expect to see you from time to time you know, Annie. You and Beatrice must come to visit us. We are going to be a couple of oldies, rattling around in a large and near empty house! You'll save us from getting too set in our ways.'

'Eh, that'll never 'appen Mr H. And not so much of the 'oldies' if you please. Don't forget I'm a year older than you.'

They laughed at Annie's remark and after hugs and just the sign of a tear in Annie's eyes they left her to her new life.

So now Philip and Flora were alone in the large and beautiful house in which they had lived for over thirty years. Flora had no intentions of their 'getting set in their ways' as Philip had put it. Her plans were slowly ripening.

Her first plan was that they should go away for an extended holiday.

'It will make the break from your daily routine easier,' she had said to Philip. 'I think we should travel.'

Philip had been surprised, and pleased, at Flora's deliberation on the subject of his retirement and how they might adjust to the change. He thought her idea of travel was a good one, providing, he said, that they started in Spain.

'There's no question of that,' Flora had said with a smile. 'We'll spend a few weeks with Connie and the family and then perhaps go and see more of Spain before we move on.'

'And does Connie know of these exciting proposals?' he asked laughing at her.

'Well...I have already broached the subject. She seems keen that we should pay them an extended visit.'

'I see, and what have you organised for us to do next?' Philip said with a grin on his face.

'Go places, see things, enjoy the sunshine and...each other's company,' she had responded.

'We have come a long way, haven't we Flora? Over a long and rocky road. But now we are cruising on calm seas. Are you happy Flora?'

'My words Philip, rocky roads and calm seas, you are becoming quite poetic aren't you?' she laughed as she teased him. 'Yes Philip, I am happy. Thanks to you. I don't know why you didn't abandon me some years ago. I did a terrible thing, I can't forget it, and I speak about it now because I want to tell you how much I love you. You have been a constant in my life during and since that awful time, and you didn't forsake me. I don't know why.'

'I loved you Flora. I love you still.' He took her in his arms and they embraced one another.

'I love you too,' she said.

They took out the maps, the brochures, the timetables; and started to plan.

***

A three week stay with Connie and family was the beginning of an extensive tour of Spain. Philip marvelled at Flora's ability to converse with restaurant and hotel staff and she took great pleasure in seeking out interesting places off the beaten track. She loved the responsibility of making bookings, ordering meals and planning each stage of what she dubbed their 'expedition'.

The route planned was to return via France, most of their travels to be by train, with a flight home from Paris. Flora still did not enjoy driving much and she had declared it wasn't fair for Philip to have to do it all by himself. Travelling by train meant that they had to keep their luggage to manageable proportions which was becoming increasingly difficult as Flora acquired a few souvenirs, but Philip could relax.

Flora recognised that those first twelve years of marriage had not been happy years. She held no-one responsible for that but herself. Now when she looked back on the time of the breakdown, twenty-four years ago; Connie's heart-rending departure to Spain; and the years it took for her own recovery; she felt as though she had mislaid a huge slice of her life. These were the years when she should have been involved with the girls, encouraging and advising them, watching them grow up. Instead, one of them was sent to a foreign country and the other to boarding school.

Now at the age of sixty-three Flora felt more like the girl who, without parental love and support, had made her own way in life. She felt strong, she felt happy. Now she was enjoying her family and being with Philip.

Flora astounded Philip once again, this time speaking French with ease.

'How is it I never knew you were such a linguist?' he teased her one day after she had ordered a delicious meal in a rather smart restaurant.

'This is easy,' she replied. 'The whole menu is written in French. Even you could do it!'

'Silly, you know what I mean. I suppose you never had the opportunity to show off your skills after we got married.'

'No, but I could have helped the girls. I was so foolish Philip. I realise now that I was afraid of speaking either French or Spanish, those languages were loaded with memories that I couldn't face.'

'My mother always said that whatever you learn in life comes in useful one day. And here we are reaping the benefit of your hidden talent.'

It was cold in Paris, the late summer warmth had seeped away. Pre-Christmas fever was in the air and decorations were already in the stores. Both Philip and Flora were apprehensive about having a quiet Christmas at home, just the two of them, until Philip suggested writing to Annie and inviting her and Beatrice to join them on Christmas Day.

'What a good idea Philip, but we'll have to cook. No letting Annie do the work! This is probably the first Christmas in her life since coming to live with us, that she will not have cooked a turkey on Christmas Day.'

'Will you manage darling? I'm not being funny when I say that, but you haven't cooked much over the years, have you?'

'But I shan't be doing it alone, shall I? You will be helping me. We may yet prove to be *bons cuisiniers*. That's *'excellent cooks'*, to you.'

When Philip and Flora reached Paris they telephoned Connie to tell of their safe arrival. It was opportune that they did so because Connie had some good news for them.

'Hold your hats on,' she bellowed down the telephone. 'Are you ready?'

'I hope it's good,' Philip hesitated.

'Nettie and David are going to get married, in London, in the New Year.

'That's marvellous news. Oh your mother is going to be thrilled to bits.'

Flora was jiggling up and down next to him, pulling on his arm,

'What am I going to be thrilled about?' she hissed. 'Give me the 'phone, let me talk.'

Connie gave her a few more details of the 'when' and the 'where' and said that Nettie would be telephoning them at home. She was sorry not to be giving them the news herself, she had phoned Connie as she wanted to share the news immediately and had asked her to tell them straight away.

'That's done it, I can't stay in Paris any longer, we must get home as soon as possible.'

After scrambling out of the booth in the main foyer of the hotel, where they had made the call, they turned with huge grins on their faces and threw their arms around each other. The hotel porter glanced at them, he was immured to such goings-on; honeymooners, lovers, affectionate greetings and emotional goodbyes were all in a day's work, after all they were in Paris, the city of love, and sometimes *tristesse*.

'We shall follow our plan Flora, the one you worked out and booked, we are not going to cut short our stay and miss all those

264

wonderful sights and delicious dinners. There is no point in hurrying home, after all, there's no-one...'

Philip stopped.

'You were going to say there is no-one there waiting for us, weren't you Philip?' He nodded.

'We are in a new phase in our lives my dear. Just think, now *we* are the oldies, and that's how the grandchildren will think of us. We are lucky we have them all and must make the most of our good health; we'll visit Connie and family as often as we can; and you never know, one day we may even go to Hong Kong! Now we have much to look forward to; Christmas – I shall be pleased to see Annie again – and then a wedding!'

***

January 1977

The wedding was a quiet affair, this time there were no surprises; no Special Licence, no secret pre-arranged hotel bookings, but a simple church ceremony in London. Philip and Flora were there, with Vicky, Garnet's school friend, who was thrilled to share the event. David's closest friend Ken flew in from Hong Kong the day before to act as Best Man.

Garnet did not wear a 'frothy white dress' as Jonathan had described it, some ten years earlier, but a cream wool suit and chic brimmed hat with a wide apricot coloured ribbon. She looked radiant and serene. She was carrying a small bouquet of deep apricot coloured roses, surrounded by small cream flowers, which before getting into the taxi she managed to launch in Vicky's direction. Vicky caught it expertly with a squeal of amusement until she suddenly realised the significance of Garnet's deed.

'You...you did that on purpose,' she shrieked.

'Of course not,' Garnet smiled back, 'it's tradition.' But turned away laughing at Vicky's bewildered expression.

They dined at the Savoy that evening, where all of them stayed overnight. Garnet and David had arranged another day in London before joining them all back in Harrogate. Philip and Flora invited Ken to return to Harrogate with them and await the newly married couple's arrival the next day. One day in London was not much of a honeymoon

265

Flora had said, but David was adamant that he wanted to see Garnet's home, about which she talked often.

'Besides, it will be good for Garnet to spend some time with you both before we return to Hong Kong.'

Later Flora said to Philip 'This will be such a good opportunity to get to know David a little. And with Ken as well, we can invite Vicky over for dinner.'

'Now, now, matchmaking, are you?'

'I don't think I will have to do much in that direction. Didn't you see the looks between them.'

'But Flora, they've only just met!'

'Listen who's talking! Isn't it wonderful?'

Philip smiled, he didn't have a leg to stand on.

'Yes darling, it's wonderful.

44

October 1980

Diary

The whole López family is in a state of high excitement. Preparations are in progress for a wedding and a birthday celebration.

Juan Luis is to marry Lucia on the 4th of October. The celebration of Isabella's ninetieth birthday will follow on the 16th. Lucia had insisted that they return from their honeymoon in time not only for Juan Luis' birthday, but in particular for Nana's celebration. His typical self-effacing response was that they would play down his birthday. 'I'm not going to upstage Nana's very special day' he had said.

Juan Luis is reluctant to stay away for as long as two weeks now that he is so involved in the business but there is no denying that he is looking forward to having the time alone with Lucia.

All decisions with regard to the wedding are, of course, the right and duty of Lucia's parents. That's not to say that Lucia doesn't have her own ideas too, which are revealing themselves as the arrangements take shape. Good for her I say!

Ramon in his usual, generous way wanted to share the financial burden of a grand wedding, because it was already certain in his mind that it would be such an occasion. Lucia's parents were relieved and grateful for his offer, knowing that the López family was not only numerous, but that they also had many friends.

It was Lucia herself who asked Juan Luis whether it would be possible to have the wedding reception in the grounds of the bodega. Her own house, situated not far away, was a beautiful property with attractive gardens but she realised it would not be adequate for the entertainment of so many people. He was happy to go along with whatever Lucia wanted, and realised the practicality of the suggestion.

'Just one thing though,' he said to her. 'You must ask Papa yourself. I don't want him or anyone else to think that the López family is taking over this whole event.'

Ramon was overjoyed, he had thought it would be going too far to suggest such a thing himself but he never passed up an opportunity to put his bodega on display. He was proud of his achievements in making what had become a renowned wine, along with the help of a few others he had been reminded, but his pleasure at receiving the request from Lucia was no less profound.

Ramon and Carmen were already very fond of this attractive and intelligent girl. She was gregarious and energetic and fell into the midst of Juan Luis' life like a twinkling star, the perfect balance to his quiet, modest personality.

What a contrast this girl was to the looks and characteristics of the López family. She was petite, and blond. She had bright blue eyes, a rare characteristic for a Spanish girl, which glistened almost as though there were tears lying in wait. She stood out against them as a new and different person and they were all captivated by her looks, her charm and the freshness of her.

Though Juan Luis now had much more responsibility, and was becoming the energetic force in the business, Ramon was not yet ready to retire. Juan Luis instigated the purchase of stainless steel vats and thought of himself as a modern wine-maker. The one thing he was determined to do was produce better and better wine, until their family name was on all wine merchants' lips.

Throughout his years of working alongside and learning from his father, Conchita too had worked with him whenever possible, in between the arrival of her babies. Her knowledge was not as technical as his but she was good with the clients and visitors to the bodega. She organised tours of the vineyards and the wine-making sheds and put on special lunches, all of which helped to put their name and their wine before the public.

The wedding day arrived, a mild October day. The ceremony in the local church was long, Lucia a devoted Catholic had been firm on the style and content of the marriage service. She was rigorous in her attendance at mass on a regular basis and had made her continuance of the practice a condition of accepting Juan Luis' proposal of marriage. This was yet another dissimilarity between her and Juan Luis' family. The López family addressed their religion on all the festive occasions, with attendance at church on holy days but beyond that they were lax in their faith. Ana Maria from time to time professed with fervour her religious convictions, but she along with the family did not feel the compulsion to attend mass more often. Isabella was the only exception to this family practice. She was a regular attender at the church though she did not see the necessity to go three times a day on a Sunday!

'Confessing my sins once is quite adequate' she declared. 'God doesn't want to hear me repeat myself!'

The question of becoming a Catholic had bothered Conchita when she had first arrived in Spain and it was Isabella who had advised her to follow her heart.

'Pray for guidance,' she had said. 'And follow what you hear in your heart, not what you hear in your head. The Catholic faith is not the only route to everlasting life, though I think I would be excommunicated if I were heard to say that! As long as you have some belief, something – and I suppose I mean

God – to lean on and of course to thank from time to time, then you will not go far wrong.'

Conchita had been grateful for her words and as she grew older began to join Nana Isabella occasionally in church, to keep her company, she said. She kept her Protestant upbringing but she went with Nana to give thanks, as Nana had suggested she do.

Nana's birthday party was a quiet family gathering, well, as quiet as any gathering of the López clan could be, twelve of them round the table, including Ana Maria. There were no gifts, she had expressly wished it so, other than flowers and congratulatory cards. Ana Maria no longer did all the cooking, despite her protests; there was now a young woman who came in daily to help. After the dinner Ramon stood and clapped his hands.

'I want to say a few words,' he pronounced. Everyone jumped to attention, this was not typical of their celebratory gatherings. Isabella looked uneasy and lifted her hand as though to stop Ramon in his tracks. He ignored her and continued,

'*Madre*'s wish that her 90th birthday should be a quiet affair has been granted but we cannot let her get away with just that.' Isabella tried waving again, to no avail.

'First we wish you a happy birthday Madre; everyone raise your glasses please.' There was a general chorus of 'Feliz cumpleaños' and clinking of glasses.

'Secondly and perhaps more importantly, I wish to say what I think the whole family feels. You have been and still are our lode star. With your wisdom, tolerance of our somewhat demanding personalities and your patience, you have guided us quietly through the years. We are all aware of it but never mention it, now is the time to thank you for it.'

Isabella was smiling as she brushed a tear from her cheek.

'Enough Ramon,' she murmured. 'Whatever has come over you?'

Her question was valid, Ramon was not in the habit of expressing his feelings and the whole family was a little surprised but glad that he had spoken in this way. He left the table for a moment to reach for some bottles set to one side.

'Now, a special wine, our award winning 1975 Grand Reserva, to celebrate and to wish you good health and once more a Happy Birthday.' Juan Luis had opened the bottles earlier and now he rose to help pour the wine. The good wishes rang out as the family again raised their glasses, clapped and one by one gave Isabella a kiss and a hug. There were tears in more than Isabella's eyes, mixed with the smiles and congratulations.

45

Diary

I am about to lose my two darling boys. They are to go to England in September to take up 'A' level studies in order to qualify for entry into university in England. They have set their hearts on it. They have been talking about it for over a year now. Daddy made several enquiries on my behalf, visited the schools and had a talk with each head, then he sent me details. Now comes the surprise; he made the suggestion that they join the 6th form at Donningtons! It had never occurred to me. Daddy gave them the boys' reports and assured them they spoke English fluently, adding that they would have difficulty discerning any trace of an accent and that their grammar is impeccable, thanks to their mother! He is so proud of the twins. Daddy added that although they would board they would be near enough to visit and already he and Ma were anticipating some happy get-togethers. So to quote Rodrigo, it's all settled.

Rosita has no wish to study in England thank goodness. I couldn't bear all my chicks to go away. It's young to have made up her mind but at fourteen she has decided her future. 'You know Mama,' she said one day, 'I'm quite good with little ones, don't you think?' 'Mmm, and what's this little confidence leading to, my dear?' was my reply. 'I want to be a teacher, I want to teach the very young in first school. What do you think?'

'I think it's a nice idea,' I replied. 'But you don't need to make up your mind yet. You've plenty of time.' Her only concern was that Rodrigo and even her grandfather would expect her to work on the bodega like the rest of the family. Not like the twins, they are absolutely sure that they will come back armed with up to date skills and knowledge and start modernising the vineyard and the business. It's quite amusing, as yet they don't know much about wine production but that doesn't seem to trouble them at all.

I also pointed out to Rosita that Catarina, having recognised her own talent, had followed her natural feelings. She is now working in a large art gallery in Bilbao, having very successfully studied art at college. Rosita heaved a sigh of relief when I reminded her of that and just nodded, saying 'good'. In this respect, like the twins, she knows what she wants in life. I suppose that's a good thing.

***

Diary

Nana Isabella is very tired these days, it seems to have come over her quite suddenly. She says it's time she left. I asked her 'And where do you propose to go?' She laughed and said, 'I'd like to join Luis. He's been waiting for me for a long time.'

It scared me a bit, I've never heard her speak like that before. She says she's not ill, just weary of waiting. He was only fifty-four years old when he died so Nana has been a widow for over forty years. What a dreadful thought. She says she hasn't been lonely, but has felt alone and has only been able to bear it through the comfort of her family, who have filled the void as she watched them grow, marry, have children, and given her great grandchildren.

She is grateful that we have allowed her to share in their growing up, to participate in everything, she said, as if we would have done anything else! She even thanked me for accepting her as an abuela, my Spanish grandmother. I almost cried when I said 'but it was you who accepted me Nana'. She has been such a friend to me, I have so valued her support and unconditional love. What a stabilising influence she has been on this family. I can't bear to think that one day she won't be there for any of us.

***

272

Diary

Nana Isabella fell asleep last night and sleeps on peacefully now, forever. I hope she is in the arms of her beloved Luis. How did she know that her time was near? Or was it her strong desire to join her husband of forty years ago that made her yield to her tiredness. She has always been so steadfast, calmly giving her strength to the whole family.

The boys are in the middle of year-end exams, their return for the funeral would disrupt their studies so we have suggested they do not come. They are sorry but I think are relieved as they are working hard.

I shall telephone Ma and Daddy with the sad news and suggest that they come later for a holiday when we have all got over the formalities and sadness.

Nana had been discussing with Juan Luis and Lucia the possibility of her living in a small flat so that they could have her house. They wouldn't hear of it of course, but I expect when everything has been sorted out they will move in. It would be a great solution for them as up until now they have stayed in the annexe of Papa and Carmen's house, which is not ideal. A newly married couple need their own space, as I well know.

***

Christmas 1982

Diary

The saying goes that when there's a death in the family there will follow a birth. And so it is. Lucia has just given birth to a daughter, three and a half kilos, fortunately not a struggle for her, even though small in stature; she has good child bearing hips the midwife told her. Lucia wasn't sure that was a compliment! She's a little worried already about putting on weight. We are all longing to know what they are going to call her. There has been so much discussion. Perhaps Isabella. It would please Papa enormously and would be very fitting, having been born in Nana's house. How she would have loved yet another great grandchild, especially named after her.

We were all a little anxious about Nina until recently. As much as we love her we knew we couldn't keep her indefinitely. She said to me

273

wistfully a few months ago that' her' babies had all grown up. It was obvious that she missed them. I spoke to Lucia about her and without my having to ask, she immediately said, "Oh please, may I have her?" Nina screamed with delight when I asked how she would feel about living with Juan Luis and Lucia. She moved across some weeks before the baby was born to settle in and get used to their house. It was of real benefit to Lucia as she plodded around during the last few weeks of her pregnancy. We are all delighted with the arrangement though Nina shed a few tears as she packed up her belongings. I told her, you're only going to live a kilometre away, you're not going to the other side of the world!' At that she laughed, and said yes of course she would still see us, often.

46

Diary

I no sooner get my boys home again when I will have to part with darling Rosie again this autumn. I can't believe it's a whole year since she went away to university in Bilbao. It was such a quiet year without any of the children around. It sounds funny to call them 'children', the twins 21 and Rosie 19. They have told me quite firmly they are not children any more but my reply was you are, and always will be my children for ever more, no matter how old you are!

Luis has graduated in Business Studies and Carlos in Spanish and French. We are really proud of them both. They have only been home a matter of weeks and they have already found themselves a job. This not inconsiderable achievement has in fact ruffled a few feathers in the family. Papa feels a slight resentment, though he pretends it's not so and Rodrigo is anxious about their prospects. The reason is that they have gone to a rival bodega. "Abuelo didn't really expect us to beg for a job, did he?" they had declared when Rodrigo spoke to them about the wisdom of stepping outside the family. Of course Papa would have offered them a job but it's a little more complicated than that. Papa even at seventy-four hasn't officially retired but we all know that Juan Luis is at the helm, and making a great success of it too. Juan Luis came to me some months ago and told me that the business couldn't carry two more people 'at the top' as he put it. After all, as he pointed out, they are well qualified in certain areas but not yet at making wine. And for the moment, he said, that's what he has to consider. He was very embarrassed and hoped that I and the twins wouldn't be offended about it. I agreed that they had to stand on their own two feet, they couldn't expect to inherit a job. Juan Luis was visibly relieved at my reaction. When the boys got home he talked to them frankly, "so that you know where you stand" he had said. They appreciated his honesty about the situation which immediately gave them permission to establish themselves elsewhere.

The bodega they have gone to is not a very large one but needed some management skills. Luis proved to be ideal not only because of his studies but also because he comes from a wine-making background. This business is involved with exporting their wine and Carlos' ability in three languages is definitely an asset. Having been separated whilst at university, the boys are delighted to be together again. They can't believe their luck at being employed by the same company. I do wonder if the proprietor thought they came as a package and he couldn't have one without the other! They are bursting with confidence but they are in for a challenging time I think.

Now that the young ones are more or less independent Rodrigo and I are thinking of going away for a holiday. We fancy somewhere exotic but can't make up our minds. We must get down to it so that as soon as Rosie returns to university we are free to go.

***

October 1986

Diary

That holiday was a disaster, my darling Rodrigo has come home desperately ill. The doctors don't know what it is but think it's some kind of infection. I'm going to the hospital every day but he just lies there looking pale, and doesn't feel like talking. I'm very anxious and am wondering if I should ask Rosie to come home. This morning they called in a Consultant in tropical diseases; it would be a relief if he discovered something, at least then they would know where they stand and, one hopes, will be able to treat it. Rodrigo just seems to get weaker every day.

***

December 1986

Diary

I waited as long as I dared before calling Rosie, but I'm glad I fetched her home in time to spend some days with her father, at a time when he knew her and could say a few words. We sat by his bedside for hours every day watching him slowly slide towards his end. Together during the last week, we held his hands. He's only sixty-one, much too young to die. This is going to be a very subdued Christmas.

I think back to that Christmas dinner at home with Papa and Carmen, family and lots of friends, it all seems so long ago. That's when I first really remember Rodrigo. That Christmas was special. A very young Juan Luis quizzed me as to whether I liked Rodrigo; that observant little fellow had watched Rodrigo talking to me and I being captivated by his charm and impeccable manners. I didn't like the teasing at the time, but I knew I liked Rodrigo. It wasn't long before I knew I loved him.

I'm too young to be a widow, what am I going to do without him? Work I suppose, drown my sadness in the business. Thank God for my children.

Garnet's letter to Conchita was timely. Conchita had been thinking she could not cope with Los Reyes, her own children were beyond the age of putting their shoes on the doorstep to be filled with gifts from the Three Kings, but there was Isabella, at five years old, already showing signs of knowing her own mind – the family trait! And Fernando, almost four, so the family tradition would be upheld, especially if little Isabella had anything to do with it!

***

January 1987

My dear Con

You are constantly in my thoughts and I am feeling so sorry that David and I could not be with you for Rodrigo's service. I know you understand that I cannot break a contract, unless I'm ill, or without a voice, as once happened a long time ago, even so it has laid heavily on my conscience.

I am due for a break, the present run of ' La Traviata' ends in a week's time and I want to see you so much. Why don't you come and stay with us for a few weeks? After leaving London we will be going back to Hong Kong. You have never been there, I think you would like it. Please, please say you will come. Come to London and stay with us in our flat for two or three days and then the three of us will fly out

277

together. I know your role on the bodega is valued but they can manage
without you for a while and the change will do you good.

I shall telephone you in a few days' time, when you will have had
time to think about our suggestion. Until then, my dear sister, keep
well.

Lots of love
Nettie

***

Connie didn't need to think about the invitation for long. She realised it was a way out of her present melancholic state. She knew that on her return she would have to pick up the threads of life again, without Rodrigo, but she decided to face that when she came to it.

What Garnet did not mentioned to Connie in her letter, was that she was trying to persuade their parents to come to London and be with them for the few days before she and David flew to Hong Kong. Philip had been unwell precluding him and Flora from attending the funeral but they had not told either of their daughters about that. They felt Connie had enough to cope with without worrying about them.

It was a bit of a squash, five of them in Garnet and David's small London flat, but Connie was happy to sleep on the sofa-bed in the sitting room which left the twin room for Philip and Flora.

Garnet and David had booked dinner at the Savoy to celebrate their tenth wedding anniversary and Garnet's forty-seventh birthday. By now pregnancy for Garnet seemed more than unlikely but as David had said, Garnet's career as a world class soprano was central to her life, apart from him, he had added with a grin. They were happy whirling from east to west and back again, in between Garnet's singing appointments and David's business commitments.

They had a surprise awaiting them in the foyer at the Savoy. David had secretly invited Ken to join them, but what even David didn't know was the surprise Ken had for all of them. They proceeded to the table which had seven place settings. Connie's heart missed a beat; Nettie had miscounted - there were only six now, even including Ken. How could she make that mistake? As they sat down Ken remained standing.

'Before I sit down, I would like to point out there are seven places set.' Connie dropped her head and could feel the blood draining from her head, afraid of what Ken was going to say next.

But Ken was smiling broadly and continued,

'That is because I have a guest.' The party suddenly focussed on Ken's evident joy.

'I would like to introduce my wife,' he announced. As though led by a conductor's baton, as one they gasped, turned their heads their eyes following Ken's outstretched arm, pointing to Vicky, walking across the dining room towards them.

As Flora had predicted those years ago, Vicky and Ken had been attracted to one other but it had taken them rather a long time to finally decide to marry.

Garnet leapt from her chair and rushed towards Vicky, regardless of many eyes on her, she hugged her there in the middle of the rather formal dining room.

'You secretive soul, why didn't you tell me?'

'I couldn't tell you anything that I didn't know myself, could I?' she said smiling.

'When? How? Tell me now,' Garnet demanded.

It was Ken who told the story. Each time he had come to England on business he had called Vicky. On one occasion he had been in Paris and telephoned her to say that he couldn't get to London, but wondered if she would like to fly to Paris; they could spend the weekend together. Vicky just couldn't leave her job as a specialist nurse in the children's hospital at Great Ormond Street, not without prior notice. Ken had thought it an excuse, and assuming that she wasn't interested in him did not call her again for months. Vicky was indeed interested but was afraid of making the next move.

'How ridiculous we were,' Vicky said, 'at our age we should have known better and not pussy-footed around. I admit I was afraid of making a fool of myself. After all, our meetings were few and far between over a long period of time.'

It was a wonderful evening bringing each other up to date and reminiscing. Connie was surprised to find herself laughing and recognised that this break, and being with the English side of her family for a while, would go some way to assuaging the pain of her loss.

47

Diary

A milestone – my fiftieth birthday! My party was a surprise, organised almost entirely by Rosie, Luis and Carlos, with a little help from the rest of the family. Rosie invited my friends from all around and throughout the years. Needless to say Ma and Daddy were invited too, she had to tell me that they were coming because of course they stayed with me, but not a word about the rest!

So that I would see nothing of the preparations I was whisked away by Luca, Ma and Daddy (obviously in on the secret) for a birthday lunch. I must be very slow on the uptake not to have realised that something was going on. Rosie had led me on with the promise of a dinner with family in the evening and that it would be really nice if I took Ma and Daddy for a short sight-seeing run. It was good to be with them and for them to meet Luca. Luca is rather good looking, quite stocky, not as tall as Rodrigo. He has thick dark hair which curls almost into ringlets if he doesn't have it cut regularly! He's a rather dynamic character, hard-working and enthusiastic about life; completely different from Rodrigo, but I mustn't make comparisons, it's not fair to Luca, he has some great qualities.

Ma kept looking at me and then at him and I know she's wondering what's going on. I can't tell her anything, because I haven't given Luca my answer yet.

The important business deal with Juan Luis is going through. I've told Ma and Daddy all about that. Luca's neighbouring vineyard, Castillo Blanco, is to be incorporated into our own. It's not very big, compared with ours, but he's worked hard on it for years and produced some very nice wine. Papa thinks it's a good move and he's hoping that the twins are going to be part of the new concern. Luca asked them a little while ago if they would be prepared to leave their present jobs and join him in running the new branch of the Bodega Lopez to be called Bodega Blanca. They aren't sure, not because they don't want to join Luca but because they don't want to desert their employer who has been so good to them, however they are seriously considering it. Luca has no children, he's never been married. He told me one day that he worried about the future and what was going to happen to his land and his company. It's amazing how things come together, such as the possibility of the twins returning to the fold and perhaps being part of the family business in this way. Only Rosita is away from us, teaching in Bilbao, loving her job.

***

Christmas 1988

Diary

The Christmas celebrations seem to come round sooner these days, I can't believe it is two years since my darling Rodrigo passed away. I don't cry anymore but I think about him a great deal. The children talk about him as though he were out at work and will be back soon. I suppose it's their way of coping with his absence.

I still haven't made up my mind about Luca. He is being very patient. He says he is virtually a member of this family anyway now that Luis and Carlos work for him, and his vineyard is part of the overall company.

We've been seeing each other regularly for several months and Papa and Carmen are obviously watching the situation closely. Papa started to talk about Luca the other day with raised eyebrows, praising his self-motivation and good-humoured manner as though trying to provoke me into some sort of declaration. It reminded me of the time when Papa praised Rodrigo and I challenged him, asking him if he was 'trying to sell him to me'. I'm older and I hope a little wiser now and I didn't rise. I did notice that Carmen didn't say much except that it was none of their business, which I thought was rather odd. She felt I ought to know more about him. Papa shut up then and there was a bit of a silence. Anyway, though I like Luca a lot - it's true he is full of life and easy to be with - I can't say that I have fallen in love with him, not yet anyway.

I have far more important things to think about in any case. Rosie has announced her engagement! He's a teacher in the same school where she works. They want a summer wedding. Here we go again! This time I have to do all the planning. I hope Rosie will come home soon to help.

***

April 1989

Rosie did come home in good time to help organise the wedding. And Eduardo came too, I'm glad to say.

It became all too obvious within days of their being with the family that Eduardo was going to fit in with everyone. A likeable and cheery fellow he announced that he had already applied for a post as head of a secondary school, not too far away from us.

He quietly announced, 'I can't have Rosita pining for her family; she tells me she has lived too far away from you all for long enough. I don't mind where I live, I have lived in many places in Spain and as long as I am with Rosita then I shall be happy.'

Conchita heaved a great sigh of relief. Her darling Rosie would be coming back.

Eduardo returned to Bilbao after a few days, but Rosita stayed on having already worked out her term's notice. It occurred to Conchita that these two had been planning for some time without a word to anyone!

That was the catalyst that Conchita needed. Where would Rosie live? The family home of course. Conchita knew that she had been wavering over her answer to Luca for too long. It wasn't fair.

Conchita called Luca on the telephone and asked if he would like to come to dinner that evening. He was surprised but pleased. He was even more surprised to find that he was the only guest, Rosita having gone out to visit friends.

Conchita had asked Manuela to stay on after Rodrigo died and then even when the children left she said she couldn't manage without her.

'I know it's not the same now,' she had said to Manuela. 'But if I am to go on working as I would like to do, I will still need your help with the cooking and cleaning. What do you say?'

Manuela had not hesitated. 'Oh please, I want to stay. And Alberto? Do you still want him to continue working in the garden and doing jobs?'

'Of course, what would I do without him?'

It was true, she could not cope without their help but what Conchita could not admit at the time, was that she could not face being alone in

282

the house. Now that it was likely there would be a few changes in the near future, she was more than glad that Manuela and Alberto were still part of the household, but of course she couldn't divulge any of that until she had spoken to Rosie.

Manuela's help in the kitchen meant that Conchita didn't have to keep running in and out, interrupting her conversation with Luca, at the same time they were not in a public place so that Conchita felt she could speak openly.

Luca arrived wearing smart grey trousers with an open-necked shirt and a silver and black cravat, the ensemble highlighted his dark colouring.

'My, you are looking smart Luca, but we are only the two of us, I hope you don't mind that?'

'Mind? I am delighted,' he replied with enthusiasm. 'You know I don't often get you to myself.'

'Perhaps I should have worn a more elegant dress.'

'You wear everything with elegance Conchita. I like... I love you as you are.'

Conchita suddenly became shy and began quickly,

'I must speak to you Luca about one or two things. First, as you know Rosita and Eduardo are going to be married in June. Secondly I have decided to offer them my house, the family home, to live in.'

'That's generous of you. Is this a temporary arrangement until they find something for themselves?'

'No. You see I think... I hope... I'm going to be moving out.'

Luca placed his knife and fork on the table with a slow deliberate action and looking up saw Conchita take a deep breath.

'Just before Christmas you asked me a very important question. You have been so patient with me but now I would like to reply.'

Luca's expression was unsmiling. He was expecting the worst possible reply.

'If your question is still....'

'My question was - will you marry me?' he interjected.

'Yes Luca, I would like to marry you very much.'

Luca stood up and marched round to the other side of the table. He took Conchita in his arms and then letting go, he pushed her to arms' length keeping hold of her hands.

'Let's be honest with one another Conchita. You know I have had a few lovers over the years, don't you? Carmen is aware of that fact and may well have mentioned it to you.'

Conchita suddenly understood Carmen's remark about knowing more about Luca but she shook her head. Luca continued,

'But I have never loved anyone enough to ask them to marry me. So I'm assuming that the fact that I do want to marry you, means I am in love with you! Not a very romantic speech, is it?'

'It's an enormous compliment Luca, I only hope I won't disappoint you.'

'Impossible. I hope I won't disappoint you. So, you said you would be moving out. Does that mean you will live with me in the Castillo?'

'If that's all right with you,' Conchita replied.

'I really hoped that sooner or later you would come to live with me, even if not as my wife.'

Conchita was taken aback at Luca's remark. He saw her startled expression and quickly stepping forward again put his arms around her and kissed her. It was a warm and tender kiss and Conchita responded.

'Conchita, forgive me, it was meant as a joke. Now when I should be saying romantic things, and expressing how I feel about you, I'm hopeless. It's a new experience for me –being in love.' Conchita smiled and then whispered,

'There is something I need to ask of you, Luca,' He leaned back and looked into to her eyes. 'Could we keep this to ourselves for a little while, until after Rosita's wedding, and then perhaps we could go away and have a quiet little ceremony. I don't want a big fuss.'

'Whatever you wish.'

Conchita smiled and then became aware of noises in the kitchen.

'Quick. Sit down and eat before Manuela comes in to clear the plates otherwise she will think we don't like the meal and she will be upset. What's more, she's made your favourite dessert.' They gobbled the food just in time before Manuela popped her head round the door.

After dinner they strolled in the dark, arm in arm.

48

June 1989

Diary

Rosita and Eduardo are man and wife! The wedding was so beautiful. It was simple and dignified. I knew I would cry; tears of happiness for my darling Rosie because it is obvious that she and Eduardo are so in love, but my tears were mingled with sadness for my Rodrigo. How he would have enjoyed the day and been so proud to give away his beloved daughter. At first, we didn't know who to ask to perform this important task. Rosita thought maybe Juan Luis would like to do it, then she made her own decision.

'Luis and Carlos; they shall give me away,' she declared. 'One on my left, and one on my right.' The boys were thrilled and it worked beautifully.

And now Rosita and Eduardo are going to live in the family house. They don't know it yet and are going to be surprised when I tell them that I shall be making a new home in Luca's house, and that I shall not be far away.

June 1989

Rosita and Eduardo were overwhelmed at Conchita's offer of her house for them to live in.

'It will be such fun,' Rosita said, smiling widely. 'Almost like old times. We'll be able to have dinner together and cosy chats in the evening.'

'Well it won't be quite like that, my darling, for two reasons. First of all I want you and Eduardo to start married life in a home of your own, just the two of you. It's the best way.'

'But Mama what...?'

'And the second reason...' Conchita hesitated but smiled, '...is because I am going to live with Luca.' Rosita gasped.

'Don't worry darling, it's all quite respectable, you see we are going to be married next week.'

'But Mama you can't do that. We shall be on our honeymoon. I want to be there, I mean, *we* want to be there don't we Eduardo?'

'Rosita, don't you think first we should congratulate your mother, wish her happiness with Luca?' Eduardo said.

'Oh *Mama* , yes of course. I'm so pleased for you. He's very nice, but....'

'What a lot of 'buts' Rosita.! This is what we both want, a quiet little ceremony with Carmen and Papa as witnesses. Then we shall celebrate with a dinner at the Parador de Santa Domingo Bernardo. I'm sorry too that you won't be there, but this way, when you come back the house will be ready for you and Eduardo, and I shall be nicely settled in Luca's house.'

'*Mama* you cannot live in that dreadful castillo! Everyone knows it's dark and dingy. Luca himself told me once what a horrid place it is.'

Both Conchita and Eduardo burst out laughing.

'Has she always been so argumentative?' he asked, laughingly. 'In which case, I can see I shall have to be very firm with her.'

Eduardo stood up and came to Conchita. He took her hands and then kissed her on each cheek.

'I for one wish you great happiness,' he said simply.

Rosita burst into tears.

'I'm so happy for you too *Mama*. I'm glad you have someone to love and to live with instead of being lonely here in this house. But - oh dear, yet another 'but'. Sorry. I want to be sure you are doing this because you love him and not because...'

'...and not because I'm giving you the house. Is that what you mean Rosie? You needn't worry. Luca asked me to marry him months ago. I told him I had grown fond of him but at that time I didn't really know whether I wanted to be married again. He said he understood, "take your time, just think about it" he said. I did and now I'm sure of my answer. Poor Luca has been very patient.

'So it's settled.' A shiver ran down Conchita's spine as she uttered the words, a voice from the past.

'You know that we could all live here together, if you wanted.'

'That's sweet of you. I'm going to marry Luca and live in his house. Living here with him wouldn't be right, the memories are too strong. Besides, as I said, you and Eduardo must start out in your own home, just the two of you with no hangers-on.'

'But you know, don't you Conchita, that I would not look upon your presence as a 'hanger-on' as you call it? If you wanted to stay in this your home, then I would be just as happy as Rosita for you to do so.'

'Thank you Eduardo but I'm looking forward to a new phase in my life and a new kind of happiness. You and Rosie are beginning a new phase in your lives too and I'm just so pleased that you can do so here in this happy house.'

For some weeks before Rosita and Eduardo's wedding, Conchita, unbeknown to anyone, had been choosing fabric and ordering new curtains for her own new home, alongside the planning and making arrangements for the wedding.

Conchita had asked Luca if she could furnish his house a little more warmly, with a few feminine touches. The living quarters within the Castillo were old fashioned and dark and Rosita was right, the place was cheerless. The rest of the building had been a castle at one time but portions of it were uninhabitable and were falling down. Conchita felt she had a task ahead of her to make it a home.

'You can do whatever you wish my dear,' Luca had responded. 'My house is now your house. I know it's a bachelor's house, rather sombre and no pretty colours. I don't know how to achieve that feeling so please, make it *our* house with your touch, your own ideas and style. I shall look forward to it.'

'Don't you want to choose with me?' she asked him.

'I leave it all to your impeccable taste,' he replied. Conchita was a little disappointed. She and Rodrigo had always made decisions jointly, choosing items for the house together. She found this new responsibility daunting and was a little disheartened. What if she chose a colour Luca didn't like? A style he found objectionable? His seemingly abrupt reply brought tears to her eyes.

The week after the wedding was very busy for Conchita. She had one or two of her favourite pieces of furniture moved into Luca's house, which encouraged her in her endeavours to make the cheerless accommodation more homely. Without any help from Luca she had chosen her favourite colours. The bedroom curtains were green and cream and apricot, a light soft fabric that floated into the room on a gentle breeze and brought the room to life.

Then came their own very quiet ceremony a week later with Carmen and Ramon as witnesses. Champagne before dinner literally gave a sparkle to the occasion and that night Conchita slept with Luca for the first time.

Rosita's move into the family home had in effect already taken place when she came home from Bilbao, after resigning her teaching

287

post. Her homecoming as Eduardo's wife, was to a house filled with flowers and loving messages from all the family.

49

Diary

Rosita has been so enjoying her teaching here in the town that I was surprised when she came to me and said that she is taking a sabbatical. My immediate concern, that something was wrong, was chased away as she took my hand. She's pregnant. I'm so thrilled for them. Me, a grandmother, I can't believe it! Now I look at her I see that she has a glow about her. I've been so engrossed in my own life, still trying to make a new life with Luca that I have not recognised what was happening under my nose.

I surprise myself as I write that - 'trying to make a new life' – after all we've been married two years, if I haven't achieved that by now then heaven help me. It's much harder than I thought it would be. Rodrigo is in my thoughts every day and I feel guilty. My head should be full Luca. I do think of him, I try to please him, cook his favourite dishes and be around when he's at home. Obviously I can't be in the house all day, every day, I'm working – and I love my work. It just seems to me that lately Luca has come to resent that. He oversees the running of the wine making process but it's Carlos and Luis who are doing a lot of the work. During the four years with their previous employer they learned fast and they were very committed, and they still are, but now it's in the family. In a way, I think Luca is jealous of the fact that they are already producing a better wine than when he ran the bodega by himself. He is still nominally in charge but he knows that his input is now minimal. Unsurprisingly the twins have gone to Juan Luis for advice and maybe Luca doesn't like that. I've seen a look of displeasure cross his face when they speak about it. All credit to the twins, they read and study all the time, no wonder they are having success. I've told them, what did they expect? - wine making is in their blood! It's Carlos really who has inherited the talent and though Luis is good, he is better at the management and business end of things.

Perhaps Luca will settle down a little when this new venture he has started has taken off. He won't tell me what it is, 'just business' he says when I ask. The problem is it takes him away for two or three days at a time. He says it's something new, nothing to do with wine. He'll tell me in his own good time, I'm sure. I'm actually glad he's got something to interest him. I felt he was becoming bored with the bodega.

***

Diary

A July baby. She arrived on the 8th and Papa is calling her his birthday present.

She's a beautiful baby, but Rosita doesn't look well. She didn't cope with the hot July weather and Mercedes was a large baby, taking her time to come into the world. I'm helping out as much as I can. Juan Luis has told me not to worry about work but to support Rosita, 'She's much more important' he said. I'm beginning to wonder if I'm really needed in the business any more. I can't give up – at fifty-four? Never mind my age, I don't want to stop working for and with the family business. It's too much a part of me!

Conchita was expecting Luca home early that evening. She had cooked cod in white wine, with onions and garlic, a simple but favourite local dish. Despite the fact that Manuela had done most of the cooking when Conchita, Rodrigo and the children were one family, Conchita was in fact a very good cook. She could take a recipe and weaving her own imagination and knowledge of different ingredients into it, she would produce something new and delicious.

When the telephone rang she almost ignored it. It persisted until Conchita muttered, 'Oh, all right, I'm coming!'

'Yes?' she answered curtly. But her irritation turned to surprise at the sound of Luca's voice.

'I'm sorry darling, but I can't get back tonight. Another meeting I'm afraid.'

'But I've invited Juan Luis and Lucia,' her disappointment was unmistakable in her tone.

'Ah yes, well, they will enjoy the meal. Save some for me. See you tomorrow.'

Luca rang off leaving Conchita not a second in which to respond . Half an hour later Juan Luis and Lucia arrived, smiling and carrying flowers.

290

'What scrumptious surprise have you concocted for us tonight?' they said as they arrived.

Conchita loved having them for a meal, they were always so appreciative. It gave Lucia a little respite from their busy home, not that she didn't love her darling children, but she needed a breathing space, time to think and to enjoy others' company. After Isabella came Fernando not a year later. Then Elena Maria and José; four children within six years. Quiet moments in their house were few and far between. It was what she had wanted - a large family, but Juan Luis declared four was enough. It was a good thing that they had the delightful and hard-working Nina living with them.

Over the last few years Conchita and Juan Luis had become close, despite the gap in their ages they were now a truly devoted brother and sister. They trusted and respected one another and had long discussions on the family and their needs and wishes, as well as on business matters. It was Juan Luis who had noticed that all was not well with Conchita. So far he had not been able to identify the problem but after Conchita's 'phone call that evening to warn them that Luca would not be with them he resolved to ask a few questions.

'So, Luca has been delayed, you say,' Juan Luis began as Conchita served some easy-made tapas of olives, pepperoncini, cocktail onions and white tuna, as a starter to the meal.

'What a pity. His loss, I must say. I don't think for a moment he can be eating anything quite so delicious.'

'Yes, he did say he would be back tonight. I really don't know what it is he gets up to,' Conchita said, trying to laugh it off.

'What is this new business he has started Conchita? He's very secretive about it I gather. Come, surely *you* know?'

'I don't,' she replied rather abruptly. 'And how is José, Lucia, is he walking yet, or still shuffling along on that fat little bottom of his?' Conchita's change of subject was transparent and Juan Luis taking the cue began to talk of Carlos and Luis and their work. But that too inadvertently brought them round to the wine production on the Castillo Blanco bodega; in particular to their recent success, and of course to Luca's apparent lack of interest in the business. Juan Luis gave Lucia a meaningful look when Conchita went to the kitchen to bring in the dessert. She took the hint and for the rest of the evening she talked of the children and their doings.

'Fernando loves school and takes great pleasure in greeting Rosita each morning, boasting to his classmates that she is his aunt.'

'Now I have Isabella telling me that she is now quite grown up and I needn't make such a fuss of her when we say goodbye at the school gates. "You don't need to hug and kiss me Mama. You can kiss me when I get home," is what she said. I tell you one doesn't expect that from one's child.'

'She always has been independent Lucia and after all she is ten. Don't be upset. You'll probably be glad of it at later.'

The conversation flowed on with talk of Ramon's diminishing involvement in the company and Carmen's pleasure at the fact that they were now able to go away from time to time. Their latest plan was to have a holiday in England.

Philip and Flora had been delighted to receive their 'phone call to ask if they might visit them in Yorkshire. Plans were made to show them not only the county of Yorkshire but to take them farther afield.

50

Diary

Luca is away on business again this week for three nights this time. It would seem that this new 'venture', as he calls it ,has been growing, he is certainly spending more and more time on it as the months go by. He has now said it's something to do with building development; new houses, I think he said. I'm not sure why he should be involved with the building industry – as far as I know he doesn't know a thing about it. I thought it must be something to do with the wine trade and after pressing him he at least told me that. But he was very dismissive and said not to trouble my pretty head about it. My head would be less troubled if he told me; it's all too mysterious for comfort. He has just about handed over all the responsibility to the boys. They are thrilled about that. They think it's because they have shown they are capable of carrying on without him and that he trusts them. I'm sure that's true but Luca knows that Juan Luis is there in the background keeping an eye on things. Nevertheless, I'm uneasy but I don't know why, I can't put my finger on anything specific.

October 1993

Diary

I'm so fed up with Luca's business trips. It's been going on for over a year now. I suggested I went with him for a change. I said I needed a break I had been working quite hard and it would do me good. He was quite angry with me. I got really upset and almost cried. I'm sure he saw the tears well up in my eyes even though I turned away. He blustered on about my not understanding his commitments, and the fact that he had to work. That's not what he said when we married; he said then he didn't need to work ever again, he had quite enough money. Even so, he said he would work, he couldn't bear people to think he was a lazy good-for-nothing. He suggested I go away and see a friend for a few days. Who? I wanted to know. 'I don't know, surely you've got a friend somewhere,' he said. 'You spend far too much time with Rosita, back at your old house. Perhaps you're sorry you left it!' That really hurt. We have never had harsh words like this before. Anyway it all ended with my saying it didn't matter. It does matter though, because it made me think hard about my life and the fact that I don't go anywhere anymore or visit friends. I seem to spend all my time here on the bodega, with the family or in this miserable Castillo. I must admit I do visit Rosie and I look after Mercedes quite often, which I love. Rosie is going back to teaching to take up her old job at the primary school. Even so I think Luca's accusation was unfair.

***

This wasn't the first time Luca had accused Conchita of spending too much time looking after Mercedes. The first time she hadn't been upset about his remark, she thought he was a little envious of her having a grand-daughter and this was his way of expressing his resentment at the time she spent away from their own home. Conchita loved looking after Mercedes, feeding her, putting her in her cot for a nap, and filling the house with baby talk. It reminded her of days gone by, except that there was no Rodrigo in and out of the house. In any case Conchita felt there was an element of duty on her part to help Rosita, who was so keen to go back to teaching. Conchita knew she had been very lucky to have Nana Isabella around, and Carmen and Papa, to help her. This was her way of being grateful for what had been such a happy time in her life, by doing what she could to help her daughter.

Conchita did her best to put behind her the unpleasant words of the last week, just a 'marital tiff', she told herself. Even so, she was aware that she was dwelling frequently on her years with Rodrigo and the fact that they had never had a tiff of any kind. They disagreed, even argued, but their words to each other had never been hurtful. Conchita found herself making comparisons more and more often between Rodrigo and Luca, which only resulted in her feeling guilty. She came out of her feelings with the thoughts that she shouldn't be doing this. It must be she who was at fault and therefore she must try harder to be what Luca wanted. The trouble was she didn't know what he wanted.

It was a month later that Carmen called round to see Conchita. It didn't happen very often, Conchita was pleasantly surprised to see her but did wonder what had prompted the visit.

'I've come to see what improvements you have made lately on the house. It looks much better,' Carmen began.

'Do you think so? I like it but I'm not sure...'

'What does Luca say?'

'Well, he's not home a great deal at the moment. He recently had some meetings and stayed over longer than he expected. So I don't think he really noticed the changes.'

'I gather he goes to Pamplona, isn't that right?' Conchita didn't respond; she didn't know where he went.

'I was there this week, I went to meet a friend from long ago. We've just got in contact again after all these years. It's a really interesting town, steeped in history. Have you ever been?'

'No. They have bull running don't they? That doesn't appeal to me. I don't seem to go anywhere much these days.' Conchita's tone was lacklustre which gave Carmen the opening she wanted.

'That's a shame Conchita. I think you should get out more. After all if Luca can go calling on someone in Pamplona, why shouldn't you go out to see your friends?'

Carmen wondered if jumping in with such a remark so early in their conversation was clumsy. How else was she to get round to telling Conchita that she had seen Luca enter a house and be greeted by a young woman. Conchita was silent but fussed over a flower arrangement that needed no adjustment at all. Carmen waited and when Conchita still didn't speak she continued in as natural a tone as she could manage.

'I expect he was inspecting one of the houses that have been built on this new development.'

'Oh that's interesting, where are the houses?' Conchita asked.

'Oh don't you know? It's a small development as you go into the town, with their own supermarket and a shopping mall, and buses into the centre of the town to the larger stores. Quite nice really, if you like that sort of thing.' Carmen's tone was a little scornful. She stayed for a while and had a cool drink, sitting on the veranda with Conchita. No more was said about Luca.

Conchita decided not to speak to Luca of his absence nor the fact that Carmen had seen him in Pamplona. It wasn't the first time that Carmen had expressed concern that Luca spent so much time away from home and the significant message that she sent Conchita that day was not lost on her.

Conchita worked hard both at home in the house, cooking and making the house welcoming when she expected Luca home, and she threw herself into her work. It was interesting and the bodega was receiving more and more visitors whom were her responsibility. Her tours round the winery were now polished and knowledgeable and she loved meeting people of all nationalities. Her greatest fun was with the English, they always congratulated her on her command of the English language, until she told them she was born in England. They were amazed to find that she was not Spanish and then the Spanish visitors congratulated her on her proficiency in the language. It always made her smile and at the same time gave her a little lift to think that she fitted in so well. Then she would remind herself that she had lived in the country for over forty years, of course she fitted in.

Where had the years gone to? What a silly old cliché. It seemed on reflection that the years had come and gone in a repeated pattern; she climbed a mountain of pain and sadness, reached the summit of her suffering and slowly descended into a valley of calm and happiness below; mountains and valleys over and over again during those forty years. As she stood preparing the vegetables one evening, waiting for Luca's return, she pondered on Carmen's words and recognised that she was about to climb yet another mountain.

***

It wasn't difficult to arrange a break from work. Juan Luis was actually pleased to hear that Conchita was asking for a few days off.

'It's about time you had a rest. You've been working flat out for weeks. The grape harvest is over so now is an ideal time for you to take a break before we have another rush of 'wine-tasters'. What are you going to do? Just sit and read, enjoy some peace and quiet and the sunshine?'

'Well yes, but not at home. I've decided to go away for a few days, maybe to the coast. I haven't seen the sea for....for a long time. Go on, tell me the sea air will do me good,' she laughed.

'It will Conchita. You've been looking rather tired of late. I think this is just the right thing to do. What does Luca think?'

'He's quite happy about it. You know he comes and goes to...' Conchita faltered, she didn't feel she could mention that Carmen had seen him in Pamplona. '...to his building activities,' she filled in. 'He says he doesn't mind at all.'

'Drive carefully then. We'll see you when you get back.' Juan Luis leaned forward and took her in his arms. 'Take care,' he whispered.

296

Conchita was moved and had to turn away so that he did not see the tears forming in her eyes.

Conchita returned home to collect her suitcase, maps and handbag, the notepad and file. She had guarded the file, even going so far as to hide it in the house. It contained some disturbing information.

Her climb up the emotional mountain had begun with an action she could never have envisaged she would make. She had contacted a private investigator.

'All I want you to do,' she had told him, 'is find out where he goes to in Pamplona, the dates and times. Nothing more.'

The report of his findings was in the folder. Now that Conchita was in the car she began to have doubts. Whatever was she doing stalking her husband like this? She felt ashamed. What if he had been aware of it? He would never forgive her. But the notes were there; 'entered house at 16.00 hrs, Tuesday 23rd October, left 09.00 hrs Wednesday 24th October.' That was only one of a list of similar arrivals and departures. The street name and house number were recorded alongside the entries.

'Perhaps Luca is renting a property to stay in instead of booking in and out of a hotel. At least that way he can leave his clothes and papers,' Conchita whispered to herself as she drove along. She sighed deeply and concentrated on the road ahead.

It was a warm, bright day and as she began to settle into the rhythm of driving she began to enjoy the scenery. She found she didn't need to keep consulting her map and she relaxed. It wasn't until she saw the sign indicating 10 kilometres to Pamplona that her earlier nervousness returned. She hadn't even formulated a plan. As she entered the outskirts of the town she saw the hoarding proclaiming the new properties.

'This is it; the development.' She slowed down and drew into a car park serving a large supermarket. She could hide here, anonymous amongst all the shoppers. She got out of the car taking only her handbag with her, securing the folder safely in the locker of the dashboard, and began to walk towards the nearby housing estate.

'What if he's at the house? What am I going to say? Oh, why did I come?' she muttered, but she kept walking as though drawn by some force outside herself. She began to tremble as she saw the house number in front of her.

Conchita approached the house but it took all her courage on reaching the door to knock, her heart was beating so hard it hurt in her chest. The door was opened by a small girl, with long hair, the dark curls tied back in bunches. She was smiling widely as she said,

'Hello, my name's Arabella.'

'Well, er...hello Arabella, I'm...' Conchita stopped. For an instant she was disarmed, momentarily forgetting why she had come to this place. The child continued to smile and asked,

'What's your name?'

Conchita hesitated. How could she could say her name without revealing her identity and the reason for the visit? It didn't occur to her to give a false name. Recovering slightly she said,

'Perhaps you can help me, I'm looking for Señor Luca Goncalvez...' but again Conchita's courage failed her, she didn't finish her sentence.

'Oh you mean my Papa. He's not here today. He's gone to work a long way away.'

Conchita stood there in front of the door, unable to move. Her mind registered 'Papa' and 'gone to work'. There must be some mistake. Then she heard a voice calling from inside the house and footsteps approaching.

'Who is it Arabella?' and a young woman came and stood behind the child. She smiled at Conchita.

'Can I help you?' she asked. And then with a sudden knowing smile she said,

'Oh, I know you, you are from the Bodega López, in Haro, aren't you? Luca has told me about his business connections with your company. You've just missed him, what a shame. He left only an hour ago, and you've come a long way, he'll be sorry to have caused you such inconvenience. He told me about the important meeting.' All this, in a pleasant manner and with a smile, Conchita felt light-headed.

'It's all right, it's fine. We....we'll catch up with one another...' Conchita was trying to think of a reason for calling instead of waiting for this ' important meeting' but her brain seemed to have closed down.

'Oh good, then I'll tell him you came, shall I?' the young woman asked.

'No, no it doesn't matter. I'll see him... at the...meeting. Thank you.'

As Conchita turned away Arabella called out,

'Bye, bye pretty lady, see you soon.'

Later Conchita did not know how she had managed to walk away from the house. Her legs felt like soft dough, she could barely put one foot in front of the other. It seemed like hours to reach her parked car and climb in. She locked the door as though afraid that someone had followed her and would get inside the car. She grasped the steering wheel with both hands and her head fell forward between them. It wasn't until a man rapped on her window, mouthing something to her

298

and gesticulating, that she became aware of a blaring sound. Her head was pressing on the centre of the steering wheel and suddenly she realised that the sound blasting forth was her car horn.

She raised her head to see the man walking away still mumbling and waving an angry arm. She sat for a moment and then started the car. She drove without thinking, following the road signs out of Pamplona, turning almost automatically as though it were a journey she made every day instead of a place she had never visited.

She drove for some time, with tears trickling down her face like melting icicles dripping unheeded until she felt the cool dampness of them soaking through her blouse.

51

Diary

I'm in despair. I don't know what to do. If only Nana Isabella were here I would go to her, she would advise me, without judgement. Oh, how I miss you Nana! There's no-one else to ask for help. Rosie – but you have your own worries and work to cope with. I can't discuss this with the boys either, they have some allegiance to Luca, it would destroy their view of, and affection for him. And I can't speak to Papa or Carmen, they're getting on now and I can't burden them with such worries. I don't dare tell Juan Luis; he's so protective of me I think he would kill him!

Luca, what have I done to deserve this? I knew about your affairs, you were honest with me and told me yourself, but you said unlike any other woman you had met you loved me enough to marry me. Is it my fault? Have I expected too much? I should have known I could never love another as I did Rodrigo. It is my fault. Now what is going to happen?

Luca returned from the business trip in a good mood to find Conchita already back home.

'That was a short break darling,' he said as he came into the house. 'Did you relax and enjoy your trip?'

Conchita could not lie, she knew she would give herself away and so she said,

'Yes it was short, but it was enough.' It was the truth but the statement silently mocked her.

'Good. Let's go out for dinner, have some time to sit and talk and enjoy one another's company without your having to cook and hop to and fro from the kitchen. We need time together, don't we? I have been spending quite a lot of time away on business.'

Conchita was taken aback by the suggestion and immediately thought 'he must know where I've been. The woman has told him. Or perhaps the child, Arabella, but before she was able to form any sort of reply Luca said,

'Off you go then, put on your glad rags, we'll go somewhere smart, it'll make a nice change for you.'

They drove some distance, indeed it was a smart restaurant, Conchita had never been there before. The meal was first class, it was tranquil, the service discreet but it was not the sort of place where Conchita could even begin to talk of their relationship and what she had discovered. She hadn't even decided when she might speak or what she would say, only that sometime soon she would have to face him with her knowledge. It was, despite Conchita's underlying disquiet, a pleasant evening but Luca's behaviour bewildered her; he was attentive, smiling and affectionate. She pleaded a headache on their return home and left Luca reading as she went to bed.

Luca stayed at home for four days and then left on business again with the remark that he would not be back for possibly as long as a week, but 'I'll let you know' he said. 'I'm sure you've got lots to do and I know you won't be lonely with all the family around you,' he added.

October 1933

Diary

Luca's gone away again. I have to talk to someone; I need help. I'll write to Nettie – no, I'll phone her. She's in London at the moment so I can speak to her this evening.

Conchita's telephone call resulted in Nettie booking a flight to arrive in three days' time. Conchita met her at the airport, Conchita's confidence in driving had been given a boost with her trip to Pamplona and she decided she would meet Nettie herself. Besides, it had occurred to her that she might be able to talk as they drove along. Having to concentrate on the driving she would have to remain calm and matter of fact, it would help her keep her emotions under control. As it was, they did not touch on Conchita's worries at all, Garnet herself had unhappy news to impart.

'Daddy's poorly Connie, did you know?'

'What kind of 'poorly' Nettie? No-one has said anything to me at all, is it serious?' Garnet nodded. Conchita felt the movement rather than saw it, keeping her eyes on the road ahead.

'Tell me when we get home,' she said. Conchita felt the personal mountain confronting her rising higher and steeper than any before; she felt she did not have the strength to climb again. She sighed and felt Nettie's hand on her arm. She knew the only way she was going to come through was with Nettie's help.

***

There was no time to talk when Conchita and Garnet arrived at the house. Rosita was standing at the door. Her face was tear stained and her arms were wound tightly round her body as though she were trying to hold herself together. Conchita gasped at the sight of her.

'Something's happened. Oh my God, Mercedes?'

They sprang out of the car and Conchita ran towards Rosita.

'What is it? What's happened?'

'Oh *Mama*, it's terrible, an accident...'

Conchita turned pale and Garnet grasped her arm as she rocked unsteadily.

'Who?' she asked in a whisper.

'Luca,' she said flinging her arms around her mother.

Conchita's legs gave way and she sank to the ground. At that moment Eduardo came up the pathway to the house.

'She's fainted,' Garnet said. 'let's get her into the house.'

Eduardo bent down, lifted her up in his arms and carried her inside.

October 1993

Diary

I have been given an answer to my question 'now what's going to happen? No, not really, it's not an answer at all. In fact there are more questions than before. They haven't told me everything, I can tell. They're eking out the information little by little, afraid I will react again from shock. But I wish they would just tell me and have done with it. It wasn't shock that made me faint, it was relief. That's a terrible thing to say but I thought it was one of the children. That would have been unbearable. Now I feel horribly guilty.

It was a car crash. The woman in the car has a broken arm but Luca...Luca was killed. The steering wheel crushed his chest. What a ghastly thing to happen to anyone, it's a dreadful end. But they are

302

telling me he would not have suffered – he died instantly. He didn't deserve it, no matter what has happened between us. Was I subconsciously wishing something would happen to end my misery? If I was, it certainly wasn't death.

I have hardly cried, not because I'm not sad but the tears just won't flow. All the family's worried; they think I'm being brave. If only they knew that what I feel is a reprieve. Whatever comes out at the inquest and police investigation, yes they tell me that will follow after the funeral, I will not now have to face Luca; no questions, no excuses, no lies.

No, I don't have an answer to my question; I have only exchanged one kind of unhappiness for another.

***

October 1993

Diary

We've had to wait two weeks before we were allowed to bury Luca. The Coroner's inquest recorded an accidental death. His car had veered off the road, the sudden spin brought about by Luca suffering a heart attack. The attack itself was not severe and had the car not crashed into a concrete wall it is likely that he would have recovered and the Coroner's report said that he might well 'have been restored to a reasonable level of health.'

Conchita's tears at last began. Through her black veil she could not distinguish the faces of many who were present in the church, their sad and anxious expressions were hidden from her. At the graveside she could not look into that murky space as the coffin was lowered. She lifted her head, adjusted the veil and began to look at the black clothed forms around her; Rosita, Eduardo, Juan Luis, Lucia, Papa, Carmen, and on her left Luis, Carlos on her right, each holding an arm to steady her. All around were so many friends and neighbours, and behind, standing back, she saw a young woman with her arm set in a plaster cast, conspicuously white against her sombre jacket. She looked familiar, but Conchita could not think who she was, but then there were many she did not recognize.

After the gathering of family and friends had left the house following the interment, the house fell silent. It was the hushed voice of

303

Garnet speaking on the telephone that reminded Conchita that the worrying family news which she had brought with her from England had never been mentioned. She waited for her and then said,

'You're 'phoning home, aren't you? When are you going to tell me?'

Garnet had been biding her time but all the while keeping in touch with Flora.

'I was waiting until...well, I don't know what I was waiting for but I just felt I couldn't burden you with yet more sad news just now.'

'It's Daddy, isn't it? He's....'

'Yes, very poorly. It was after Ramon and Carmen's visit last year that Daddy finally went to the doctor. He wouldn't go at first, but Mummy put her foot down when she realised that he was having difficulty moving about. I know Ramon told you how worried he was about the trembling. Well now we know, it is Parkinson's disease and it's bad. I feel so guilty that I didn't insist on doing something about it last time I was home. It's a bit late in the day to do much about it now, it has progressed faster than was expected. All they can do is prescribe a drug to help control the trembling. But he's rather fragile.'

'Why wouldn't he go to the doctor? Surely he recognised that it was serious?'

'He says not. And now he hates anyone mentioning it or making any kind of a fuss. Mummy's not strong enough to look after him, after all she's seventy-nine so I don't know how she would manage if ....Sorry, you can see why I didn't want to tell you all this earlier. I'm sorry I've got to saddle you with even more sadness.'

'I'm glad you've told me. It's only right that I should know. After all he is my f......' Conchita stopped and looking at Garnet she smiled wanly.

'Strange isn't it, after all this time. I still think of him as Daddy.'

The two sat quietly for some minutes until Conchita asked,

'Shouldn't you be going back? I don't want you to, of course, but I'm thinking about Ma, as well as Daddy?'

'Yes, I should. But they have help; I booked home support to come in from an agency to make sure that Daddy had help getting up in the morning and going to bed at night. And of course the doctor calls regularly.'

'My God, it's as bad as that? I never realised. I seem to have lost touch with what's going on. Not Dr McAllister anymore I suppose?'

'No, he retired quite a while ago. You know, I hadn't planned on staying for two weeks, but under the circumstances it was the right thing to do. Besides, I can't leave yet, you haven't told me why you cried for help.'

'Did I really cry?'

'More or less. Tell me Con.'

Conchita related what she felt were the facts; Luca's frequent absences, her trip to Pamplona, and her visit to the house where she had met the woman. She tried not to imbue the facts with anything other than their face value. Garnet listened.

'You saw her didn't you, at the funeral? The one with the broken arm.' Garnet nodded her head. She had not interrupted Conchita's long story but now she said,

'What will you do?'

'That's what I've been asking myself,' she said, 'but if you can spare yet another day or two I would like you to help me on a quest.'

'Of course, whatever you need.'

Conchita drove this time knowing the route to Pamplona without reference to a map and wondering at her own audacity in wanting to seek out the young woman. Conchita knew she must face the truth before she could leave this phase of her life behind and allow the pain to subside. She only hoped that the woman would understand and would talk to her honestly. Her only fear was that the child, Arabella, would be at home, then they might not be able to be open with one another. That is if she would speak to her at all.

Conchita parked the car, this time in the square opposite the supermarket.

'Perhaps you should meet her alone, Con,' Garnet said. 'She might feel threatened if there are two of us standing on the doorstep.'

'No, I need you. Suppose she's uncooperative? If it were me I would be wary, even scared.'

There was no need for either of them to be wary or scared. The door was opened by a small neat woman in her early thirties. She was fashionably dressed in blue jeans and a pale pink shirt, the left sleeve rolled up over the cast, her abundant hair was scooped up in an unruly cluster of dark curls.

'I saw you arriving. Please come in,' she said, and with one hand she opened the door wide for them both. 'I wondered if you might come.'

As they moved into a small tidy room she said,

'Would you like a coffee, or perhaps a cup of tea. The English love their tea, don't they?'

'Coffee would be very nice,' Conchita said quietly.

305

'Excuse me for a moment, I will switch on the machine,' she said as she turned towards her kitchen.

'I think I should leave you Con, she's obviously not going to hit you over the head. She seems a pleasant young woman. Besides I don't understand much of what's said and I don't think she speaks any English.'

'Stay, just for a few minutes. I'll explain, when she comes back.'

After a few minutes she came back into the room,

'Perhaps one of you would carry the tray. I'll bring the almond biscuits.'

Garnet leapt up and took the tray from the kitchen.

'My name is Alicia,' she said as she began to pour the coffee. 'And you are Conchita, I think.'

'Yes. How do you know?'

'Luca told me about you. That's why you have come isn't it? To find out who I am and why Luca comes...came to my house.' She dropped her eyelids for a moment and tightened her bright red lips.

'Please, I'm sorry, I don't want to cause you any more pain or sadness, surely there's enough without our doing that to each other. Perhaps I shouldn't have come after all.'

'Yes, it's good that you've come. I realise that you must have been troubled and hurt by Luca's absences. You have a right to know the truth, after all he was your husband, whereas I....' There she stopped. The coffee was poured and ready to drink, the pause giving her a moment to compose herself.

'Connie, please explain who I am,' Garnet urged.

'I know who you are,' Alicia said in accented English. 'I speak a little English you see. Luca told me about the whole family. I am happy to meet you too.'

Both Conchita and Garnet caught their breath and looked at each other.

'But why?' Conchita asked, 'if you were his.........'

'His mistress, you were going to say. Yes - I mean no, I was once, a long time ago. Luca was very honest with me and he told me about you; the large happy family, the grandchildren, the bodega and its success. I feel that I have met you all already.'

'I think it was unkind of him to talk to you of me, of the whole family in that way. Are you not resentful?'

'At first, I was a little. But I reminded myself that I made my choice, long ago. I could have told him that I was pregnant, but I chose to be independent. Please, let me assure you that I was no longer his mistress for some time before you and he married, and definitely not after. Mine is a little story – may I tell you?'

'I'd be grateful, I'm at such a disadvantage. It seems you know all about us but we know nothing of you, or of...Arabella.'

Alicia placed her coffee cup on the small table in front of them. She sat back in her chair and placed her hands in her lap. She began, as though telling a story.

'I was twenty when I met Luca ten years ago, as I say long before he married you. Arabella is his daughter, you met her that day you called, and then ran away.' She laughed lightly as she said it.

'I had no idea,' Conchita said.

'No, neither did he. We had been together for nearly four years and then just after we had broken off our relationship I found out I was pregnant. I didn't tell him. The last time we met was here in the town, he really was here on business, he told me he was getting to know you, after his bodega was sold to your father. He also told me that he wanted to marry you, if you would have him. A year later I read that you had married. We did not see one another again for about two years and during that time he came to Pamplona several times. His visits were without intent to see me, he didn't know where I lived. It was by chance that we met. He recognised me. I had Arabella with me and he invitied us to have tapas with him for lunch. He wanted to know how I was, "Have you married?" he asked as he looked at Arabella. When I said no, he asked me quite pointedly who her father was. I was wrong footed and in my hesitation he guessed.'

'I remember, when I asked for Señor Goncalves, that day that I came here, Arabella said "Papa" was not in,' Conchita said.

'Oh she didn't know he was her father, it was her fantasy! She thought it was fun to go to school and say she had a new 'papa'. I asked her not to do it but she just laughed, a very precocious six year old, I can tell you.'

Throughout this exchange Garnet had remained quiet, partly because there were things she had not understood when Alicia had returned to Spanish. She also did not want to break the flow of this young woman's story, which seemed to Garnet to be recounted in all honesty.

'So that's why he kept coming to Pamplona, to see you and his daughter,' Conchita asked.

'Only partly, remember he was coming on business. He was involved in this new development of housing but his visits were longer than was really necessary, I know because he stayed with us. Please Conchita, I may call you Conchita?'

'I have to tell you, we never slept together. He came, he said, because he felt guilty, and he wanted to help us. That's how we have this nice house.'

Conchita began to cry, her tears slipped quietly down her cheeks.

'I feel ashamed of myself, that I mistrusted him. I was convinced that he was being unfaithful. I was hurt, all I could think of was myself. Not for a moment did I consider that he had a justifiable reason for being away so often. But I can see now, that he had.'

'No, not really, although in some small way perhaps yes.' Alicia responded. 'He was fascinated by the fact that he had a daughter. He wanted to see her frequently and 'watch her growing up' he said. I told him he couldn't do that. It was wrong of him to expect to be a part of her life now. His responsibility was to you, and he admitted that he loved you. We had reached a crossroads, you might say. You see, Arabella was growing fond of him and I saw that she could be hurt if the situation continued. I gave him an ultimatum. He must either leave you and marry me, and recognise Arabella openly as his daughter, or he must stop visiting us.'

'You loved him?' Conchita said softly.

'I was fond of him, but no, I did not love him. And he did not love me either. I knew he would never marry me. I did not want to marry him! It was a threat, I only wanted to frighten him into some action, to try to resolve the situation before it became too complicated. I was afraid for Arabella all the time.'

'But this wasn't the solution we could ever have imagined, either of us, is it?'

'No. Fate can be cruel and humane in the same single stroke. I am sorry for you, you have lost your husband. I am a little sad too, because for a short while he and I were happy together. But I also feel guilty. You see, I accepted the gift of this house, in a way that gave him permission to come and see Arabella any time he wished. It is hard bringing up a child alone, but I should not have accepted it.'

'No-one could blame you for doing so,' Conchita said.

'Maybe not, but there will be those who think I am mercenary, accepting such a gift. Perhaps you will too when I tell you that I have just received a letter from the bank to say that he also put aside a sum of money for Arabella's future. So I have come out of it all in a favourable position. You must not feel sorry for me.'

'Thank you, Alicia. You have been honest and frank, which I appreciate. I feared you would not want to see me that you might even hate me.'

'On the contrary, I find that I like you. You are brave to come here in search of the truth, not knowing what that truth might be. I'm not sure I could have done that in a similar situation.'

'So now that we have met and there are no hard feelings, shall we stay in touch with one another?'

'Perhaps, we'll see. You must first learn to live without Luca – as I did some years ago. I feel for you.'

52

Diary

I've decided to go home – I mean to Yorkshire. Isn't that silly, my calling it home. My home has been here for over fifty years, and yet where Ma and Daddy are I still think of as being 'home'. They even still live in the house I grew up in, well almost grew up. It took me quite a while to grow up I know. My family here might be upset if they knew I had these feelings. It's not as though I'm unhappy – oh I have been, especially recently, but I'm getting over it.

Nettie's latest letter is worrying me. She has flown back from Hong Kong twice since early December and describes Daddy's condition as precarious. I must go, dare I say it, before it's too late. I've written to Nettie to tell her that I will be there before the end of the month.

I'm asking Juan Luis to let me go for a while, as if I needed to do that! There's a knowledgeable young woman working for the bodega now, Maria, who is more than ready to take up some of my work. She speaks English and French and comes from a winemaking background, albeit French wine from the south west! We pull her leg about being a defector but she laughs it off with the comment "I work for Spain, and all wines Spanish. Yesterday Bordeaux; today Rioja. Tomorrow who knows?" She can give as good as she gets but with a twinkle in her eye.

I'm relieved and reprieved for as long as I want, Juan Luis has said. He keeps telling me, 'I'm not your boss, I'm your brother. You don't have to ask permission for anything.' But Juan Luis is definitely the boss now, a much respected one I'm happy to say. I heard an old man talking in the village the other day, sitting at a table with his buddy, the pair of them with their wrinkled, nut-brown faces wreathed in smoke, talking about the bodega. I'm not ashamed to say I loitered in order to catch the words. 'That boy is just like his grandfather,' he said. 'Acuerdo, you're right, I'd work for him any day,' his companion said. 'Bad luck, chum. He wouldn't have you – you're too old.' And they dissolved into giggles like misbehaving schoolboys. I smiled all the way home.

***

Email: 22.00 Hong Kong/ 7 am Haro   *February 1994*

Dear Con

I'm so pleased you are going to Harrogate. I shall come as soon as possible. I have some free time from mid-February until April.

I'm not quite ready to retire yet but as you know I'm not singing so often these days. I've been asked to work with some up and coming youngsters, I think that's rather exciting. Just think of it – me taking Masterclasses, training the young ones! I can't believe it. It doesn't seem long ago that I was such a youngster myself. I have been so lucky in my career and lucky to have had someone like David who has put up with the comings and goings, and periods of separation. David's sixty this year and thinking of taking early retirement. He's even talking of buying a house in England, but I'm not sure any more that I could live there permanently. It's only talk at the moment.

Email me your flight times and Flight No. and I will try to arrive at about the same time.

Mummy 'phoned last night. She said Daddy's calm and reconciled to the inevitable. But she is not, she's frightened of her future without him. Aren't we all. See you soon.

Much love
Nettie

***

Conchita arrived in Harrogate first and had two days with Philip and Flora before Garnet's arrival. It was a quiet time which gave Conchita the chance to talk to her father, or he to her would have been more the case if she had allowed him.

'There are a few things I need to discuss Connie,' he began, almost as soon as she arrived.

'There's plenty of time Daddy. I'm going to have a nice long stay, so we can sit and chat every day.'

'Yes, good. Because you see arrangements have to be made.'

311

'Now Daddy, let's just enjoy one another's company for a while. We'll get around to whatever it is you want to say all in good time. Why don't we wait until Nettie arrives, the day after tomorrow. In the meantime, would you like me to read the newspaper to you? Or just sit here?'

'No, tell me about the family, all the children. How old they all are now. What they are doing. And Ramon, and...........er...you know, C...!'

'Carmen,' Connie slipped in as she saw him struggling to remember her name.

Conchita spoke softly, recounting the children's activities, their escapades, their successes in school.

'I'm just closing my eyes,' Philip murmured, 'I'm not asleep, keep talking.' Conchita spoke softly until she saw the slow rhythmic breathing as he drifted into sleep.

The next morning Garnet arrived. She had not telephoned but had taken the train from London to Harrogate and a taxi to their home.

'Why didn't you phone? I could have met you at the station?'

'Didn't want to disturb the peace with that jarring 'phone bell clanging through the house. Last time I was home the noise upset Daddy.'

'More like his fury at not being able to answer it himself,' Flora said smiling, as she hobbled into the hall from the kitchen, leaning heavily on a stick. 'He's so afraid he's missing something. So nice you're here darling,' she said, hugging Garnet. 'Fancy, both of you. Can't remember when we last had both of you here at the same time. Dump your things and get in there to say hello, he'll have heard your arrival – there's nothing wrong with his ears!'

Garnet knew exactly where she would be sleeping. Not in the single room she had occupied on her last visit but the twin room where she and Connie had slept all those years ago. She had asked Flora, 'Please can we be together?' There never was any question of it being otherwise. Flora had anticipated their need for each other.

Nursing help was arriving every day now, even though Connie and Garnet were there.

'We can't cancel it,' Garnet had explained. 'Otherwise we'll go back down to the bottom of the queue. There aren't enough resources to be able to send help to everyone, even when it's desperately needed, so you have to keep on the list. Besides, it gives us more time to spend with Mummy. She needs lots of support too.'

As Philip slept one morning, Flora made coffee and asked the girls to join her in the sitting room, she wanted to talk.

'Daddy wants to sort out some 'arrangements' as he keeps calling them. What he means is, how am I going to manage when he...' she stopped.

'Ma, you don't have to go through this.'

'Yes, I do. When he dies, because he is going to die very soon, we all have to face up to these 'arrangements'. Poor Connie, you have just been through a state of grieving, probably still are, and now you are going to have to cope with this.'

'I'm here Ma, to be with you and Daddy, and Nettie so that we can all face up to it together. This is quite different from – from what I've just been through. I was sad, of course, but not as sad as I thought I might be. It makes me feel guilty to think that I already feel I've got over it, well almost.'

'So, my two lovely girls, I want you to listen to what I have to say before Daddy tries to give you your instructions! Because he will, he's determined to extract promises from you both that you will carry out his plan.'

'My plan is this. This house will be sold and the money will go to you my children, and my grandchildren.'

'Mummy, we don't need any money. We are both very comfortable.'

'Well, hang on a minute, not all of it. I've already made enquiries about going into a retirement home.'

'No, you can't do that Ma. We won't let you.'

'Yes you will, as soon as you realise that it's what I want. It's a lovely 'residence' not a 'home for the elderly'! And they have a place reserved for me. I've been to see it and I really like it.'

'Wouldn't you prefer to come to Spain and live with me Ma? You would love the warmth and I would love to have you.'

'It's a beautiful thought my Connie, but no, I'm too old. I want peace and quiet. Oh by the way, they have lovely rose gardens and I'll be able to potter and prune to my heart's content.' Flora laughed at the thought.

'You seem to have it all sorted,' said Garnet with a very solemn expression. 'So what is Daddy going to 'instruct' us on?'

'He's going to ask you to find a nice place. I couldn't tell him I've already done it, it looks as though I can't wait for him to...' Flora began to cry.

'I haven't told anyone else,' she sobbed, 'Everyone would think it unseemly to be doing what I've done before... before he...' Flora could say no more.

313

'It's not unseemly Ma. You're very brave. If you're sure this is what you want...'

'Absolutely. And, I can have as many visitors as I like, there are guest rooms, so there will be no problem when you come to visit.' Flora smiled again.

That night Connie and Garnet, as they climbed into bed, the same beds they had occupied fifty years earlier, began to discuss their mother's intentions.

'What do you think?' Garnet said.

'She seems to have made up her mind. But you know I would willingly have Ma to live with me, if she would come.'

'I think she's right. She couldn't move away from here now. She does still have some friends in the area. By the way, did you know, Rhonda has been writing to her?'

'Rhonda? Why? I would have thought that woman has done enough harm without bothering Ma now.'

'Apparently, after Ma's breakdown, all those years ago, she went to her and apologised. She did help, after all, when Ma was found wandering in town.'

'Apologise! She was more or less responsible for everything.'

'Not everything, Con. But she did take advantage of Mummy, out of jealousy.'

'I'll say!'

'Mummy told me she couldn't forgive her at first. But later, when Mummy was recovering, Rhonda got in touch again to ask if she could help her. I believe she did, she took Mummy out and helped her get back into the set, you know, golf, bridge, coffee mornings. I met her by chance, at that time, and she said, "You must hate me." I said "No, but I can't say I like you." She laughed. "That's honest enough. I don't blame you. But I'd like you to know that I really want to help, if I can. I have to."

'What do you mean – 'have to?'

"As selfish as it may seem, I need to salve my conscience, yes after all these years. But my motives are also altruistic. I always admired your mother. Not that she would ever have thought that. The truth is I was jealous of her at university. She was attractive, she was bright and she worked hard. Believe me I was bright, well off, and I had everything going for me, except I wasn't as attractive as your mother, nor did I have such a nice personality, but I threw it all away. What I did was unforgivable. But I think your mother has forgiven me."

'What an admission.'

314

'Anyway, Rhonda is around now, a little younger than Mummy, drives a car, wants to take her out.'

'How does Ma feel about it?'

'She says fine, if it makes *her* feel better she'll be delighted to be taken anywhere.'

'I'm not sure I'm so forgiving.'

'Well you couldn't be, could you? After all, your life changed radically because of ...all that. Con, let's talk of other things. How are you really?'

'I'm going to be fine Nettie, I promise. After all this is over. And you?'

'Likewise.'

'Come and stay with me soon in Haro, won't you? And David too?'

'We will, I promise you.'

Philip Hampton died in his sleep ten days later.

53

Diary

It was sad circumstances that took me to England and imposed such a long stay. Despite our grief and many tears the time together with Ma and Nettie was so good for all three of us. We talked as we never have before, easily and with sincerity.

Thank goodness David came over from Hong Kong. Nettie only has to ask and he drops everything to be with her when she needs him. He's a marvellous husband to her. He was a godsend when it came to all the practicalities but also a loving support to both of us. He was so kind to Ma too.

To our amazement the house was sold within ten days of it going on the market. It was quite a shock but it took our minds off our sorrow and stopped us becoming despondent. Ma was remarkable in her courage and kept up our spirits with anecdotes of Daddy's years at the bank. She cried a little but I don't think she has let go, it hasn't sunk in yet that for the first time for over fifty years she is going to be alone. I know from experience the tears can come later and sometimes with greater force. I'm worried that she will be alone when it happens. Nettie and I have made a pact that we will return to England as often as we can and of course we shall talk to Ma on the telephone.

Such a lot has happened in a month and now I'm home again. Yes, it is my home, even though I said I still thought of the house in Harrogate as home. Not the house, but where Ma and Daddy were. Now they are no longer there. But it's not that that makes me feel it isn't home any more. This is where my children are and my grandchild, and this is where I have made my life. I must settle down again and be thankful that I am loved and have so many to love.

Juan Luis greeted me so affectionately. He and Lucia are there whenever I need them and I have told them how grateful I am for their love and support. Even if I wanted to I can't lean on Rosie, not now, with a two year old and her teaching, which she loves. She and

Eduardo both love their work. I shall take care of Mercedes whenever I can but I too want to continue working as a wine guide. I'm really quite good at it, even though I say so myself! Of course it's a great help being able to speak both English and Spanish.

Juan Luis has asked me if I would like to update the leaflets we give to visitors and the information sheets we send to wine merchants in England. He said, teasing me as usual, that my English is probably better than his. Cheeky boy! I think I'll enjoy doing that.

Conchita was determined to make better known that the official mark of quality, *denominacion de origen,* for Rioja wine had been upgraded in 1991 to *denominacion de origen calificada.* This should be on all their labels and publicity which she would incorporate in her new designs of leaflets and information sheets.

Conchita knew that was what really put Rioja wine on the map. The improvement in the quality of Rioja wines was a consequence of the more stringent testing and the regulations under the new mark, which ensured the high quality of the wine produced. Now, with the family's knowledge and hard work, their own bodega, Bodega López, building on their past reputation and the growing popularity of Rioja wine, was going from strength to strength. Its export business was booming. They were in the news again with a '*Medalla de Oro*' – a gold medal for their 1986 Gran Reserva.

Ramon López, and his father and grandfather before him, had been at the forefront of testing, experimenting, learning to produce better and better wine. 'One never stops learning,' Conchita remembered her Papa saying to her on one of those early tours around the bodega on her beloved horse Alvaro.

***

2000

Conchita had to think hard when she looked at the year; she could hardly believe she had been in Spain so long. Her thoughts often flew back to her father's words as they rode around the bodega. She had never found another mount like Alvaro but the gentle mare Otono was perhaps better suited to her now. Conchita found her evening rides alone in the cool of the evening comforting and peaceful. She gloried in the sight of the neat, straight lines of the vines, diminishing until they

317

joined the line between the sky and the land. She delighted in the view of the peaks of the Sierra de Cantabria in the distance which after all these years still fascinated her with their white crests, and dark patches that looked from a distance like yawning caverns. It was on these rides that she mulled over her present situation; she felt contented.

She was happy that she was able to spend time with Mercedes, not only reading together, but taking walks and rides with her on her pony Belleza. She felt there was something of the relationship that she had had with Nana Isabella, she hoped it was so.

'I'm like you, aren't I Nana? I read lots and ride round the bodega like you do.'

'Do you know little one, when I was a young girl your *bisabuelo*, my Papa, used to take me out riding all over the land. He was trying to teach me about the vines, how they grew and what one must do to make good wine.'

'That's what I want to do Nana. I want to learn how to make wine.'

'Well, when I was a girl I hated those rides. I didn't want to learn. But you, as young as you are, it seems you do want to learn.'

Conchita could hear her father's voice now, repeating the date of the forming of a Regulatory Body in 1926 which gave the wines *denominacion de origen.* She had been so unresponsive at the time but that fact had stuck and she smiled to herself.

'Nana, why didn't you want to learn?'

'That's a long story,' and she sighed.

'Is it in your special story book? Can I read it?'

'My special book? Oh, you mean my diary. Yes I suppose it is a story.'

'When can I read it?'

'Well this kind of book is not usually for other people to read.'

'But if it's not for people to read why do you write it?'

'I might have guessed you'd ask me that! I suppose it is a sort of story book - about me, and you, and all the family, and what we do. It's the kind of story that ends when ....well, it might be rather some time before it's finished.'

'When it's finished I can read it, can't I?'

'Maybe.'

'Tell me about the bodega Nana.'

'Well, it was your *tatarabuelo,* your great, great grandfather, who started making wine, long ago. His son learned how to make wine from his father and so it has happened over the years, the son learning from the father for four generations.'

'But what if there isn't a son? Why can't a daughter learn to make wine?'

'No reason at all. I have a feeling you may be the first lady *viñadora* in the family.'

Mercedes nodded as though to say, 'Yes, I shall be.'

54

2002

Conchita felt sad sometimes that neither of her parents could know of the accolades Bodega López was receiving. Sometimes as she rode in the quiet of the evening she wrote descriptive letters to them in her head telling them not just about the wine but also about Mercedes who at ten years old already determined to follow in the family's footsteps and become a winemaker. She wondered what they would have said and thought. No doubt they would have been proud of her and the family. But now that Flora had died there was no one left in Harrogate to whom she could write.

However, there was Garnet. Letters, but more often emails, flowed frequently between them. Conchita's latest message had been difficult to write.

Email: nettie@hotmail.co.uk   *2002*

My dear Nettie

I know… emails don't start with 'dear' do they? It's 'hi' or some such modern jargon. But over all the years (so many years) you have been so dear to me. So I begin, as always; My dear Nettie…

I'm wondering when you will next come to Haro? It's been four months since we've seen one another and I'm not in a position to come to Hong Kong just now. It's not just my work, which goes well, and which I thoroughly enjoy but I have a small health problem of late and I need to talk to someone. No, not anyone, someone special. You are the only person who will hear what I say and keep it in confidence and yet you are the one person I would not tell because I love you so much. But I need you Nettie. Can you come?

Much love
Con

Conchita had already been to see her Doctor.

'I'm going to make an appointment for you with a Consultant Oncologist at the hospital in Bilbao,' he told her. 'A lump in the breast is a cause for concern. However, at this stage let us not worry unduly, we will hope that it is benign.'

Conchita's calm nod in response to his words belied her anxiety. It was her tightly clasped hands in her lap that revealed her fear; a picture that was probably not lost on her doctor.

'I suggest you ask someone in your family to accompany you. A little moral support, you know,' and he smiled.

'Perhaps. Yet at this stage I don't want to start worrying anyone unnecessarily. Please will you keep this confidential? As you say, it might be nothing to worry about.'

'Of course, patient confidentiality is always observed my dear. You need have no concern that any of your family will learn of this consultation, as you say - at this stage.'

Conchita drove herself to Bilbao. 'Be brave,' she said to herself. 'After all there might be nothing to worry about.'

Hearing her own encouraging words her mood was lifted until she approached the hospital. By the time she entered the cubicle for the examination she was trembling.

It was at the word 'malignant' that a soft blanket seemed to wrap itself around her mind. She blanched and swayed in her seat, a nurse took her hand and held it until the Consultant rose to say;

'We will meet again, after we have some more results from the tests and then we will arrange your longer visit to the hospital.'

The Consultant had carefully avoided using the word 'operation' but as Conchita drove home the terrifying words; '...surgery, chemotherapy, radiotherapy...' seeped from time to time through that blanket. She remembered little of the return journey, the car seemed to roll along on automatic pilot requiring no effort on her part.

As she stepped into her house the word 'surgery' again surfaced in her mind and a cold shiver ran through her. What had he meant? Why didn't she ask? It was at that moment her courage failed her; she burst into tears.

'I can't do this alone,' she sobbed. 'I need Nettie.'

She went straight to her computer and logged on to her email.

***

The response, bearing in mind the time difference between Spain and Hong Kong, was remarkably quick. Nettie replied that she would be on the next 'plane, arriving in Bilbao at 14.30, within twenty-four hours after Conchita's plea.

Conchita was relieved but at the same time felt guilty that she had preyed on her sister's love and kindness to come when needed. It was not the first time she had done so. Conchita recalled her cry for help six years ago after her trip to Pamplona. Here she was again counting on Garnet's support.

How fortunate it was that Juan Luis had to make a business trip to Bilbao that very day – 'How my guardian angel is looking after me,' Conchita had whispered to herself when Juan Luis had told her of his visit. So she felt no misgivings in asking him to collect Garnet from the airport. She knew he would be delighted, doting on this 'other sister' as he jokingly called her, she who held a special place in his heart. Had they not made music together some years earlier? which Garnet had generously told him was the catalyst to her returning to her singing career. Conchita knew that Garnet's unselfish and immediate response was a sign of her concern for her sister and that she had understood the importance of her need. It was not long before she would discover the nature of her cry for help.

* * *

'I've been through many upsets in my life Nettie, but I couldn't face this one without your loving support,' she told Garnet. 'I'm sorry I've pulled you half round the world and dumped this problem on you, especially as I have other family members who perhaps could have helped me. But it's no good, I can't ask them. I know it's silly, I just wanted you, the English bit of me. I'm sorry.'

'Never be sorry Con, for anything. We've kept each other's heads above water all these years, why should we stop now? Enough of that, what are we going to do to get you well again?'

Garnet accompanied Conchita to the hospital to talk to the Consultant Surgeon to arrange the timing of the operation and the period of convalescence. No-one thought anything of their going off for a day out and so for the moment Conchita's problem was a secret.

The answer was immediate surgery, it would be a mastectomy and removal of lymph glands.

'I don't want to tell anybody Nettie, so can you keep this a secret?' Conchita asked her as they drove along.

'For the moment, yes I can. But we shall have to tell the family what's going on Con, you can't keep something like this to yourself. They have a right to know and…well, you are going to need their support too.'

'I know I can't expect you to stay on and on, you have commitments and I have been selfish enough making you come all this way for me. Nettie, how long can you stay?'

'Until you are out of hospital, I can promise you that. Then we'll have to see what the next stage is.'

On their return Conchita spoke again of keeping all this from the family.

To her surprise, Garnet refused.

'I can't do that Con and neither can you. How would you feel if I kept from you something serious in my life?'

'You did once.' She said quietly. Garnet was silent for a moment.

'Yes, you're right. But I was ashamed and afraid. This is different. You are shutting out the very people who love you and will want to help you. You can't do it Con, they'll be terribly hurt. And what's more you'll need them, I can't be here all the time.'

Conchita drove on in silence for the rest of the journey home. As they arrived at Castillo Blanco, Nettie broke the silence with another candid but truthful remark.

'And you can't go on living here, either. It's dark, dingy and you were never happy in this house.'

'I was, sort of, but never as happy as I had been, but I never expected to be. But where will I go?'

'I don't think that's a problem knowing your family. Once every-one hears that you want to move they'll find somewhere nice. They have lots of contacts and they'll only have to put the word out and something will turn up. You'll see.'

'You seem to be getting me all sorted out Nettie.' Con said with a smile.

'That's what I'm here for, isn't it? In any case, it's not so altruistic as you might think. When I go back I want to know that you are being looked after and in a nice place. I never did like Castillo Blanco – what a ridiculous name; it should have been called Castillo Negro!'

Connie couldn't help but laugh at Nettie's joke and they went into the house smiling.

Conchita decided she would tell Juan Luis first.

'Do you want me to be with you when you tell him?' Garnet had asked. 'I will if you really wish it …but I think this is something you should share with your brother without my help. He loves you so much Con he will be deeply affected. He will be shocked and he will need *you* to help *him*.'

Jean Luis sat pale and motionless as Conchita explained the reason for their visit to Bilbao. Tears ran down his face which he wiped away angrily with the flat of his hand.

'Conchita, what can I do to help you? Please let me help you.'

'Yes, you can help me Jean Luis. I'm not very brave and I don't know how to break the news to Rosita. And then everyone else.'

'Of course, I will. I'll do anything that will help. I'll even do the telling, if you would like that.'

'That's good of you, but no Juan Luis. Nettie and I have talked about it and I'm prepared now and I think it's better coming straight from me. I'll be honest with you, I did think at one point that I wouldn't tell anybody, I'd fight this out by myself, but Nettie talked me out of that. She's right it would have been unkind and foolish to think that I could hide such a thing from you all.'

After all these years the family had grown used to Conchita's reference to her sister as Nettie, but they all still called her by her proper name - Garnet. Juan Luis himself had asked, 'Garnet is the name of a gem, is it not?' and Conchita told him of her mother's reason for giving her such a name when she was born; Garnet is the gemstone for the month of January. 'But it's true, she is a gem,' he had declared, 'and we are lucky to have such a precious sister.'

***

Conchita was in hospital for two weeks and the tumour was successfully removed but as had been discussed with the Specialist a course of chemotherapy was to follow, after which she told Jean Luis;

'I'm so disappointed, I thought I might get away with just one blast of the beastly stuff. They're going to give me a little time to build up my strength they say, before it starts again.'

'Then we shall make sure that you get plenty of rest and good sustaining food. We all want your smiling face back on the job.'

'That's another thing, I miss my work and talking to everyone every day. I'm so sorry I'm not pulling my weight at the moment,' Conchita gave a forced laugh. 'Even if I tried it wouldn't achieve much would it? I'm such a skinny thing now.'

'You need some of Lucia's cooking,' he laughed, 'that will put the kilos back on again.'

Jean Luis went away determined to get every member of the family to visit Conchita regularly and to make sure that she ate well.

'At least one of us should pop in every day,' he told them. 'She needs the contact and the conversation. She's missing her job and feels she is letting us down.'

Over a period of a little more than six months, Conchita struggled through two lots of treatment, its side effects – the nausea, the tiredness, the discomfort - depressed her. The loss of most of her lustrous hair grieved her.

Evidently the tumour had been aggressive but frequent tests showed the treatment was having a beneficial effect. However the news that she was to go through a round of radiotherapy brought her almost to breaking point.

It was Mercedes, as young as she was, who understood that her Nana needed not only people but also some kind of pastime to help fill the empty hours.

'I'm going to take a jigsaw round to Nana's,' she told her mother. 'We can do it together.'

'Nana hasn't got much energy Mercedes,' Rosita replied.

'Well, all she has to do is lift a piece now and then and add it to the picture. I know she's too tired to talk sometimes but she still likes to have company, so we can chat as we go along. Besides she needs something to make her think, I mean of nice things instead of thinking about how awful she feels.'

Rosita wondered at her daughter's perceptiveness. It was true, Conchita needed a distraction.

'Mercedes, you mustn't be hurt if Nana doesn't want to do it?'

'Of course not. If she gets tired I can do the jigsaw by myself, I won't talk but I'll still be there with her.'

Conchita was delighted to have Mercedes' company. The jigsaw puzzles reminded her of her childhood in Yorkshire.

'We used to do jigsaws,' she remarked to Mercedes when she first arrived with one under her arm.

'When? Who's 'we' Nana.'

'When we were children; I mean my sister and I.'

'You mean Nettie, don't you? Tell me about Yorkshire Nana, and you, and Nettie.'

The challenge of the simple jigsaw stimulated Conchita and triggered memories that had lain quiet for years. She talked about Granny and Grandpa Hampton, her school and Bella.

'Bella came to Spain with you, didn't she?'

'No, in fact she came later. It was Nettie who understood how much I missed her and she managed to persuade daddy, I mean...'

'It know about your English daddy, Mama told me. I hope you don't mind.'

'I'm glad you know Mercedes.' She smiled and sat back in her chair. Mercedes continued placing the colourful shapes until she saw her abuela's eyes close. She tore a corner from a newspaper that was lying on a side table and wrote:

Have a nice rest Nana. See you tomorrow. Don't do too much of the puzzle without me!

***

The treatment had taken its toll on Conchita's energy levels and also on her appearance. Her clothes hung on her like a rag doll, and her skin was sallow.

It was a combination of the love and care, good food and Mercedes' uplifting visits which helped Conchita to feel better and look happier. Gradually, she gained a little weight and started to walk about, in and around the bodega.

***

2004

During the next twelve months Conchita gained more weight and the roses came back but faintly to her cheeks. Her hair had regrown, dark and thick as it had been as a child.

'It's the fresh air, the good food and above all the company of my family,' she proclaimed to everyone when they complimented her after a while on her improved appearance. She began working again conducting visiting parties around the bodega, explaining the winemaking process and proudly showing them the countryside she loved. She spoke English often revelling in the visitors' compliments on her command of the language smiling to herself about her 'secret' nationality.

She took to riding again with Mercedes in the early evenings, but she no longer read to her at bed time, approaching thirteen years old Mercedes was more than happy to read by herself!

Over the next three years Conchita paid regular visits to the hospital in Bilbao for tests. She felt glad that she had not kept the news of her illness from the family. It was true, it would have been a cruel deception and as Nettie had said, she needed their support which they gave unstintingly. She worried from time to time that she was not pulling her weight, she had cut down on the hours she spent taking visitors around the wine-making process and there were days when she was exceptionally tired and went home. Fortunately, there was Maria who had stopped joking about one day returning to her beloved Bordeaux region and had become almost one of the family. Conchita was happy to hand over some of the tours to a young and attractive girl, knowing that she was efficient and knowledgeable.

Juan Luis had secured a small house for Conchita, light and airy, only a short distance from Rosita and Eduardo, which with help from all of them had been made comfortable and colourful. Not until Juan Luis reminded her that most people had retired by the time they were sixty-six did she stop being troubled by her shorter working days. It was the three young men; Juan Luis, and the twins Carlos and Luis, who took turns at what they called a privilege to take her to the hospital for the continuing check-up visits.

On one of the early trips Juan Luis had asked Conchita to make him a promise.

'I want you to tell me what is said each time you have a check-up. Not the details, just... 'all is well'or 'no change', or something like that. If for any reason there is a change...' he stopped and took her hand.

'They have told me if I reach five years after the surgery without any problems, I stand a good chance of a few more years after that. So I'm doing quite well, aren't I? Three years since my surgery and no signs of anything untoward.'

'But promise me, you will tell me, won't you?'

It was a promise that Conchita kept.

55

2007

It was during the summer of 2007 after the latest check up at the hospital, that Conchita received an unexpected telephone call from the hospital. She had grown so used to them saying 'see you in six months' time' that the request to return for further tests shook her. She called Juan Luis the same morning to ask if he could come and see her at home. That in itself was unusual. He arrived, knowing that something was amiss.

'After my tests only a week ago I've been recalled to the hospital. I'm scared Juan Luis.'

'It could be nothing, just a verification of the test results, some extra information they need. We're not going to start getting upset Conchita, are we? Positive thinking, right?' Conchita nodded. 'So, when do you have to go?'

'Straight away. Well, as soon as possible they said.'

'Right, I'm ready, are you? We'll go now. I'll just 'phone the office to tell them I will be out for a few hours.'

They were quiet on their return journey late in the afternoon, until they were almost home. Juan Luis stopped the car outside Conchita's house.

'I am going to tell Rosita, please let me do that,' he said as Conchita began to demur. 'Then tomorrow we will make plans, you and I and Rosita, together.' Conchita nodded, holding back the tears, pretending to herself that this would be a question of working out the practicalities. Then Juan Luis took her hands, that was her undoing. She dropped her head onto his shoulder and sobbed.

The next morning she walked to Rosita's house. She was grateful to Juan Luis for going to Rosita first. She realised she could not have spoken the words.

'The cancer has returned,' Juan Luis told Rosita. 'It seems no more treatment is possible.' Rosita, sitting opposite Jean Luis, poured him a cup of coffee. Her hand was steady but her lips were set in a tight line. As she looked at him he reached for her hand.

'Be brave,' he said, 'your mother will be here in just a moment.'

'Juan Luis has come over for coffee and a chat,' Rosita said as her mother stepped through the door 'and to work out how we all are going to help you...' but her voice broke and her eyes began to fill with tears. To hide them, she took her mother in her arms.

Earlier Conchita had been afraid their greeting would be emotional, but with the words out of the way, their embrace was gentle and loving.

'Coffee for me too? I need a little pepping up this morning,' she said. She immediately realised that the sub-conscious thought had risen into the spoken word. Conchita knew that it would be seen like an attempt to be cheerful, not lost on Rosita, or Juan Luis, particularly as her voice came out brittle rather than bright.

Rosita sat to pour coffee for Conchita. She spilled a little on the table, her hand unsteady this time, as she strove to hold back the tears.

'Now, there's something I would like...'

'Of course Mama, whatever you want we'll...' Conchita put out a hand to each of them across the table.

'It's just that I'd like to stay in my own lovely little house for....as long as I can,' Conchita said. 'But I know the time will come...when...I won't be able to...manage.'

'That's when you will come here Mama. I'm going to get the little downstairs room prepared for you.' It was the room the whole family referred to as the magic room, where exceptional and happy things had happened.

'You see, Mama this is where you are going to...going to get better.' She said, with a brave but unconvincing smile.

***

September 2007

Diary

I was so afraid of the surgery. A mastectomy! The idea appalled me. Some of me would be missing, forever. I would not be a whole woman. And then I began to harbour the hope that it would clear out the vile canker (a far better word for this ghastly disease) once and for all. Then came the chemotherapy and radiotherapy; well, they were but a stop gap. I think we all knew it but we hoped for more.

How long has it given me? A little more than three years; time to put my house in order, as they say. Not that there was much to do. I missed seeing Carmen for a while after Luca's death. I felt ashamed that I didn't know why Luca went away, as though it was my fault and I blamed Carmen for coming to tell me that she had seen him in Pamplona. Then I felt guilty at having Luca followed. I soon realised it was through concern that she had come to me and I went to her to make things right between us. We were friends again, as we always have been.

The bodega is going well; Juan Luis and the twins are born wine-makers. Rosita is happy with a darling daughter, my grand-daughter! What a marvellous life I have had here in my adopted country. If I had known how it would turn out perhaps I would never have been that naughty girl who made life difficult for everyone.

Conchita's days passed, some quietly when she needed more rest, others she was able to go out and visit family or friends. She did not conduct visitors around the winery anymore but now and then she followed Maria and her entourage.

'What a godsend that girl is,' she whispered to herself one day as she listened to her explanations in English, 'But equally at ease in Spanish and naturally in French,' Conchita's thoughts continued. It seemed certain now that Maria would never leave Bodega López and the whole family was happy about that.

For a while Conchita was able to ride Otono in and around the vines. Mercedes continued her visits as often as she could but now her studies took up much of her time. The late summer evenings were pleasant, not too hot, and then Mercedes called her Nana on the telephone.

'I was just wondering Nana if you would like to ride with me this evening, if you feel like it,' she added.

'I would love it,' she said. 'It's time I saw you on that new mare. I began to wonder if you would ever part with Belleza. Lovely as she was she was far too small for you.'

'It's true. Did I tell you she hasn't gone far away? A friend of papa's wanted her for his seven year old son. I'm so happy, and Belleza will be very pleased to have a young child on her back.'

Their rides were shorter now than in the past but somehow Mercedes always found time to bring the conversation round to Yorkshire.

'Tell me some more Nana, I've never been to England.'

330

'There isn't much more to tell Mercedes. Don't forget I left England when I was younger than you are now. I did most of my growing up in Spain and I didn't do it very well!' She laughed at her own words.

'Is it in your story book Nana?'

'Yes, it is. My 'story book' as you call it, helped me work through some of those difficult times.'

'Mama has told me a little bit about what happened. Are you…well, resentful Nana that you were made to come to Spain?'

'It was very hard at the time and I have not forgotten that I was very unhappy and I behaved badly. After a while I did find happiness and now when I look around me I know what an amazingly happy life I have had.'

'It's strange isn't it Nana…?'

'What's that?'

'If you hadn't come to live in La Rioja I would never have been born!'

'What a terrible thought! How could I have lived without you?' Conchita shook her head in mock horror and laughed.

'Nana!'

***

As the weeks passed Conchita began to wonder if she would see Christmas. Even though the increasing pain was kept under control she grew more tired each day. The evening rides with Mercedes were no longer possible . She was determined not to go to bed for an afternoon nap it smacked too much of giving in. Her comfortable chair served very well for a while.

None of this went unnoticed and Rosita spoke to Jean Luis.

'I think it's time Mama came back to her old house. How am I going to suggest it Juan Luis without upsetting her?'

'Just invite her Rosita. I think you'll find she's ready. She knows she can't manage by herself now. And after all, she'll be 'going home'.'

That is exactly how Conchita saw it. In her old house, where she had been so happy with Rodrigo and her three children, she occupied the magical room where Garnet had stayed, learned to walk again and pick up her life once more. For Conchita there would be no taking up of her life; she was climbing the last mountain. She watched the days come and go, sometimes as clear as ever, sometimes in a mist when the pain

331

broke through and the morphine cocooned her in a blanket of warm forgetfulness.

It was October but there were still warm days when Rosita drew back the flimsy curtains and opened wide the French windows. The bed faced out onto the terrace and gave Conchita a clear view of the vines and the mountains in the distance. Occasionally she would pick up her diary, which had been her companion nearly all her life. From time to time she turned the pages, stopping here and there. The words sent her thoughts into the past, her life unfolding, page by page. Sometimes the words became images, she could close her eyes and watch the inner pictures roll like a film.

In these lucid moments she marvelled at bygone times. Was she really that young English girl who, sent to Spain, an unknown country, and an unknown language, acquired a new family and learned a new way of life? And became happy? She read of the conversation she had had with Mercedes years earlier when she had told her of her own youth, riding round the bodega with her father, not wanting to learn about vines and wine. 'Why?' Mercedes had wanted to know. 'Well, that's something of a story,' she remembered replying. But Mercedes wasn't content with this undefined answer.

'Oh, when can I read your story book Nana?'

'Oh, the story isn't finished yet. Maybe someone will tell you some of it one day.' It wasn't written for reading, as she had told Mercedes. She had laid bare her soul on those pages, perhaps it would be better if some of those thoughts were never read.

Some days the memories passed slowly through her mind, she felt her story was coming to an end. On this day she did not write but held the diary against her heart.

'My story,' she whispered and then her eyelids closed. There was a deep sigh as her last breath left her body. Her arms fell to her sides and as she drifted gently into a deep sleep her story book slipped to the ground.